Praise for the novels of M

"*Shards of Glass* is a spellbinding fantasy with a powerful tale of friendship at its beating heart. With vivid world building and compelling characters, this is a treasure of a book."
—Kylie Lee Baker, author of *The Keeper of Night*

"Ideal for readers looking for stories of complex political maneuvering in fully realized fantasy worlds, with earth-shattering events told through complicated, sympathetic characters. This origin story for a well-loved character from the world of Elantra will get new readers up to speed while telling a story that long-time followers have been waiting for. Highly recommended." —*Library Journal* on *Sword and Shadow*

"This world feels so complex and so complete."
—*ReadingReality.net* on *The Emperor's Wolves*

"Enjoyable, entertaining, engaging fantasy."
—*Tor.com* on *The Emperor's Wolves*

"Exciting… Both new readers and Sagara's long-time fans will be delighted to visit the land and people of Elantra."
—*Publishers Weekly* on *The Emperor's Wolves*

"Full to the brim of magic…beautiful and intricate…a breathtaking read."
—*Word of the Nerd* on *Cast in Wisdom*

"This is a fast, fun novel, delightfully enjoyable in the best tradition of Sagara's work. While it may be light and entertaining, it's got some serious questions at its core. I'm already looking forward to the next book in the series." —*Locus* on *Cast in Oblivion*

"Readers will embrace this compelling, strong-willed heroine with her often sarcastic voice." —*Publishers Weekly* on *Cast in Courtlight*

Also by *New York Times* **bestselling author Michelle Sagara**

The Chronicles of Elantra

CAST IN SHADOW
CAST IN COURTLIGHT
CAST IN SECRET
CAST IN FURY
CAST IN SILENCE
CAST IN CHAOS
CAST IN RUIN
CAST IN PERIL
CAST IN SORROW
CAST IN FLAME
CAST IN HONOR
CAST IN FLIGHT
CAST IN DECEPTION
CAST IN OBLIVION
CAST IN WISDOM
CAST IN CONFLICT
CAST IN ETERNITY

And "Cast in Moonlight" found in HARVEST MOON

The Wolves of Elantra

THE EMPEROR'S WOLVES
SWORD AND SHADOW

Look for the next story in
The Chronicles of Elantra,
coming soon from MIRA.

SHARDS
OF
GLASS

MICHELLE SAGARA

mira

If you purchased this book without a cover you should be aware
that this book is stolen property. It was reported as "unsold and
destroyed" to the publisher, and neither the author nor the
publisher has received any payment for this "stripped book."

mira™

ISBN-13: 978-0-7783-0522-4

Shards of Glass

Recycling programs
for this product may
not exist in your area.

Copyright © 2023 by Michelle Sagara

All rights reserved. No part of this book may be used or reproduced in any manner
whatsoever without written permission except in the case of brief quotations embodied
in critical articles and reviews.

This is a work of fiction. Names, characters, places and incidents are either the product
of the author's imagination or are used fictitiously. Any resemblance to actual persons,
living or dead, businesses, companies, events or locales is entirely coincidental.

For questions and comments about the quality of this book, please contact us
at CustomerService@Harlequin.com.

Mira
22 Adelaide St. West, 41st Floor
Toronto, Ontario M5H 4E3, Canada
BookClubbish.com

Printed in U.S.A.

This is a late birthday party favor, because I am, as usual, completely disorganized in real life.

I wanted to thank people for coming out to celebrate my sixtieth birthday; with COVID and my general Oscar the Grouch tendencies, I wasn't certain people would want to. I'm so grateful you took the time to join us, and I'm grateful for your company. (But not for the speeches. I'm not as thankful for speeches.)

So, thank you to:

Debbie Ohi & Jeff Ridpath

Ruth Ohi & Kaarel Truuvert

Reid Ellis

Ronnie Ellis

John & Kristen Chew

Jamie Chew

Liam Chew

Katherine Arcus

Karina & Greg Sumner-Smyth

Daniel West

Ross West

Tami & Ken Sagara

Gary & Ayami Sagara

And Thomas, who planned it all

1

Raven loved glass. When foraging through garbage at the edge of the warrens, it was the glass pieces she loved best. She handled them with care—she'd cut herself a few times, and once her hand got so swollen she could barely move her fingers—but there was nothing like glass. She'd found one piece that was, jagged edges and all, almost three inches across. She'd been so lucky.

Some of the kids in the warrens would gather glass and take it to glassmakers, where—at the back door, in the various alleys—they could sell the bits and pieces. She'd been allowed into a shop once—a young apprentice had let her sneak in—and she'd watched glass melt, had seen bottles created from it, liquid becoming something harder with the passage of time.

She hadn't stolen anything, but even so, she'd never been allowed in again.

Today, she was waiting for rain. When glass and water collided, the water did interesting things. Or the glass did. Or the light through the glass. Most of the people in the warrens who were a threat didn't like the rain. The trick was to hide until rain was certain to fall, and then leave the hiding place before others crowded into it, seeking shelter.

Besides, maybe if it rained hard enough, she would see Robin.

Robin was her only friend, and he had disappeared. She hadn't seen him for a long time. No one had seen him, although it had taken her a while to get up the courage to ask. People were just as likely to kick her as answer, but she was used to being kicked, and they mostly did it to make her go away, not to cause her pain.

There was the old woman by the well—the one with the pipe and the eye patch and the terrible temper—the grey crow. That's what Robin called her sometimes.

Raven weighed the broken piece of glass before tucking it into a dirty cloth and hiding it in her pouch. She'd picked up some garbage from the other side of the warrens' border—a couple of tin pieces, a pocked, carved wooden horse that had seen better days—because no one talked to the grey crow without having *something* to offer.

None of this would be worth much for barter or trade, but Raven sometimes ran errands for people outside of the warrens, as well. Not often anymore. She didn't like to talk much—she wasn't good at it. Robin had been much better. Raven suspected that the old woman had *liked* Robin, which was an odd thought, because the grey crow didn't like anyone.

But that made her safer: she hated everyone equally. None of the gangs in the area were stupid enough to tangle with her—although maybe they'd tried when the old woman was unimaginably young. She wore the eye patch for a reason. She had friends—some old, like she was, some younger—but they didn't seem to take *orders* from her. They passed news and information; sometimes she even smiled when they did.

Raven had never liked her smile, so it was good that she so seldom showed it.

"You, bird girl," the grey crow barked. Raven had not yet

approached her; she'd lingered on the edge of the crowd that often gathered by the well. In crowds, there was a bit of safety, although in truth not much; if someone wanted to hit her, no one would interfere as long as they didn't try to kill her. Maybe not even then.

Raven hastened to reach the old woman's side, because that one-eyed frown was etched deeper than usual.

"Where's the bird boy been?"

Raven's shoulders fell.

"You haven't seen him around, eh? Wait, is that why you're here? You managed to dig up some courage?" She laughed. Raven tried to smile although she didn't understand the joke. The laughter left the old woman's voice and face as she studied Raven. "Girl, what's my name?"

"Your name?" Raven was confused.

"Yeah, my name. I have one. Your friend used it from time to time. Never heard you say it, though." She glanced at Raven's hands, and the bits and pieces of gathered metal. "I have no use for that, but—good girl, to understand that you have to bring something to the table."

There was no table here, but Raven nodded anyway.

"I won't take it amiss that you've brought garbage, but I want something else today before I'll listen to your questions."

Raven tensed. Had the old woman noticed her piece of glass? Is that what she wanted? She froze, greed warring with greed—for glass, for Robin. They were perfectly balanced, and she struggled with them until the old woman rapped the top of her head with a fist.

"You don't have Robin so *pay attention*, bird girl. Are you listening this time?"

Raven paled. She'd been listening, but the thinking part had overwhelmed the words. It wasn't safe. She had to pay attention. "Y-yes."

"Good. I won't repeat it again. I want you to say my name.

Say my name, and I'll answer any question you want to ask today." The fist was withdrawn and the old woman crossed her arms, leaning back against the wall. "But it's a onetime offer, and it's good only until the sun sets."

"Grey Crow?"

The woman snorted. Raven could have said *One Eye*, but knew that wasn't what she wanted, either.

Raven walked to the wall against which the old woman was leaning; she then crouched, bending her knees and bowing her head so that her forehead touched them. She curved her arms around her shins, rocking.

The Old Woman was what most people called her, if they were far enough away she couldn't hear. Everyone knew two things: avoid her when she was deadly silent, and be respectful when she could hear you. Raven had never understood names well—they didn't carry information. Even her own name was like a verbal gesture, something meant to catch her attention. It wasn't who she was.

Robin called her Raven. Robin said that was her name. He said his own name—Robin—was a bird's name, and he thought Raven was better than Crow. She couldn't remember being called anything else; only Robin used her name. The grey crow called them both birds.

What's your name? Robin had asked, the second time they met.

She'd considered the question. *Person?*

Robin's expression made clear that this wasn't the correct answer.

I'm a person.

Yes—but that's not your name.

What is this? She held up a piece of glass.

Glass.

She nodded. *That's its name. It's what it is.*

But Robin hadn't accepted that answer. He explained that

a name was what a specific person was called. His name was Robin. He was a person, yes, but he was a person *named* Robin. She must have a name. He told her he didn't mind if she didn't want to share it.

She didn't mind sharing, but she had nothing to offer him— she couldn't remember being a person named something. She told him some of the things she'd been called, and that made him very unhappy. He insisted that she must have had a name. If she did, she didn't remember it. He asked about parents, and she didn't remember those, either—although she knew other people had them.

She knew it was safer to have parents—but she understood that parents were not things that appeared simply because they were wanted. Parents were adults, and some were not happy to have children. Many of those children were abandoned. Most died. Some didn't.

She didn't.

She knew how to watch. She didn't want anything from the strangers she could see, and she avoided them. She could; she knew the warrens' alleys and yards better than anyone. Robin sometimes hid with her. He was often afraid.

Raven was seldom afraid because fear would change nothing.

But…she was afraid that she would never see Robin again. Wasn't that fear? She puzzled over it. She wanted to find Robin, if Robin was still alive. And to find Robin, she'd come to the old woman with the eye patch. That's right. She was supposed to be finding the old woman's name.

She crouched in the woman's shadows, watching those shadows move, attached to feet. She watched them shorten, and then watched them begin to lengthen. It was sun's light that did that, although outside of the warrens there were lights on poles in the streets that also cast shadows, like tiny moons raised partway to the sky by people's hands.

No, no. Name. She had to think of the name. She watched

people walk by and hoped that someone would approach the old woman, that someone would call her by the name Robin would have known. But she couldn't remember Robin using a name, because most people didn't. If they knew you, if you knew them, the name was unsaid; if you didn't know them, the name was irrelevant.

She had never asked anyone else for their name. She hadn't asked Robin, either. But…she thought of Robin by his name now. She called him by his name. She wouldn't have known it if he hadn't told her.

She had never asked the old woman for her name. She knew where the old woman could be found, if she needed to find her; she knew what she liked and what she hated; what she nodded at and what she cursed. She knew how long her legs were, how quickly she could lash out with a kick; knew to stay outside of that range if the woman's face was full of frowns.

But she didn't know her name.

The shadows lengthened as Raven watched them, trying to remember any interaction in which a name had been invoked. She couldn't. She could remember almost all of their interactions, even the ones that included Robin. No name.

No name.

She finally unlocked her arms, lifting her head to look at the old woman, who had barely moved or spoken. Raven rose slowly, turned away, and headed to the alleys; it was getting late. There was a trick to finding empty shelter, and it relied on the time between sundown and night. She had no answer to give that would serve as payment for the question she wanted answered.

"Giving up?" the old woman said to Raven's back.

Raven shrugged.

"You don't look at people when you're talking, do you?"

Raven understood the subtle command in the question, and

pivoted, aware now of the passage of time. "I do," she said, a hint of exhaustion in the words. "But I wasn't talking."

The woman chuckled. "Fair enough. You're giving up?"

"I don't know your name. I don't think I've ever heard it. You have a name, so I can't give you one the way Robin gave me mine."

"Robin named you?"

"Robin gave me a name." Raven shrugged.

"And what about the name you were born with?"

"I don't know it."

The woman frowned. "I remember seeing you around when you were a kid. I never saw parents or grandparents. You were always alone."

Raven nodded.

"I thought you'd disappear one day. I thought the warrens would devour you, you know? Even kids with parents aren't guaranteed to survive." She spit as she said this, as if the word *parents* didn't belong in her mouth. "And you were a strange kid." She straightened as she spoke, removing her back from the wall. "Go wherever it is you call home. I've got nothing for you."

Raven nodded again. But as she turned, she said, "What is your name?"

She could hear the old woman snort. "That's your question?"

This time Raven shook her head. "I forget, sometimes. I never asked you. But I'll remember it now, if you tell me."

"Turn around. Look at me if you're speaking to me. You're not on the take; you don't have to pretend there's nothing between us."

Raven's frown traveled up her face, folding forehead and eyebrows as she obeyed.

"Definitely a strange one. My name is Giselle. It's a name I chose for myself, not the one I was born with." The woman's arms were now loose by her sides, her hands slightly clenched.

"Giselle." Raven turned the two syllables over, rolling them across her tongue as if they had texture or taste. "Your name is Giselle."

"Yes. You could have asked before sundown, you know." The old woman stretched. "But you said my name before nightfall. What was the question you came to ask?"

Raven blinked rapidly. What had the old woman said? She wanted Raven to say her name. She'd never said Raven couldn't ask what the name was. Raven had made an assumption because she didn't understand the rules of the game. Robin would have known.

She'd waited for him. She'd listened in on conversations that might touch on him. Had he died? Had his body been found? Had the Hawks taken him away on one of their infrequent patrols?

"Do you know where Robin is?"

Giselle smiled. "Have you eaten?"

"Yes?"

"Today?"

Raven considered the question. "Yes?"

"I haven't. Spent all day waiting for you. Come on, keep an old woman company."

Raven tensed. There was a reason the old woman was feared. Raven knew—she'd always known—that being on the inside of someone else's space, someone's *permanent* space, was dangerous. Sometimes people went in and never came out. Sometimes they came out as corpses, carried somewhere in the dark and left by the roadside.

The only person she had ever met who might help her if there was danger was Robin, and Robin was gone. Robin was the reason she had come. She didn't understand it, not really. He wasn't the first person who had vanished from the streets and the alleys. She had barely noticed he was gone for the first week or two. It happened—sometimes he found work, and sometimes she did, running errands and delivering things for people who had food and money to spare.

But it had been more than a week. More than a month. Long enough she'd lost track. She found herself haunting the places in which they'd once met, found herself listening for the sound of his voice, the sound of his steps. Sometimes she lingered beyond the safe time, her pockets heavy with food to share, pieces of glass and metal and stone to show him. He did not come.

She had started to search in earnest. She had started to listen to other people talking, to take in their words and conversations as if they had something to teach her. Nothing. Nothing.

She had finally come to the old woman, the grey crow, Giselle.

She had not come here to disappear. She had not come here to enter a cage. Nor to eat, nor to accept any favor she couldn't pay for.

She had come to find Robin.

"You've always been a cautious bird, but that's no crime—no cat's ever eaten you. Well? What will it be?"

Raven nodded and remembered belatedly to speak. "Yes. Yes, I will come with you."

Giselle had killed before. She had had people killed, as well. Robin considered these to be the same. Raven didn't. She found much of what Robin said was too blurred around the edges, and she was always forced to ask questions just to make sense of it. The difference between Robin and any other person she had met in her life was that Robin was always willing to answer.

Because he answered, she learned how Robin thought and—far more important—how Robin used words. His words and her words could be the same but they didn't *mean* the same thing. Even if they were speaking the same language.

It had occurred to her only after Robin disappeared that maybe other people were the same: their words and her words didn't mean the same thing. Perhaps she would have learned more, but people were *hard*. And most didn't want to talk to Raven.

Giselle lived, as Raven expected, in an actual house. The house itself was in decent repair; it had actual glass windows rather than warped shutters, although one window was boarded up. All of the windows had cages around them, and Raven hesitated at the foot of the stairs that led to the front door. Had the door been guarded, she might have turned and fled.

She took a deep breath.

Giselle didn't speak until she'd opened the door—and she opened it by touching its center at the height of her shoulders. To Raven's surprise, the interior was lit, and the light was far brighter given the darkness. Giselle entered, turning to look over her shoulder at her guest.

Raven followed.

Raven didn't spend much time indoors. She recognized the dining table for what it was, but had never sat at one herself. The interior of Giselle's home was almost empty. It seemed a waste, because it was so large and it was in decent repair, but Raven kept this observation to herself, as she did most observations.

"Sit," Giselle commanded, indicating a chair at the table. "I'll make dinner. You drink?"

"Yes?"

"You drink anything besides water?"

"Oh."

The old woman chuckled. "I don't know how you've survived this long. You're like a stray cat. How did you meet Robin?"

How? Raven frowned. How had she met Robin? She knew, but didn't know how to answer. She didn't have the words.

Giselle chuckled. "You were always together when I saw you. Fine. What's your first memory of Robin?"

Memory. Raven closed her eyes.

"Child. You must like the boy. Tell me a good memory."

Raven hid frustration; she had an answer for this. "I was watching water on glass—I had a curved piece—in the sun, and he asked me what I was doing."

"And you answered?"

"Yes, but… I had to answer many times because he didn't understand. But when he did, he wanted to join me, and he wanted to try different things."

"So you *can* smile."

Raven frowned.

"You know about the disappearances in the warrens that started a couple of years ago?"

Raven nodded. She'd been aware of it because Robin knew, and Robin worried. For her. For himself. She'd told him his worry for her was pointless. She'd done her best to teach him all of the hidden nooks and crannies of the warrens—the places that were most likely to be safe, the places that were only safe at the right time of day, and the places to which he might flee in desperation.

But they changed with time. It had been so long.

Raven didn't interact with most people. But she could see the pattern that people, moving and living, etched into the streets just as surely as the roads themselves, and she could move with or against their subtle tide.

"Some enterprising people came into the warrens with coin. Or drugs. They wanted people. They didn't seem to care which people; they weren't looking for anyone specific. They'd come to the warrens because they didn't want their victims to be people who'd be missed." As she spoke, a ripple of expression shifted the lines of her face. "If they'd been normal people, I could have dealt with it. But they were Barrani."

Raven knew that Barrani upset the pattern in the warrens. Barrani and humans didn't mix well; the humans avoided their normal routes if the Barrani were on the same road. So did Raven. "Did you help them?"

"Would you believe me if I said no?"

Raven frowned. "Why would I not believe you?"

"Because most adults lie."

"Most adults have to have a reason to lie," Raven replied. "I have no power. I have no weapons. I have no gold. There's no reason for you to lie to me—unless you work for them, and I'm one of the people you mean to sell."

The woman laughed. Her laugh was at odds with her expression, but it was not entirely unkind; Raven had had plenty of experience with unkind laughter. "Robin always said you were the smartest person he knew." The laughter left as suddenly as it had arrived, as if it were a summer squall. "Let's say no. I'm not a fool; they're Barrani. Their flavor of polite political games is assassination and death. Usually in much fancier streets than ours.

"I suspected the warrens' missing people was their work." Her grin was sharp and deadly. Raven didn't understand why Giselle avoided Barrani—she seemed a lot like them to Raven's eye.

"Happens I was right." She frowned, pulled out a chair, and sat. "I told you to sit. You're free to leave at any time. I won't cage you here."

Raven stood beside the door, as if she might open it and fly out at any minute. She didn't want to sit down. But Giselle was dangerous; she sat.

"You probably didn't notice, but I kept an eye on Robin."

Raven was surprised. "Why?"

Giselle shrugged. "Why did you?"

Raven frowned. "Robin is my friend. Was he kidnapped?"

"The evidence is circumstantial—but we're not a court of law. He disappeared after the Barrani moved in."

"But they left."

"The Barrani hired a mortal crew from the warrens to do their dirty work. Those people should never have allied themselves with outsiders—and Barrani outsiders at that." She spit to the side. "We made sure they didn't add much to their trafficking after that—but Robin was already gone. They had no idea where he'd been taken. They had no idea if he was still alive.

"Those disappearances? They're done now. They're over. I don't know where you've been hiding the past week, but it isn't in the places you used to hide."

Raven nodded. "Someone found them. Hiding places grow and die all the time."

"You don't visit the ones you used when Robin was here."

She shook her head. "Because Robin is gone. If he was taken by people, it means they could find him—he was never as good at hiding."

"No. No, he wasn't. But I think hiding is like a dagger; double-edged. And listen to me. The warrens will eat people alive, but you know that. Robin isn't coming back."

Raven frowned. "You know where he is."

"It happens I do—but it's not in the warrens. The disappearances served a purpose, or so I'm told."

"You were told? By who?"

"Good girl. By a very grouchy old man who came to the warrens with a couple of Hawks. I'd've turfed him out if they hadn't also brought a very familiar young man with them."

"Robin?"

"Robin. The old outsider offered me a job, but it was Robin who talked me into taking it. He'd been taken out of the warrens by the Barrani—sold to them. But he wasn't the only one, and some of the people who disappeared were returned to us."

"What's the job?"

"Finding people," the woman replied. "Just that. I get a price for every person I find that's of use to the old man; I get a smaller price for every person I send his way, regardless. I don't kidnap them off the streets; I don't march them there at knifepoint. I offer them a cut of what I'm offered. We're pretty suspicious in general; some don't take the cut if it seems too high." Her grin exposed yellowed canines.

"What does he want?"

"Students, apparently."

Raven blinked. The answer made no sense. "Students?"

"Students. You look confused."

"Suspicious," Raven replied, frowning. "Students like in rich kids' schools?"

Giselle nodded. "Yeah, I didn't believe it, either. Or I wouldn't have if Robin weren't front and center. Robin said they want students. They have classrooms—large rooms dedicated to lessons—and bedrooms for the students. And food. Three meals a day."

Raven took a risk. "What's the downside?"

Giselle chuckled. "Girl, if you weren't so bloody odd, I'd've taken you in myself. You've got half the cunning necessary—you'd have to, to survive. Can't tell you what the downside is. I know roof overhead and solid meals would be a boon to a lot of the street kids here, but some people came back. Robin won't."

"But he came with them?"

"Yeah. He was looking for you."

"What did they offer you?"

This time Giselle laughed. "For you? The old man offered ten times the head cost. *If* I can get you there, I'll get ten times the price for an unknown. So, how about it? I'll give you a cut."

Raven frowned. "What percentage were you offering anyone else?"

"Does it matter? They're not you. I'll give you a third."

Raven's frown deepened. "Half?"

"A third. I'm keeping the twenty percent as a finder's fee. You wanted to know where Robin is. I'm giving you that information. And if you accept my deal, I'll even make sure you get there myself."

Raven met and held Giselle's gaze; Giselle failed to look away. "Have you taken anyone else there?"

"No. You'd be my first. I've handed people over—voluntarily on their part—but I haven't gone down myself. Robin was doing well enough. I'm not selling out my own. We were born here, we survived; if we don't watch out for ourselves, who will?" At Raven's expression, she added, "Sure, we have to watch our own backs and our own wallets most of the time, but there's more than that.

"That old man was interested in you, girl. Too interested, maybe. I just want to see where you end up."

"You don't trust Robin?"

"I don't trust anyone—but neither do you. If you're willing to enrich me by taking a walk out of the warrens, be here in the morning."

In the morning, Raven crawled out from under a fence; it was still dark, but the dogs were sleeping. They were accustomed to her; they didn't bark or attack when she approached. She could sleep safely here, or think safely, because they *would* attack almost anyone else. Not the owner of the place, though. There was a reason he didn't let strangers into the yard.

I don't trust anyone—but neither do you.

The words flopped about in her head, interrupted by bits and pieces of memory. The warrens were all she'd ever known— all that she remembered. She knew them as if they were part of her body; she knew the parts that were broken, knew when they were healed as much as they could be, knew how to find things if they were here.

She trusted her knowledge.

People, she didn't trust, because they were so hard to know. She looked for similarities, but it took effort and concentration. People behavior was a language she'd never properly learned. Danger signs? She'd learned those.

But safety signs were harder to know, to trust.

She'd never needed people before. She didn't really need them now. Robin had disappeared, and she'd gone on as she always had.

But she couldn't show Robin her glass pieces; couldn't show him how oil and water formed different drops along their surfaces; couldn't *share*. Robin was the only person she'd met who was half-interested, not in Raven, but in what she knew, in her interests. And when there was no Robin, things felt half-finished, half-empty. She hadn't felt like this before, and it took her a while to understand it: she missed Robin. Robin was, inasmuch as Raven understood the word, a *friend*.

She'd looked for Robin. It had taken a while. She'd hoped he'd come back on his own, and she'd gone out of her way to visit less safe spots that he might seek out. He hadn't come.

Yesterday, she'd taken the risk of approaching Giselle. Giselle had answers, if they could be believed. Giselle could take Raven to Robin, if she wasn't lying. If she was, Raven might never escape. She might never see the warrens or her precious hiding spaces again. But if Giselle wasn't lying, Raven might never return. Robin had never returned. Not on his own.

Raven hadn't slept that night. Her thoughts were loud, like a swarm of angry wasps; they buzzed and buzzed, breaking the quiet that sleep demanded, although Raven herself didn't make a sound.

When dawn's colors began to stretch toward the indigo of night sky, she dusted herself off and headed back to Giselle's home.

She wanted to see Robin again.

2

Giselle was waiting for Raven, the door of her house at her back, her hands bunched in jacket pockets. Raven glanced at the sun's shadows, which were still quite long. She wasn't late. She was aware, however, that people felt the passage of time differently. Perhaps Giselle expected people to be early in order to consider them on time.

Giselle straightened, her shoulders coming away from the door. She didn't waste time with greetings, which was a relief to Raven, who could remain silent. "You've got everything you need?"

Raven nodded.

"Come on; let's hit the bridge before the merchants reach it—we'll waste too much time, otherwise."

Raven waited. When Giselle began to walk, she glanced around. No one followed. No one but Raven.

"I don't need guards if that's what you're worried about. Where we're going they can cause offense to the wrong people. They're warrens born and bred. The old man we need to meet isn't."

Old man? Oh, the old man who had offered Giselle the job. Raven nodded.

"Don't lag behind. You're not carrying much—you know how to avoid cutpurses?"

Raven nodded more firmly.

"Good. It isn't only in the warrens that they're a problem—the nicer neighborhoods have their share of thieves. We're just more open about it." She smiled; it wasn't a friendly smile, but it offered no threat to Raven. Giselle's clothing did, though—she dressed the way she did around the well in the warrens.

The warrens, Robin said, weren't respectable to most of the people in the city. So that meant Giselle...wasn't respectable? But the old man had come to her. Ah, no—maybe Robin had come to her and the old man had followed. Had the old man been disrespectful, Giselle would never have accepted his work.

"You really aren't much of a talker, are you?"

Raven nodded. Belatedly she realized that this could be a criticism, that she was expected to speak. To speak and not give offense. Robin never expected her to speak, but conversely never expected her to shut up, either. He didn't find her words mystifying or boring. It wasn't his acceptance of her silence she missed; it was his acceptance of her words.

It was the sharing of her thoughts, her ideas, her experiments, her hiding spaces. Her sense of the warrens. She had shared things—or tried—with people she met in the past, and it had never gone well. But conversely, total silence had often caused offense, as well. There was a line between silence and speech that she'd never learned how to walk.

Better to avoid people entirely.

But she couldn't avoid Giselle today. What if Giselle changed her mind? What if Giselle left her here, on the outside, with no places to hide? Thinking this, Raven lengthened her stride.

"Which bridge are we going to?" she forced herself to ask.

"It's one of the bridges into the fiefs." Giselle stiffened but kept moving. "The fief of Tiamaris, to be precise. Tiamaris's lord is a Dragon; he is close to the Dragon Court, and the Eternal Emperor. The streets of Tiamaris are...very unlike the warrens now. Wasn't always the case. Once, it would have been death for a child like you to cross this bridge. Now, merchants cross it. Merchants and craftsmen. And us."

Raven said, "Will we see the Dragon?"

Giselle smiled. "Look at you—you almost sound normal." The smile dipped. "No, we are not likely to see the Dragon unless something goes badly wrong. Seriously, you *want* to see a Dragon?"

Raven nodded, her chin bouncing long after it should have stopped. "I've only seen them up in the air—too far away to reach."

"You're a strange one. A Dragon could swallow you without biting, you're so small. Probably wouldn't because you're in desperate need of a bath." Her smile was warm, in contrast to her words. Raven found people who meant what they *didn't* say very difficult to understand.

But... Robin.

"I don't think they're allowed to eat people."

"What does 'not allowed' mean to a Dragon? Who's going to stop them? Men aren't allowed to kill each other—but they do. If the Imperial Hawks catch them, they might hang, but there are a lot of killers in the warrens who've never graced the gallows, more's the pity.

"The Hawks who catch the killers are people—Barrani Hawks, a rare breed among their kind. No one else is guaranteed to survive us." Her smile was like a blade's edge—narrow, but almost glittering. "Who could punish a Dragon? There's a reason the Barrani lost their wars against the Dragons."

Raven nodded, having nothing to say; she had learned that nodding was enough of an acknowledgment for most people. People liked to know that you were paying attention, according to Robin. And people did like Robin, so Raven assumed he was right. What she didn't often understand was the why of it. Why was it important to be liked?

Robin said it was safer to be liked, but Raven knew from experience that it was far safer to be unseen, to be almost invisible.

Maybe, Robin had said. *But it's a lot lonelier. Don't you get lonely?*

No. No, she did not get lonely. Raven had been alone all her life, for as long as she could remember. She'd been a child in the streets of the warrens, only occasionally leaving when she'd been given a job. And she always returned. Robin asked her if she'd ever dreamed about leaving for good. About somehow having money or power that would allow her to live in the richer parts of the city.

Robin then had to explain *dream*, because the dreams Raven had weren't dreams she could control. She explained that she'd had nightmares about the world outside—the world she didn't really know—but accepted them for what they were.

So many answers to Robin's odd questions were *no*.

But *no* meant explanations, and Robin's explanations were always interesting, even if they were hard for Raven to understand. If she didn't, he'd try again. He'd answer her questions until she had no more questions to ask. Or no more questions he could answer. But even if he couldn't answer immediately, he'd come back later, he'd try again. She'd never spent so much time in another person's company before. She was used to passing people by—and being passed by, which was her intent. She'd lived like that for as long as she could remember.

Robin spoke to her, not at her, and he *listened*.

Don't you get lonely?

She didn't know. Lonely wasn't like cold—which led to death— or hunger or heat. It wasn't like breaking a bone. It wasn't *real*. She couldn't put her fingers on it. Couldn't hear it. Robin's absence didn't physically harm her. It didn't threaten her.

But she'd gotten used to Robin. To the sound of his voice. To the way he could keep his distance without physically being distant. When she found new things, she wanted to share them with him, to show them to him, to explain them to him. Or to ask if her explanation made sense, because sometimes it was hard to tell.

And he wasn't there anymore. He wasn't anywhere in the warrens.

She missed him. That was the word he'd used.

Maybe, she thought, she could understand his question now. Maybe this odd yearning, this strange discomfort, the sense of the empty space beside her, which had never, until Robin, been filled, was being *lonely*.

"Raven."

Raven startled as a hand found her shoulder; she looked up to meet Giselle's eye. "Robin always said you were a dreamer. Pay attention for a bit. We're almost at the checkpoint."

Raven nodded. She wanted to slide into Giselle's shadow to remain unseen, but Giselle wasn't worried about the checkpoint. The grey crow wasn't afraid of the men who were responsible for keeping the wrong people away from the bridge. She expected them to look down on her, but that had never mattered to Giselle, except in the warrens.

Raven found it uncomfortable because she wasn't used to talking to people. And guards often asked questions that had a *right* and *wrong* answer; they weren't really questions. She had never been good at saying the right thing. It was better not to talk at all.

But Giselle answered questions, and when she mentioned the Academia, the guards stepped back and waved them through.

Tiamaris. Raven could hear the word the moment she stepped foot on the fief side of the bridge. She murmured it, and Giselle nodded, raising brows slightly, as if surprised that Raven had paid that much attention. "Yes, this is the fief of Tiamaris. According to Robin, we can reach the Academia from any fief—

but Tiamaris is the safest of the six fiefs connected to the rest of the city."

Raven nodded. Had she been with Robin, she would have asked him if he'd heard the fief's name, because they didn't always hear the same things. Sometimes they heard the same words, but understood their meaning differently; sometimes he didn't hear what she heard at all.

Giselle began to walk down the road that the merchant wagons traveled, looking to her left. Here, there were signs with words on them. Raven could sound them out slowly; Robin had taught her that. She'd often wondered how it was Robin could read—and write—but the only time she'd asked, a shadow had crossed his face.

"I'm sorry, I don't want to talk about that," he'd said. He'd been quiet for the rest of the afternoon, and Raven had never asked again. But because of Robin, she recognized the letters on the signs.

So did Giselle. It occurred to Raven that Giselle could also read. Most in the warrens couldn't.

"I think we need to go further in. According to Robin, normal geography doesn't apply to the Academia—it's why it can be reached from any fief, but only by certain streets."

Raven nodded. At any other time she would have been curious about the Academia. Now she wanted to go to wherever it was, because that's where she'd find Robin. In spite of that, she wondered how a place could exist that could be reached from any of the fiefs. She didn't know a lot about the fiefs, but knew what every child knew: all of the fiefs bordered *Ravellon*, the place where Shadows lived. The fiefs weren't part of the city, but their streets were supposed to be like the warrens. Except no Hawks, no Imperial Laws that everyone mostly ignored anyway.

She didn't know if that was true, but the fief of Tiamaris looked nothing like the warrens.

She doubted that the Academia was in *Ravellon*. If it were, Giselle wouldn't be here. Giselle was smart about jobs and money—she didn't take the ones that were likely to end in her death. Or so Robin had said. Robin had always liked Giselle.

Her feet felt lighter as she walked down the road; the wagons and the guards and even Giselle were almost forgotten. She thought about running, but decided against it; Giselle knew which street she was looking for. Raven didn't.

Or Raven hadn't. But the street itself seemed to make her feet tingle. She thought, if Giselle got lost, she could find the Academia on her own.

Why? Robin would have asked. Robin had always asked questions—mostly about the hiding spaces in the warrens, about the way they grew and died, as if they were weeds or flowers. *Why* was a good question. One of Raven's favorites. It invited Raven to talk about what she knew. And Robin always tried to understand her. He always believed her.

A shadow passed above the streets; Raven looked up instantly, her eyes welded to the wings of the large Dragon that circled in the air above their heads. Giselle had said they probably wouldn't see the fieflord. Raven hadn't been so certain.

If it weren't for Giselle, she would have toppled over backward; the grey crow caught her before she could fall. Anywhere else, she might have lain down and looked up, but Raven knew better than to do it in this road. Too many wagons.

The horses that pulled the wagons became skittish when the Dragon landed, because Dragons were big, and this one blocked the road. But even as she thought this, Raven saw the most amazing thing: the large Dragon, gleaming bright red—she'd give all her glass and metal for just one piece of the Dragon's scales—began to dwindle in place, wings folding across its back and melting into it as the tail disappeared and the neck shrank. The Dragon looked melty, like candle wax—but when it had finished, a man stood in the road wearing armor the color of Dragon scales.

The man's eyes were orange, but seemed redder as they reflected the armor. Beside him, as if conjured out of thin air, was something that looked like a woman. The drivers relaxed as they caught sight of her, some waving, some shouting their greetings.

Raven just stared.

Sometimes she didn't know what she was looking at. Sometimes she saw something that she had no words to describe, because until Robin, words were mostly irrelevant. Words were meant to communicate with other people and there hadn't been too many of those. Raven knew how to ask questions related to the few jobs she'd been given, but she'd never tried to talk with her employers the way Robin had tried to talk with her.

The Dragon looked at Raven, his brows momentarily folding. He then noted Giselle. Usually it worked the other way around. But Raven understood that it was the person standing beside the Dragon who was the power here, red armor notwithstanding.

"You are Raven," that person now said. She smiled. Her eyes were brown, and her clothing wouldn't raise brows in the warrens. "I am Tara, and this is my lord, Tiamaris. Why are you here?"

Giselle cleared her throat. Giselle was the one who was supposed to do the talking here.

But Raven knew that the question, asked of her, had to be answered by her. Giselle seemed to be aware of it, as well, if belatedly; she opened her mouth, but no words came out.

"I am Raven," she said.

Tara smiled. "That is not the name you were born with."

"No. Robin gave me my name. Do you know Robin?"

Tara frowned for a moment and then her expression cleared. "Yes. I believe he came with the chancellor of the Academia."

"Do you know the way to the Academia?"

"Yes. You are...oddly loud."

Raven flinched. She'd been told many times that when she talked, she spoke too loudly. If she concentrated, she could lower her speaking volume—but she had to concentrate. And some people just didn't like it when she talked, so she mostly didn't talk. She was confused because she hadn't spoken much to Tara, but she didn't assume Tara was lying. "I won't speak."

Tara shook her head, her lips turning in a genuine smile. "It is not that kind of loud. I don't doubt that some people might be disturbed by the volume at which you speak, but I will never be one of them. Nor will my lord. You could be shouting until you were hoarse, and you would still never be as loud as a Dragon when he is conversing with his kin. My lord cannot hear as I do, but thought it best to meet you in person. You are with the...grey crow?"

Raven nodded.

"And you are here voluntarily."

Giselle was unamused but unsurprised. She was from the warrens and Raven was young enough to be sold. She was aware of the assumptions outsiders could make. Clearly she thought the fieflord had made those assumptions—and disliked what he assumed was happening.

"I am here voluntarily. Giselle is taking me to meet my friend. He's at school," she added, the warmth in Tara's eyes encouraging her to do something she seldom did: speak out loud.

The Dragon's eyes narrowed, although he didn't blink. He was staring—perhaps glaring—at Giselle. Raven wasn't certain what she could say to absolve Giselle of suspicion. She was afraid to try because sometimes her words got so tangled up.

Tara, however, turned to the Dragon. "If it will set your mind at ease, we can accompany them to the border."

The Dragon's eyes were orange. He failed to reply.

Tara reached out and set a hand on the Dragon's shoulder.

"There is only one road that leads to the Academia. We can escort them there, and we will know if they immediately diverge. But I do not believe they will." She then turned to Giselle. "We have had experience with Elantrans attempting to sell their daughters, or girls they claimed were their daughters. Tiamaris observes Imperial Laws, saving those that involve Draconic flight, form, and speech.

"The children thus brought across the bridge have remained within Tiamaris. Those that brought them here have not."

"Are they dead?"

The Dragon's eyes darkened slightly. "Yes."

Giselle's smile was sharp but genuine; Raven thought she wanted to burst out laughing. She didn't. "We will gratefully accept your escort," she said instead. "We really are going to the Academia. An old man entered the warrens where we both live. He had a young man with him, and I recognized the young man. Robin. He was looking for his friend.

"And it happens she'd finally started to seriously look for him. The old man wants students. He doesn't care about money if he feels they belong in the Academia—and he's offering them a home, clean rooms, actual food."

"And what do you get out of it?"

"A finder's fee," Giselle replied, her smile both deepening and shifting. "I'm from the warrens. There's something in it for me."

"This *old man* came to the warrens to deal with you directly?"

"He did. Probably Robin's suggestion."

Tiamaris and Tara exchanged a look before the fieflord nodded. "Tara and I will accompany you to the border. And I will personally accompany you to the Academia."

To Raven's surprise, Giselle ended up speaking at length with the fieflord. Tara fell back to walk beside Raven, which was not as uncomfortable as expected. The only other person who'd been willing to speak with her at any length had been Robin.

"I'm not technically a person," Tara said, although Raven hadn't spoken aloud.

"You look like a person, though?"

"Yes. This is an Avatar. I am actually the Tower that guards the fief."

Raven didn't know a lot about the fiefs.

"No? If you want, I can explain what I am and what I do."

At Raven's vigorous nod, Tara explained. Towers existed in all the fiefs—that part, Raven had heard. But it was knowledge that was never going to impact her life or her survival, so she had filed it away as *maybe later*. Later was now.

The Towers were sentient. They were alive. They'd been created by the Ancients. That word sent a shiver through Raven, as if it were a physical object and she'd been hit by it. The Towers existed because *Ravellon* existed: the city that had once been the center of the world. It had fallen to Shadow, and Shadow had slipped out to destroy or transform the rest of the world.

The Towers had been created to prevent that. The Ancients had chosen living people, and those people had become eternal, immortal, the living hearts of the Towers themselves. Tara was the heart of the Tower of Tiamaris.

She couldn't leave the Tower because she *was* the Tower. But she could extend her awareness and create a physical form to contain it so she could interact with people.

Raven's brow creased. "Is that why you can't come to the Academia?"

Tara smiled. "Exactly. I can only traverse the domain I guard. I can find people within it, although the farther they are from the Tower itself, the more work it takes. And much of my attention is diverted by the border we were created to guard against."

"*Ravellon.*" Had Shadow not been a threat, the Emperor would rule the entirety of the city, the way he theoretically ruled the warrens. But not even the Dragon Emperor dared to interfere with the Towers or the fiefs in which they stood.

The Towers were necessary if all of Elantra was not to fall to Shadow.

Tara nodded. "Yes. Lord Tiamaris is part of the Dragon Court. He continues to support the Emperor. The citizens of Tiamaris are grateful that our fieflord is a Dragon. As am I."

"What did you mean by oddly loud?"

"I could find you anywhere in my lord's fief without concentration, were you to be lost here. I can see you far more clearly than I can see most of my citizens. You are almost as clear to me as my lord, and that should not be possible. But... I have no sense that you are doing this on purpose. Only a sense that you are...looking at the lands in which I am situated. Your curiosity is perhaps the loudest thing about you." Her smile deepened. "Your friend was right, I think: there is definitely a place for you at the Academia."

"Giselle really did make the offer," Raven said quietly, as if Giselle would ever need her defense.

"I know. But my lord has survived by being more suspicious than you are. I am suspicious only when any hint of Shadow is involved. And if I am the Tower that protects the fief of Tiamaris, he is the captain. He is the lord."

"Why?"

"Because that is the way the Towers were created. Shadow is infinitely flexible, infinitely capable of surprise and attack; it is constantly developing new methods of infiltration. The Towers cannot freely leave their domains; they are not always apprised of new research, new information. But the Tower lords can. That is their responsibility: to provide new guidance in the unpredictable changing landscape."

"You like him?"

"I do. I chose him." The Tower's eyes crinkled at the corners. "But that is irrelevant. As I said, Towers need captains; it is built into us as an imperative. We can survive without one for some time—but not forever. It is not that I chose him that is significant. It is that he chose me."

"But…wouldn't anyone choose you?"

"Would you?"

Raven shook her head. "You already have a lord."

"And if he were to perish, would you then come to choose me?"

Raven seldom made commitments to people. Robin was her friend, yes—but they lived separate lives. She had not taken responsibility for people; she was well aware that she was socially awkward and lacked power to protect anyone but herself. Sometimes she wasn't so good at that, either.

"I think I see what you mean," she finally replied.

"Yes. Some people might choose me as they'd choose a convenient shelter from the rain. That has happened in the past. But that is not a commitment; it is merely a happy convenience. Some people look at what a Tower can do, and they want that for themselves. They think of what I might do for them. But they do not think of what I might need, and they do not consider what they might do for me.

"Lord Tiamaris does. Often, and perhaps too much. I am grateful, now, for all of the pain of the past, because I learned from it. I learned to understand the difference."

"But you didn't know, before?"

"No. I thought if people needed me, they would never leave. It is different now. My lord does need me, and I need him. But it is…balanced. And now, we must part."

Raven nodded. She could see the street clearly; there was a vivid quality to the color of the road and the air and the trees that reminded her of some of her best hiding places. This road was safe to walk. This road was unlike every other road they had passed. Giselle didn't seem to notice the difference. Nor did the fieflord. But perhaps the fieflord walked these streets so often, they were almost mundane to him.

"Ah, no. I do not think either of them see the street as you see it."

"Do you?"

"I don't know. I don't see as you see, even when we observe the same things." Her smile deepened. "But I agree with your absent friend. I think the Academia will suit you, should you choose it."

Raven froze. She looked ahead, and then looked at Tara. "What if it doesn't choose me?"

"Was your life terrible before?"

Raven shrugged. "I didn't used to think so. I'm still alive. I haven't starved. I haven't frozen in winter. I know where to hide to stay safe."

"What changed?"

Raven considered the question for a long beat; Tiamaris and Giselle grew distant as they talked, because they hadn't stopped beside Tara. What had changed?

"Robin," she finally said. And then she offered Tara a clumsy bow, an awkward bob of motion, as if she understood that Tara was worthy of deep respect but didn't quite know how to signal it properly.

She then turned to the dwindling backs of her companions and scurried after them, forcing herself to look only at them, and not at the buildings, at the foliage, at any other part of the street itself. She knew, if she took her time, they would vanish completely. Maybe they would forget her, because most people did.

This time, she didn't want to be forgotten.

She had almost reached Giselle when the curved street joined a road that ran around grass and trees in a giant oval.

"This," the Dragon said, "is the Academia."

On the external curve of the oval road were buildings of various heights and sizes; on the interior was a park. She didn't see those in the warrens. People sat on the grass, on the benches, and beneath the boughs of trees; she could hear them as they spoke to each other, some voices raised in anger, some in open, riotous laughter. Some of the people were silent; they sat, books in lap, foreheads furrowed in concentration or eyes crinkled in amusement or delight.

She was accustomed to crowds of people—the well was always crowded—but had always avoided them except at need.

She noted that everyone here wore similar clothing, although they were of different heights, weights and even races. Some were Barrani, and the rest of the students seemed to avoid them. Only in one case did she see Barrani seated on the grass beside regular people.

As if they could hear the thought, one of the Barrani looked up. Although she was tens of yards away, Raven could see her clearly; their eyes met, and the young woman's brows rose slightly.

Raven had never seen a Barrani with green eyes before. She had thought all Barrani had blue eyes of various shades, but no: this one had eyes of emerald. She rose as Raven came to a halt to process this new information, and before Raven could start moving again, the Barrani made a beeline across the grass to where Raven stood. Before she could reach Raven, Giselle intervened, coming to stand between them.

"She is not in danger," Lord Tiamaris said, his voice a rumble of minor annoyance.

"The girl's Barrani."

"Ah, yes. But she—and her friends—are highly unusual for Barrani. Or any other race, if it comes to that. I assure you she means no harm to your young charge."

"Not mine," Giselle said. "I'm seeing her here for my own purposes."

"Of course you are," the Dragon replied. He had the trick of saying words that somehow implied the opposite. Robin said it was sometimes called *sarcasm*, but Raven had always had difficulty identifying sarcasm. Why would people say the *exact opposite* of what they actually meant?

"I would prefer that we take Raven to the chancellor. I have business at home that's waiting, and I'd like to be quit of this place to get back to it."

"That won't be a problem."

The Barrani woman came to a stop in front of Giselle. Raven peered around the grey crow. Her first impression had been right: the Barrani had green eyes.

"Are you a new student?" she asked.

Raven blinked. "I… I don't know. Maybe?"

"Have you come to speak to the chancellor?"

"I think so."

"I can take you to the office. I'm a student here. My friend—" She glanced behind her, as if only just aware that the other Barrani student seated on the grass hadn't followed.

But Raven forgot all that, because one of the people in the park unfolded, straightened out, and turned around. She recognized him instantly.

It was Robin.

3

Robin wore the same black robes as the green-eyed Barrani. Raven thought he'd gotten taller, but his hair was shorter and his cheeks had filled out a bit. His clothing was clean—city clean, not warrens clean—and he had shoes that were entirely in one piece; the soles seemed to be attached to the uppers. His clothing even fit, although with robes it was harder to tell.

He moved quickly, but his feet made almost no sound. That was the thing she'd first appreciated about Robin. He liked to talk, but he didn't hate silence. Raven was full of silence. She was silent now, although once she'd caught sight of Robin, her gaze never wavered.

Neither did his, but he smiled, the corners of his lips dimpling, his eyes crinkling. His eyes were brown. They'd always been brown. Raven's were an odd color; they looked different depending on the light. She wondered what they looked like now. Wondered what Robin saw when he looked at her.

She supposed she could ask.

But she had no words; she'd used so many in the past two days, there were almost none left. She stood in the road, Giselle and the Barrani forgotten. Robin had to move past them to reach her.

"Raven!" He stopped short of hugging her, but that was good. She didn't mind physical contact when it was cold. In the winter it was sometimes necessary. But she avoided it most other times. She thought, though, that had he hugged her now, she might not have avoided it.

Robin clearly remembered her. Not just her name or her appearance, but the her she was in the silence.

Robin then turned to Giselle. "You found her."

"Actually, boy, she found me."

His eyes widened. "She went looking for you?"

"She did." Raven couldn't see Giselle's face, only her back, but she could hear something like amusement in the old woman's voice. "She was looking for you."

Robin swiveled to Raven, his eyes changing shape again. "You went to Giselle looking for *me*? By yourself?"

Giselle had just told him that. Raven didn't understand why he needed to ask, but clearly he did. She nodded.

"Really?"

"I didn't see you. I didn't see you for long enough that all the hiding places changed. I thought you might have died. People die in the warrens."

"People die everywhere," the young Barrani woman said.

"The grey crow would know." Raven looked only at Robin. "She knew who you were. If you'd been found dead somewhere, she'd know."

"Raven gives me entirely too much credit," Giselle said.

"We came to the warrens to find you," Robin then said, his words faster and easier than Raven's. They always had been. He laughed. "We went to Giselle. I did check the old hiding places first, but…it had been long enough I didn't expect to find you."

"I tried," Raven whispered. "I tried to keep them. Just in case."

"You won't need them anymore." Robin had come close enough that a whisper could be heard. "But knowing you, you'll find way better hiding places here."

"Giselle says we won't need 'em here."

Robin's expression shifted; it became what Raven called *complicated*. "We shouldn't, no."

As if aware of the sudden darkening of mood, the Barrani woman's eyes shifted color, becoming far more blue. Raven blinked. Maybe Barrani eyes changed color all the time? She'd heard that they *could*, but it was rumor; she'd never seen it herself until today. "We have class," the Barrani woman said.

Robin, however, caught her arm before she could turn. "This is Serralyn."

Serralyn grimaced. "Sorry—I forget introductions when I'm distracted."

"Me, too," Raven murmured. "I'm Raven."

"Robin has told us a lot about you—I've been dying to meet you. That guy just getting up off the grass is Valliant. It's a name, not a description; students seem to find that confusing. He doesn't talk much."

"And the other Barrani near Robin?" A Barrani man stood to one side of Robin; he was glimmering faintly. It made her eyes feel itchy.

Serralyn laughed, black brows rising into her hairline. "That's Terrano. Most of the people here can't see him right now."

"Oh. Does he not want to be seen?"

"I don't," Terrano said. "I'm not technically a student, so I'm not supposed to be on the Academia grounds."

"So...why can I see you?"

"That's the question, isn't it?"

Giselle had stiffened. It must be true. Giselle, at least, couldn't see him. Everyone could hear him, though.

"Serralyn could see you."

"Yeah, but that's a special case."

"Because she's Barrani?"

"Oh hells, no. Both Serralyn and Valliant are like family. They can always see me."

Valliant, the silent one, stepped on Terrano's foot, his eyes narrowing; they were blue. Terrano's eyes were blue, as well, but lighter.

Serralyn's eyes drifted back toward green as she shook her head. "Robin, we should take her directly to the office."

"You just pointed out we have class."

"The chancellor will forgive you if you miss a class. And I missed the last one, so I've already got a mark on the record this week." She folded her arms. "I think we'll be forgiven if we get an absence slip. Eventually." She grimaced. "It's Melden. You know what he's like."

"Yeah. I don't even know why he's here, to be honest—I don't think he enjoys teaching much."

Terrano grinned. "He's probably here because he hates students."

"True. Maybe boring us to tears is his subtle revenge." Serralyn exhaled in a huff of annoyance. "Fine. Valliant, you hate seeing the Dragon anyway—can you go to class and make excuses for us?"

"Or you could just ask Killian to take her to the office while we do what we're supposed to do?"

Serralyn laughed, as if Valliant's words were a deliberate joke. Raven didn't think he was joking. This was part of the reason she found people so tiring. It wasn't hard to understand their words—but it was often impossible to understand what they *meant*. "I think this is important," she added, her tone more serious.

"She's new. She can't possibly be part of this."

"We don't even understand what *this* is. I'll go with Robin and his friend."

Giselle cleared her throat. "I can escort her if there's a native guide. The chancellor seemed to feel that lessons—that classes—were of grave import."

"It's fine."

"He owes me money if he accepts Raven here as a student."

Terrano laughed. Serralyn grimaced. Robin, however, snorted. "If? There's no if about it."

Valliant and Serralyn crossed the park, the oddly glimmering Terrano between them; Robin remained beside Raven, changing the length of his stride to match her pace. It was familiar, he'd done it so often in the warrens. She'd had so much to tell him, but she couldn't remember most of it right now. Everything was new here; everything was strange.

Giselle followed them, walking beside Lord Tiamaris.

To the right and left, small clusters of people seated on the grass or the occasional bench looked up as they passed, but no one else made any attempt to approach or speak with them, which was more comfortable for Raven.

She wondered if Robin was right about hiding places here. She felt like she needed one now. But instead, exposed to open sky, she climbed the wide stone steps that led to large peaked doors. The doors opened before she'd made it all the way to the top.

She froze; Serralyn and Valliant didn't. Robin stopped because he was accustomed to Raven's sudden stops. He'd even accepted her sudden detours, when she fell utterly silent and veered to the left or right. He'd follow, becoming as silent as she; he understood that this was her way of avoiding a danger she had suddenly recognized—even if he hadn't.

But this time, although he stayed by her side, he said, "There's no danger here."

Raven hesitated. Her feet felt heavier with each stair she climbed.

"That is not entirely true at the moment," another voice said.

Raven looked up, forgetting to breathe until Robin poked her. "Robin, what have you brought to the Academia?"

Robin frowned, his eyes changing shape as if these weren't the words he'd expected to hear. "This is the friend I told you about," he said. "Raven."

"This is your friend?" A stranger stood in the open door. He was the height of a Barrani man, his skin pale and flawless, his hair long and black, but something about him was *wrong*.

Raven wanted to ask Robin who—or what—this man was, but she didn't want to attract any more of the stranger's attention. She would have turned to run if Robin had been afraid of him. But he wasn't. At all.

The man stared at Raven, forgetting to blink. "You met her in the warrens?"

Robin nodded. "The chancellor said we need new students. I told him about Raven. He came with me to the warrens to try to find her."

"Raven?"

Robin's brow furrowed in confusion. "Yes. Raven."

"Come here."

She wanted to run. She wanted to grab Robin's hand and drag him with her. She needed to find a hiding place.

"He's safe," Robin told her, his voice soft. "Raven, I *trust* him. You don't have to stay here if you don't want. I thought you'd like it here—there's food, and there's a library I think you could spend the rest of your life in."

Raven looked down at her feet, pretending that this stranger was like any other stranger in the warrens. Robin did the talking. Robin approached the friendly ones. Robin could tell if they meant harm—he could tell when they needed to run, to hide. He didn't think they needed to hide here.

But as his words sunk in, she lifted her chin. "Library—that's a house full of books?"

Robin nodded. "But if this feels like a bad place to you, no one will make you stay. It's not a prison. You can go back to the warrens. I'll—I'll try to visit you on the day we don't have classes."

"Who is he?"

"He is—he's Killianas. He's the heart of the building."

"Heart?" She frowned. "Is he like Tara?"

Lord Tiamaris cleared his throat. "Yes," he said, voice grave. "He is like—and unlike—Tara. Tara is the heart of the Tower of Tiamaris; she is the heart of the defenses of the fief. Killianas is the heart of the Academia, but it is not in defense of a physical threat that he was granted his long stewardship."

"Lord Tiamaris is correct," Killianas said. "But your name is Raven? It is an unusual name."

Raven wanted to tell him that it was the name Robin had given her. She didn't because she might draw more attention to herself.

Robin, however, said, "She didn't have a name when I met her. Or she didn't remember the name she'd been given."

"Ah. You named her?"

Robin nodded.

"But why Raven?"

"Her hair is the color of raven's wings, and she likes shiny things."

Serralyn coughed. Loudly. "Magpies like shiny things," she said. "You've got the wrong bird."

"Serralyn." Killian's tone was reproving. "Ravens are also known to collect shiny objects that catch their eye. Personally, I would prefer to be called Raven than Magpie. Perhaps you should attend ornithology classes to better familiarize yourself with facts."

Serralyn did not seem to find the correction embarrassing.

"Very well, Raven. Robin wishes to take you to the chancellor's office. I will accompany you."

Raven nodded and took a deep breath. Her feet were heavy, and her legs, trembling. Robin looked at her with serious concern. He didn't ask what she feared; he'd learned, years ago, that she had no answer beyond *danger*. She knew Robin would never knowingly endanger her, but danger existed, regardless.

Killianas frowned. "There will be no danger to your friend, Robin."

Robin continued to hesitate. Serralyn's eyes turned blue. Tiamaris's eyes turned darker orange. Giselle's and Robin's stayed the same color, but Giselle had narrowed hers in a way that implied she'd be the danger, if necessary.

Robin offered Raven his hand. She took it and tried not to hold it too tightly. She believed him: she wasn't going to be imprisoned. This was where Robin was. Robin was happy here.

Raven wasn't certain she could be as happy. But…a house full of books, and new places to hide. Robin was right: she could almost sense them. But that meant she would need to hide, at least some of the time. She was frozen for three long breaths, and then, tightening her grip on Robin's hand, she entered the building.

The halls were stone. The walls were stone. The floors were stone, although in some halls, she could see the glint of polished wood. There were windows that were taller and wider than Raven—or any other person present—and smaller closed doors she assumed led to rooms she had no business in.

She marked them all. She noticed the branching halls, the narrower ones, the shorter ceilings that could be seen in the distance; she noticed the stairs, the stairwells, and the windows. She stopped twice to kneel on long rugs, to look at their edges, to run her fingers through them, but she didn't let go of Robin's hand.

"I told you," he said—she wasn't certain to who, "Raven's curious about almost everything."

Killian said, "I see." Raven found his voice a bit odd. People's voices sometimes echoed, especially near stone, but Killian's echoes were different. It was as if the sound of his voice was like a deep well; you could only see the surface. When he spoke, there was an undercurrent, a different sound, something farther down in the darkness.

She rose, looking slightly guilty. "Sorry," she said, remembering belatedly that all these people were waiting for her.

Killian didn't seem irritated or disapproving. He simply waited, moving when she moved, and pausing when she paused, almost as if he were Robin. He wasn't, she knew; he looked nothing like Robin, and there was a harshness to his face, his form, that Robin would never possess.

Still, if he wasn't friendly, he made no attempt to harm her—and that was generally the best she could hope for from strangers.

There were strangers in these halls. What had been almost empty became instantly crowded—a flow of bodies moving deliberately toward a destination Raven couldn't see. She froze, becoming entirely still. Robin squeezed her hand. "It's okay," he said, voice soft. "These are all students. Their classes have ended, and they're on their way to the next one."

She nodded. She was surprised; Giselle said the old man had come because he was in desperate need of students—or so Raven had inferred; no one came to the warrens who wasn't desperate for something, and no one stayed if they had a choice. But it was crowded here. People—humans and Barrani—jostled each other as they walked quickly down the halls, their steps a cacophony of sound, their words bouncing off every exposed wall.

In the warrens, no one jostled Barrani. If Barrani were on the streets, people found different streets to stand in, as far from the Barrani as possible. Here, it was different.

She moved to avoid being hit or touched, sliding sideways, stepping quickly but carefully to find the few spaces that existed in a dense crowd. Robin let go of her hand as he always did when there were too many people, matching her movements but falling slightly behind. He was cautious, had always been cautious, but he wasn't afraid.

Here, in the open, with so many people in all directions, Raven struggled with fear. She had always had a difficult time with people, especially crowds. She glanced at Robin, saw his expression, and tried to take her cues from that: he wasn't afraid. He wasn't even particularly cautious. This was normal to Robin.

Valliant turned to Robin. "Time for one of us to actually attend Melden's class." He took a step into the flow of the crowd and walked away.

Raven watched him leave, wishing she could leave, as well.

"The halls will empty again," Robin said, voice slightly louder. "It's not like this constantly."

"Does it happen at the same time every day?"

"At the same times, yes."

Times. More than once. She exhaled. Robin had never lied to her. Sometimes she didn't understand his words, and sometimes she misinterpreted them—but when she finally understood what he said, or what she thought he said, she found he was truthful.

Serralyn, who had heard the brief conversation, said, "This is as safe as it gets in large crowds that include Barrani. From what Robin's said, the Academia is way safer than the warrens."

"It looks to be," Giselle added, her voice quiet. She was frowning at Killian.

Killian said, "I am not like the Tower of Tiamaris. The power given to me was not absolute. Even had it been, I have grown weak over the centuries of disuse; it is partly to empower me that students have been welcomed in almost alarming numbers. Should our growth continue, in perhaps two decades I might be able to offer the assurances of complete safety for our students.

"But there are…holes in my vision at the moment. Where there are unsupervised people, seeds of danger often grow. Ah, we are here."

Here was a set of closed double doors. Killian frowned. "The chancellor has guests at the moment. Please wait here." He glanced at both Serralyn and Robin. "You are now officially late for Professor Melden's class."

Serralyn glanced at Killian and then sighed. "I'll leave you with Raven," she told Robin. "And I'll make excuses if Melden complains."

Robin nodded. When the crowd had dispersed, he had once again taken Raven's hand. Raven was staring at the closed doors, her eyes narrowed. "Can we touch this?" she asked, although she didn't look away.

"I have," Robin replied. "And I still have both my hands."

Killian cleared his throat. "People generally touch closed doors to either open them or knock at them."

"Yes?"

"Why are you curious about the doors?"

Raven tilted her head. "I just want to feel what they're made of. They look like wood, but…they aren't."

"Interesting. Tell me, do the floors and the walls of this building strike you the same way?"

Raven frowned. She had begun to look at them, but she'd lost focus when forced to navigate the crowd. "Maybe? It's strongest here, at the doors."

"I see. The doors are reinforced magically. But as you imply, they are not made of wood in the traditional sense; the wood is…reconstituted. Terrano?"

"I see doors. I see warding. They don't look that different from any other doors—just more ostentatious." Terrano lost the light that surrounded his body. Raven wondered if that meant he could now be seen by other people who weren't his family. Or Killian.

"I think it best that neither of you touch these doors for the moment." Killian paused and then added, "The chancellor bids you enter." As he spoke, the doors rolled open. The wide frame revealed a desk some distance from the doors; the desk was occupied by an old man with a long beard and a neutral expression. He did, however, look up from the papers that cluttered the desk's surface.

When he caught sight of Robin, his expression relaxed. A subtle smile tugged at the corners of lips that were almost hidden by facial hair. "Robin. You've come with your friend." It wasn't a question.

Robin nodded. "Giselle brought her."

"I see. Come in. Come in, Raven."

She stepped into the room, and was surprised to see a second version of Killianas. Turning, she saw the Killianas who had escorted them vanish. She blinked.

Robin understood that blink. In a low voice, he said, "Yes, he can exist in two places at the same time. He can have two separate conversations at the same time, as well. I think he can exist in a dozen places at once if he considers it polite or necessary."

"You live in a very strange place," she replied, at her normal volume.

Robin was accustomed to this. "It's a *good* very strange place." He then took a step forward; as he was attached to Raven by hand, she came with him. She wanted to examine the room—there was a globe on a side desk, and something that might have been a globe but had other things around it, suspended by thick wiring. There were shelves to the side of the desk—and behind—that contained nothing but books.

She frowned. Looking up at the man behind the desk, she said, "Is the floor not safe?"

"I assure you it is."

"But the rug here…" Her voice died down as the man's eyes went from gold to orange as he observed her. She was talking too much. She always talked too much once she opened her mouth.

"Please, continue."

"Well...the rug is for protection. But...it's not protection of the floor."

"Tell me, Raven, have you ever been taught the fundamentals of magic?"

"I don't think so?"

"You're not certain?"

"I...don't know what you mean by *fundamentals*." She pulled her hand free of Robin's, as if to separate the stigma of ignorance from her friend. She then clasped both of her hands together.

"Ah. Robin has told me a little about you. He has all but demanded that I speak with you, even going so far as to coax me to visit the warrens in person. I am the chancellor of the Academia.

"We do have rules about admission. The first, and most important: we are a place of study, not a prison. You cannot be brought here against your will. Ah, no. You can be, but you will not be forced to remain, and those who did bring you will face consequences.

"Let me tell you about the Academia."

Raven's clasped hands had unclasped; they were now buried in her pockets as she touched the surface of glass—the piece she'd wanted to show Robin. It was smooth and its texture was comforting.

"Tiamaris," the chancellor said, "I believe that I may well be occupied for the next several hours. If you are concerned that the child may have been brought here against her will, I assure you she was not." He then turned to the grey crow. "Regardless of the child's suitability, we will pay your fee. Go to the administrative building—Killianas will guide you."

"I'll get the finder's fee for an acceptable student?"

"Yes. My intuition tells me that she has genuine potential.

Should she choose to leave, that would still be true; you have not wasted my time. The remainder of our interview is personal; it holds little relevance to you." *And it should remain that way*, his tone implied.

Raven wasn't good at reading and understanding tone most days, but she understood this one. She'd've left at a run if she'd been Giselle. But the grey crow didn't flee. If she could be intimidated by simple words, she'd never have survived in the warrens.

Raven frowned. Raven was intimidated easily, but she'd survived. She did it by avoiding people, because people were always the heart of true danger.

Giselle didn't flee, but she did retreat, offering the chancellor a nod. She turned toward the open doors and glanced back before she stepped across the doorjamb. "I am fond of Robin and Raven; I have an interest in their safety." There was a warning in the words. Raven would never, ever have offered it, but Raven wasn't Giselle.

Robin, however, winced.

"I will keep that in mind," the chancellor replied, as if he couldn't hear the warning—or didn't have to care. He had orange eyes. Tiamaris had orange eyes. Tiamaris was a Dragon.

"Are you a Dragon?" she blurted out before Giselle had left.

Grey brows rose. "Yes. Yes, I am a Dragon."

Tiamaris was smiling.

"Lord Tiamaris was once my student. He has changed since those days, but he still has difficulty taking a gently worded hint. Tiamaris: *leave*." The last word was *loud*. Raven would have covered her ears, but her hands were still clutching the odd treasures she'd found, and no one jammed pieces of glass or metal into their ears if they wanted to be able to hear later.

Lord Tiamaris chuckled. "Very well, Lannagaros. I have overstayed my welcome and must report to my lady that we are not, in any way, facilitating human trafficking." He was smiling, his eyes almost gold. "Raven," he said as he rose. "Take care of Lannagaros."

"*Tiamaris.*"

"I am certain we will see each other again in the future—possibly the near future." Lord Tiamaris offered the chancellor a brief bow before he walked out of the office. That left Robin, Raven, Terrano, and Killianas in the chancellor's office when the doors closed. Killianas who was also escorting Giselle somewhere else. Raven thought it might be convenient to be able to create a duplicate of herself at need.

To Raven's surprise, the chancellor looked to Killianas. "Well?"

"I believe she will be an intriguing and unusual student."

"You believe?"

Killianas closed his eyes, which most people didn't do in the middle of a conversation or a report. Robin accepted this as normal. "Do you wish me to eject Terrano?"

"I always wish you'd eject him, but it seems an enormous effort for very little practical purpose. Killianas, if you cannot eject Terrano without strain, at least see that he does not interrupt this interview."

"As you command," Killianas replied.

"Hey!" Terrano said.

Killianas caught Terrano by the shoulder. "The applicant is entitled to some privacy."

"Why? I don't get any!"

"Your lack of privacy was your choice. You chose to name-bond with your friends so that you would *not* suffer from excessive privacy. You are not a student; you are tolerated because of your close association with genuine students."

"Hah. I'm tolerated because it's impossible to get rid of me permanently—short of killing me, and that wouldn't be easy, either. He'd lose Serralyn and Valliant, and you can't afford—"

Raven didn't hear the rest of his words. The doors opened and closed on Killianas and Terrano.

"My apologies, Raven. It has been a long and trying day. I assure you that this is not the norm for applications to the Academia."

"Oh. What is normal?"

"You would head to the administrative building and fill in an application. If you are not able to write—or read—a verbal interview is offered."

"But...this is a school."

"Yes."

"And the students—they know how to read and write."

"We have one that is learning. It is not the ability that concerns us, but the potential."

"Do they like it?"

"Like?"

"Learning."

"Robin says learning is what you do. The world teaches you, and you listen. What have you learned, Raven?"

Raven shrugged. People of power asked questions and *expected* answers. Raven always took time to answer, as if testing each word to make sure it was solid, and by that time they were often angry. She hadn't finished testing the first tentative sentence when the chancellor shook his head.

"That's fine. It's not important. We have students here who might once have been considered scholars in their own right; we have students like Robin, who wouldn't. But Robin has much to offer the Academia—very much. And he believes that you do, as well. Killianas?"

The Avatar had walked out the doors without leaving a copy of himself behind. Raven didn't expect him to answer. Given the fold of the chancellor's brows, he did—and the lack of answer didn't anger him. It darkened the color of orange eyes; she could see red in them. So could Robin.

The chancellor cleared his throat. "I would like to take more time to discuss the Academia with you, but I fear that that discussion will have to wait. I will, however, say this: if you are willing to stay with us, we would be both honored and delighted to have you join the student body." He rose. "Robin, I will excuse you from class today; take Raven and show her the rest of the campus. Answer any questions she might have if you feel they *can* be answered."

Robin nodded. The nod was stiff; Robin was afraid of something. Before she could ask—and she wouldn't have asked him here, in front of the chancellor—the doors flew open quickly enough they banged into the walls and bounced off.

"Chancellor!" a young, out-of-breath woman shouted. "Killianas asks for your presence *immediately*."

The chancellor nodded. "Take care of Raven, Robin." He didn't look back. Instead, he joined the out-of-breath student. "Take me to him now."

4

The chancellor almost flew through the doors, which was odd given his apparent age and the fact that he walked—or ran—on two feet. Raven watched his graceful movements until he could no longer be seen, which didn't take long. She then turned to Robin.

Robin's face had paled. His hands, when her gaze drifted to them, were balling into fists. She reached for one of them to offer what comfort she could.

"You're worried," she said. It was a statement, but Robin always understood when her statements were questions that invited answers. She didn't know enough about the Academia to understand why Robin was so worried.

He nodded. "Killian didn't come," he whispered. "He sent a student."

Raven frowned. "I don't understand."

"Killian can be anywhere. I told you he can be in two places at once, right? But he sent a student to tell the chancellor there's an emergency."

"He doesn't do that?"

Robin shook his head. "If this were normal, Killian would

have come himself. Or at least his voice would have arrived. The chancellor is worried *because* Killian didn't come. It means he can't—or he thinks there might be danger if he does."

"Do you want to follow the chancellor?"

Robin took a deep breath. "No. There's nothing we can do. If there's actually a danger, we'll only get in the way."

"I know how to hide," Raven said. "You can hide with me. We can watch from a safe distance."

Robin shook his head. "I'm sure the chancellor would notice us, no matter where we hid. He really cares about the safety of his students. A lot. If we're in danger, we'll be the first thing he worries about, the first thing he tries to protect—even if he's in danger himself."

"He's not going to be in danger," Terrano said. He was peering in through the open doors, as if to make certain the Dragon had left.

"Can you go see what happened?"

"Where do you think I was?" Terrano glanced down the hall, and then back to Raven and Robin. "We should get out of the office."

"Why?"

"The office when the chancellor isn't present can be a bit dicey." To Robin, he added, "The chancellor told you to show Raven around the Academia. I don't think anywhere else is going to be dangerous at the moment, so we should probably do that."

"Do you know what happened?"

A ripple of uneasiness crossed Terrano's face. "I know why he was summoned. Another body was discovered in the quad."

Once again, Robin froze, his mouth slightly open as if he'd meant to speak and had lost all the words. "Whose?" he finally asked.

"Lykallos."

"Was it—was it like Barrios?"

"Almost exactly like Barrios." Terrano exhaled. "So far, two murders, two Barrani deaths. Sedarias is worried. She wants Serralyn and Valliant to come home."

Raven didn't recognize the name, but Robin clearly did; he winced. "But not you?" he asked.

"She knows I won't listen." Terrano grinned. "She doesn't *like it*, but she knows it's a waste of time."

"Robin says it's safe here." She gave Robin the side-eye.

"It's safer than where Robin grew up. A lot safer."

"But she wants Serralyn and Valliant to leave?"

"We live in a sentient building," he said. "Serralyn and Valliant used to live with us. The building's name is Helen, and within her perimeters, she has almost absolute power. No one gets in—or out—without her knowledge. And none of us can harm or kill each other." At Raven's expression, he winced. "We're mostly Barrani," he offered. "We have vile tempers when we lose them, and people can get hurt—but not when we're living with Helen.

"The Academia is a sentient campus—Killian. So it shouldn't be possible for students to die like this without his knowledge. Or at all. But Killian isn't at his full strength yet."

"Killian said he wasn't built the same way as other sentient buildings." Robin hesitated. Raven noted it. It probably meant Robin agreed with what Terrano was saying, but didn't want to.

Terrano shrugged. "We don't know enough about the history of the Academia to judge. But Killian was injured and in stasis for a long time, and even when he woke, he was only half-awake, half-aware.

"But regardless, we now have two corpses when it should be impossible to even have one."

"That doesn't bother you?" Raven asked.

"Not really—they're not mine, and they're not my friends. We're Barrani. We grew up on stories of murder and death. We just work hard to make sure it's not ours. Does it bother you?"

"I lived in the warrens," she replied. "There were always deaths."

"Did those bother you?"

Did they? She considered the question. "I didn't like it," she finally said. "But it's like weather—it happens. Sometimes it's good. Sometimes it's bad. But liking or hating it doesn't change the weather."

"Why did you stay in the warrens?" Terrano asked.

Robin answered before Raven could. "We had no money, and no way to make more than enough to keep ourselves fed. Barely. And it's not like people don't die in the rest of the city. I mean, if there were no crimes, we wouldn't need Hawks."

"Fair enough."

"Where are you going?" Robin asked as Terrano began to move.

"Where do you think?" Terrano grinned. "I want to examine the scene of the crime."

"I'm supposed to be taking Raven on a tour of the Academia. To help her decide whether she'd like to be a student here."

"Well...the quad is part of the Academia, right?" The grin deepened. "Serralyn's heading there now."

"She's in class!"

"The professor kind of called the class early, though. His classroom faces the quad, so she's not the only student who was looking—but most are doing it from the windows. What's wrong now?" he asked of Raven.

"How do you know?"

Terrano grimaced. "Serralyn is one of my friends. It's a bit complicated, and now's not the time to explain it, but we can hear each other's thoughts, so I know what she means to do." He then turned, while Robin tightened his grip on the hand she had almost forgotten he was holding. He expected there would be a crowd, and Raven had never liked crowds.

Robin was right to expect crowds, but this one was different: it was an audience. Raven didn't hate audiences, in theory, because the attention of the people that comprised them were focused. Sure, some of the crowd was attempting to pick pockets or cut purses—but they mostly did that outside of the warrens, because in the warrens purses tended to be lighter, emptier, or nonexistent. Better to steal from the rich than from people you might see again.

She made no attempt to enrich herself here. Robin had no intention of stealing. He never had, even when food was very scarce, which was one of the reasons she decided, on one rainy, gloomy day, that she might be able to trust him. Trust in the warrens was rarer than diamonds. Mostly, people were willing to trust you because you couldn't hurt them. They had more power.

Giselle didn't trust people. She could treat them as if she did only when they were weak or insignificant in comparison to her. There was no risk in trust, then—but that wasn't really trust, and Raven knew the difference.

Robin trusted people. She'd asked him why, once, and he reddened. He said it wasn't because he trusted people so much, but rather because he trusted his own instincts.

He'd trusted Raven.

It was a gift. She remembered it clearly. She would never forget it. And she didn't want to lose that trust; she didn't want to break it, which might be worse.

"Careful," Robin said, slowing. "You'll trip and fall."

Raven nodded. Sometimes when she was thinking, she lost track of where her feet were. She had to pay attention. People noticed her; they noticed Robin. No one seemed to notice Terrano. She remembered that Terrano—who she could see clearly—was invisible to them. As she watched she realized it was more than just invisibility. Terrano appeared to be passing *through* robes and arms; he disturbed nothing.

As Robin moved with purpose, passage became more difficult; the crowd became a wall of shoulders. One person might have been able to easily slide between them, but two made it awkward. Robin didn't let go of her hand, as if afraid she would get lost.

He did, however, tap people on the shoulder and ask, politely, to be let through. Soon, he reached the edge of the crowd itself, bodies transcribing the rough shape of a circle. In the center of that circle stood Killian and the chancellor. Between them, on the ground, lay an oddly broken body. It was Barrani in shape and form, and the Barrani was definitely dead.

There was no blood that Raven could see at this distance, but the man's arms were at odd angles; neither the chancellor nor Killian touched the corpse, but they stood above it as if studying it, protecting it, or both.

Raven craned forward; Robin's hand held her back.

"Not here," he whispered.

Raven yanked her hand free. For a moment, the people that formed the circle, the people that stood within it, and even the body itself had become grey and almost formless. She could see a piece of glass—a large, triangular piece with uneven edges— beneath the corpse's arm. It wasn't in his hand. Maybe it had been, before. But she knew that if someone didn't grab that glass, it would vanish. It wouldn't melt—it wasn't ice. It would vanish, leaving no trace of itself behind.

She remembered the first time she had seen this happen in the streets outside the warrens. She had seen the reflective surface of glass, had been drawn by its shininess, its newness, as if it hadn't been lying around for nearly long enough to pick up dirt or dust. She had waited to one side of the open street because it had been crowded; she intended to wait until they were almost empty.

But as she waited, she realized that the reflected light was dimming. It wasn't nightfall, and it took her a few seconds to realize the glass itself was shrinking, its edges fading from view. She watched as it eventually vanished, as if it had never existed.

After that, she risked crowds. She discovered that if she could pick these unusual pieces up, they retained solidity. But she had to touch them. They had to be in her hands. She assumed this was true for other people: that if someone else had any interest in broken pieces of glass, they could pick them up, and they would also retain solidity. She'd never tested this.

She didn't want to lose her treasures. She wanted no competition from treasure hunters. Raven knew, in a competition, she would lose. But she would have tested it with Robin, had Robin not disappeared.

She had pieces in a pouch in her pocket now, because she wanted to show them to Robin. She wanted to add this piece to her small collection, and it would go away if she didn't reach it first. It was the largest piece she'd ever seen.

Robin wasn't used to holding people captive. He tried to reach for her hand again, to hold her back—and she forgave him; she knew he was worried *for* her. She didn't want his worry, but had never quite figured out how to turn it off: it was Robin's worry, not her own, and he held on to it as if it, too, were some kind of secret treasure.

But when she pushed her way through the last of the crowd, a smattering of annoyed words followed in her wake—and so did Robin.

She was aware of the chancellor. She was aware of Killian. She was even aware of the corpse whose name she had been told and whose name she had almost instantly forgotten. None of these things were as important, in the moment, as that stray piece of glass, because if she hesitated, it would be lost.

Robin knew he couldn't stop Raven, not when she was like this. He tried anyway. She'd been offered a berth as a student, and he was certain that here, her oddity would be a benefit; here, she could be Raven and still flourish. He had always been drawn to her strange way of living in the world—even if that world was the warrens, which regularly spit on the naive and the ignorant. He'd seen his share of corpses in the streets of the warrens; he'd almost become one himself, crossing the wrong streets at the wrong time.

Raven, for all her strangeness and her reluctance to speak—as if speaking was a commitment she was only rarely willing to make—had saved him. She'd caught his sleeve in trembling hands, mutely shaking her head. When knives came out, she'd drawn him away before he could be caught in a skirmish between rival gangs.

There were signs, she'd told him.

Gestures and codes passed between residents of the warrens. Sometimes they could be seen in the arrangement of the sparse goods at merchant stalls, or the way specific foods were put on prominent display; if an apple sat in the center—a red apple, and Raven pointed out that it was probably wax—it meant danger in a certain quarter, or the advent of war in the warrens. It was a wordless language, a wordless warning, offered to people who understood the warrens because they lived there.

Robin hadn't been born to the warrens, but he'd entered them as a child, fleeing from a different type of violence, not that the end of that violence was any different than the skirmish he'd almost entered. Death was death. Still, he'd known that people wouldn't follow him into the warrens, not the way they might anywhere else in the city. The warrens were mythic to those who had not been born there.

Robin had grown up in the warrens, because he wanted to live. He had almost no memories of life before—only that there had been a before, and the rules of that before were different. He could read. Raven couldn't.

Raven couldn't read *words*. But she could read the warrens, she could understand their geography, she could understand the storms—both literal and metaphorical—that raged through their streets.

She had never been able to teach what she instinctively

understood. She understood power, to a greater or lesser degree, but couldn't see that it was power that defined the tone of the streets. Power and its structures existed everywhere. Understanding the ebb and flow meant safety. Failing to understand might mean death. Raven almost never left the warrens. The odd jobs she took were confined to the warrens, with rare exceptions; one or two of the people who threw work her way would send her as a courier to the streets outside.

The chancellor was looking for people who were unusual: focused on learning as much as they could about the things that drew out what he called passion. There was something about Raven, when she was focused and engaged, that made her so compelling to Robin. Compelling and enviable.

She didn't care what anyone else thought. She wasn't even aware of it. He'd often wished he could be the same—but, as she always said, Robin was Robin, and Raven was Raven.

And Raven was currently rushing toward a corpse between the two people who would decide her fate, seemingly unaware of their import, the weight of their ability to make decisions. Both Killian and the chancellor could be tolerant; they more or less accepted Terrano as a part-time student. Then again, they probably didn't have a lot of choice. Even the librarians said it was impossible to keep Terrano out if he put his mind to entering.

With Raven, they had a choice.

Robin readied his excuses. He would have stepped in front of where she now crouched, but that would have meant standing on an actual corpse. Or the chancellor.

He therefore stood beside Raven, half of his attention on her as she knelt by the side of the corpse, and half on the chancellor, on whose decision her fate rested.

None of his attention was on Killian. Even if Killian was sentient, something about his presence felt so much a part of the environment it was ridiculously easy to forget he was there.

Until he spoke. "Lannagaros, what is that child doing?" The words were louder and sharper than his norm.

The so-called child did not apparently hear the question.

The chancellor, however, shook his head, beard swaying slightly at the force of the gesture; the building's Avatar fell silent.

Robin watched. When he realized Raven wasn't going to be grabbed and thrown out, he knelt by her side, as he'd often knelt in what she called hiding places.

Raven reached for the arm of the dead man. Ah, no. She reached beneath that arm, pulling up the elbow to get to the grass under it, flattened by the fall. She then stopped, acknowledging Robin's presence for the first time since she'd shoved her way through the standing crowd.

Her voice was hushed in a way that spoke of excitement. "Robin, Robin, Robin."

"I'm here."

"Can you pick this up?" She pointed to the grass.

He frowned. "The grass?"

She shook her head at a speed that made him wonder—as it often had—how she didn't lose her balance from dizziness. "This." She pointed again.

"I'm sorry, Raven," he replied. "I can't see anything but grass." And the arm of the dead student.

"You can't see it?"

"What am I supposed to be able to see?"

"The glass. The glass piece. It's—it's the biggest glass piece I've ever seen. But it'll…melt. It'll go away unless someone picks it up. Can you pick it up?"

This wasn't the first time Raven had asked Robin to do something impossible, but as he had the first time, he felt almost guilty. "I'm sorry. I can't see it."

"But—but it's right here. Here," she added, stabbing air with a finger. He could see the disappointment she never bothered to hide transform her features, and as always, it made her look so much younger. He felt like a terrible older brother.

No, he thought. No, not terrible. Not that.

"Raven," Killian said, his voice a very unfamiliar rumble. "What do you see?"

The chancellor looked at Killian, not Raven, as the question hung in the air.

"It's glass," she replied. If she'd heard the shift in texture and tone of voice, she didn't react to it—but that was Raven.

"Glass?" the Avatar asked.

"Killianas. I do not see what young Raven sees." The chancellor gestured, his eyes narrowing; they were now a dark orange. Robin knew they could get far darker. If Raven hadn't been crouching here, he would have stepped back. "I do not see it when I actively look. There is the faint trace of magic, as one might expect, but nothing specific. What do you sense?"

Killian was silent, the entirety of his attention focused on Raven. He didn't answer the chancellor's question, which was almost shocking. Instead, he turned to Robin, and when he did, Robin saw that Killian's eyes were entirely black; there were no whites, no irises; they seemed to be all pupil. All pupil with small flecks of iridescent color that whirled around too quickly to be identified.

"Do you understand what your friend is doing?"

Robin hesitated, mouth suddenly dry. "She's picking up a piece of glass."

"That is not what she is doing."

"It's what she thinks she's doing. She collects glass pieces and metal bits—she's done that ever since we first met. It's never seemed dangerous before, more like...picking up someone else's garbage." He hesitated again.

"You often can't see these pieces?"

"She has better eyes than I do for that kind of thing."

"But she can walk into people without noticing them?" he

asked. He was clearly listening to Robin's thoughts, but Robin's thoughts were chaotic, not calm. Robin wondered why he didn't listen to Raven instead, and a shadow, a hint of fear, crossed his thoughts.

"Yes," Killian replied, as if Robin had found words to express that sudden uneasiness. "I cannot hear Raven at all. What have you invited into the Academia?"

Robin was silent for one long beat; his hands had curved into half fists, and his shoulders were rising almost to the level of his ears. He forced them back down, although he couldn't completely unclench his hands. "My friend," he replied. He had intended the words to come out strong; they came out shaking instead. But he said them. He meant them. "I trust her with my life, because she's saved me so many times. She would never do anything to deliberately harm anyone—even people who mean to hurt her."

He wasn't worried that Raven would be embarrassed by his words. He was certain she hadn't really heard them. Raven was in her own world, her eyes crinkled by a smile that was a pure expression of joy, of delight. When she withdrew her hand, she held a piece of glass, and as she had said, it was possibly the largest piece he had ever seen her retrieve.

But in Killian's shadow, Robin watched. He saw the moment her fingers made contact with the glass no one else could see, saw it suddenly reflect daylight, sunlight. She handled it with care—it had sharp edges—as she brought her treasure closer to her chest.

Only then did she turn to face Robin. She held out her hand; in it, carefully extended between two delicate fingers, was her newest acquisition. "Robin, look!"

"Go ahead," Killian said.

Robin turned to Raven, feeling vaguely like a traitor.

She noticed. "What's wrong?" she said, blinking. She then

looked at her surroundings: at black-eyed Killian, at the orange-eyed chancellor, and even at the dead person she'd almost been kneeling on. "Oh. I did it again."

At the sudden fall of her voice, Robin reached out and caught her shoulder. "Yeah, a little. It's okay. Let me see what you found."

When Raven failed to move, he exhaled. "And let me see the pieces you never got a chance to show me."

She hesitated for a long beat, as if teetering on the edge of awareness. But Robin's invitation was enough to pull her back; she dug into her pockets and found the small pouch she had always carried.

The chancellor cleared his throat. "Raven, Robin, I must ask you to save show-and-tell for a more appropriate place. We have, as you might have noticed, a crisis to deal with."

Killian said, "I would not advise it, Chancellor."

"I am willing to consider your advice in a less precarious situation," the chancellor replied. He exhaled as his eyes slid to an orange so dark it was almost red. Robin was grateful that his ire appeared to be directed toward Killian.

"Then may I make an alternate suggestion?"

"You may."

"Allow me to accompany Raven and Robin to your offices; I wish to make use of the east conference room."

Robin had never been in the east conference room; the chancellor clearly had. "If you insist. Make sure to offer them food."

"We've eaten."

This seemed irrelevant to the chancellor. "Yes, but in all likelihood you will miss both dinner periods. Follow Killian, and pay attention to what he says."

Terrano waited until they had cleared the quad and entered the building which housed almost all of the dorms and classrooms. He then materialized in front of Robin. "What did she just do?" he asked.

"She picked up a piece of glass. She collects them. Or were you hoping for a different answer?"

Terrano grinned. Almost nothing ever fazed him.

"Killian is *right here*."

"Yeah, but he can hear your answer no matter where you are if he cares to really listen."

"I've never knowingly lied to Killian."

"No—you're a terrible liar. And even if you wanted to, Killian would know."

Raven was frowning; she'd caught a sentence that she needed to think about, and had therefore missed all the rest. "He can hear you even if you don't speak?"

"Uh, no. He hears the words we're thinking to ourselves because we're supposed to have decent manners," Terrano replied. "I'm used to it. I live in a sentient building, and she can hear everything we're thinking, so it doesn't bother me. It does bother some people, because the inside of your head is supposed to be private space."

"But…"

"But? Are you worried that he'll hear what you're thinking?"

Raven shook her head. "I would like it. I would like it very much. Words are hard. All the time, they're hard. If I say something, people don't understand what I mean. I try to choose the right words. I try and try. It's better not to speak.

"But if he could understand me even if I didn't speak…"

Killian glanced at Raven, his eyes still black as the void. "I cannot," he said. As he spoke, color returned to his eyes, his face.

"But you can hear Robin? You can hear Terrano? When they don't speak out loud?"

"Yes."

"But…but why not *me*?"

"I do not know."

Robin held his breath.

Raven said nothing further, but looked openly disappointed, and Robin understood. Raven was, and had always been, an outsider—a person who fit almost nowhere. Robin had been her first friend. He still was. But even in the Academia, Raven wouldn't fit in. What Killian could do with others, he could not do with—or for—her.

Worse, Killian was suspicious of her. This wasn't what Robin wanted. He had thought—had believed—that Raven could truly be at home in the Academia. That she could, at last, be at home *somewhere*.

Killian's voice was gentle when it interrupted Robin's thoughts. "But is that what she wants?"

"We won't starve here," Robin said, voice low. "We won't freeze. We won't lack shelter in bitter storms. Even if home has different meanings to you and me, safety shouldn't. She can be safe here."

Killian fell silent as he continued to walk them back to the chancellor's office. He glared at Terrano, but he often did that, and Terrano's response was a cheeky smile. "It is not a question of her safety," Killian finally said, "but of ours. Come. Let us have show-and-tell in a room that has been created to survive almost anything."

5

Killian's words echoed in Robin's thoughts, growing weight and dimension because they absorbed Robin's fear. Had he been speaking of any other person, the fear would have dipped into suspicion.

But he was talking about *Raven*. Raven, the least malicious person Robin had ever met. He couldn't trust her to have his back in a fight—but he couldn't trust anyone to do that when the chips were down. Not until the Academia, and its chancellor. Not until Killian. Terrano. He was certain he could trust Serralyn and Valliant not to abandon him in a pinch.

He valued that.

But Raven didn't abandon, either. If she couldn't stand and fight—and she couldn't—she could do something smarter: she could grab him by the collar and force him to run. To run and to hide. That was a risk. It had always been risky to flee. There were so many dead ends in the warrens, so many places where escaping one danger meant landing into an even worse one.

She was willing to take that risk. She'd been willing to extend a hand. She'd shared what little food she'd scrounged, and in the winter, that had probably saved his life.

Raven had never, ever asked anything of him. Except for this: to share her excitement at her discoveries. To listen to her when she held something precious to her in her hands. She didn't have a temper. She didn't have any sense of what she was owed. She existed in the warrens, but she'd always inhabited a world of her own.

He couldn't believe that Killian was suspicious of her. He couldn't accept it.

"I find it comforting," Killian said, smiling, his eyes entirely normal. "You are, unlike many of the Barrani—or even the mortal students—remarkably straightforward."

"Robin doesn't lie," Raven said.

"No," Killian replied. "No, he does not." He paused in front of the chancellor's closed doors and lifted a hand.

Raven's gaze was torn from the treasures she clutched tightly in her hands. She took a step back and ran into Robin.

"He's just opening the doors," Robin told her.

"Yes," Killian said. "But Raven has apparently noted that I am not opening the doors to exactly the same location."

Robin turned to Raven, whose eyes were wide. He very carefully touched her arm, and she shook herself, looking at the hands that had fallen, and what they contained. She nodded too many times. She was aware of Robin. She was even willing to trust that all of this was somehow necessary. But she was now afraid.

"Killian won't hurt you unless you try to hurt him first. I promise."

Raven inhaled. "I don't know what will hurt him, though. Maybe he's like an ant. Maybe I'll step on him when I'm running away."

"I am not like an ant," Killian said before Robin could reply. "And even were I, you cannot accidentally crush me."

"But you won't know it's an accident. You said you can't tell."

"That is true. Robin, however, understands you better than I can yet. It is to Robin that I will listen."

"Not me?" Terrano asked.

"One can hardly help but hear you," Killian replied, in a different tone of voice.

Terrano laughed.

"Come, Robin." Killian gestured and the doors opened. "Enter. I believe if you do, Raven will be less afraid of following." He turned to Raven. "I can see what you now hold in your hands. Until you touched it, I could not. This room is built with special walls. They will not allow entry—even Terrano would find it very, very difficult—to any save us. Nor will they allow dangerous magicks to leave. Robin believes you are not a danger, and I have chosen to trust him—but some caution is required of me, because I am the Academia.

"Robin is not our only student. Should he miscalculate, he will suffer the unfortunate consequences—but no one who does not choose to take the risk of entering should likewise suffer them. Does that seem fair?"

She puzzled over the question, even after Robin had nodded his agreement.

"Yes?" she finally said.

Robin, who'd waited for her reply, now walked past Killian and through familiar doors into an unfamiliar room. The chancellor had called it the east conference room, and it conformed to its name: there was a long oval table, beneath which several chairs were tucked. Enough chairs to accommodate Raven, Robin, and Terrano with ease.

"Do you know how he died?" Raven asked. It wasn't the question Robin would have asked; not even Terrano was that cheeky. But there was no cheekiness in the question, just... Raven's focus and her furrowed brow. As if there was an answer to be found, and she had started to search for it, gathering stray strands of information to weave them into a whole.

"No, Raven, we do not. On the surface, the previous death and this one seem very similar. The bodies were not discovered in the same location."

★ ★ ★

Everyone took a seat, except for Raven. Her forehead was etched in her worried frown as she looked around the room. Her eyes finally settled on the farthest right corner facing the door, and she moved toward it as if she intended to sit there. This wasn't the first time Robin had seen this behavior. Normally, he would join her—she seldom chose out-of-the-way corners without cause—but she was the reason they were in the conference room in the first place.

He did follow, but only to take her hand and lead her back to the table. "No one will be able to see your treasures if you're sitting there." This was true.

"I don't want everyone else to see them." Also true.

"Killian wants to see them."

Silence.

"Killian won't steal them. He won't take them away."

Killian cleared his throat. "Do not speak for me. I wish to see the item she found beneath the corpse. It may prove critical in our understanding of the cause of death."

Raven's finders-keepers attitude caused her hands—now empty—to tighten. Her lips compressed. She was unwilling to have the argument in words, but it *was* an argument.

"I don't want to," she finally said, because Robin had not returned to the table. "I'll show you later. I promise."

Robin exhaled. "I told you the Academia was safe, right?"

She didn't nod, but she'd heard him. "You were wrong."

"It's been safe. We're fed, we're warm, we get taught things I would never, ever have been taught if I was still in the warrens."

"Like what?"

"Mostly? Portals, and portal spaces."

Her fear of losing her treasures warred with her instant desire to know more. It was a close-fought battle. "What's a portal?"

"Portals are really, really interesting. If I'd known how to create one in the warrens, we'd never be in danger from gangs again."

"Would it kill them?"

"No! No. It's like a…door. Portals are like doors that open into different spaces. But you can create them—if you know how—anywhere. If I could create portals quickly, I could create one in the middle of the street and we could run to it, enter it, and leave pursuers behind."

"Doors are attached to walls, though?"

"Yes. *Door* isn't quite the right word. It's just—it's like opening a door to a different room, except it's not a room—it's a different place. It could lead to a room in an entirely different building, or a room that wasn't behind the door. I could create a portal right in front of where we're standing, and we could both walk through it and end up somewhere else."

"Where?"

"That's the part I'm trying to learn."

"Can you create a portal?"

"Ummm, no. Not yet. Maybe not ever—it's magic, but it's a complicated magic that isn't like normal magic." Robin realized his mistake only after the words left his mouth.

Raven frowned. "What's normal magic?"

Terrano snickered, which didn't help. Raven probably wouldn't think Terrano was laughing at her—but mostly, she didn't care about laughter, even when she was the unintentional cause of it. Ugly laughter, yes—but that was often an early warning sign of violence to follow.

Terrano's laughter wasn't kind, but it wasn't ugly.

To Robin's surprise, Killian said, "That is a very good question." For the first time, his regard of Raven lost its edge, and his smile seemed genuine.

Raven turned to Killian's Avatar in confusion. "Is it?"

"Yes. I consider it a good question. But perhaps it isn't what you meant."

"What do you think I meant?"

"I think you meant to ask: *What is magic?*"

Raven frowned; the frown cleared slowly. She nodded. "Can you tell me?"

"It is a very broad question. In fact, at base, the attempt to answer that question is the reason for perhaps half of the classes taught in the Academia. Some people are born with a talent for magic—it is perhaps like mortal eye color, or height. But the study of magic and its nature is undertaken by many scholars who might otherwise be unable to wield magic."

Raven's frown was familiar to Robin; she was disappointed with the answer, but the answer had already begun to spawn more questions. She was trying to figure out how to word those questions—how to ask them to get the answers she wanted.

Killian, however, was ahead of her. "Tell me, Raven, what is water?"

His question interrupted hers. She blinked. "Water is wet?" But she knew this wasn't the right answer. She just didn't know, until she'd said it, that it wasn't, that she didn't have an answer to the question. Or maybe, given her expression, Robin was wrong. Maybe she had too many answers. He didn't know. It wasn't a question he had ever asked her. Water was water.

"You will find," Killian said into her silent struggle, "that there are many, many questions. The Academia attempts to answer them—but complete answers often require decades of research and thought, even when the subject seems, on the surface, quite common." He smiled; something about the smile was unusual for Killian. "But I understand, now, why Robin thought of you.

"Come. You meant to show him your treasures, and I have interrupted you."

Raven blinked, shook her head, and turned to Robin. There was no better way to interrupt her thoughts than the one he had chosen. But Killian couldn't read her thoughts.

"No. But I can hear you very clearly, Robin. I always have."

★ ★ ★

The table on the conference room seemed the perfect place for Raven to spread her treasures. She looked at it carefully, its pristine surface otherwise empty. She held her pouch and her newest acquisition but hesitated.

"Is there a difficulty?" Killian asked.

"This table," Raven replied firmly.

"Is the table the wrong size? The wrong shape?"

"It's...not really a table."

"Is it less of a table than the floors are flooring?" he asked.

Her frown deepened. She looked past Killian to Robin, her brows subtly creased. Robin reached out and placed a flat palm against the table's surface. "It feels like a table to me."

"Are you sure?"

"What does it look like to you?"

"A table," she admitted. "But." Robin waited as she gathered words. "It seems blurry. More like a reflection of a table than a table. No," she added, frustrated. "More like a table would look if it were underwater and I was above the water."

"Do the rest of us look like the table?"

She shook her head.

"The chancellor's desk?"

"That looked like a desk. A *big* desk."

Killian said, "The east conference room is a room, as I mentioned, into which magic cannot easily enter and from which magic cannot easily escape. Allow me to adjust the table."

Nothing happened—that Robin could see. But Raven's eyes rounded as she stared at the tabletop, and then slowly settled into their usual shape. She exhaled. "This is a very strange place," she muttered, for Robin's benefit.

"Strange is sometimes good," Robin replied. Smiling, he added, "You're very strange, but you aren't dangerous."

"Things you don't know can hurt you," she murmured.

Robin nodded. "You don't have to put them on the table," he told her. "We didn't have tables in the warrens."

She exhaled, but her shoulders, which had been hunched, lowered as she took a deep breath. She turned to him, her troubled expression warring with the excitement of sharing; it was the latter that won, but Robin had never seen such a close contest. Maybe Raven couldn't be at home here. Maybe he'd done her no favor seeking her out. She'd always survived in the warrens. She was smaller than Robin, and she wasn't very good with people—but she had an uncanny knack for avoiding deadly trouble.

She was skinny; in the warrens that was the norm. But she'd neither starved nor frozen in the bad winters. Maybe it was the warrens that were her home.

Robin had never been at home there in the same way.

But he felt a tiny bit of home when Raven held out her newest acquisition, because her eyes almost sparkled. She shed the discomfort, the tension of being in a strange environment, like seabirds shed water. In her hand lay a large, almost flat piece of glass. Its edges were sharp—it was a miracle she hadn't cut her palms when she'd gripped it so protectively.

"You're right. It's the largest single piece you've ever showed me."

Killian watched.

"I got others while you were gone," she said. She hesitated, and then gingerly handed the new piece to Robin. Robin took it with at least as much care as Raven opened the pouch she'd carried.

Killian watched them both, frowning. "Raven." When Raven failed to answer—probably because she'd failed to hear him—he repeated her name with more volume. The third attempt caught her attention. Her pouch was now open, the strings loosened to allow her to remove her gathered treasures.

She looked at Killian, her hands paused.

"Where did you get that pouch?"

Raven's hands tightened at the force of the question. She could hear the echoes of it, rebounding off walls that seemed impermanent, shimmering in place without achieving true solidity. She immediately pulled the pouch to her chest, tightening the strings; the only thing that prevented her from squirreling it away was the fact that Robin held her biggest acquisition. Robin's eyes were frowning eyes, but the frown was directed at Killian.

Raven didn't want that, either.

She'd never been asked that question, and because she'd never been asked it, she didn't have an answer ready. She didn't have the words. She struggled to find them, and settled on words with which she was familiar, she'd used them so often.

"I don't know." This wasn't a *how are you today* type of question—a question that was asked to mark time, a kind of longer hello. She knew that; she knew she should have had words ready.

"How long have you had that pouch?"

Robin winced. She turned to him, almost mute in the face of the question.

He exhaled. "Raven's sense of time isn't like ours," he said, understanding what her look meant. "Yesterday, last week, last month, last year—those don't have a fixed meaning for her. If you wanted her to conform to that sense of time, you'd have to make a schedule and you'd have to be there to help her follow it until she got used to it.

"She can't answer the question because she literally doesn't know how to answer it."

Raven nodded, relieved. But her gaze was fastened to Robin, not to the person who'd asked the question.

"Then let me ask you. How long have you known Raven?"

Robin frowned. "Seven or eight years."

"Do you know anyone who might have known her for longer?"

"Known of her, maybe? That would be Giselle. But Raven didn't interact with Giselle. It's just that Giselle knew almost everything that happened in the warrens. And she didn't hate Raven."

"The grey crow," Raven added. "The grey crow always flies." She had to tell Robin, had to remind him.

But sometimes her reminders didn't work. Sometimes she hated words. They didn't say what she meant. Not all of it. And then she had to make more words, speak more words. But for Robin, she had tried. Not at first, but gradually. Slowly.

And Robin had given her words, ways of making sentences, ways of reading sentences. He had taught her quietly; he was never loud. He was never angry. Sometimes he was surprised, and sometimes there was a tang of the unpleasant in that surprise, but it never lasted.

"Giselle, the woman who brought Raven to the Academia?" Robin nodded.

"I believe I need to speak with Giselle, but she is no longer on the premises." Killian's eyes were narrowed.

Robin didn't speak; finding Giselle wasn't hard, but he'd have to leave the Academia to do it.

"Yes. If you would do that, it would be appreciated." He frowned and added, "Tell her we will, of course, pay for her time."

Robin grinned. "Then she'll definitely come."

"Show me the piece of glass you are holding so carefully."

Raven tensed. She wanted to reach out and grab the glass back. Robin looked at her, as if seeking permission, and she struggled. She couldn't say yes. She couldn't nod.

"I think Killian wants to see it," Robin said, speaking slowly and with care, "because it was found beneath the body of a murdered man."

"Are all of your pieces found that way?" Killian asked.

Raven shook her head. "Not most of them."

"But some?"

She hesitated, thinking. Trying to remember. The thing that had caught her attention was the glass—although sometimes it was bits of shiny metal. How many had she found near corpses? How many had been under corpses that someone else had kicked out of the way? How many had been lying in the streets or near garbage?

She didn't know. If she opened her pouch, if she took out all of the pieces, one at a time, she could probably answer that question, because each piece was like a bit of story, or at least had bits of what Robin called story attached.

But she no longer had any desire to do that anywhere Killian could see. And she definitely didn't want to do it here, in a room that wasn't quite a room. There were no places to hide in it. She was almost certain that she could find hiding places in the Academia itself—it was the first thing she looked for when she was in unfamiliar terrain. She'd been too impatient. She hadn't been careful. She had never needed to be careful around Robin.

Robin, however, turned to Killian. His shoulders were tense, and his expression was what Raven called complicated. He was afraid. Not of Killian—Raven understood that fear, and she recognized fear *of* in the people she knew. But that wasn't quite right. He was afraid of Killian, but he wasn't afraid of being hurt by Killian.

She found herself clenching her jaw, and her hands were fists, but fists wouldn't hurt because Robin held the newest piece of glass. She didn't trust herself to speak, but she could say Robin's name, and did.

Robin turned to her.

She nodded.

It didn't seem to help his expression, but he did turn to

Killian then. He held out his hand; the glass rested above it as if it were made for Robin's palm. The idea struck her and held: it fit Robin's palm. Maybe she had found it, maybe she had found it *here*, because it was somehow meant for Robin?

It was a new idea, to Raven. She had always wanted to show him her treasures. She had never wanted to give him one. Had never thought that maybe it wasn't her treasure, but his.

"Thank you, Raven," Killian said softly.

She frowned.

Killian held out his hand, and Raven stopped breathing as she realized what Killian intended. Before she could intercept him, Robin carefully placed the piece of glass across Killian's palm.

Light exploded in the room—light bright enough to blind. There was sound, but it was dimmer, and mostly it was composed of voices as Robin and Terrano made noises. Raven did, too, but she couldn't help that—she knew the piece of glass wouldn't survive.

Robin blinked rapidly, his eyes tearing. He'd felt neither pain nor heat, but the sense that something had exploded in his face remained. His first impulse was to touch his face, to bring his palms to his eyes. But his face was unmarked, and after blinking rapidly, his eyes adjusted to the ambient lighting of the conference room once again.

His second impulse was to check on Raven. Raven, who would be crushed. She'd given that treasure to Robin because she trusted him, and it was gone. It was lost. She might never trust him again.

But when he could see again, when he could see Killian, he saw that the piece of glass was still whole; it still existed in Killian's hand. Killian's hand was red, raw, and weeping beneath it, but he'd preserved the glass.

"Raven," Robin said, catching her by the shoulder to stem

the babbling sounds of near hysteria, all shorn of actual words. "Raven, look. It's still there."

Raven stilled instantly at the sound of Robin's voice. She was, like Robin, blinking rapidly, but when she saw that Robin was right, she immediately grabbed the glass from Killian, her movement so swift it was back in her hand before Robin could speak another word.

"That was interesting," Terrano said in his lamentably normal voice as he turned to Killian. "You're hurt."

"I am aware of that," Killian replied. His eyes were black. Black and opaline. His face was the white of death. He looked at Robin. "I do not believe Raven should show you any of her other treasures at this time."

Robin risked a glance at the walls; they had buckled, as if half collapsing before righting themselves as much as they could. The end result was something that didn't really resemble walls or a room.

"Robin, I would like you to continue your tour of the Academia. Raven, please refrain from taking your treasures out of your pouch for the moment. If you accompany Robin back to the warrens when he goes to speak with Giselle, you may show him safely there.

"But I believe Raven would like the library, and I would prefer that she remain in the company of others. The chancellor is currently occupied, and will be occupied for several hours."

Terrano shrugged. It was Serralyn who loved the library; he could take it or leave it. Unless the librarians tried to bar his entry, in which case he had to enter to prove a point. "Serralyn says he's interviewing the students. I don't see why he can't just interview you."

"No," was Killian's soft reply. "You do not. You may tell Serralyn that she has permission to join Robin and Raven if they visit the library. The librarians approve of her." Killian gestured and the room itself dissolved; they were all dumped back into the corridor, without the excuse of a door to slow their progress.

Serralyn was delighted at the prospect of a visit to the library, but she couldn't use portals; they waited in the hall until she joined them. That gave Robin time to attempt to process what had just happened. Killian had been *hurt*. Judging by Serralyn's eyes when she joined them, she already knew. They were Barrani blue.

Terrano, choosing visibility, nodded. "I didn't think that was possible."

"It shouldn't be." Serralyn exhaled. "Robin?"

He nodded.

"Where did you find Raven?" In this particular case, speaking about Raven—who was present—in the third person wasn't the rudest choice. Raven's shoulders were now hunched around her ears, and her gaze was firmly on her feet. Robin knew that if she could find a convenient hiding place, she'd flee to it, to gather her thoughts or better hide her treasures. In such a posture, conversation was beyond her.

"She found me. My family had just…moved to the warrens. I was lost."

"Lost?"

He winced. "I'd been noticed by a group of people who didn't have my best interests at heart—I wasn't likely to survive. But when I ran, she caught me and dragged me into one of her hiding places. She didn't speak—she made clear I shouldn't, either, and we sat huddled together while they ran by. They came back three times, but finally gave up.

"I literally wouldn't be here today if it weren't for Raven."

"How long ago was that?"

"I think I was seven? I might have been eight. It was a long time ago." His brain caught up with his words, and he flushed. "I mean, for a mortal child, it was a long time ago."

"She doesn't make that glass, right?"

"No. Her treasures are things she's found—much like she found the piece she picked up today. I don't think all of the pieces she values are like...like that one." He glanced at Raven and felt a pang of pure guilt.

"Why do you think Killian wanted you to take her to the library?" It was Terrano who'd asked. Serralyn might wonder the same thing, but she wasn't going to risk losing unlooked-for library privilege.

Robin, who was fast giving up on the idea that Raven could find a home here, shrugged. "Maybe he does think she'd be a good student—maybe he thinks she's like Serralyn." He hesitated, and then added, "Neither of us can read ancient languages."

"But she can read yours?"

"She can—but it was the warrens. It's not like we had a lot of supplies or books there. I tried to teach her what I'd been taught—but I didn't learn much before my family was forced to relocate. The chancellor didn't ask for remedial lessons for me for no reason."

It was a class that none of the Barrani students—not a single one—had been asked to take.

He reached out and caught Raven's left hand with his right; it was shaking, but it was now empty. The pouch had disappeared into her clothing. The piece of glass had not. She carried it in her right hand, but she didn't look at it. No, it was the floor that had her attention. She didn't withdraw her hand. Robin wondered if she'd noticed him at all.

This was no longer the day for a tour of any kind.

But she surprised him.

"Can we see the library?" Her hand tightened around his. He shifted his grip so their fingers entwined. "I'm sorry."

"You have nothing to be sorry for."

"I didn't know it would hurt him. It never hurt you." Her voice was a whisper. She was still searching the floor, but Robin took comfort in the tightened grip; if she found a hiding place, she meant to take him with her. She didn't mean to hide from him.

"No one knew. Killian didn't, and he was the one who was injured. Do you think he'd've asked to see it if he knew what would happen?" But the image of his blackened hand returned.

Raven shook her head.

"It's not because you picked it up," he told her.

The doors to the library were, if not open, then at least present. This wasn't always the case. If you could see the doors, you were theoretically allowed to open them. Raven hung back, still attached to Robin's hand. Robin therefore turned to Serralyn.

Serralyn glanced at his occupied hand and nodded. She approached the doors and placed one palm across their surface; with the other she grabbed the handle of the right door.

The door dissolved beneath both hands.

Raven's hand grew slack as she watched Serralyn. It tightened on Robin's when the doors faded from view and the library itself became visible.

Robin hesitated. He hadn't warned her about the librarians, which was the first thing he should have done, because one of them was a gigantic spider.

That spider was closest to the door. Of the three librarians, he was the friendliest. He lifted his forelegs in the Wevaran gesture of greeting. Robin usually tried to return it, even if mortal limbs weren't nearly as flexible, but today he only had one free arm. He turned to Raven to tell her—quickly—that the spider was not, in fact, a spider, but a person named Starrante, but froze.

She was staring at Starrante, her eyes round, not with fear

but with delight. Yanking her hand free, she lifted both arms, just as Robin would have done, and waved them. The movements were almost an exact mimicry of Starrante's, if Wevarans only had two limbs.

6

If Robin was shocked—and he was—it was nothing compared to Starrante. Barrani had eyes that shifted color, depending on their mood. Dragons had similar eye color shifts, although the colors for each race were different.

The Wevaran, like most of the other races, had eyes that functioned in the same way, but they had a lot more eyes, and the shifts were more subtle. Their base color seemed to be a reddish brown; scarlet implied surprise or panic—but in those cases, eyes rose from the central body on slender stalks. It was the motion of those stalks that was the clearest indication of Wevaran mood, in Robin's experience.

Starrante was surprised. Two eyes rose as the Wevaran, wordless, faced Raven.

She didn't speak. Nor, once she'd finished the greeting, did she move. But there was no fear in her expression as she regarded the librarian. Serralyn's gaze jumped between the two mortal urchins and the ancient Wevaran, before she shrugged.

She was the first to speak. "Can we come in?"

Starrante's stalks swiveled toward her. He scuttled to the side. "Of course."

"All of us?"

"You have been given the chancellor's permission. You are welcome to enter. But I don't recognize one of you."

Robin cleared his throat. "This is Raven. Raven, this is Arbiter Starrante."

"Starrante?" she asked, in some confusion.

"It's what people with vocal cords like ours call him."

"Him?"

Starrante emitted a series of clicks that Robin now recognized as laughter.

"Raven," he said in that clicking, crackly cadence that was Wevaran speech, "are you a prospective student?"

She failed to answer immediately, considering the question with her usual care. "I think so?"

"She is," Robin said. "I told you I had a friend I thought would be a good student here."

"Ah! And she is the one?"

Robin nodded.

"You look troubled. Did the chancellor not approve?"

"He…told me to show her around the Academia before she made her decision."

"I see, I see." His eyes swiveled to Raven. "Have you disliked the Academia? Is there anything that concerns you?" He paused, and then added, "Ah. Are you concerned about the murder?"

She frowned, but failed to answer. Robin could have answered for her. Murders were common where they came from, although they weren't generally called murders. Wars between gangs were still wars, but those wars were like terrible weather: a fact of life.

Serralyn looked toward the endless walls of shelves; they towered above the heads of any of the students, although ladders were in place that could be easily moved—they had wheels. Raven's greeting and Starrante's reaction were interesting, but in a distant way; nothing had exploded, and no one seemed angry, so they didn't have the pull for Serralyn that the library itself did. She glanced at Robin, mutely asking permission to leave. Robin nodded.

He wasn't surprised when she headed immediately toward the towering shelves; on the few occasions they'd been given permission to enter the library together, she'd vanished almost immediately.

Raven hadn't apparently noticed the books; she was staring at Starrante, head tilted to the left. Robin knew Raven wasn't like most other people, but her pure excitement at meeting a Wevaran was the strongest expression of that difference he could remember seeing.

"Robin, where did you meet your friend?" Starrante asked.

"In the warrens."

"Have you met her parents?"

He shook his head. "By the time we met, she didn't have any." Shortly after, neither had he, the two facts being entirely disconnected.

"Where in this warrens did you meet her?"

He could remember the exact location, but it didn't come with names or landmarks Starrante might readily recognize.

Raven, however, answered. Or he thought she answered. He didn't recognize the word she used. Had it been Wevaran in origin, he probably would have; it wasn't.

"How old are you, child?" Starrante asked.

Raven blinked. It was a question she'd never been good at answering. Nor could she answer simple questions like *when is your birthday* or *what is your name*. She'd been surprised when Robin could answer both, although they weren't questions she'd asked of him to that point. She'd asked a lot when he'd answered someone else, though she'd waited until the person who asked had continued on their way.

"It's not important," the Wevaran said into her silence. "I could not accurately answer that question when Robin asked it of me, either. I would have to sit down and attempt to construct an answer, given various events."

"It would remain an inaccurate number," a new voice said as the second librarian appeared.

Raven's eyes were practically glued to Starrante; Robin wasn't sure she'd heard Arbiter Kavallac, the Dragon librarian. But her focus didn't imply deliberate snub. She wasn't speaking, but when in the midst of discovery and its excitement, she almost never did—and that, given her expression, was where she was.

What he wanted to know was what she saw when she looked at Starrante; clearly it wasn't the giant spider anyone else saw. She'd understood instantly that the two raised limbs were a greeting, and because the greeting didn't contain words, she had mimicked it as well as any human could.

Kavallac's eyes were bright, but her expression showed hints of genuine curiosity. When Raven failed to notice her, she turned to Robin. "I heard Starrante speaking about a possible new student and it caught my attention. Is this the student in question?"

Robin nodded.

"She seems quite taken with Starrante."

Robin nodded again.

"Where did you find her?"

Robin repeated the answer he had now given more times today than he had ever given. He then paused and turned to fully face Kavallac. "Have you heard about the second death?"

The Dragon's expression made clear that Robin was now the bearer of bad news.

"The chancellor was at the site of discovery; the body hasn't yet been removed."

"But what we'd like to know," Terrano added, materializing beside Robin, "is how investigation is necessary."

"If there is a murder, investigation is always necessary," the

Dragon replied. Robin noted that she kept her gaze on him, not Terrano, who had asked the question.

"Look, that may make sense to Robin. It may sound good to all of the other students—but it won't work on us. We live with Helen. Before that, we lived with—were imprisoned by—the Hallionne Alsanis. We have a pretty good idea of what sentient buildings are capable of. In either Helen's or Alsanis's case, any murder we discovered would have had to be committed *by* the buildings themselves. They don't allow harm to come to their occupants.

"Killian's a sentient building. He should at least be aware of the danger to students."

Kavallac's eyes darkened, but she kept her gaze on Robin. "How much experience do you have with the High Halls?"

Robin blinked. "None."

"She was talking to me," Terrano said, annoyance coloring the words. "I have enough."

"I was speaking with Robin," Kavallac snapped. Robin had no doubt that if she could easily eject Terrano, he'd be gone. But he'd only come back; it was very hard to keep Terrano out for long.

"Why would he have any experience with the High Halls? He's not Barrani."

Robin wondered what it would be like to be as fearless as Terrano.

"I've heard about the High Halls—it's the Barrani center of power. It's where the High Lord convenes his court." Robin kept his tone as even as possible. He *liked* Kavallac. He liked Terrano. He just wanted them to be in two completely separate buildings.

Kavallac nodded; her eyes remained a steady orange. Often, in Robin's presence, they were gold, the Dragon color of happiness. "The High Halls, as the Academia, were created by the Ancients; they are a sentient building.

"Terrano believes sentient buildings should prevent murders. Perhaps he is naive."

Terrano bristled. "What she is *trying* to say is that murders occur in the High Halls."

"To listen to some of your kin, more frequently than weather," Kavallac said. "The nature of the Barrani defines the tolerance of the High Halls. The Hallionne would not allow guests to murder each other in any fashion; they were built as sanctuaries.

"The High Halls might consider such overt protection infantilizing. Barrani die at each other's hands all the time."

"Not in as great a number as they did by the hands of your kin." Terrano's eyes were now dark blue.

Robin turned to Terrano then. "That was war. Historical accounts of the start of each war seem to differ depending on which racial accounts we read or hear."

Serralyn sprinted from the distant shelves toward Terrano; she slowed only when she reached his side, and stepped neatly between her friend and the librarian. Her eyes were blue, but green could still be seen. She turned to Robin, standing between Dragon and Barrani. "This is the problem with immortal memory." Her voice was soft, her expression absent any joy. "We remember everything as clearly as you remember yesterday."

"More clearly," Terrano said, but his voice had lost some of its edge. He exhaled slowly. "What the Arbiter is attempting to point out is that the High Halls doesn't supervise its occupants the same way Helen or Alsanis did. The High Halls was created as a home for the High Lord and his court, and the lords have always intrigued. The High Halls allows the Barrani within to lead lives of their choosing.

"There's only one Barrani against whom no Barrani would survive attempted harm."

"The High Lord?"

Terrano rolled his eyes. "I told you: intrigue. I'm almost certain the High Halls believes any High Lord that can be assassinated by his underlings deserves to die. Only the strong should rule. No. The High Halls wouldn't interfere there. The lords of the court are free to play their deadly games. If they were conspiring with Shadow, it would be different—they'd all die. But killing our own kin? Time-honored tradition." The bitterness in those words was unusual for Terrano.

Serralyn placed a hand on his shoulder. Lifting her head, she said, "The High Lord rules; there are powers granted only to him while he lives. But there will always be a High Lord. It is The Lady that the High Halls protect.

"The Lady—the Consort—is protected by any sane Barrani. She is sometimes called the Mother of the Barrani. Without her presence, no new children wake. If harm were to befall her, we would be just as worried for the High Halls as we are for Killian; it would mean something was dangerously wrong or broken within the High Halls themselves.

"But the High Halls have welcomed Barrani company in the very recent past, and Terrano has been spending too much time there."

"Not enough time, in my opinion," Kavallac added. "We would all be better off if he spent a few decades there." Her eyes, while not gold, were less orange.

Serralyn was a peacemaker at heart. And she was Barrani.

Kavallac turned, at last, to Terrano. "You have spent time speaking with the Avatar of the High Halls."

"And playing chess, yes. I win," he added, his signature grin returning. The grin fell away. "In those discussions it was clear that the intervention—that the lack of intervention—was the High Hall's choice. The Avatar was aware, but did not choose to interfere.

"I don't think that's the case with the deaths in the Academia."

"Killianas has said that the imperatives with which he was created are unusual."

"The imperatives of Helen, Alsanis, and the High Halls are *all* different. Murder could happen in only one of the three—but the Avatar of the High Halls would know who had committed the crime, why, and when. He wouldn't disclose the information; he feels that it's the business of the Barrani. But he would know. Killian doesn't seem to know."

"This is not a subject you should discuss with librarians," Kavallac said.

Robin noted that she didn't disagree. She hadn't disagreed with anything Terrano said, and she wasn't prone to polite agreement, or even silence, for the sake of peace. Neither was the absent third librarian. Starrante was the only one who might deflect politely. He hated conflict.

But he seemed as distracted by Raven as Raven was by him.

"You have not mentioned the Towers in the fiefs in your experiences with sentient buildings—buildings created for specific purposes." Kavallac's eyes were orange, her expression the disapproving glare of a teacher at a recalcitrant student.

Terrano shrugged. "I haven't lived in one. I've only visited."

"No—I imagine you would be destroyed or severely injured should you attempt to visit the Towers the way you visit the library. I am not saying you intend harm, but most of the Towers would look askance at both the attempt and the nature that allows it."

Terrano opened his mouth.

Kavallac lifted a hand before words fell out of that mouth. "Have a little patience. The Towers, just as the buildings you have mentioned, have their own imperatives: they encircle and imprison Shadow. By the time the Ancients considered their construction necessary, they were far more familiar with the changing nature of Shadow and the harm Shadow could do to the fabric of reality.

"They therefore created Towers whose existence and function required a captain. A lord. With the passage of time, the lords would change; they would bring changing knowledge and information to the Tower, and work in concert with the Tower to protect the fiefs from invasion."

"Don't see what that has to do with Killian's lack of knowledge."

"Knowledge is not unlike Shadow in its changing nature."

"Facts are facts," Terrano said. "Why didn't Killian know about the murders? Why doesn't he know now?"

"Facts are, as you put it, facts. But our understanding of the context of those facts shifts and changes with knowledge. Some things considered promising in a past so distant even I did not experience it firsthand were later disproven, or proven far more insidious and dangerous than early scholars had anticipated. The direction of knowledge, the use to which it might be put, shifted and changed in response: learning is not a fixed study of simple facts; it is an understanding of those facts in the context in which they were learned; it is the way facts blend with other facts and suggest knowledge that was previously hidden.

"There are dangers when new knowledge is unearthed; those who seek power have often threatened or pressured the Academia. Before I accepted my position as librarian, there were even attacks meant for the library—which, as you must suspect, Killianas could easily deflect. What he could not, however, deflect, was the murder of the students under his care when they were not on the campus."

"The two dead Barrani were *on campus*, Arbiter."

Kavallac continued as if Terrano hadn't spoken. "Those who sought the power knowledge brings—specific, useful knowledge—understood that the Academia required students to function. Students are not born and raised within the confines of the Academia; they arrive at our doors. If they could threaten the Academia with a lack of new students, it was a danger; those prospective students were held hostage in the lands beyond the campus."

"Just in case you've forgotten because it's been so long, the question was: How can Killianas not know?" Terrano's response was impatience personified. Robin, however, found all of Kavallac's information fascinating. Possibly frightening.

"You are not even a student here. Let me remind you that I am not required to treat any of your rude demands with respect." Her expression made clear she was irritated, not angry. "But I believe the answer will affect those who *are* students, and for whom we bear some responsibility.

"Very well. The chancellor is to the Academia what the captains are to the Towers. The chancellors can leave the campus; the Avatars cannot. It was the chancellors who ended the threat to students who were attacked outside of the Academia's campus; I believe it was the second chancellor who decreed that all students must occupy the dorms. It was the chancellors who dealt with the political machinations that occurred beyond Killianas's reach. Our current chancellor, I believe, would be up to that task.

"It is therefore the chancellor you must ask. If the chancellor grants permission, Killianas will be more free to discuss what he knows."

"That doesn't answer anything," Terrano grumbled.

Robin had to agree. But he understood Terrano's concern now. Terrano had more experience with sentient buildings. Terrano thought Killian *should* be able to prevent murders on campus. Killian *should* know how they occurred, and why, and by who. Investigation was only necessary if Killian didn't know. Or couldn't.

Robin's strong desire to turn heel and march directly to the chancellor's office was offset by Raven. Or rather, it was offset by Starrante's sudden rapid clicking, shorn of syllables. A chitter of sound, it was higher in pitch than normal, and it also immediately drew Kavallac's attention.

It also, unfortunately, drew the attention of the third librarian, the one who in general held students in some contempt. He appeared a little ways off from Starrante. He looked like a Barrani, but he wasn't—he was of a race the Ancients had created before the Barrani. The Barrani called them Ancestors. Or death.

Arbiter Androsse, eyes sharp and darker blue than was safe, snapped, "What is this cacophony?" He glared in Kavallac's direction, which was the real reason Robin wasn't happy to see him; the two Arbiters often disagreed, and when they did, things got *loud*.

As Kavallac wasn't the source of the noise, it wasn't surprising that she responded with a reddening glare. "Perhaps age has finally caught up with you," she snapped in return. "And your ears are failing if you mean to glare at me. It was clearly Arbiter Starrante's voice."

Androsse then turned his glare on Starrante, or so Robin assumed; Starrante was generally excused from the ill temper that governed the interactions of the other two.

Starrante had barely managed to contain his wordless screech, but his eyes—all of them—had lifted right out of his body and were waving and weaving in something that seemed, to Robin, to be near panic.

"He *is* excited, isn't he?" Androsse said.

Kavallac's eyes, now red, agreed. "Starrante," she said, her voice a rumble that implied the far larger and deadlier form she could assume at need.

Half of Starrante's eyes swiveled toward the two Arbiters. The other half seemed to be randomly waving in the air.

Androsse frowned. He gestured sharply, swiftly; Robin felt a full body slap pass through him. Terrano cursed. Everyone converged on Starrante.

No, Robin thought, they were converging on Raven. The two Arbiters—the Dragon and the Barrani Ancestor—moved toward her. Androsse raised his arm a second time, but Starrante reached out with a limb and hit the Arbiter in the chest.

Robin's jaw fell open, but words failed to tumble out. He ran to Raven, caught her sleeve, and turned to face Androsse, Starrante squarely at his back.

"Do *not* touch her!" the Wevaran snapped. "She has done nothing wrong. She is not a threat." The fact that he felt the need to shout this at Androsse was not a good sign.

Kavallac came to the rescue, in a fashion; she interposed herself between Androsse and Raven. Or Androsse and Starrante; Starrante had positioned four of his limbs around Raven without actually grabbing her and drawing her back.

Raven was blinking. She understood that the sudden noise—all of it—had something to do with her presence, but she didn't understand the appearance of the two librarians she had yet to meet. Her back was to Androsse and Kavallac, and her eyes were following the agitated weave of half of Starrante's eye stalks. As if she could hear them. As if she could see a pattern that might be like language in their movement, but silent.

"Hold on to that, child," Starrante said.

The Arbiter wasn't angry at her or even about her; his voice was gentle. It was the voice Robin most often heard when discussing his various classes—and the questions that arose from them—with the Arbiter.

"I would like to see what she is holding," Androsse said.

Raven closed her hand and shoved it into her pocket. Her pockets were deep; they ran the length of her robe. This was Raven's way of saying no.

Starrante chittered in his native tongue.

Androsse's eyes were indigo—the Ancestors' eye colors followed Barrani eye color closely. He responded to Starrante in a tongue Robin had never heard. It wasn't Barrani, nor was it the variant High Barrani Robin was learning—with Serralyn and Valliant's help—to master. It wasn't Elantran. It was higher but simultaneously deeper.

Kavallac reached out, grabbed Robin with one hand and Raven with the other. Raven froze but Robin shouted her name and nodded, trying to keep his expression as calm as possible. "Serralyn!" the Dragon librarian roared. "Grab your irresponsible friend.

"Library hours are now over!"

Killian was waiting for them when Kavallac forcefully ejected them. Both Robin and Raven stumbled; Terrano kind of… flew. Serralyn was the only person who hit the exit entirely on her own, but her eyes were a very dark blue, probably because they'd been ejected with so little warning, but possibly because the phrase *irresponsible friend* had implied, to her, that Terrano was the cause for their swift expulsion. She didn't get angry very often, and it wasn't—as it was for most Barrani—her base state.

The door didn't slam shut at their backs, which was what Robin expected given the manner of their ejection—but perhaps that was because Killian moved to stand in the frame.

Kavallac spoke to him. Robin didn't understand a word she said, but he both felt and heard her; Draconic roars shook the stones beneath his feet. Killian answered in kind; Robin cupped hands over both his ears, but then turned to look for Raven. She was standing to one side of Killian, back to the door, her eyes wide and almost vacant, her shoulders trembling.

He lowered his hands again, preservation of hearing momentarily forgotten.

He'd dragged her here. He'd thought she'd be safe because he'd been safe.

He'd never seen the expression she wore now—the lack of expression, the vacancy—but he knew she was afraid. Possibly terrified. He moved instantly toward her, passing before her vacant gaze. She didn't notice him. It was bad.

Raven didn't like to be touched; the only exception was her hand. She was willing to let Robin hold her hand. He reached—gently but deliberately—for her hand now.

"Raven. *Raven*. It's Robin. I'm here."

She turned slowly to face him, her eyes round and unblinking.

"Robin," Killian said. "Take Raven away."

"Where?"

"Anywhere but here. *Now*."

"Raven," he said, deliberately gentling his voice. "I think we should leave. Let's—can I show you my room?"

She blinked. Blinked again. And then, to his relief, said, "You have a room?"

"I do. We all have our own rooms. Want to see mine?"

For a long, long beat he thought she would refuse. Once or twice in their childhood, she had refused, pulling her hand, shaking her head, and vanishing around a corner before he could catch up. The first time it had happened, he'd been afraid—for her. For himself. She had been his first real friend in the warrens.

But she was by the well two days later, looking a bit sheepish; she approached him carefully, almost backing into him rather than facing him. And he'd talked to her the way he always had. She'd brightened then. He knew, when she vanished or ran away, that she had to do it for reasons he didn't understand; if it was dangerous, she'd've grabbed his hand and dragged him with her.

He'd learned to follow.

It took two years before Raven was willing to return the favor of looking at the things Robin wanted to show her. Robin believed he had finally earned her trust—which was fair. He'd trusted her almost from the beginning. But he realized shortly thereafter that it wasn't her trust he'd earned—it was her curiosity. At some point in the very slowly built friendship, she'd become curious about Robin.

What's a friend?

He took her hand. She followed.

At their backs he could hear the discordant sound of Dragon roar, Wevaran chitter, and an entirely foreign tongue. And he could hear Killian responding to each in kind.

Serralyn followed them. Terrano had been thrown down the hall, but had managed to pick himself up off the floor by the time their path brought them together.

"He's fine," Serralyn said before Robin could open his mouth to ask. "He wasn't very corporeal when we were thrown out. You know how you can drop a mouse off the tallest building in the city, and when it lands it's fine? Think of Terrano as a mouse."

"Please don't," Terrano said. He glanced at Raven, and then at Robin. "You certainly riled up Starrante—I've never seen him that excited."

"Didn't sound like excitement to me," Serralyn said. "It sounded almost like fear."

"Yeah, it looked that way to me, too." Terrano grimaced. "It certainly looked like that to Androsse—I was afraid he was going to—" He stopped talking. Robin was grateful.

Terrano was so strange. He wasn't normal, even for a Barrani; he was too chaotic, too unregulated to become a student. He didn't like other people's rules when they were applied to him, and the Academia had a lot of rules. But he could be sensitive, he could notice hesitance and anxiety that had no obvious outward signs.

He'd noticed it with Raven, just now. Had Raven not been here, he'd've finished the sentence. Had Androsse been angry with either Serralyn or Robin, he'd've finished it with grim delight. But he had the sense that Raven couldn't or wouldn't handle it well.

"What did you do?" Serralyn asked Raven.

Raven hung her head. "I don't know."

Robin couldn't see Raven's face, her head was bowed so deeply. But he did see the tears that splashed against the floor. He froze. He'd almost never seen Raven's tears.

He looked away in discomfort. Robin didn't cry in public. He didn't want people to see him cry. He almost dragged Serralyn and Terrano away to give Raven privacy, to give her space.

But before he did, he remembered that Raven wasn't Robin; she didn't have many of the social fears, the fears of being judged, the fears of being weak. She was…just Raven, and she was upset.

Drawing a deep breath, prepared to be told to go away, Robin gently tugged her hand. "My room?" he said softly. "I'd like to show it to you."

She didn't lift her face, but she did nod, and she tightened her hold on his hand.

Serralyn followed, as did Terrano.

The one thing about his Barrani friends that Robin sometimes found difficult was their concept of privacy: they just didn't have it.

They weren't hypocrites; if they walked happily into Robin's room at all hours when they had something they wanted to share, they truly didn't mind if Robin returned the favor. They just… didn't seem to have a need for privacy, for private time or space. He'd discovered that he could just tell them he wanted to be alone, though. Valliant wasn't terribly interested in Robin. He'd nod and walk out. Serralyn often asked why before she left. Terrano, however, nodded and vanished.

Probably. Terrano being Terrano, it was hard for Robin to know if he'd vanished or just become invisible.

Regardless, Serralyn and Terrano followed Robin to his room. They didn't like that he lived alone; Valliant and Serralyn shared a room, and Terrano was there half the time even if he wasn't officially a student. Maybe that was why they didn't really understand the concept of privacy. Raven understood it better, and she needed way more of it than Robin ever had.

Raven had never needed people. She seldom needed company. The only things that brought her to Robin's side were danger—largely to Robin—and discovery. She wanted to share those discoveries with someone, and that someone had become Robin.

Raven came in and sat down on the floor in the corner just beneath the one window the room possessed. She bent her knees, wrapped arms around them, and bowed her head to hide her face. He knew he would have to show her something to get her to raise it again.

But he had questions, as well. He waited, but Raven didn't move. She was trying to become as invisible as Terrano often was, but in her own particular way.

"Do you know what the chancellor discovered when he examined the body?" Robin looked at both Serralyn and Terrano.

The two friends exchanged a glance; Terrano shrugged. It was therefore Serralyn who answered. "Nothing beyond the obvious: someone is dead in the quad. Again. The cause of death has 'yet to be determined,' but obvious things have been ruled out: no wounds, no poisons with which the student body might be familiar, no strangulation or broken neck. If it weren't for the position of his arms and the lack of breath, he might have been sleeping." She turned to Terrano. "You asked the librarian why Killian can't tell us when, how, or who killed Lykos."

Terrano nodded. "She seemed to think Killian couldn't answer my questions without the chancellor's permission. But she also seemed to know something."

Serralyn nodded and turned back to Robin. "But there's a

different problem now. Your friend picked up something that no one else could see. I didn't, Terrano didn't—and he was looking for anything out of place—and the chancellor didn't. Killian didn't see it, either. Raven did. She not only saw it, but she ran to the body and moved the dead person's arm out of the way in order to pick it up.

"It was glass—it looked like glass once she'd retrieved it. But it's not glass. Whatever it is, it injured Killian, and it caused Starrante to lose all composure."

"You don't know that." Robin didn't, either; he'd been talking with Terrano and Kavallac. But he thought Serralyn was right. Raven hadn't been afraid of Starrante, and Starrante had been delighted to see her, to converse with her—or at her, sometimes it was hard to tell. He'd seldom seen Raven so instantly effusive, but if it was exposure to Wevaran that caused it, he'd never have had any reason to—there were no Wevaran in any part of Elantra except the library and the fiefs.

Serralyn exhaled. "Raven, you showed Arbiter Starrante your piece of glass, didn't you?"

7

Raven wanted to go back to the warrens.

Robin didn't like the warrens, but he hadn't been born there. He hadn't grown up hearing the cadence of the warrens' many streets, the punctuation of weather, the sudden tremors of violence and death. He hadn't watched the way buildings had slowly given way to age, little cracks and splinters forming in wood; hadn't seen the way the water rose or dried up in wells. Not the way she had.

He hadn't learned to *listen*. He hadn't learned how to find hiding places, hadn't learned how to sink into the warrens. She thought he *could*. She'd thought he could the moment she first laid eyes on him. She thought she could teach him.

But instead, he'd taught her. He'd taught her about people. He'd taught her how to talk to them—people were *hard*. He'd taught her how to read—to read signs posted near the warrens, to read the street signs that still had enough letters they could be read. He'd taught her about names, but she understood names. It's just that most people didn't use them.

And he'd given her a name of her own—a name that other

people could use. A name that meant they were aware of her, or they wanted her attention.

Raven hadn't wanted attention.

Isn't it lonely?

Robin taught her that, as well. Loneliness. Because Robin was the first person she could share things with, and in the end, she *wanted* that. She wanted someone who was interested in the things that caught her attention. She wanted to show him the things she found. No one else had ever cared.

And there were more people here who wanted to see things. Who wanted her to share them. Starrante had. She could tell.

She shouldn't have shown him. That was the truth. She shouldn't have shown him after Killianas had been injured. She should have hidden that treasure among her others, so painstakingly gathered over such a long time. She should have shown them to Robin, and only Robin. And then she should have gone back to the warrens.

She could always come here again, when she found something new. When she found something worth sharing. Robin meant to stay here, and she knew the way now.

But Robin thought it was safe here. Here, where there was no Raven, and where Robin didn't know how to hide.

She was torn.

When Serralyn asked her if she'd shown Starrante—and that name was *wrong*—her treasure, she cringed, burying her head further into her knees, as if bony knees could be cushions. Now she was tangled in all the things. Now she could feel the weight of the question, the weight of guilt, of doing harm, of living as if…as if…

She inhaled and lifted her head. "Yes. Yes, I showed him."

Terrano's eyes were so wide they would have fallen out of his head if they weren't attached. "After what happened to Killian? After that, you wanted to show that piece of glass to an Arbiter? In the library?"

Serralyn ignored him. Her eyes were blue. Raven decided she didn't like blue. "Is that why he was…so loud?"

"I don't know."

Robin moved to stand in front of where Raven crouched, his back toward her. "She means it. She doesn't know. But I think we can assume that whatever it was Starrante saw was the cause of his excitement."

"This might be a problem," Serralyn replied. "Raven's never been here before. I'm certain we'd all remember her if she had. She hasn't even applied to be a student. But she found something that no one else could see under a corpse that died for no known reason. Killian can't hear her. He can't read her."

Robin nodded.

"You'd better show her whatever it was you wanted to show her, because I'm not sure it's going to be safe for her here. Given what happened to Killian in the conference room, I'm not certain the chancellor would consider it safe to accept her application.

"If she'd managed to pick up whatever it was she found when there was no crowd, it might have been okay—but people are on edge. She stands out," Serralyn continued, voice softening. "And people are terrible when they're afraid."

"As long as there are no other deaths," Terrano said, "it should be fine."

Serralyn exhaled. To Raven's eyes, she looked exhausted. People sometimes did. "We've never been that lucky. Come on. I think Killian will be looking for us soon." She grabbed Terrano's arm.

Raven's eyes widened when Serralyn's hand passed through his arm. But Serralyn's eyes narrowed. She was annoyed, not surprised.

"It won't be us he looks for first, and I want to hear what he has to say," Terrano told Serralyn.

"I think they need a moment or two," Serralyn replied. "A *private* moment or two."

Terrano frowned.

"Invisibility doesn't work on Raven," Serralyn snapped, her eyes darkening. Raven lowered her head again. She thought they might fight, and she wanted no part of that. But she hadn't explored this campus enough to know how to avoid it. So she stayed on the floor, arms curled around legs.

She wasn't certain how long their argument took; she only heard bits and pieces of it, but even then it felt muted, distant. In the end, Terrano left with Serralyn.

Robin closed the door behind them. He then walked to his bed and sat on it. It creaked. Raven wondered how much it would creak if she sat on it. Or if someone larger—like the chancellor—sat on it. Would it make the same sound? Would the sound be louder?

She shook her head. The floor didn't creak at all when people walked on it. Why did the bed? She unwound her arms, lowering her legs until they lay flat across the floor. The floor was wood, with cloth bits—a rug?—on top. But it didn't *feel* like a normal, wooden floor. It was entirely flat; the wood seemed new. Giselle's floors hadn't been like this. The glassmaker's floors had been stone. She tried to remember other floors, but failed. She just knew they weren't like this one.

"Are all the floors like this?" she asked.

She heard Robin exhale. "I think so, but I haven't checked all the other floors."

"The library floor was different."

"You noticed it?"

Robin always asked strange questions. How could she not notice the floor? She'd been *standing* on it. She found it easier to breathe when she had questions, but knew most people didn't like it when she asked them. She only asked them until she got answers, but most people also didn't have answers.

Robin was different. He'd always been different. He didn't mind when she shifted position, lying flat on the floor, her head to one side as she looked at the woodgrain. "It's all the same," she told him.

"The floor?"

"The woodgrain. That's why it looks strange—all the planks are the same. Is this what you wanted to show me?"

He shook his head. "How was the library floor different?"

"It wasn't wood. It wasn't pretending to be wood," she replied.

"And no, I didn't think about showing you the floor."

"Oh." She pushed herself up. "What did you want to show me?" In spite of herself, she was interested. Robin didn't consider glass a treasure, but he understood that it was Raven's treasure, not his. He told her that different people had different treasures—different things they valued. It had been hard, at first, to understand, although she knew people could be very different from each other on the outside.

The bed creaked again as he rose.

He walked over to a…table of some kind? It had four legs, but it had drawers, as well, and the top seemed to be…a rounded half dome. Wooden. Raven followed.

"It's my desk," he told her before she could ask. "This part rolls up. Look. And this part? It pulls out. So if I need to write, or if I need to read a heavy book, I can place it on the surface. These over here are small drawers. I think we use them for quills or wax. You can put a small candle in this one—but there's usually light here. Killian keeps lights on. They're up in the ceiling."

He moved his chair so that Raven could stand on it because she wanted to see the lights. She'd liked lights for as long as she could remember; they were like little bits of captured sun, but different.

"If you wanted to stay here," he told her, his voice soft the way only Robin's voice had ever been, "Killian would make you a room of your own."

"Would it be like this one?"

"I think so. Most of the student rooms look like this—at least the ones I've seen."

"And that—that desk?"

"All of the rooms have a desk. Some have two. All have beds. All have a window."

"Can you open the window?"

"Yes."

"Can I open it?"

"Yes, if you want."

It was the desk she wanted. A small table with drawers and a lid. A place she could put her things. She knew, looking at Robin's desk, that her things would be safe, because the desk felt like Robin. Like his clothing, it seemed part of him.

"And there's edible food in the dining hall. I know today's been rough, but I think you'd really like some of the classes."

"Why?"

"Because the professors *like* questions. And they're trying to teach us how to use *magic*. They know about the history of magic, how it might have been developed, why we have it at all—I think you'd like that stuff."

Raven turned to look at Robin, to study his expression. She liked his face when it was like this; his eyes were dark, but even dark, they were almost shining. He wasn't smiling—he was too serious for that. No, not serious; that wasn't the right word. Raven didn't always understand Robin. She hadn't expected to—people had always been hard.

But Robin was the first person she truly *wanted* to understand.

Maybe more than he wanted to understand magic. More than his classes, his teachers, his certainty that she would have good questions or the right questions. Robin didn't want Raven because she could find hiding places he couldn't. He didn't want to be with her because she could keep him safe.

What he wanted, she didn't know—but she wanted to know. *You wanted to go back. To the warrens. To where it was safe. It's not safe here.*

But Robin wasn't in the warrens. Robin would never be in the warrens again.

You can always come back. You know where he is now. You know where Robin's home is.

Oh. Robin had a home now. This place—it was Robin's home. He wasn't alone anymore. He had friends who weren't Raven. He had Killian, who didn't like her, and Serralyn and Terrano, and the chancellor.

Raven only had Robin.

If she left, would she still have Robin? Would Robin still be her friend?

She turned to Robin's desk. Her hand slid into her large pockets; she grasped her pouch and withdrew it. She walked to the desk, opened a drawer on top of the surface he'd pulled out, and placed her pouch inside it. She then closed the drawer. And opened it again. Her pouch was still there.

"Killian doesn't like me."

"Killian doesn't know you," Robin replied. "You didn't like me when we first met, either."

"I did."

Robin smiled. "You didn't. It took you a long time to like me."

"That's not like—that's trust. I liked you. I observed you. I learned about you in different situations. I learned to *trust* you. But I did that because I liked you. Killian doesn't like me. Killian likes you, though."

"I think Killian's afraid to trust you."

"But if he doesn't like me, why would he try? If I didn't like you, I wouldn't." There was no resentment in Raven. She wasn't hurt by Killian's lack of "liking." She accepted it the way she accepted everything else.

"Because you'll be a student. You'll be one of his students. He doesn't understand why you're different, but he'll accept it. And once he gets to know what you're like, he'll be glad he did." Robin spoke firmly and with complete conviction.

Raven said nothing, but she looked at the desk for a long time. She believed that Robin believed what he said. Robin did not lie. But Robin could be wrong.

Robin wasn't surprised when Killian appeared at his door. Killian seldom entered the student rooms unless invited; Robin didn't invite him in because Raven was there.

"The chancellor wishes to have a word with you."

"When?"

"Now."

"Just me?"

Killian nodded. "Raven may remain in your room, if she is concerned about the state of the campus. It is what I would recommend."

Raven didn't appear to hear Killian. She was busy opening and closing drawers.

"I have to speak with the chancellor," Robin told her, tapping her shoulder to get her attention first.

She nodded as if the chancellor had very little to do with her.

"Wait here for me, okay? I have more things I want to show you after I finish talking with the chancellor."

She nodded again. This didn't mean yes, as Robin had discovered in the past; it meant that she had heard him. He didn't press for *yes*. Instead, he walked out of his room and quietly closed the door behind him. He hoped—but wasn't certain—that Raven would be distracted enough that she would stay in his room until he returned.

"She is wrong," Killian said as they walked away.

"About?"

"I do not dislike her. But it has been a long, long time since I last met people who I could not hear in the fashion I hear you. Some of the Barrani students are good at obfuscating their thoughts, but I hear their presence regardless. When I was alive as you are alive, I did not have the benefit of such hearing. I met people, as you meet them now, and made judgments about them based on their behavior and our interactions."

"It is strange to have to do that again." Killian's smile was almost self-deprecating. "I did not react well to Raven upon our initial meeting, and for that, I apologize."

Robin shook his head. Killian's reasons for suspicion made perfect sense. "Is your hand okay?"

"It was not my hand that was injured; it was your perception of the injury, given the form I have chosen to take. Yes, I am fine now. But I gather Raven chose to show what she found to Arbiter Starrante, and that has caused…a stir. The library remains closed, and some of the older students are not happy with this state of affairs. It is fortunate that we have so few seniors at the moment.

"But that will change in the future, and not the far future. We have hope, Robin." He stopped at the familiar doors to the chancellor's office.

The doors rolled open.

"Enter," the chancellor said.

Robin had never been afraid of the chancellor. He had never feared this room; he had never been sent here for breaking any of the Academia's student rules. While the chancellor looked intimidating, he was far more forgiving than his usual facial expression suggested. This was not the first time he had visited the office, not even the first time he'd visited it at the chancellor's invitation.

Today he was nervous.

"Come," the chancellor said. He'd been seated behind his desk, but before the door had closed, he left the desk and walked toward Robin. "I did not ask to speak with you because you are, in colloquial terms, in trouble. I do not intend to browbeat you into some form of compliance. You have done nothing wrong.

"Join me." He indicated the chairs nearest the bookshelves; a small, round table separated them.

Robin sat after the chancellor was seated. The chancellor's eyes were orange. "I heard there was a disturbance in the library."

Robin nodded.

"I would like to hear what happened from your perspective. The librarians are still arguing somewhat vociferously, and they have yet to open their doors. I am the chancellor of the Academia, but the library is not directly under Killianas's auspices. Killianas controls access to the library doors, but he does not, and cannot, make demands of the librarians."

"Did Killian not tell you?"

"He mentioned that there was difficulty, yes. He said Starrante, in particular, was far more upset than he has been in quite some time."

"I think he was angry with Arbiter Androsse."

"Indeed." The chancellor seemed content to wait for Robin to speak.

"I didn't see what happened." Robin hesitated and then plunged ahead. "Did Killian tell you what happened in the conference room?"

"Yes." The chancellor's expression was now like a wall.

"What did he say?"

"If I were interested in hearing Killianas's report again, I would ask Killianas. I am asking you. If you wish to start in the conference room, I accept that, but I asked about the library."

"I didn't see what happened in the library until the end. I was speaking with Arbiter Kavallac and Terrano."

At the mention of Terrano, the chancellor pinched the bridge of his nose. "I see. Continue."

"Terrano wanted to know how it was that Killian didn't know about the death in the quad. Killian is the heart of the Academia; he's a sentient building. If something happened, Killian should know. He should know how the student died. If the student was murdered, he should be aware of the murderer."

The chancellor nodded.

"But clearly he isn't. Terrano's not like us. Like me. He's… pretty strange, but he's seen a lot. And he says he knows three other sentient buildings—and every one of them would have known what had happened."

"What did the Arbiter say?"

"She…told me to talk to you. Sir."

"Did she say why?"

"She said she couldn't speak about Killian, and Killian couldn't answer Terrano's questions without your permission. So…if Terrano wanted to talk to Killian, Killian wouldn't answer. And Terrano isn't likely to ask your permission."

"He is not foolish in that particular way, no, as the general reaction to most of Terrano's requests is *no*. Regardless, that would not cause Starrante's ire."

"Raven was excited to meet Starrante. Excited, not afraid. When he greeted us, she immediately greeted him back, waving her arms the way he does, but…almost precisely. Better than I can normally manage."

"That is not usually the way new students respond to their first meeting with *Arbiter* Starrante."

"It's not the way Raven usually responds to anyone the first time she meets them. I think she was happy. Starrante—Arbiter Starrante—seemed happy, too. But I think Raven showed Arbiter Starrante the glass she found."

"Ah, yes. The piece of glass. I will have more to say about

that in a moment. Raven showed Arbiter Starrante her piece of glass and that caused the commotion?"

"I think it caused the noise, yes. Arbiter Androsse took one look at Arbiter Starrante—and Raven—and moved toward Raven to intervene. Arbiter Starrante hit him. He was trying to protect Raven. Arbiter Kavallac joined the fray before it could get out of hand—I think she was trying to calm Arbiter Androsse down."

"Not Arbiter Starrante?"

Robin frowned. "I think she thought she'd have better luck with Androsse—they fight all the time. But it was Arbiter Kavallac who opened the door. She threw us all out."

"I see."

"After that, Killian talked to them—in their own languages, so none of us understood what he was saying. Well, Terrano might have understood some of it. But Serralyn didn't and I didn't."

"Did Raven?"

"She…she wasn't listening. I don't think she was even aware of her surroundings for the first little bit."

The chancellor nodded, his face expressionless. "Let us now turn to the subject of Raven's piece of glass."

Robin flinched.

"I am aware that Killianas chose to sequester you in the east conference room, with my permission. Did he tell you the nature of that room?"

Robin nodded. When the chancellor failed to continue, he exhaled. "It's a protective room. Nothing dangerous can escape it; nothing dangerous can enter."

"Indeed. You were in the room with Raven and Killianas's Avatar?"

"Yes."

"Did Raven give Killianas the piece of glass?"

"She didn't want to," Robin said in a rush. "Killian insisted."

"I see. Was there a reason for her reluctance?"

"She doesn't like to show her treasures to anyone. She collects stray bits of glass and metal, and she keeps them close, in a pouch. She shows them to me. She shows them to me the way she showed them to Starrante. But Killian *asked*. He pretty much demanded. So she gave permission for me to hand it to him."

"You have no reason to believe that she knew the effect it would have."

"No!" Robin swallowed. "No. Killian didn't even know the effect it would have—and to Raven, they're bits and pieces of other people's garbage. She calls them glass. She had no reason to expect that it would injure Killian in any way."

"And Arbiter Starrante?"

"Arbiter Starrante wasn't injured. He was shocked, I think. More than surprised. But he wasn't hurt."

At that, a dry smile tugged at the upper corners of the chancellor's long beard. "Perhaps that was the case before his disagreement with Arbiter Androsse became more heated.

"Robin, what have you brought to my school?"

"You told me—you told us—that you wanted students who were interested in learning. In book learning, but also in other fields. As long as they had curiosity and passion and…and other words." His voice trailed off, but he hadn't surrendered. "Raven was the first person I thought of. I know she's weird. Most people ignore her, when they're aware of her; some try to hurt her, but she manages to avoid them.

"If you leave her alone, she looks for things most wouldn't care about, but…she's probably in my room right now examining every element of my desk. She noticed that the floor was strange—and realized it was because the woodgrain is identical across all of the planks. She just—she notices things. She thinks about them.

"I mean—a floor's a floor, right? Not to Raven. I thought

she was what you were looking for. I thought she was what you said the school needed."

He'd grown up in the warrens, but he hadn't been born to them. He knew better than to throw away his future in defense of a stranger. He'd known Raven for years, but how much time had he actually spent with her? How much of a friend was she? How important could she be?

Enough to offend the chancellor? Enough to lose the hope of a decent life?

He struggled with fear for one long breath. *Raven saved my life. I owe her my life.* "And I think she *is* what the Academia needs. I've never seen Starrante so excited."

"Or shocked?"

"Before that."

"You haven't answered my question."

"I have, sir. I've known Raven since I was a child. If she's not human, it might explain a thing or two—but she's always been human to me. She's never done anything that would make me suspect she was some other race." He hesitated.

"You suspect she has some rudimentary knowledge of magic, perhaps?"

"No." Robin frowned. Thought followed on the heels of the single syllable. "I didn't. She's just Raven." But was she? Was her ability to find hiding places—convenient, unseen, safe— just instinctive? Was it only because she avoided people so much she was bound to trip over places they just didn't go?

"You are thinking. It is such a refreshing change from most of the student body, I am reluctant to interrupt you." The chancellor sat back in his chair.

"Has Killian said anything about Raven?"

"A surprisingly small amount given her obvious ability to inadvertently cause him injury. I am aware that in terms of his normal functioning, she is almost a blank space. A very different blank space from that created in the quadrangle. Yes," he added, "we come at last to the question of Killianas."

"As you experienced for yourself, Killianas is capable of controlling the base essence from which the Ancients built the Academia's campus to create a space like the east conference room. He is capable, with effort, of creating a space that is almost impregnable. He is capable of preserving the lives of students in emergencies." The chancellor frowned, his eyes narrowing.

"This is meant to be a private meeting, if the word *privacy* has any meaning for you at all. Perhaps I should speak in my native tongue." He glanced at Robin, having offered this warning, and roared. Robin had time to cover his ears; he could make out syllables in the overwhelming sound of spoken Draconic.

Terrano appeared midair, close to where wall met ceiling just above them, and fell immediately. Given that he could have landed on carpet, but hit the stone in front of the fireplace instead, Robin guessed that the chancellor was annoyed.

"If Killianas's concentration were not required, I would tell him to remove you and keep you out."

"He can't."

"He can't *yet*—but everyone has to start somewhere. I do not believe you were invited to this office."

"I'm not a student." Terrano grinned.

The chancellor's eyes were orange, but they hadn't darkened to the red that meant danger. Robin wondered how long it would take.

"Killianas," the chancellor barked.

Killian didn't appear, but Robin had come to understand it wasn't necessary. Avatar absent, he nonetheless replied. "Chancellor."

"Tell Serralyn and Valliant that Terrano is likely to survive his intrusion. I am certain at least one of them is now very worried."

"She is," Killian replied. "Should I allow them to enter?"

"They are already at the door?"

"Only Serralyn was concerned enough to run here."

"No. Simply tell her to go back to her room."

Robin glanced at Terrano, who was slightly red in the face as he forced himself off the floor. It seemed that he'd gained far more weight than he was accustomed to carrying—no doubt at the whim of the chancellor.

"I told her not to worry. The chancellor wasn't likely to kill me. Or try," he added quickly.

"Serralyn no doubt expended much energy attempting to restrain Terrano. It was wasted effort, but I also imagine she knows that. Terrano, on the other hand, has strong reason to suspect that I would never harm—or allow harm to come to—Serralyn or Valliant.

"He is willing to take his many, many foolish risks because he understands that consequences will be visited on him, and him alone."

"I'll hide behind Robin," Terrano said.

"That will not do you any good should I be determined. I am not. I did not immediately eject you because many of Robin's possible questions come from you. I wish to avoid the possibility that you will hector Robin—and through him, me—with those questions. *Sit down.*"

Terrano sat. It didn't look entirely voluntary.

"I assume you were eavesdropping on our conversation and are therefore up to speed." He turned once again to Robin. Robin was surprised to see flecks of gold in the chancellor's otherwise orange eyes; he would have expected red. Gold was a good color for the chancellor's kin, although it was clear he was still speaking to Terrano. "Don't feel that you have escaped all possible consequences. When we are done, I have a task for you. I expect you to fulfill it to the best of your admittedly untested abilities."

8

Terrano reddened, not with humiliation, but genuine anger. His hands became fists on the armrests, his eyes narrowed. They were an odd color. Had he been any other Barrani, they would have been very dark blue.

So many new things to see today. Robin wished he had seen none of them, but cleared his throat.

The chancellor did not hear the fainthearted attempt at distraction as he glared in Terrano's direction. "Do not even try. Unless you wish to leave permanently, I suggest you join the conversation in a more corporeal form." He then turned to Robin. "As I was saying, Killianas is capable of creating impenetrable defenses when he so chooses.

"This, Terrano understands quite well. He has seen similar situations in other buildings of similar construction; many of those defenses were aimed at him, I'm certain. Killianas finds Terrano interesting enough that he does not put in the effort."

"It wouldn't make a difference if he did," Terrano snapped.

"In his current state, I concur. And that is the difficulty we now face. In Killianas's current state, his defenses are...porous. He can be attacked; he cannot keep the Academia entirely safe."

"Why?" It was Robin who'd asked; Terrano was trying—and failing—to rein in his temper.

"I admit my knowledge of the architecture of sentient buildings is lacking. I attended the Academia as a student in my distant youth, but Killianas's health was not my concern. There are differences in the building itself, as one might expect given the passage of time, but the significant differences are not cosmetic.

"You are aware that there was a period in which the Academia, for all intents and purposes, ceased to exist. Its return to accessibility is relatively recent."

Robin nodded again.

"The person who discovered the Academia in its injured and barely functional state was a fieflord—a lord of one of the fiefs' Towers.

"I remember the day the Towers rose. They were almost the last act of the Ancients who had been our creators, our progenitors. No arguments could be made that would sway them from their chosen course. Shadow had all but destroyed *Ravellon*—the crown jewel of this world, and the gateway to many others; the gates to other worlds have fallen silent—or worse.

"The Academia had been constructed in the vicinity of *Ravellon*. Scholars, researchers, students—all desired to be close to that ancient city.

"On the day the Towers rose, the Academia fell. We watched, we students whose truest home, whose truest calling, was this place. And we went to war, to the wars decreed by those who were not so affected, who had not chosen to bear witness. Some of us excelled in war; some perished." As he spoke, the chancellor's eyes shifted in color, orange becoming browner, but not darker. Copper.

It was not a color Robin had seen before, and given the chancellor's voice, not a color he wished to see often.

"We grieved; we said our farewells. We lost the dreams the Academia had engendered in us. The world became a greyer, and bloodier, place. But the Academia, unbeknownst to us both before and after the wars had ended, had not been entirely destroyed. The Towers themselves had created the thinnest of nets, the weakest of anchors—to preserve what could barely be preserved.

"The Barrani fieflord of one of those Towers became aware of the very tenuous survival of the Academia. From the Tower he captained, he learned some part of what Killianas required to become partially functional.

"Lord Candallar did not have the heart of an academic. As he and his confederates were not particularly interested in learning, in studying, they assumed that students simply meant bodies."

"Who were his confederates?" Terrano's voice was sharper but less angry.

"The assumption that the fieflord was in contact with Barrani confederates is reasonable—but he brought a mortal lord to the Academia grounds, as well. Regardless, they believed that students were bodies. Anyone who was breathing and was unlikely to be missed was dragged into the suspended building to serve that purpose. Many were mortals from rougher parts of town. Some, however, were Barrani. None of the Barrani were lords of the court.

"We have not discovered all of those who kept counsel with the former fieflord; nor do we believe that we are now safe from interference. What Candallar wanted was not necessarily what his comrades wanted; I would assume, in fact, the opposite."

Robin frowned. "They wanted the library."

"That would be my guess. There are those who study purely to gain power, and their interests are narrow. The library is said to contain every book that has ever existed. Some of those texts are likely forbidden or illegal. I do not believe the books can simply be stolen or removed; in order to study them, those who seek that knowledge would have to have some control—or permission—from the Arbiters." Which would never happen.

"We could investigate," Terrano offered, less ire in his tone.

"No. No, thank you. The work required is subtle. Your suitability for such investigations is low—your manners would make survival in the High Halls difficult. And I believe your cohort is already in some danger there. Most wish to see Sedarias unseated."

Terrano shrugged. "True. But if they live in the High Halls I don't have to talk to them directly. And the human contingent is probably trying to gain immortality. Again."

"Terrano."

"What? All the worst trouble humans get into is usually about that."

The chancellor grimaced, but didn't disagree. He exhaled a thin stream of smoke. "The kidnappings started with a few students; the earliest were Barrani." Robin grimaced. Of course they were, if Barrani were involved. Mere mortals were inferior in every way. "But those early victims did not have the desired effect."

"The kidnapper's desired effect?"

"Indeed. That pattern continued for decades of your time. We surmise that these Barrani students did not have a notable effect on Killianas or his consciousness.

"My knowledge of Killianas's requirements comes from Killianas himself; he does not recall similar conversations with the deceased fieflord or his confederates. They had been given rudimentary information; the source remains unclear, although we have some suspicions.

"They expanded their student body; they moved from Barrani to mortals. In the case of mortals, there are far, far more available. Wealth is not, and has never been, evenly distributed; no more has power. The warrens is a small corridor within the city proper that is almost a tiny fief unto itself—lacking a fieflord or a Tower. While the rumors of certain death should one enter the warrens is, demonstrably, untrue, the force of law is thin there.

"Mortals were taken from the warrens, as you know very well."

Robin nodded. It was where he'd been kidnapped.

"What those mortals achieved in terms of Killianas's waking was significant in comparison to the Barrani students similarly transported. Some students were also taken from the streets of the fiefs where they were unlikely to be missed; some were sold to Lord Candallar, or offered in trade. Killianas began to stir.

"It is to our advantage that the fieflord and his confederates assumed that it was the number of students, the numerical factor, that actuated the change they desired. Killianas stirred. Their lack of understanding aided Killianas, and his partial wakening aided one or two of the professors who had been trapped since the Towers rose. The library remained untouched—and the library was one of their goals. It might have been their only goal; we do not know. But the library cannot be reached except through the corridors of the Academia.

"I believe the former fieflord intended to keep the student body at a certain number—just enough to allow him and his confederates to enter the Academia grounds and begin to search for useful knowledge, useful information, by which they could augment their own power, but not so many that Killianas would be possessed of all of his faculties.

"That is, of course, not what happened. They had accidentally acquired a handful of the right students, which allowed Killianas to fully manifest." His smile was sharp. "Had the Academia not been accidentally discovered by one of the Hawks from the Halls of Law, I believe they would have realized their mistake and removed some of the students. They did not have the time.

"But unless they removed specific students, it would not have made a difference. Do you understand?"

Robin nodded.

Terrano, however, snorted. "He doesn't. I mean, he understands your words, but you're being *way* too subtle."

"Very well. If they removed you, Robin, Killianas would not have recovered as much as he has. You are not singular, but your interest and your presence allowed you to see the cracks in the daily routine, to begin to work around them; you were taught more of how to write, how to read Barrani, in a setting where that was impossible. You learned. You listened to the lectures; they were in large part above your comprehension.

"But not entirely. What you wanted from the Academia, the Academia was created to provide. Killianas woke far more fully because you were present. You are not the only one, but your influence on others has been noted." The chancellor exhaled. "Killianas drew strength from both your presence and mine.

"He required a chancellor; I desired that office. In the future, I wish the world to see the Academia as its best and truest self. Killianas *is* awake; he is aware. But if he is aware, he is not yet at full strength."

The chancellor exhaled again, his eyes darkening. "It is my current suspicion that Lord Candallar's surviving confederates are responsible for the two deaths upon the campus. On some fundamental level they assume it is the Barrani students that empower Killianas."

"So they're Barrani?"

"Not necessarily. It is in the nature of those who seek power to assume the superiority of those who have that power; they may believe the Barrani students are more valuable, more necessary, to the functioning of the Academia. Many mortals would make that assumption, or accept that assumption—Barrani are immortal; they offer eternity."

Terrano coughed. "Immortal and invulnerable aren't the same thing."

"No. But it is clear that they consider Barrani more valuable, and therefore more likely to cause damage by their absence."

"But...the early students didn't help wake Killian."

"Indeed. But if mortals are involved in this enterprise, that is experience they would not necessarily have. The fieflord is dead. His knowledge presumably died with him. The Barrani do not share information except at need, and they mix lies into most of what is offered—subtle lies and misdirections."

"What does anyone gain by bringing the Academia down?"

"Control of its remains. But the opportunity to wrest that control from us—from *me*—is slender, and it grows smaller with each passing day." The chancellor's eyes were definitely orange now, but red flecks had started to appear. As if aware of the effect this could have, he raised his eye's inner membranes, muting the color. "Had one of those deaths been yours, they would have done far more damage to Killianas.

"We have been lucky so far, but luck is not something on which we can depend. I would not be surprised to see similar deaths occur within our human cohort. At the moment, we have accepted most—but not all—of the applications we have received. Understand that that is necessary. If Killianas is to regain the strength required to perfectly defend the Academia, we have no other choices. I am aware that some of the students are here for political reasons; you assume that those are Barrani. Not all of them are.

"But the politics of the situation should be our problem, not yours. I told you that we require students with a genuine capacity for curiosity, focus, for asking questions in their need to understand. I have also told you that that capacity is found in all walks of life. In the past, those students naturally gravitated to the Academia.

"They will begin to do so again, but I do not believe we will have a fully operational Academia for at least a decade. I was prepared for that, as was Killianas. It had not occurred to either of us that the Academia would once again be considered a target in the fashion we believe it is: someone wishes Killianas to once again slumber.

"Without students such as yourself, I believe they have a chance of success."

Terrano frowned. "Are you certain that's what's happening?"

"No. It is the most likely conjecture, given known information. It is also true that Robin's death would cause the gravest harm, but it is not only Robin's death that could achieve this. I would give you the names of the rest of the students, but I do not wish to create a victim list for our enemies."

"And you're telling Robin because?"

"Because he is your friend. I am certain none of the three of you—Serralyn, Valliant, and you yourself—would murder him; I am certain that you would do all in your power to prevent his death.

"The only physical clue we have was discovered by Raven. She could see what we did not; she could touch it, retrieve it. In her hands, it appears to be a large shard of otherwise broken glass."

Robin nodded.

"Killianas was concerned; what he saw in Raven's hands was not what the student body saw. Or sees. She let you handle the piece of glass, and no harm was done to you. But Killianas's attempt to examine the glass was not successful."

"What does Killian see?" Terrano asked. The chancellor failed to answer. "Killian?" Killian also failed to answer.

"Well, that explains why you wanted me to hear this—but why did you summon Robin?"

"There is an unfortunate request on my desk from Arbiter Starrante. He apologizes for the...what did he call it? Fuss. The minor misunderstanding. He would like to speak with Raven again."

"The library is closed, though," Robin pointed out.

"Indeed. But of the three Arbiters, Starrante retains the ability to leave that space. Given the difficulties faced by at least two Barrani students, I consider his presence in the halls of the Academia a risk—to both himself and the library he guards. I do not wish him to be seen traversing the student dormitories. If he is spotted entering your room, you will become a target."

"What did Starrante say he thought the glass was?"

"*Arbiter* Starrante has not yet answered that question." The chancellor pinched the bridge of his nose, looking momentarily as exhausted as he sounded. "It is difficult for me to deny his application. He wishes to speak with your friend. Do you know where she currently is?"

"Probably in my room."

"Probably?"

"Raven's not used to having rooms like these."

"Where does she live?"

"In the warrens. But if you're asking for an address or something similar, I don't have one."

"You don't know?"

"She lives in the warrens. She's survived there for her entire life. But I'm not sure that living there meant living in rooms or apartments or anything like that. I've asked her to wait in my room, but Raven's sense of the passage of time is…a little bit odd. She might be there when I return. She might be wandering around the halls or the campus looking for a hiding place."

"Hiding place?"

Robin shrugged, his shoulders stiffening. "She's good at finding places to hide. I probably wouldn't have survived if she hadn't been. They're real places—she doesn't make them or anything—but she can find them. And when they're no longer hidden enough, she finds different places. It's what she's always done."

"She appears to be very interested in your desk," Killian said.

"She's still in my room?"

"She is. She has, however, emptied every drawer and removed it; she has examined the seams, the wood, and the handles; she has rearranged the contents of the drawers several times, but I believe she has hit upon one that does not disturb her. Ah, no, apologies; apparently I was premature."

"She'll be in my room for a while."

"Does she normally do this?"

"I haven't had a desk of my own since I was a much younger child." And not much of a place to live, either. "So I doubt she's really seen one that's safe to touch." He exhaled. "She's odd, I know that. But she's the best friend anyone could have in a pinch." He sounded defensive, which was fair; it was how he felt. "She'll understand that desk better than the person who constructed it by the time she's finished."

"I agree," Killian said. "She is unusual, if the glass taken from the scene of the crime did not make that clear."

"You would advise me to admit her?"

"I am torn. But there is something about her—it's become very clear to me as I watch her examine Robin's desk—that I believe we need. Her manners—or lack of manners—are irrelevant for our purposes. I foresee some difficulty with some of the teachers if she is to enter the junior year alongside Robin. But I would advise that they be on the same class schedule for the time being should you choose to accept my recommendation."

The chancellor was silent for a long moment. "I dislike having students share rooms; I was young once, and I understand the conflicts and troubles that arise from a lack of privacy. You were promised a room of your own."

Robin nodded.

"I would be grateful, for the moment, if you would take Raven as roommate. I understand that you are not, and would not be, her keeper—but life on campus will be exceedingly strange for her, and she appears to be comfortable in your presence.

"I will, however, make certain she has a desk of her own."

"I told her she'd have her own room."

"If that is her preference, that can also be arranged. But from the sound of things, she is unlikely to notice a great difference. You are not her keeper, although perhaps that is not yet clear given the burden of responsibility you clearly feel.

"We are done. I will respond to Arbiter Starrante's request. Killianas?"

"It shall be as you request, Chancellor."

"Good. See Robin safely to his room."

"What about me?" Terrano demanded, struggling to leave the chair in which he'd been deposited.

"I am not finished discussing things with you." When Robin failed to rise, he said, "Robin, we are done now."

"But Terrano—"

"Terrano is neither your problem nor your responsibility. I do not intend him harm; I merely wish to ask a few questions. His answers are frequently headache inducing; in the worst case, nausea inducing. You are to be spared that.

"Arbiter Starrante is fully capable of creating a portal that leads directly to your room; he will not be followed and his destination will not be easily noted. Please wait in your room until he arrives."

"Can you tell?" Robin asked Killian—or Killian's voice—as he made his way back to the dorm.

"Tell?"

"Which students are so-called special students."

"No, Robin. To me, you are one of dozens of students. I find you interesting; I find your very different view of life fascinating. But there is nothing that marks you as special in the way the chancellor believes you are."

Robin grimaced. "The only special thing about me isn't something most people would consider valuable." He'd grown up in the warrens. His mother had died when he was still young.

He'd learned how to survive. His mother feared the warrens, but she'd never lived in them. She'd fled *to* the warrens to survive. The warrens were therefore, in his young mind, safer.

And he wouldn't have made it if it weren't for Raven.

Killian nodded. "I understand the gratitude you feel toward her."

"But you can't tell if she'll be a student that helps you?"

Killian shook his head. "The chancellor has a clearer grasp of what is necessary. I told you—it has been a long time since I have had to approach people as if they were entities entirely separate from me. It is true. I cannot gauge potential in the way the chancellor can. I can evaluate students as they are now, but I cannot see the possible paths those students will take; I cannot see the students they might become.

"If the chancellor told you chancellors were deemed necessary in order to safeguard the Academia from the politics and fury of the world outside my boundaries, he was correct. But he underestimates the value of his own perception. It is not uncommon. You, too, underestimate your value in a similar fashion.

"I have made peace with the oddity that is Raven; had there been no deaths, I would have been less suspicious, less cautious. Possibility has its own imperative, its own beauty—but there is never just the positive future; it walks hand in hand with the negative."

Raven was in the middle of attempting to fit drawers into different empty spaces when she felt the floor move beneath her feet. She understood that these were Robin's drawers, the contents were Robin's; she quickly abandoned her experiment and put the drawers back where she'd first found them.

She considered the corner, but the floor was moving and she didn't like it when ground moved beneath her feet.

In the end, she jumped up on the bed, bracing herself against the headboard as the mattress began to move. There was an odd pulse to the movement, a steady beat; the bed followed that beat, and because Raven was sitting on it, she was forced to keep time.

But she didn't curl up or hide her face; she watched.

She watched as the floor changed, the odd, identical planks multiplying in number; she watched as the walls receded, as if being pushed by the planks and the changing shape of the floor. The walls retained their pale color, the ceiling remained at the same height. But she heard a popping sound, a crackling buzz, and watched as a bed appeared against the far wall. A second bed.

She had never seen a room behave this way before. Nothing dangerous emerged from the floor or the walls, and the bed looked identical to the one she sat on, although the sheets were tidier. She watched the floor until the rhythm of its motion was completely quiet. The room had become larger. Had she walked into this room the first time, she wouldn't have noticed the sound.

But there were two beds. Two.

Was one meant for her?

Raven was aware of Robin almost before he opened the door. She very gingerly stepped off the bed to place her feet flat against the floor; after a moment, she frowned and removed her shoes. The floor was warm. It was solid. It felt like wood, like she thought new wood should feel. She walked from the bed to the wall with the door in it; that wall had grown in length, but the position of the door remained the same, as if the door were an anchor. Everything else had shifted.

How many steps wide was this room now?

And where was Robin's desk?

She shoved her hands into her pockets, clutched the familiar pouch, and slowly exhaled. Panic was bad. Panic was always bad. Panic could eat you.

"Raven?"

Oh, right. She'd heard Robin. She'd got distracted again. She turned to face him immediately.

Robin looked around the room; he didn't seem surprised.

"The room changed on its own," she told him. "I didn't do anything."

"No, of course not. But…the chancellor asked if we could room together. He thought it might be easier for you than having a separate room."

She blinked. "Why?"

"I don't know. I did try to tell him that you're used to being alone. If you don't like it, you can have your own room."

She looked down at her feet, trying to find words. She knew Killian didn't like her. Maybe, because he liked Robin, he wanted Robin to keep an eye on her. Maybe he thought she would steal something—people sometimes thought that. She didn't know why.

Did she want her own room?

She'd never, ever had a room of her own. She wasn't sure how to keep a room. It didn't fit in pockets. It wasn't something she could just pick up. It wouldn't fit her hiding places—none of them were big enough.

There was one.

No. No. *No.*

She turned to Robin. "Don't you want a room of your own?" He had seemed happy with it. To Robin, a room was important. And it was normal. He had a room here. He wanted her to have a room of her own. Had she ever explained how ridiculous it was to own a room? She couldn't remember.

"I'm happy to share a room," he answered. "But only with you. I think I'd be kicked out if I had to room with Terrano—I'd strangle him. Or try."

"Really?"

"Ah, sorry. No, but I'd be really, really irritated. Terrano isn't a student. He doesn't believe in homework. Sadly, he doesn't believe in any of our homework, either—but we're the ones who get in trouble if it's not done."

"What is homework?"

"It's—" Robin exhaled. She thought he was frustrated with her; sometimes he was. "I told you we have classes, right?"

She nodded; classes were also mysterious, but she had a sense of what the word meant.

"The teachers stand at the front of the room—well, not Lascar, but the rest—and they try to tell us things we don't already know. When something is new, it's hard to remember it all, so we *also* get homework. We're supposed to do the homework assigned us, because it's supposed to help us remember and understand the lesson better.

"The Barrani don't have to worry about that. I swear, I don't envy them immortality, but I'd kill for—I mean, I really, really envy their memory. They remember everything."

"So they don't have to do homework?"

"No, they do—but not to help them remember. It's to prove that they understand. If you don't understand something, remembering the exact words and phrases doesn't really help—or so Serralyn says."

"My writing is bad."

"I know. Mine isn't great, either—so you'll probably have to take classes with me to learn how to write better."

"Are there others?"

"In that class? No—before it was just me. It'd be nice not to be alone there."

Raven tilted her head. She liked Robin because he didn't lie. He tried to help. He wasn't always helpful—he didn't understand the way the world worked, which was frustrating when there was an emergency. And his words—sometimes he said things that weren't lies but *made no sense*. Like strangling Terrano. He liked Terrano. He would never try to hurt him.

But—even if it was *like* a lie, it felt different.

"You're not happy with it," Robin said.

She hesitated. She wasn't happy, but didn't know why. She had to think, and think, and think. Robin would wait; he always waited. Eventually she found words, found the thing that felt wrong or disappointing. "I wanted a desk of my own."

"Is that it? You'll have a desk of your own. It's like the beds, and the shelves. Did you notice? There are two of everything. Even windows."

"But there's only one desk."

Robin frowned. He looked at his desk. There wasn't another one.

"No," Killianas's disembodied voice said. "But Robin is correct. You will have a desk of your own. I wasn't certain if you wanted any say in the design and composition. You might want more drawers or fewer drawers; you might not like the rolltop. You might like a flat desk, a desk that's more akin to a table with drawers. I didn't want to make your desk without asking you first."

She blinked. "I can have a different desk?"

"Yes. You can have a desk identical to Robin's, or you can ask for a different desk."

"Right now?"

"Right now."

Raven started to think about desks. About drawers, about drawer sizes, about what she would want or even need. She was excited, happy, and utterly impervious to Robin's dinner warning.

He did manage to reach her eventually.

"Oh, I'm not hungry. I want to stay here and think. Is that all right?"

"It is," Killian said. "But it is not recommended that you skip meals."

"Just today?"

"I will allow that today is a special day. Robin, however, will go to the dining hall."

Raven heard the door open; she heard it close. She knew she was now alone in the room. She rose instantly, the desk uppermost in her mind. But the desk was a new impulse, a new *wanting*, and the old ones still held sway.

She moved to the windows and stared up at them, stared beyond them to the outside. "These windows," she whispered. "They're *glass*."

9

Robin almost missed dinner; the cooks were cleaning up the kitchen.

Martin raised a red brow when Robin skidded to a dismayed stop. "A bit late, are we?"

"Yes, sir."

"You know the rules, boy."

He did.

"But dinner started late; little bit of ugly excitement. So I'll give you a pass today—you arrive late tomorrow and you go hungry. Clear?"

"Yes! Thank you so much!"

Martin grinned; it was a tired, sweaty grin. The kitchen was always hot. "I didn't think twice about accepting this job— better than sweating in a noble's kitchen. I didn't realize I'd be cooking for Barrani." He made a face. "I thought I'd be cooking for kids like you. Go, eat, learn to be on time."

Serralyn and Valliant were waiting for Robin when he emerged from the kitchen. Terrano was not. Serralyn's eyes were green, but shading toward blue. She looked exhausted. Valliant looked like his usual, buttoned-up and reserved self.

"I've never understood the chancellor's decision to hire actual cooks and kitchen staff," Serralyn said. "Killian should be perfectly capable of feeding everyone."

Robin shrugged. He'd eaten in the Academia dining hall as a captive student, and during that time, there had been no cooks. But he liked the food now better. Chewing, he thought about it. "Maybe it takes energy to provide food, and the chancellor wants to conserve that energy?"

Serralyn shrugged. She was moody; it wasn't like her. Robin glanced at Valliant, but Valliant didn't appear to be concerned. Then again, Valliant almost never looked concerned. Or interested. On occasion, his eyes could light up with green, but it was seldom.

"Do you think the students were killed by other students?" Robin asked, joining the conversation he was certain she was having with herself in her own head.

Serralyn shrugged. "We did—for the first death."

"Why?"

Her smile was tinged; there was an edge to it, but also a grief. "You know that Valliant, Terrano, and I are part of a larger group of friends. We're family, even if we share no blood."

Robin nodded.

Valliant placed a gentle hand on Serralyn's shoulder. She shook her head, but he left his hand where he'd placed it, not to restrain, but to comfort. It surprised Robin a bit, because Valliant was so silent, so separate, most of the time.

"There's a reason we can hear each other talk, a reason we can see through each other's eyes. It's not something your people can do. We tell each other our names—but those names are the words that woke us at birth." This time Valliant's hand tightened. Serralyn shook her head.

"Our people don't *do this* for good reason. We don't trust each other. We can't."

Robin hesitated before he asked her why.

"You live a handful of decades. And you change a lot during those decades. That's mortality. You trust—or you don't trust—but you only have to be trustworthy for a small handful of years. We live forever, if we're careful. And we *do* change. Just not as quickly. Trust of that kind? It means the other person has to be trustworthy forever. What you wanted when you were four years old and what you want now are totally different. What you might want or need in ten years will be different again. That's living, that's growing. But forever is a lot to ask, a lot to expect—it's why we're taught never to do it, if we have any choice.

"But…we did. There were twelve of us. Twelve chosen to venture to the West to hopefully be transformed by the ancient power of the Green and its *regalia*. We were only barely considered adult at the time, and with a single exception, we were expendable. If we gained power, great. If we died, no great loss."

"But your parents—"

"Who do you think chose us?" was Serralyn's uncharacteristically bitter reply.

"Who was the exception?"

"Sedarias of Mellarionne. In her family, there was a contest in her generation to see who was strongest; the strongest would be sent. Most of us aren't fond of our birth families or our family line."

"But she is?"

Serralyn's shrug was tight, her eyes narrowed, as if she were looking at something the dining table didn't contain. "No. Her brother has tried to kill her. Her sister has tried multiple times. Her cousins have tried. She's in the direct line of the family seat—or she was. She had the potential to become the ruler of Mellarionne. But so did her siblings, and a handful of her cousins. Understand that for the Barrani, it comes down to power. She wanted power. She wanted to rule Mellarionne.

"In theory, she now does. She's Sedarias An'Mellarionne. In

practice, until she kills her cousins, and some of her aunts and uncles, the seat is still up for grabs. She's too new to the title. So she's had to build alliances within the High Halls, and allies are tricky. Some offer allegiance because they want personal gain."

"All," Valliant said quietly.

Serralyn exhaled. "Maybe. But we're allies."

Valliant shrugged. "Because we want something personal." Before she could speak, he added, "Family. People we *can* trust. People who will have our backs. I have everything I ever wanted."

"So does Sedarias." Serralyn's eyes had shaded to green as Valliant spoke. And Valliant spoke, Robin realized, for Robin's benefit, not hers. "But becoming An'Mellarionne gave her more enemies. Or maybe it just made the enemies she always had far more dangerous.

"I'm not much of a fighter. Teela is. Sedarias is. I can wield a sword at need—but I'm never going to be good at it. But I'm here, at the Academia. If I were still living with the rest of my cohort, I'd be absolutely safe; Helen is the most effective guard anyone could ever have.

"If we're here we're at risk because we're her allies. If we're killed, it will weaken Sedarias—or that's what her enemies will believe."

"You don't?"

"It will enrage her. It will throw her into a cold, eternal fury. That fury won't be quenched until every single member of our killer's family—and anyone who supported that killer—are dead."

Robin hesitated. "The first death was Barrios."

Serralyn nodded. "He was of Sendallan, and Sendallan has chosen to publicly support Sedarias. We thought it might be a warning to anyone else who might. Not all of the students present are present because they want to learn; some have been sent for other reasons. That's true even among the new mortal students.

"But Lykos was from an insignificant and unallied family. He had no power; even if he did well here, he wasn't going to change his family's status. He said two cousins were coming from the West March. He was really looking forward to that." Her hands were curled around fork and knife, but her knuckles were white. "Now we're less certain it's political. All of our cohort's investigation to date has been from the political angle. Lykos doesn't fit that."

Robin wasn't surprised when her fork bent.

He ate his own food while he watched his companions; the meal was almost funereal. But food was food, and food was necessary. He hesitated. He wanted to say something that would be helpful—but he couldn't think of a single thing. Lykos wasn't like Valliant or Terrano to Serralyn; those three were family in any real sense of the word.

But clearly she'd interacted with him enough to know that his cousins were coming to the Academia. The first death—Barrios?—had angered her but hadn't surprised her, and in the end it caused little grief. Barrani students, for the most part, stayed away from Serralyn and Valliant. Robin had asked why once, and Serralyn, green-eyed and cheerful, had said, *They don't consider us Barrani.*

Robin didn't understand why; anyone with eyes could see that they were Barrani.

But then he thought of Terrano and hesitated. Terrano looked Barrani—when he could be seen. But his eyes were sometimes the wrong color, and on a couple of occasions, the wrong *shape*. The chancellor tolerated Terrano, and Killian seemed to actively enjoy his company. But he wasn't a student, and the chancellor had made clear that he would never be accepted as one.

Serralyn wasn't eating. She was gripping her cutlery as if she wanted to stab something, but wasn't certain what.

Robin exhaled. Lowering his voice, he said, "Would you like to come back to my room to study? We have a test in three days."

She frowned. In general, group study was done in the study hall. In any other building, Serralyn said it would be called a library—but there was only one library in the Academia.

Valliant said, "Go. You've been gloomy all day. It might be entertaining. Robin's friend is there."

"She is," he said, grinning. "The chancellor is giving her application consideration, and while he is, she's rooming with me. I don't think she'll mind."

"Do you think she'll even notice?" Serralyn's smile was more natural.

"Maybe? Killian said he would make her a desk of her own, and she got lost in thoughts about what that could mean, which is why I was late for dinner and she's not here."

"Then yes. I'm sorry I'm so glum. I didn't know Lykos well. But—" She shrugged. "I guess I was too naive. I thought here— where the purpose was learning and study—the political games and resultant murders wouldn't happen. We'd just all be people who wanted to *learn*." She rose, food abandoned. "Are you finished?"

He mostly was, and *mostly* became *finished* in a matter of a minute. He then rose and headed toward his room.

Raven wasn't the actual draw; she wasn't the reason he'd invited Serralyn to come study. Valliant excused himself long before they reached Robin's room. If Serralyn found Raven interesting, Valliant found her discomfiting. It was a very normal reaction.

Only when Serralyn and Robin reached Robin's door did Robin pause. "Starrante wants to speak with Raven again. So he's likely to come directly to my room tonight. I don't imagine I'll get much sleep while they're talking, so please feel free to stay."

Her eyes did brighten then. Her shoulders relaxed; until they did, he hadn't noticed just how tightly drawn in they'd been. "Thanks, Robin. You're one of the biggest—and best—surprises in the Academia."

Raven was not in the room. Or rather, he couldn't see her immediately; he discovered her in the corner behind the newest bed. Her arms were wrapped around her legs and her knees were beneath her chin. This was her hiding posture, if the hiding space she'd found was small. The room wasn't small.

Robin exhaled.

"What happened?" he asked. He wasn't asking Raven; he didn't expect she would hear him. He was asking Killian.

Killian either didn't hear the question or chose not to answer, which was disturbing.

Robin frowned, turning toward the wall closest to the beds. There were no windows. When he'd left the room, there had been two.

Serralyn was looking at the walls, as well; she approached them, lifting her hand to touch the space that windows had occupied before dinner, as if she could see their faint outlines, given the expanded dimensions of the room.

She then turned to the crouching ball that was Raven.

"Raven—the windows here, they were made of glass, yes?"

Raven didn't answer. Robin thought she hadn't heard. But when Raven's legs slid to the floor and she looked up, he realized that she'd been *crying*. He was frozen—tears always had that effect on him. "Yes. They were. They were real glass."

Serralyn nodded, as if this was the expected answer. "What's the difference between real glass and fake glass?"

This was a question Robin had never asked. He'd assumed it was all glass, shattered remnants of windows or mirrors that she'd found while sorting through garbage. It hadn't occurred to him that there was invisible glass that only Raven could see, because when she came with her newest treasure it *was* a piece of glass. He could touch it, hold it, examine it under her watchful eye, and return it.

But the most recent treasure had been illuminating. Because until Raven picked it up, there had been no glass. Killian couldn't see it; the chancellor—who'd no doubt used magic to examine the body—hadn't seen it, either. The only person who could was Raven.

Killianas created the dorms and the dorm rooms. Killian's windows were glass, in Raven's view. Real glass. It had never occurred to Robin to wonder what would happen if the windows in his room were broken.

He hoped that wasn't why there were no windows.

"Fake glass?" Raven asked.

"You said the windows were real glass. But *real* implies that there's *fake* glass, don't you think?"

The question caused her brow to furrow. Robin was grateful that he'd asked Serralyn to join them, because Serralyn was patience personified. There was something about her that was always gentle.

"Did you touch the windows?"

Raven shook her head.

"Did you tell Killian that the windows were made of glass?"

Raven nodded. "But I wasn't going to break them! I wasn't going to take the glass—it was in the right shape. It wasn't broken." Her voice dropped. "But he made the windows disappear. He unmade them.

"And he didn't make my desk."

Robin could speak now. "Did you decide what you wanted your desk to be?"

She looked at the ground.

"Raven?"

She nodded.

"Did you tell Killian?"

She shook her head. "He took the windows away. He hasn't come back." She lowered her chin, but didn't raise her knees again. "Maybe I should have just asked for a desk exactly like yours."

"When did he leave?"

"After I asked him about the windows. And now there are no more windows." She looked up. "I'm sorry, Robin. I'm so sorry."

"It's not your fault. We still have a room, we still have beds. We still have one desk—you can share mine until we get this sorted out." He exhaled. "I'm certain Killian isn't angry at you. I'm certain he'll give you a desk of your own. There might have been an emergency somewhere." Given his discussion with the chancellor, Robin believed it could be true. But he wasn't certain.

Serralyn, however, was now looking at the windowless walls. "Did you try to touch the windows?" she asked, without looking back.

Raven shook her head. "It's not the kind of glass you can take. Or keep. It's not broken."

"Wait, you only pick up broken glass?"

Raven nodded.

"Could you break these windows?"

Raven's brows disappeared into her shaggy hairline, the question was obviously so scandalizing. Robin had never seen that expression on her face before. But he realized it wasn't an answer to Serralyn's question.

"Could you?" he asked—of Serralyn.

"I've never tried. I live in my dorm room—why would I want shattered, broken windows? But I admit I'm now curious. To my eye, the windows look like normal windows. When we look out of them, we see what's actually outside of the building—it's not like Helen's windows. I know that buildings can create almost anything within their own fixed boundaries, but…it never occurred to me to really interrogate the composition, the physical object itself." She exhaled. "We can't take most things Helen can create off the property; she can change our clothing inside of it, and she can clean clothing we bring in.

"But I'd imagine that none of the furniture would persist beyond her borders, either."

In spite of herself, Raven was listening, caught by Serralyn's tone—or maybe subject.

"Do you pick up splinters of wood, as well?"

Raven shook her head. "Glass and metal bits."

"Oh. Why?"

"Those are shiny; they're easy to see. I've never looked for wood bits. Or cloth bits. Or other things." She tilted her head as if considering this.

"No—it's fine, it's probably harder to store them safely, if they can be found at all." Serralyn turned toward Raven, back to the wall, hands behind her back. Her eyes were now green, although her expression wasn't sunny; she was thinking. She looked at Raven, whose eyes were clear. "What do you do with the shiny bits?"

"I keep them. They're my treasures."

"Is that why you started to collect them?"

Raven frowned. "I don't know."

"Do you know if you could do anything with them? Make something from them?"

Raven shook her head. It wasn't clear if the answer was *no, she couldn't*, or *no, she didn't know.*

Serralyn continued to think. "I guess my only pressing question—well, only two—are: Why was there a piece of glass beneath the body that no one else could see, and why did that piece of glass cause damage to Killian?"

"I don't know," Raven replied. "I don't understand Killian."

"That is to be expected," a familiar voice said. The clicking between syllables announced the arrival of Arbiter Starrante.

Both Raven and Serralyn turned instantly toward the Arbiter, the giant somewhat hairy spider who had appeared—utterly silently—in the middle of Robin's room. He lifted forearms in greeting, and Raven immediately stood to do the same in return. She smiled.

She hadn't been smiling a lot today, otherwise.

"Ah, Serralyn," Starrante said, weaving the air in the Barrani student's direction. "I apologize for the hour—I know it is late. But I wished to wait until after the late dinner hour was concluded."

"Did you expect to find me here, too?" Serralyn asked, eyes shining green.

"I did. I had a suspicion that Robin might invite you to attend."

"Is there something I shouldn't hear?"

"I am not the Arbiter of Academia rules; I am an Arbiter of the library. I cannot therefore answer that question in good conscience. For my part, were I in the library, no. There is nothing I can say that you should not hear.

"It is the advantage to having so many students from such varied backgrounds. I speak, I offer my thoughts, and they return with questions. Some of those questions, I will have heard a hundred times. A thousand. And some, I will never have heard, and it will start me thinking of new strands, new possibilities. I therefore welcome your inclusion.

"I don't sense Terrano."

"He's not here," Serralyn replied. "I'm not sure what he's doing—do you want me to check?"

"It is not necessary." He turned some of his eyes in Raven's direction. "I came to speak with Raven. She showed me her treasure, and my reaction was perhaps too effusive."

"Arbiter Androsse certainly seemed to think so."

Starrante made a noise that sounded similar in tone to a human snort. "I was not anticipating his intervention. He tends to act first and consider after—if he considers at all. If you wish to forgive him," he added, his tone and words implying that they shouldn't bother, "it is very, very seldom that I react in such a fashion. He perhaps considered your presence a threat to the library."

Raven frowned, tilting her head. "Why?"

"You would have to ask him. Had I considered you a credible threat, my response would have been quite different."

Both Robin and Serralyn caught the use of the word *credible*, which implied strongly that Starrante knew exactly what Androsse feared. Given Raven's presence, neither were willing to point this out. If they didn't, they wouldn't get answers. Maybe that would be better. It would certainly be better right now. But it was information Robin felt they might need.

Serralyn went to the library every chance she got—she'd probably get a chance to speak with Androsse first.

Robin avoided him. He liked Kavallac, and he liked Starrante; there was something far too old about Androsse. It wasn't that he looked down on Robin—or rather, not that he looked down on Robin more than he looked down on any other student—it was that he seemed to look at students in general as if they were all insects. Insects that he could paralyze and pin to boards to display.

If any forbidden knowledge was to escape the library, it would be because of Androsse. He didn't care what occurred outside of the library space; indeed, he sometimes seemed to relish the prospect of chaos.

Serralyn, who had been raised by political Barrani, didn't find Androsse as intimidating as Robin did. She did, however, avoid him where possible. In this case, it wouldn't be possible.

Starrante was clicking, but he was speaking his own language; Robin knew because he'd heard Starrante talk with other Wevaran before. He could generally identify languages he couldn't speak, but the Arbiter's spoken voice made that more difficult.

Serralyn glanced at Robin. "She can understand Wevaran."

"Looks like," he whispered back. He found it fascinating to watch Raven interact with Starrante. He had never seen her interact with other people for any length of time, and of those people, none had been a giant spider. But she was more effusive, she moved more, her facial expressions were far more animated.

Or maybe that was an artifact of conversing with Starrante; the Wevaran used their limbs as a kind of emphasis or punctuation. Maybe she was doing the same.

"Can you understand what they're saying?" he asked Serralyn.

She was focused on the movement of limbs and the syllables of Wevaran speech. Raven wasn't making an attempt to speak Wevaran; she was hardly speaking at all.

"I think—I can't be certain—that Starrante just mentioned webs. Terrano says he definitely mentioned webbing."

"Is he here?"

"No. Killian asked him to remain outside. He's listening in. He's too focused to be irritated that I wasn't asked to leave." She grinned. The grin faded. "He's better at Wevaran than I am, and he can manage to enter the library without the requisite permissions—but not reliably. Starrante finds him interesting. Kavallac and Androsse do not."

Robin watched, his curiosity deepening; he was unwilling to interrupt Raven because she was in a much happier place. But it became harder to keep his distance; he knew, if he were standing beside Raven, Starrante would speak the clipped Barrani with which he interacted with students.

"Where do you think Raven learned Wevaran?"

It was a question Robin had avoided asking himself. He grimaced. Avoiding questions had become a habit in childhood, while his parents had still been alive. Some questions wouldn't be answered. Some would be answered with a smile—a fake smile, carved by will and focus, not by anything resembling happiness or joy. And some would be answered so effectively he wished he had never, ever asked.

But no questions about Raven—until this moment—had been off-limits; he questioned, even if he didn't bother her with them. He knew she had trouble answering most questions, even harmless ones; she struggled with words, and with a sense of time. He expected, should she choose to stay, he'd be reminding her of classes, of mealtimes, or she'd be late—if she remembered to show up at all. And maybe that was unfair.

She laughed. Raven laughed. He stood, frozen, watching her. Had he heard her laugh before?

"You found her in the warrens?"

Robin nodded. And then added, "Maybe it's more accurate to say she found me."

"Where did she live?"

"I don't know. She tried to answer, but I thought it was a bit garbled. When I first met her, I thought she was simple."

"Simple?"

He shook his head, embarrassed. "She wasn't good with words. I assumed she couldn't really use them. But…she learned. She still finds it difficult."

"Maybe it's just Elantran she finds difficult," Serralyn said, her eyes never leaving Raven and Starrante. "Her family?"

He shook his head. "She was like me."

"You had no family?"

"No. But I lost mine the normal way." He could say that now. It had been years. "It was something we had in common. No parents. No fixed place to live. She found us a place to hide. A perfect hiding place, she said."

"Was anything unusual about it?"

"Unusual?"

"Was it normal? Was it part of the warrens, but overlooked by your pursuers?" Serralyn's brows were angled down. All of the questions she couldn't ask Raven or Starrante were now focused on Robin, as if curiosity had to have a place to go, or it would drown her.

Robin started to say yes, but stopped. Raven *always* found hiding places. But part of the reason she wanted to find him was because those places moved. Hiding places had to be found, and it was a continuous process. They didn't just disappear once she'd found them—but they didn't persist.

He'd assumed this was because other people had found them; to Raven, other people weren't safe.

"I don't know," he finally said, his voice soft as he considered what he did know, attempting to untangle the threads of his assumptions. "I know we could see out from them; I know we could hear people passing—and shouting. And screaming, once." He shuddered. "I assumed it was normal. There was nothing strange about it; it wasn't like..." His voice trailed off.

"Like our dorms?"

He nodded. "They were run-down places, places beneath buildings, rooms in buildings that looked like they would fall down on us at any second. Once, a basement with a broken window. Sometimes it was just a corner of an alley that had enough junk in it we could hide behind it. None of it seemed out of the ordinary."

"But people didn't find you."

He nodded. "No one found Raven, either. Anytime I tried to find her, she found me. Sometimes I didn't see her at all, though." He glanced at Serralyn, whose gaze remained fixed on Raven.

"She helped me. Honestly, she saved my life, probably more than once. She taught me about the warrens—things my parents couldn't teach, or didn't, before they died."

"Have I ever asked you about your parents' death?"

He froze.

This time she glanced back at him. "Sorry. We talk about ours a lot."

"Your parents are dead?"

"Valliant's, Teela's, Annarion's, Mandoran's. I'm not sure you've met all of them, but they're part of us. A lot of our parents died in the wars between the Dragons and the Barrani. Some died in other ways."

"Did any of them survive?"

"Yes, more's the pity." The words were soft, her eyes blue. "Dead parents can't cause more pain. Sorry. We were older when our parents died—in some cases, much older. That's lamentably normal for the Barrani, but—most of the Barrani don't consider us normal." The blue receded as she grinned. "Which is fair—we're not."

Robin didn't talk about his parents' deaths. He didn't talk about his past, the life before the warrens, which he could only barely remember—most often in nightmares.

"Did you ever ask about Raven's?"

Had he? Maybe in the very early years—but that was when she'd been learning how to speak. "She's been the best friend the warrens could offer," he said. "And even if she weren't, I owe her my life. But I've never seen her harm *anything*. The glass she finds? She doesn't break anything to get it. She's shared food, and sometimes when she's willing to take jobs running errands, she'll share coin.

"I did the same, when I could—but some of those errands came through Raven. If people thought she was simple, if they thought she wasn't quite right in the head, they thought she was trustworthy. Inasmuch as anyone could be, living in the warrens."

"You wanted to bring her here."

"I did." His voice was soft. "I thought she would fit in, somehow. I thought she would find a home here—a place where she could show off her treasures and ask her hundreds and hundreds of questions."

"Looks like you weren't wrong."

"I guess. Things are more complicated than I thought they'd be."

Serralyn chuckled. "That," she said, "is the anthem of our lives. But—she looks happy." She froze.

Raven had carefully removed her pouch, and from it, she had drawn a piece of glass.

Both Serralyn and Robin forgot to breathe.

This time, however, Starrante's eyes—stalks lifted and almost at full extension—didn't immediately start a frenzied, terrible dance above his body, although their color did shift. Robin had closed the gap that he'd forced himself to make—and maintain—before Raven was able to hand the librarian the piece of glass.

She blinked as Robin stepped into her field of view, her expression rippling into something apologetic. "I forgot."

"Forgot?"

"You were here. Sorry." She hung her head.

He hated it. He hated to be the cause of it. "We didn't mind, Raven. We knew Starrante came to talk to you. We didn't feel left out."

Serralyn said, "I did." But she was smiling broadly, her expression at odds with her words. Robin could have told her that Raven would find this confusing, but today she was focused on glass and Starrante; she probably hadn't heard Serralyn.

"Is it okay if I show him the glass?"

Robin wanted to say yes. He said nothing, because *yes* wouldn't come.

"It is safe," Starrante said, in words Robin could understand. "It was safe in the library—but my reaction caused consternation in Arbiter Androsse—a man not known for his thoughtful approach to concern or disagreement." Some of Starrante's eyes shifted color, the normal reddish brown becoming not the scarlet of fear or anger, but almost burgundy. Annoyance?

Raven looked to Robin. He realized that she often looked to him when other people were involved—and in this instance, that was ridiculous. She could speak to Starrante in a way that he couldn't.

"If he says it's safe, it's safe."

She nodded. Robin stepped to the side, this time facing the librarian.

"I almost didn't recognize this," Starrante said as he held out a limb. "It is so broken."

"Does it belong to you?" Raven asked, in some alarm, the glass in her hand.

He took it gently. "No, child. Not now. It is yours. You found it; none of us would have seen it at all were it not for your intervention. I will not take it from your keeping, but I am grateful that you were willing to share it with me."

"But what is it? What did you recognize?" It was Serralyn who'd asked. Normally Robin would have, but he felt uncomfortable now, the terrain of the familiar and much-loved Academia giving way to an uncertainty that made everything feel unstable.

"Glass," was the soft reply. "It is, as Raven says it is, glass."

"But you said it was broken almost beyond recognition?"

"And so it is." He had not answered the question. This, too, was unusual. Starrante, of all the librarians, was the one who encouraged the asking of questions; he seemed delighted to hear them. Some he could answer; some he would not. He felt that the finding of answers would heighten—or deepen—their relevance.

This felt like neither of those.

As if aware of this, the eyes across Starrante's body lowered until they nestled against his skin. Wevaran eyelids closed on all but three.

"I have more," Raven said. "Do you want to see them?"

"Yes, child. Yes, I would. I will handle them with care; they are—as I said—yours, not mine."

"It's not all glass," she told him as she once again opened her pouch.

"No?"

"Mostly it's glass. But sometimes there are metal bits."

Eyes rose on stalks, but were otherwise still. "Metal bits?"

Raven nodded. "They're like gold, I think—but not that color. But they don't rust. I don't have many of those—it's mostly glass." She turned to Robin. "Can we use your desk?"

He immediately turned to the desk, pushing the rolltop up. Raven extended the writing surface as far as possible without breaking anything. Her hands were shaking as she carefully opened the drawstrings on the pouch.

"Where did you find that pouch?" Starrante asked.

She looked confused. "I've always had it."

Starrante rumbled. One eye turned toward Robin, who nodded.

"I don't remember a time when she didn't have it. But she doesn't take it out very often." Holding it anywhere it could be seen by others was risky; no one would assume that its contents were broken glass and stray bits of metal. But if some of those bits were actual gold… Robin wasn't certain. Raven talked sometimes about bits of metal, but what she showed him—what delighted her most—were the pieces of glass.

Serralyn cleared her throat as Raven very, very carefully began to empty her pouch, one piece at a time. Robin would have upended the bag on the desktop, and then spread the resulting pile out. Raven was more precise and far more careful, but that made sense. To Robin, the things were already broken. He couldn't imagine that handling them would do more damage. But he didn't touch other people's treasures without invitation and respect.

Piece by piece, all smaller than the one she'd found on campus, she spread out those treasures.

When the first piece of metal came out of the pouch, Starrante started to cough. His eyes extended and once again began to flail. Robin was reminded of young children then, although Starrante was in no way young or a child: it was the flailing of pumping arms, the brightness of fully open eyes, the air of excitement.

His limbs rose; he reached out to lift one of the metallic pieces, but caught himself before he made contact. "Raven, may I look at this one?"

Raven nodded.

10

Robin once again held his breath, remembering what had happened to Killian when he had asked—or demanded— to examine the single piece of glass.

Raven clearly remembered it, as well; a shadow crossed her face, dimming her excitement. Robin realized that while she always showed him new pieces of glass, she seldom showed him pieces of metal; he had assumed that she'd picked up tarnished pieces of broken things, but they weren't as important to her.

He reassessed now. She had no problem handing Starrante pieces of glass; she had not wanted to give even glass to Killian.

Had she known? Had she somehow suspected that touching this glass would cause Killian harm?

He opened his mouth, but shut it again; Starrante was waiting for Raven's response. There was no demand and no threat—or no more threat than one would generally feel from a giant spider. That hadn't been the case with Killian. Then again, Killian was responsible for the safety of the Academia—a responsibility that he had failed, given the fact of two dead students. It made sense that his caution would have an edge to it.

Raven turned to Robin, her brows folding in silent question.

"I don't know," he told her. "But Arbiter Starrante thinks it'll be safe for him."

Starrante rumbled again, lowering his arm. "It *should* be safe." He made noises that had no obvious words attached.

Raven took a step back. She was willing to leave her treasures exposed, but there was a current of fear in her posture that was new.

"She doesn't want you to take the risk," Robin told the Arbiter, apologetically.

"Can Robin touch it?" he asked.

Raven nodded immediately.

"Robin?"

Robin nodded as well, but moved slowly, the shadow of his arm passing over glass, and dimming its reflection. Raven had said the metal was like gold, but a different color. Some of the pieces were so small Robin was surprised she'd seen them at all; they were slender, narrower and shorter in length than a pin.

But they were different colors; some were gold, some silver, but some were purple, green, radiant blue, yellow; one or two were white. All, however, looked metallic to Robin's eyes. He wondered if there was, or had been, cloth of a similar kind. It was a stray thought.

"Robin?" Starrante said again, and Robin reddened. He wasn't as easily distracted or overfocused as Raven, but there was a reason he had always felt comfortable accepting her as she was.

He looked for Raven's permission again just to make certain. She nodded.

Robin then let his hand hover over the pieces, landing at last on one that was a deep purple. He chose one of the thicker pieces because he wanted to avoid embarrassing himself; he wasn't certain he could pick up the slender, needle-shaped pieces without making multiple clumsy attempts.

The metal was cool to the touch, not cold, and as Robin

lifted it closer to his eye, he could see that the purple color was a blend of blues, greens, reds, and black, all folded together, as if the original object had been composed of slender metallic sheets of different colors.

Starrante observed. He then turned to Raven. "I better understand your caution. I will leave the inspection to Robin for the moment."

Robin would have dropped Raven's treasure in any other circumstance. He set it down carefully because it was Raven's. But his hand didn't hurt, nothing had exploded, nothing had changed. Raven had believed it would be safe for Robin, and it had been. He turned to Serralyn to say as much and grimaced: she had Terrano's eyes.

Which is to say, her eyes no longer looked like normal Barrani eyes. Terrano transformed his eyes all the time, Serralyn never. But she'd chosen to do so now. Her eyes were therefore the wrong shape, the wrong color; they had no whites, no pupils, no irises. From the wrong angle, they seemed like windows—windows into a terrible pool of chaos, an alien landscape.

"What do they look like to you?" he asked, avoiding that wrong angle.

"Glass," she replied, in her normal voice. "Broken glass."

"The metal?"

"That's a bit different. It...doesn't look like metal to me— not when I look at it like this." She grimaced and closed her eyes. "I seriously have no idea how Terrano does this for any length of time; it gives me a wicked headache."

"Because he *is* a wicked headache?"

She laughed. "It looked more like...wax. Like candle drippings."

"Even when I was holding it?"

She nodded. "It was hardened; it didn't look like your hands were going to melt it. But it doesn't look metal when viewed

that way." She shook her head. Wicked headache appeared to
be accompanied by nausea; she was pale and slightly green as
she opened the eyes she usually had. "But it looks like metal to
Raven, and to you. It looks like metal to me now." She turned
to Starrante. "How do you see the metal bits?"

"I do not see them as you saw them when you attempted to
avail yourself of Terrano's spell, but it is a closer approximation."

"What do you think would have happened to you if you
picked it up?"

"I am uncertain. It is not metal as you understand it; it is not
as inert. Ah, no; *inert* is the wrong word. I believe that if the
metal comes into contact with the right—or wrong—material,
it will change."

"The metal?"

"And the material."

"You mean...you."

"I am uncertain, Serralyn. But I am not—at this particular moment—willing to become the subject of such an experiment." He clicked and whirred to himself. "I would have
been in my distant youth." His voice contained nostalgia and
amusement. Robin still hadn't clearly defined what *smile* meant
to a Wevaran.

Robin smiled.

Serralyn didn't. Folding her arms, she said, "What did you
think this broken glass was when you first saw it?"

Starrante clicked. "I will discuss that with you later. I am
uncertain, and the matter may be delicate; I will have to con-
fer with the Arbiters."

Robin stiffened.

Serralyn's arms tightened. "When you say 'with the Arbiters,' do you mean..."

"I do. It is very seldom that a full council of Arbiters is called,
but I feel the situation may warrant it. Until we have convened

and discussed the issue, it is not a matter to be discussed with students."

"But students are the ones who have the glass."

"Raven is the one who has the glass," he replied, "and at the moment, Raven is not a student. Her application is being considered, but in these difficult circumstances, the consideration may take time." Before Serralyn could speak again, he lifted both forearms. "I have no intention of removing any of the treasures Raven has gathered. They are hers, and I will make that absolutely clear.

"I have even less intention of removing Raven. Killianas has been somewhat nervous, but it is clear to me that he considers Raven an important applicant: she has been given space in the dorms—in Robin's room. He is fond of Robin; I do not think he would risk Robin's safety."

Robin said nothing, because he'd never felt Raven was a threat to his safety. He'd felt that *absence* of Raven in the early years was a threat. Never her presence. He'd shared hiding spaces with her before; he could share a room this big without difficulty.

And maybe, just maybe, he wanted that—he wanted to protect her because she had offered him safety when he'd had none, when all the safe places had been destroyed by death.

He shook himself. That was not a place he wanted to go. Not now. Not ever.

Starrante touched his shoulder. "I will return, with your permission. But, Robin, keep her safe if you can." He glanced at Raven; she watched him, but said nothing. Her arms remained by her sides.

Serralyn continued to study the pieces of glass until Raven began to gather them up again. She made no move to interfere, and none whatsoever to touch. Robin offered to help Raven, and she nodded, wordless. She was done with words for the day.

Or so he thought. When Serralyn left for the evening, Raven sat on her bed, her hands in her lap, her head bowed. Robin realized she had no nightclothes. She had nothing but what she was wearing or carrying in her pockets. That had always seemed normal to Robin, but normal had shifted. He had never seen her wear different clothing, but her clothing wasn't rags and tatters; she wore her robes.

He would have asked Killian to help, but he wasn't certain Raven would be comfortable with that. He didn't expect Raven, head bowed, to say, "Killian."

Silence.

"Killian, you promised you would make me a desk. I need a desk. I need you to keep your promise."

Killian appeared in the center of the room. Not his voice—because he didn't speak—but his Avatar.

"Killian?" Robin said.

Killian turned to Robin, and Robin froze. Killian's eyes were black. Black with iridescent colored flecks. It was the color they became when there was danger, or when Killian was so preoccupied he couldn't maintain a Barrani appearance. Neither was a good sign.

"My desk?" Raven asked. To Robin's surprise, it was almost a demand.

"I have told you that the desk you have requested would be difficult, and it will take time."

Robin was certain his jaw was still attached to his face, but he pushed it shut, just in case. How could there be something Killian needed time to create? He'd created most of this room almost instantly. The bed. The windows—which weren't there anymore.

"I have also told you that some cooperation on your part is required. Alternately, you could accept a desk very like Robin's desk; if you do not like that style, you might have a desk like Serralyn's."

"You said."

Robin had seen Raven haggle once or twice in his life—but it was rare. Very rare. She was haggling now. With Killian.

He blinked, rubbed his eyes, and blinked again; she was still glaring up at Killian, her hands by her sides.

"I said that I would *try*, Raven. But there are difficulties for me at this present time. And I remind you that you said you would try to help me."

Her brows furrowed. "I said I would *try*. But I don't know if I can."

Killian nodded. "Robin?"

Robin felt like the world was slowly being pulled out from beneath his feet. What had seemed stable and solid was vanishing—just like his window. "Yes?"

"You have spoken with the chancellor."

"Yes."

"You therefore have some understanding of the possible difficulties the Academia is facing."

Robin nodded.

"At this time, the chancellor is doing what he can to ameliorate the difficulties—but it is not yet enough. I believe your friend might be of aid."

This, Robin had no difficulty believing. But if Raven could help Killian, it made the Academia far less safe than he'd thought.

"I wish you to accompany Raven and help her if she requires help."

"When?"

"Tomorrow."

"After class?"

"Classes can wait; you have the chancellor's permission. I have informed your teachers."

"What did Professor Melden say?"

"He said nothing."

"Loudly?"

"How can nothing be loud?" Raven asked.

Robin winced. Melden didn't approve of Robin; he was one of the few mortal teachers in the Academia, and he *expected better* from those who represented humanity in a sea of Barrani. Certainly Robin was not Melden's version of better. Skipping class—at Killian's request—was unlikely to improve his opinion.

"He has very obvious facial expressions. Killian, can you provide nightgowns or nightclothes for Raven?"

"I can, yes. I am uncertain that she will wear them. You may show her to the baths."

Raven shook her head. "I'm not dirty," she told them both. Robin knew that tone.

"I am, and I'm going to bathe."

"I'll wait here."

Folded clothing appeared on the end of Raven's bed. She glanced at it, but made no move to touch it. Robin headed toward the door. "I'll be back soon. It's safe here. We can sleep."

Raven nodded; it was her distracted nod. Most of her thoughts were no doubt on the desk that had failed to be built.

The conversation with Starrante had taken a while; the bathing room was almost empty. The water, however, was still warm, thanks to Killian. Robin slid into the bath. Until he'd come to the Academia—admittedly as a prisoner—he'd washed with cold water; in the summer he could wash himself on the banks of the Ablayne, but in the winter it was harder.

In the center of the room was a pool, sunk into the ground. There were smaller tubs—full of heated water in which one was meant to wash—with soap—and rinse. The pool itself was warm and meant for those who were mostly clean. The first time he'd entered the baths was a revelation.

He'd felt he could almost remember a time when he had been bathed in water such as this; it was clean, it was warm. He almost expected someone to come and wash his hair—which didn't happen.

But today someone did arrive, her movements so silent he didn't hear her until she was beside him. She grabbed a towel in silence; she grabbed the clothing that lay folded on the nearest bench in the same silence. He recognized that silence, although it had been years since he'd experienced it; old habits died hard, if they died at all.

He held his breath, grabbed the towel she'd shoved toward him, and dried himself off. Quickly. When he glanced at his clothing, Raven tensed but nodded. Yes, he had time—but only if he moved *fast*.

He slid his legs into his pants, slid both arms into the sleeves of his shirt; these were day clothes, not nightclothes. He wondered if Killian was aware that Raven was here.

"Killian!" he shouted. There was no reply.

He dressed quickly, ignoring buttons, and when Raven grabbed his hand, he followed instantly, almost holding his breath.

There were two doors that led from the bathing room; one led back to the hall, and one led to a balcony. Raven led Robin to the hall, which surprised him. Most of her hiding places were outdoors in the warrens.

He hadn't been certain she would find hiding places in the Academia, possibly because he hadn't believed they'd be necessary. But he knew this run. He knew this silence. He understood the urgency. Raven was on the hunt for a hiding place, and she only hunted when it was necessary.

These halls weren't the warrens. The people in them were students—and the odd teacher—not the denizens of the warrens most likely to cause the need to hide: gangs seeking to mark their territory in obvious and brutal ways. New gangs were especially threatening.

Robin had been on the edge of too young to join one. Younger kids could be adopted into a gang to run errands and keep a lookout for the Barrani Hawks that sometimes patrolled the warrens' streets. Human Hawks mostly didn't get sent to the warrens, because they weren't guaranteed to survive there. There was safety of a kind in a gang—but more fear and less freedom.

He might have joined one regardless, had it not been for Raven.

He was old enough now, but now he had the Academia. And in the Academia there was no need to hide.

It was odd to run through well-lit halls; even at night, the lights in the hall responded to the presence of people who traversed it. Their shadows—his and Raven's—were short and squat beneath those lights, lengthening as they passed them.

Raven led him out of the dorm wing, her hand white-knuckled around his, his almost numb. She passed a door that led to the quad, running faster as the glass that comprised three quarters of the door came into view. Not outside, then.

The bodies had been discovered in the quad.

She turned a corner—Raven, who didn't know the Academia, and who hadn't seen its many halls except at Robin's side—and continued her headlong run. She found stairs Robin didn't remember clearly; the area here was less well lit, and the lights that adorned the walls, less responsive—as if they were actual lights and not part of Killian.

From there, she continued her run; Robin's breath was far louder than hers. The Academia wasn't small; the building was an expanse of halls, rooms, auditoriums. They should have been close to those auditoriums, given the length of their sprint, but they weren't. He couldn't see the familiar doors that led to the largest classrooms.

She came to stairs that descended. There were no lights on the walls that led down; the darkness grew as Raven turned.

For the first time since she'd come to retrieve him, she hesitated, her running gait momentarily broken. He looked at her expression in the dimmer light; she was blinking rapidly. She didn't speak.

She didn't ask his opinion.

Robin understood: it wasn't safe. It wasn't safe yet.

Inhaling, her expression a moving set of muscles that expressed worry and determination in rapid shifts, she walked down the stairs. Robin suspected she'd have taken them at least two at a time had they not been attached by her hand—but he couldn't manage that without falling.

The stairs felt longer in the gloom. They were moving far more slowly than they had to reach this point. But the stairs ended at either a wooden wall or a door—Robin assumed it was a door. Raven reached out with her free hand, touching the door at the same time as Robin did.

The door vanished.

The flat of his palm, pressed against wood, was now pressed against nothing; he stumbled forward slightly, righting himself. Beneath his feet—his bare feet—was cool stone.

Raven didn't speak. She didn't let go of his hand. In the distance ahead, he heard sound—breathing? Possible moaning. He tensed then. Raven didn't. She exhaled—he could hear that much over the distant sound—and then once again began to move.

Beyond what had been either wall or door was a hallway; the hall was, if not well lit, at least lit. Raven sped up to a jog, not a sprint, for which Robin was grateful. Wood beneath bare feet was far more comfortable than stone—and in the more traversed halls there were carpet runners over that wood.

This hall had doors; the doors were closed. Raven walked past most of them, then stopped at one on their left. She opened it with her free hand, the door swinging in. She stepped into the room, pulling Robin behind her, and then turned to close the door.

Only then did she let go of his hand, but she was shaking her head, half in disgust, half in worry. The worry, he understood; the disgust, he didn't.

"Here," she said, indicating, by speech, that speech was now considered safe. She then looked at Robin and shook her head.

"What?"

"You said it was safe here."

"It's been totally safe. I mean, since the chancellor came. It's been safe."

"It was safer in the warrens."

"We almost starved in the winter," he pointed out.

"But we didn't. This isn't a good place."

He looked past her. The room was full of boxes. And dust. And spiderwebs. "How long do we have to hide?"

She shook her head. She couldn't answer. Robin accepted this. "Why couldn't we just run back to our room? Killian was there."

She shook her head again. "The room's not safe right now." She stared at him, frowning. "Maybe you wanted me to come here because you knew."

"I wanted you to come here so you wouldn't have to hide anymore!" Robin seldom raised his voice, but Raven's words stung.

"But we do have to hide." Her voice was calm and without the heat that Robin's had momentarily contained. It made him feel guilty. There was no accusation in her words. Even her misunderstanding of the reason he'd wanted her to become a student wasn't an accusation.

He bowed his head for a long moment. When he lifted it, he was far calmer. "Sorry. I never felt I had to hide here."

"This isn't a good place for hiding," she said. He knew she meant the Academia. "There aren't enough hiding places. I think they'll disappear faster, too. Could we go back to the warrens?"

Robin hesitated, and then said, "There's more glass here, though."

Raven froze.

"And Killian will make you a desk. You'll have your own desk. You could have your own room if you wanted." He didn't bother to mention food. Raven understood that it was necessary—but it was necessary the way water was; she drank it, but it wasn't *important*. Glass was.

"I don't want my own room."

Robin nodded.

Raven deflated. "Fine."

"Do you know what's in these?" He looked around at the boxes, the dust. If this was a storeroom, it hadn't been used in a long time.

"I don't know."

"Is it safe to open them?"

"Dust. You'll sneeze."

"Does any of it feel like it could be dangerous? Would it break the hiding place?"

She stared at him—as she very rarely did—as if he were trying to grow an extra head. This meant *no* in Raven-speak, but more emphatic.

Robin then turned to a random box—one that rested on top of three others. The boxes varied in size, and in construction, but not in the layer of dust that covered them. Or the webs that were anchored to them.

Robin really liked Arbiter Starrante. He really didn't like spiders. Raven had never cared. She didn't care about wasps. She didn't care about cockroaches. They were like birds or other animals to her. So were rats. Unless they tried to eat her food, in which case she'd boot them. She moved fast enough to connect, too.

Robin sighed. There was dim light in this room—too dim to really see clearly by—but it was better than nothing. And as Raven had decided that they were hidden enough to talk, without any sense of how long they would have to remain that way, Robin decided to open boxes in the storeroom. Even if the boxes contained food, they were clearly long past their expiry date—long enough past that the usual smell of rotting food or the maggots that it sometimes housed wouldn't be a threat.

He had to stretch a bit to reach the first box; Raven watched, and then found a place on the floor to sit; she leaned against boxes, but that was almost necessary; there was very little exposed wall.

Having not come prepared to excavate, Robin didn't have a crowbar at hand; he hoped it wouldn't be necessary. He put the retrieved box down on the floor; it was surprisingly heavy, given its size. But this wasn't a crate. No, it was a small, dust-covered chest. He could see the hinges his handling had exposed, as layers of dust transferred themselves from chest to skin.

The chest was locked.

Robin frowned. He had the clothes on his back—but not all of them; he had no shoes; and his shirt remained unbuttoned. He fixed that as he looked at the lock. "Raven—could you lend me one of your metal bits?"

"Which one?"

"One of the pins. But—a longer one. I think there was a white one?"

"It's grey."

"Sorry—it's the first time I've seen the metal." He couldn't really distinguish between glass bits, either. "But only if you think it's safe."

"You can hold them—but why?" She frowned. "The lock?"

"Yeah."

Raven snorted. "Give me the box." She rifled through her

robe and withdrew the pouch. "You weren't ever good at picking locks, you know."

"I got better. And that one lock was *rusted*."

Raven could, of course, pick old locks—sometimes there were hiding places behind them. She'd taught Robin, but he'd never been quite as good as she was. And she'd never been patient because if a hiding place was necessary, it was necessary *now*.

"Let me try. We're already in a safe place, so it doesn't matter how long I take, does it?"

She shrugged, which mostly meant he was right. Raven had never liked inefficiency—when she was aware of it. But she fished a grey, pin-shaped piece of metal out of her pouch.

Robin moved the chest toward the light, and paused. There was light, so there was a light source—but he couldn't immediately find it, which didn't make sense. There was no ceiling light that he could see, which meant the light was against the wall. But crates were piled against the walls; if there was a lamp or something similar on a wall, they'd have blocked most of it. He'd see light against the ceiling closest to the wall.

"Can you see where the light is coming from?"

Raven nodded.

"I can't."

"It's here," she said, and pointed to the room's center. To the floor. Robin frowned. She was right, but the floor itself wasn't glowing. The frown left his lips, but his brows furrowed as he moved the chest and put it down—carefully—in the center of the floor. The room didn't darken perceptibly.

He then shrugged, accepting it. This was part of the Academia, even if Raven considered it a hiding place. He expected a certain amount of magic, and this was clearly that. He moved the chest and held out a hand. Raven carefully placed the pin across his palm. She didn't hesitate, but she handled the pin with the same care she handled all of her treasures, a reminder to Robin to do the same.

The lock absorbed his attention, drawing it away from the need for a hiding place. He gently pushed the pin into the key-hole. It wasn't a complicated lock—most chests this size didn't have them. This was the size of a large jewelry box; it was the type of chest diaries might be placed in.

His hands paused.

He had no conscious memory of seeing a diary or a box meant to lock private things away from the prying eyes of family.

"Robin?"

He shook his head. "It's not hard. It shouldn't be hard. I'm fine." But he heard the echoes of a girl's voice, faint and an-noyed. *What are you doing in my room? Mom! He's in my room again!*

Small echoes. Echoes of grievance and anger. A voice he wanted to hear again, to *really* hear, even if it shouted in fury. Even then. No. *No.*

"Robin?"

He could not touch those memories. He couldn't. It had been so long since he had. Why now? Was it because he was safe here? Was it because he finally had a home again?

Raven grabbed his shoulder. "Robin," she said again.

He shook her hand off, or tried. "I'm fine."

"Let me open the box."

"No—I can open it."

She looked at him, frowning, before she withdrew her hand. "You know why I found you?" she asked as he turned back to the lock.

"You said you heard me."

"Yes. I heard you. I found you because I heard you. I helped you because I heard you."

The pin entered the keyhole again; his hands weren't entirely steady. He pushed gently, prodded gently.

"It was sad," she continued. "It was sad. I heard you and you sounded like me."

11

Robin's probing lost the steady deliberation he had barely managed to achieve. He turned from lock to Raven; she was now seated on the ground within arm's reach, her hands in her lap, her pouch beneath them.

"Sounded like you?" This was more than she'd ever said about that day.

She nodded. "Like me." She lowered her head. "But you went away."

"That wasn't my choice!"

She raised her head, eyes wide; Robin realized he had almost shouted. Raven hated shouting. He swallowed air. "Sorry. I—" Raven's words hadn't been an accusation. They never were. It was just the way Raven talked. Had it been so long he'd forgotten? "I didn't mean to leave. I didn't *want* to leave. I wasn't the only person who got dragged off the street—there were four or five men, all warrens' natives."

She nodded, lowering her head into her knees again.

"I didn't know what was happening. I thought they might have worked for Giselle."

She snorted into her knees.

Robin's half smile was genuine. "I didn't think they meant to kill me. If they wanted that, I'd've been dead." But even as he spoke, he hesitated. Raven hadn't come to find him. Raven hadn't come to drag him to a hiding place. It was the first time, in the warrens, that there was danger that she hadn't sensed in time to come to his aid.

He swallowed all of those words, because even unspoken they sounded like an accusation to him.

"They brought me to the fiefs; they crossed into the boundary zone. You should see it," he added. "It's like, and unlike, the fief streets: there are houses and buildings, but they're all kind of grey, as if they have no actual color. But there was one building there—it had no doors. We entered it through some kind of portal. I lost consciousness then.

"When I woke up, I was here. I was in the Academia."

She said nothing, but she was listening.

"I was lost here. I couldn't leave—I tried, but every road always led back to the Academia. Nothing changed here. There were classes. I was expected to attend classes; I found this out when I was threatened with demerits or detention—I can't remember which. But...there was food. The dining hall had food. And I had a room that wasn't falling apart and wasn't cold or wet."

"You liked it better."

"I liked it better than starving or freezing, yes. But even if I'd hated it, I couldn't leave. I spent a week trying. I learned what demerits were. What detention was. But everyone forgot them the following day. I'd wake up, and the same day would start again."

She lifted her head again. "Why?"

"I don't know—"

"No, I mean why did you try to leave?"

He exhaled. "Because you were in the warrens. I didn't mean to leave you alone for so long."

She nodded, a continuous bob of head.

"You were my only friend," he told her.

"No. You're *my* only friend. But you have other friends. You made other friends."

"Not really. Serralyn and Valliant weren't here then. Neither was Terrano. The chancellor wasn't here, and Killian didn't talk at all. Professor Larrantin was, and a couple of others—but I didn't have classes with them. The classes were always the same. Mealtimes. Lights out.

"Some of the students forgot. Some of the professors. I think they'd been here forever. But the newer students hadn't. People like me. I tried to work around the sameness. I started to ask questions in class. I started to learn how to read better, and how to read Barrani, because most of the classes are taught in Barrani.

"But Killian didn't start to speak, didn't start to wake up, until the end—and when he did, it happened all at once: the chancellor, Terrano, the Hawks. I think the fieflord of Candallar wanted to *be* the chancellor, but he couldn't."

"Why?"

"Because he didn't give a crap about the Academia or its students. He tried to kill most of us. The chancellor killed him instead. And then the chancellor moved in, Killian talked a lot more, and I got to spend time with Starrante. And with Serralyn—she loves libraries like you love glass—and Terrano.

"And I thought of you. I thought of you all the time. I wanted to find you."

"Why?"

He shook his head. "I missed you. I have more friends. But they've known me for weeks. You've known me for almost all of my life. I'm sorry. I'm sorry I went away. If I'd had any choice, I wouldn't have."

"It was my fault. I didn't hear you. I didn't *know*. I didn't find you—I didn't feel like I *had to* find you."

He took a risk. He knelt in front of Raven, and very slowly hugged her. They had been two kids without strength or power. "It's not your fault."

"But you don't want to come back." Not a question.

He shook his head, feeling a stab of pure unadulterated guilt. "This is home now."

"Not my home."

He said nothing, surprised that he was holding his breath.

She'd heard him.

She'd helped.

He felt, in flight, in hiding, that they were kindred spirits. They were lost in the warrens, and they were both alone. Maybe that's what she'd heard. Robin had never wanted to be so alone.

It was always Raven who found him first, even if he went looking. Sometimes she had food, which she shared. In the beginning, she'd said almost nothing—but it was a quiet nothing, a good nothing. She hadn't felt the need for words, and Robin—tired, hungry, cold, and exhausted—hadn't the energy for them.

He hadn't asked her if she'd heard him then.

She came to him the first winter. What threatened him then wasn't other people; it wasn't malice. It was the cold, the lack of a home, the lack of food. All dangers that existed without intent.

But the hiding place she'd found was a room. It was drafty; the roof had half collapsed in parts of the building, but the room itself, though the floors were warped and the shutters—or the slats that remained—too damaged to properly close, was warmer than the outside. She'd offered him clothing, a coat meant for an adult, and sparse food. But it had seemed like a feast to Robin. It had been his first winter without his parents.

Raven moved them one more time before winter ended. Robin followed. When spring came, he met Giselle. He wondered if Raven had pushed him in that direction, if she'd known—but Raven wasn't one of Giselle's kids. She did odd jobs, running things back and forth from the warrens to the outside—but people hired her if she asked because she *could* run things safely back and forth. She wasn't mugged, wasn't robbed, didn't lose things.

She continued to make her own way. Robin found shelter in a very crowded room when it was too cold. Giselle offered him work as an errand boy in exchange for that spot on the floor in the crowded room; she offered him coin and food— not a lot of food. There'd never been enough food.

But Raven still came to find him from time to time. Raven still led him to hiding places. And Raven showed him her treasures. Her pieces of glass.

He had loved the way glass transformed her expression; he loved the sudden joy, the unfettered delight. He hadn't felt that for so long it was like a foreign language—he could recognize it, but couldn't speak it. He didn't want to break it. Not then. Not now.

Her joy was delicate, it was fragile. He knew how easily broken a joyful life could be. Maybe he would have envied her. Maybe he would have resented her. But he knew, even then, that sharing these with him was Raven's way of taking a risk. And he knew, from observation, that she didn't show her treasures to everyone. Didn't even try.

It was like a secret.

It was their secret until she came here. Until she'd found the biggest piece of glass—that no one could see until she picked it up. Until Killian's hand blackened. Until Starrante was so excited he lost all control of speech.

Now it wasn't a secret. It was a possible threat, a possible danger, totally unanticipated. He'd never, ever considered Raven a danger. To anyone.

The lock clicked.

Robin turned toward Raven and held out his hand; she took

her treasure and slid it back into her pouch. She then moved to stand over the small chest as Robin opened it.

He'd been right. It was the type of box one locked and kept in one's bedroom. There was a book in it, leather cover cracked in places because it had dried out; there was an ink bottle—capped, which was a bit of a relief although he didn't expect the ink would be anything more than dried color—and a quill.

"Feather!" Raven exclaimed.

"It's a quill."

"It's a feather."

"Yes, but…it's a quill. It's used to write."

She stared at it. "Show me."

"I can't show you right here—there's no ink. This bottle is dried out. We can't use it to write."

She said, "Can I keep it?" She clearly meant the feather.

"I guess, if you want? It might have belonged to someone before."

"You can keep the book," she offered, as if negotiating. He hadn't expected she would want the feather, because feathers weren't entirely uncommon in the warrens, and she'd never been particularly excited to see them; she'd never picked them up.

He had no need of a quill; he expected it would be brittle and difficult to use. "Is it safe to go back yet?" he asked, closing the box. It was heavy, but he intended to take it with him; the book had made him curious.

"Almost."

"How can you tell?"

She gave him a *not this again* look. He almost laughed. But he closed the lid of the box—after Raven had retrieved the feather—and then sat on the floor to wait out the danger. He really hoped they wouldn't be here for the rest of the night.

Raven woke him. He wasn't certain how long they'd been in the storeroom. He was leaning against her; she had an arm around his shoulder. He didn't remember falling asleep—but he did remember sitting on the floor beside her. That had been normal in his childhood; sometimes the hiding places were small enough there was no way to keep physical separation.

"Is it morning?"

Raven shook her head. She stood, slightly jittery, as if impatient to be gone.

She'd always been like that: she didn't like to be stuck or trapped in one place. She would do it if there was danger, but the moment danger had passed she needed to move. At times like this, she would leave. Sometimes she would remember to say goodbye, but not in the beginning. The storm had passed, and they were no longer sheltering from it. So she ran off to do whatever it was Raven did when there was no storm.

He wondered if she would vanish in the same way today, and was almost surprised when she didn't. But she didn't grab his hand as she opened the door and headed into the gloomy hall; nor did she reach for him as she led the way up the narrow stairs.

She did catch his sleeve when they finally entered the part of the Academia Robin knew well. It wasn't morning yet, but it would be in maybe an hour. He was almost grateful for Killian's interference; he could actually get some sleep without having to answer to either teachers or the chancellor for his terrible attendance.

He'd definitely missed breakfast.

He wasn't certain whether he'd slept past lunch. Raven, however, was in the room. She was seated at Robin's desk, and her bed, perfectly made, implied that she hadn't bothered to sleep.

The feather—the quill—was in her hand. She had paper—from Robin's desk, although he didn't have a lot of it—and ink. But the inkwell was capped, and the paper was blank. She turned the minute Robin sat up and rubbed sleep out of his eyes, her expression expectant.

"I told Killian," she said.

He was a little too sleep-fogged to immediately guess what she'd told Killian.

"About the hiding place, I mean."

Ah. Robin cleared his throat. He was not as clean as bathing would usually imply; his clothes—he'd managed to peel himself out of them before he hit the bed—were dust-covered and lay in a pile beside his bed. He had other clothing, and rose to find it, not that Raven noticed or cared; she was mostly impatient. There were clearly important things to do right now, and getting dressed wasn't one of them.

He dressed, then walked over to the desk, lifting his voice. "Killian, have we missed lunch?"

"Not yet," the Avatar replied. To Robin's surprise, he appeared in the room. Raven frowned, but ignored him. She had clearly decided that if he didn't like her, he wouldn't hurt her, and besides, her posture implied, she had *important things to do*.

"Can we get an extra chair if we can't get an extra desk?"

Killian's eyes were still unfamiliar, but the Avatar nodded. A chair appeared beside Raven. "I came to inform you that there's been another incident."

Raven immediately turned toward Killian, quill in hand.

"The chancellor requests your presence. Both of you."

"Was it in the quad again?" Robin asked, the new chair forgotten.

"No."

"Where?"

"Apparently one of the students in Professor Melden's class made an attempt to artificially extend Professor Melden's office hours."

"Pardon?"

"The student—mortal—was found dead in Professor Melden's

office. Professor Melden is, predictably, upset. He is also out-raged, and stormed over to the chancellor's office to make his report.

"The body has not been touched or moved. I have, however, informed the Arbiters, and I believe—if you will head to Professor Melden's office—that Arbiter Starrante will join you."

He paused, frowning. "Raven."

She glanced at him.

"What are you carrying?"

"A feather," was her prompt reply.

"A quill," was Robin's; the words overlapped.

"A quill? May I see it?"

She tightened her grip but held it out, the implication very clear: *You see with your eyes, not your hands.*

It was a familiar phrase. Where had it come from? Robin shook his head.

"Is it one of your treasures?" Killian asked.

"I saw it first," Robin said quietly. "So I don't think it's like the glass. Is it glass you're looking for?"

"It is."

Raven did not perk up. She was now aware that the finding of glass was not an unalloyed delight; there were people who were watching, none of whom could see the glass before she touched it, and some of whom could be hurt by it.

Robin was worried that the joy he had found so surprising, so delightful, would now be forever shadowed. He didn't want her to go. Was surprised at the thought, it was so strong.

"There is a chance," Killian said, "that the glass itself is in-volved in the unexplained deaths. It is highly unlikely that something otherwise undetectable that is found near the bod-ies is entirely irrelevant." He glanced at Raven.

"No desk," she pointed out.

"No searching," he replied.

"I found a hiding place. I told you about it." She started to fold her arms, realized she was still carrying the feather, and shifted position in order to extract her pouch. She slid the feather into it; Robin was surprised it fit.

"Almost anything," Killian said, "will fit in that pouch."

"It's not that big."

Raven said, "Does it have to be big?"

"Yes?" But he stopped. Raven had emptied the contents of her bag across Robin's desk. If he thought about it carefully, there had been a lot of pieces. And they'd all fit in that bag, somehow.

"Exactly," Killian said. He opened the door. "This way, please."

The personal offices of the various teachers—professors, scholars, masters—were not in the main building in which all of the classes and the dorms were located. To reach the offices, one had to leave the largest of the campus buildings and cross the quad. Two murders—or two deaths—had occurred in the quad, but this hadn't thinned the crowds; this was where students often went when they had time between classes.

Robin glanced at Raven; she'd taken his hand, as she sometimes did in crowds if she meant to stay with him. Killian chose to maintain his physical Avatar as they crossed the small park and headed to the administrative building. Robin had no idea why it was called that, and hoped Raven wouldn't ask.

The woman who manned the large desk looked harried and exhausted. Killian's presence stemmed any questions she might have asked. She knew why he was here, and if he was with two students, the two students were allowed to pass the desk, which was probably why Killian accompanied them "in person."

Robin wasn't surprised to see the chancellor outside of Professor Melden's door, but tried not to flinch when he caught sight of the owner of the office.

To reach that office, Robin expected they would have to

navigate through a press of students, but there had been very few students in the halls, and those that were there had headed to class—albeit moving much more slowly than the norm.

The chancellor's expression was grim, his eyes almost red; he'd raised his inner eye membranes, which muted their color, but not enough. Melden was talking as if silence were a crime. It didn't improve the chancellor's mood.

"Robin. Raven." The chancellor exhaled a small puff of actual smoke. "Good. Professor Melden?"

"You can't possibly expect that I am to be excluded from investigation of my own office?" Melden said; his cheeks were flushed, his raised brows bracketing an expression of pure outrage. He did glare at Robin, but that wasn't uncommon. "And who is she?"

Robin couldn't cut Melden off because Melden wasn't a student, but he would have made the effort—quickly—if he had been.

"A person whose expertise I consider relevant," the chancellor said, each syllable spoken with more emphasis than conversation generally demanded. "Killianas, Professor Melden has had a taxing morning and appears to be in need of a drink and some quiet contemplation."

Killian's expression was far more neutral than the chancellor's.

"I do not need quiet contemplation time—I need answers!"

"Very well," the chancellor said, his voice a low rumble. He turned to Melden; Robin lost sight of the color of his eyes. Raven froze in place, her hand tightening around Robin's.

"It's okay," he told her. "He's not angry at us. We don't need to hide."

She was trembling.

Robin thought there was a high chance she'd turn and try to drag him off; he tightened his hand, as well. All of the words he might have said in an attempt to calm her were lost to the very

Draconic roar that filled the hall and shook the floor beneath their feet.

"Professor Melden," Killian said, his normal, measured tone audible above the chancellor's roar, "I believe the chancellor now requires quiet. I am certain he understands your discomfort, but it will be best for all of us if you accept the offer of a drink and some solitude."

Melden didn't get a chance to reply, which was probably for the best—for Melden. The chancellor respected Melden in his area of expertise, but his tolerance had limits, limits that were apparently invisible to the professor. Killian's escort was immediate. Both the Avatar and the professor disappeared. Robin wondered if Melden had been deposited in the chancellor's office, or perhaps in the common room to which the teachers could retreat when between classes.

The chancellor exhaled. "My apologies," he said. "It has been a very trying morning, and Professor Melden is understandably upset." He opened the office door and entered the room.

The offices granted the professors were much larger than the dorm rooms for students. The door opened into a small sitting area composed of two smaller tables and six chairs. Shelves adorned the walls to the left and right. There was no body on the floor— or in the chairs—of the room.

Beyond the sitting room would be the office proper, the place where Melden in theory did nonclassroom work. The door to that office was ajar, but not fully opened. It didn't matter; from this vantage Robin could see prone legs.

Killian had said the student wasn't Barrani. Robin felt like a terrible person for wishing that it had been. Melden taught two classes. Robin was lucky enough to attend only one of them. Had it been up to him, he'd've avoided the one he was stuck with. Melden's constant harping about the essential responsibility of being a human surrounded by Barrani was annoying.

You think they're your friends? You think they accept you? You think they don't sneer at you behind your back? You're mortal. *You're inferior in their minds. You will never be accepted as one of them.*

But he didn't have to be.

Melden was suspicious of Serralyn and Valliant; he assumed they treated Robin like a servant, like a lesser being—whatever that meant. Robin was certain Melden would dislike Raven. Raven wouldn't dislike Melden; she'd accept him as he was. But she wouldn't understand why he should be relevant to her life. His judgment was therefore his problem, not hers.

Melden was knowledgeable—if he weren't, he wouldn't be here. His specialty, however, was historical uses of magic and their effects. He was not a practical mage. He didn't have the talent for it. Most people didn't. Ah, no. Most humans didn't.

"Robin?" The chancellor's tone made clear it wasn't the first time he'd spoken the name in a bid to get Robin's attention.

Oh. It wasn't so much Robin's attention he wanted, as Raven's presence, and Raven was still attached to him by hand. She'd made no move toward either the office or the body it obviously contained, content to wait for Robin to emerge from his cloud of thoughts.

Robin entered the office first.

The body was closer to Melden's desk than the door, which was good; it meant the door could be fully opened without hitting a corpse. Robin, who had been silently praying that the dead student had been in Melden's other class, closed his eyes. It was Henri Alderson.

Robin wasn't fond of Henri, and Henri had despised Robin the moment he discovered that Robin was an orphan from the warrens. In that, Henri and Melden were similar, although Melden was better at disguising his disgust. But not a lot better, in the end.

Henri shouldn't have been in this office. Robin wondered

what had led him here, what he'd been searching for, and last, what had killed him. "Is it like the two Barrani?" he asked the chancellor.

The chancellor understood the question and nodded. "There is no obvious cause of death. The location is suspect—it is not a location Mr. Alderson should have been in after hours. But it begs the question: How was he able to enter the room at all?" The secondary, unasked, question was: Why had Killian not prevented it? Why had he not noticed?

Why had Raven come running into the baths to drag Robin—at speed—to the hiding place she'd had so much difficulty finding? How were these events related? Robin had no doubt—at all—that they were.

The warrens had taught Robin a lot about death, but very little about respect for a dead body; the respect he had was instinctive, not learned. And Raven had none. He felt her hand tighten, felt her start to tremble, and knew.

He wanted to hold on to her hand, to stop her from rushing forward. He knew this was why the chancellor wanted her there—but he also knew, now, that her fanatic desire to collect had drawn the wrong kind of attention. Possibly even from Robin himself. Raven had never been normal. She'd just been herself. He'd assumed that she was, like Robin, human and poor and powerless; she had knowledge of the warrens he lacked, and an uncanny instinct for danger—but he'd never assumed she wasn't human.

Didn't want to assume it. Didn't want to lose the connection that had bound two orphan children in a hostile environment.

But he let her go now, because she was Raven. No matter what else he discovered about her, she was still Raven.

She lost track of Robin immediately, as he knew she would; she forgot the chancellor, standing to one side of the body, hands behind his back. Killian was omnipresent, even if his physical Avatar wasn't in attendance.

"I still can't see it," said a disembodied voice to his right. Clearly, Terrano was also present.

Robin turned in the direction of the voice.

"What? He didn't tell me to get lost."

"Maybe he didn't see you."

"Killian knew I was here. One of us had to be here, and I don't have classes." Terrano still didn't deign to become visible. "Serralyn says she'll lend you her notes, since you're taking the day off. Now hush. I'm trying to concentrate."

Raven approached the body without apparently noticing that it was one. But this time she didn't lift any of the limbs. She frowned. She didn't ask if she could touch anything. "No glass," she whispered, the jitter in her voice not one of disappointment but excitement.

"Raven," Terrano said, voice much louder than it had been when he was speaking with Robin.

She wouldn't hear him. She would hear no one until she'd finished.

Robin held his breath when she grabbed the dead face of Henri Alderson and pried the slack jaw farther open. When Robin had seen corpses in the streets of the warrens, he hadn't stopped to examine them. He flinched.

Terrano stepped forward, becoming visible as he reached for Raven's wrist.

"Terrano," the chancellor rumbled.

"I can't see what she sees," Terrano snapped back. "But there's something there. I don't think she should touch it."

It was far too late for that. Raven reached out, her fingers skirting the edge of a dead student's lips. She retrieved a scrap that caught and reflected light, as if its black surface was covered with a thin sheen of glass. She held it up, wide-eyed, toward the light source that hadn't existed before the chancellor had gestured.

Grasped between her fingers was a piece of metal that hadn't existed before she'd touched it.

But Terrano's response, Terrano's warning, implied that it had. Only Raven had seen it clearly. But Terrano had seen something. Robin could guess how he'd done so, and he avoided looking at Terrano's face because he really found the transformed eyes disturbing. He doubted he'd ever get used to them.

Raven looked up at Terrano, who was far closer to her than Robin or the chancellor. If she even noticed the change in the shape and size of his eyes, she didn't care. To her they weren't injuries, and they weren't wrong; they were just what they were.

"Terrano," the chancellor said. "Does Raven seem harmed to you?"

"No. She's not normal, is she?"

Robin coughed. Loudly.

"I never said *I* was."

"We can discuss 'normal' at a later time. Preferably in a few centuries that are otherwise busy and productive and absent the type of chaos one would expect if you were a student. Which, I remind you, you are not.

"However, as you have encroached—"

"You let me!"

"—I wish to know what you felt you discerned. Why did you attempt to stop Raven from picking up her...scrap of metal?"

"It's not metal," Terrano snapped, annoyed. "As you know. I have half a mind not to answer that question."

"And I have half a mind to have Killian continuously eject you. I am not under the illusion that you will remain off campus without the application of more severe solutions, but it might amuse me. I can assure you that there is very, very little that amuses me currently." Although his words were sharp, his eyes had drifted toward the more golden end of orange.

Maybe the chancellor actually liked Terrano.

Robin said, "You might as well tell us what you saw."

Terrano nodded. "It was like a little vacuum. Just—something that seemed to distort the edges of the reality around it, as if drawing them in."

Robin had not seen that. "In the mouth?"

"Yeah. It wasn't large."

"Was it as large as Raven's new treasure?"

"I think it was larger. Not a lot larger; it seemed to fill the mouth. What Raven's holding wouldn't. But it was off, and I couldn't see it that way when I looked in most of the ways I know how." Before Robin could ask, he held up a hand. "I'm never invisible to Raven, as far as I can tell. I'm usually invisible to most of you. Killian can always tell I'm here—but he doesn't have to use his eyes.

"Eyes like yours and like the chancellor's are...made for this plane. They're made for the world in which we were born and in which you exist. I was born here, but when I was a child I was exposed to influences that weren't. I couldn't incorporate them cleanly into my existence at the time; I couldn't remain on the outside, looking in. The chancellor could. Someone like Master Larrantin could. I was—we were—too young.

"To make matters worse, we were imprisoned in a sentient building for almost a millennia. Sentient buildings like Killian don't exist in only one space. Their functions demand that they touch many planes of existence; they can exist in cold that would instantly kill you, in heat that would instantly melt you, and in poison that would make you wish you could die of either cold or heat. To name a few."

"Can you?" It was Raven who'd asked. Although her eyes were practically welded to the piece of metal she held, she'd been listening.

"Not the way Killian can—but close enough. There are some places I can't go and still be myself."

"How can you not be yourself?" This time, Raven looked at Terrano, head tilted.

Terrano rolled his eyes, but answered. "I guess it would depend on how you define the word. I'm Barrani. I was born Barrani. But Barrani at birth can't do what I can do. There are places I can sense, but I can't go there—not as I am now. I could if I changed. I could if I tried to be like, say, Starrante. Maybe. But they aren't places where speech works the way it works here. They're not places where sentience, for want of a better word, as we know it exists.

"They might be places full of death and only death for those of us who are actually alive. I don't know. But I do know that the changes I would have to make to survive would change something fundamental."

"Is physical fundamental?"

"What?"

"Is being physical fundamental?" She frowned. "You change. You change your shape. You change your size. You change your weight, your solidity, your eyes, your mouth—things I can easily see. You probably change things I can't. But you always look like Terrano to me. If you had to change more things, would you be not Terrano?"

His eyes returned to their normal shape and appearance; the tilt of his head almost matched Raven's. "That's…a good question. Can you see my name?"

"Yes?"

12

Both Robin and the chancellor froze.

Terrano didn't. He didn't look alarmed, either. Most Barrani would have looked terrified or murderous. Even Robin knew that names were the heart of the Barrani that carried them. If someone knew the name, if someone could speak it with will and intent, they could take control of the person to whom it belonged. Barrani didn't share their names. If a Barrani who wasn't Terrano heard Raven, if they believed that she meant that name, the *true name*, Raven wouldn't be safe here. She might not be safe anywhere.

"Can you read it?"

She blinked. "Read it?" And shook her head. "I'm not good at reading. Robin taught me. But he hasn't taught me that."

"Robin," Robin said firmly, "can't see his name. Even if I could, I couldn't pronounce it. And, Raven—never, *ever* say this where anyone else can hear you." He glared at Terrano. "It's not safe."

"What she sees might not be dangerous," Terrano said. "She can see me when I'm stretched; she can see me when I'm walking on the edge of one side of this world, just far enough away not to be visible to most people. Neither of those would give her any control over me. It's interesting," he added, and then winced.

The chancellor's eyes were now full red.

Robin avoided asking whether or not she could see the chancellor's name.

"Can you see Robin's name?" Terrano asked instead. It was safer.

"Yes?"

Terrano and the chancellor exchanged a glance.

"Does it look like mine?"

She snorted. "Is he you?"

Robin almost laughed, she looked so irritated.

Raven stood, as if the conversation were now done and she could move on to important things. She lifted the piece of metal in her hand. "Can I keep this?"

The chancellor nodded. "Killian feels that your treasures are safest in your hands."

"I'm not stealing," she told them. She turned to Robin. "Can we go back now?"

"I'm hungry," Robin began.

"Killian will have lunch waiting for you in your room," the chancellor said. "Raven, if you could be patient, we have not quite finished here."

She sighed, retreating to the nearest chair before she pulled out her pouch of treasures and added the piece of metal to it. She then frowned, retrieved the quill, and examined it carefully as if it were the only relevant thing in Melden's office. "There are papers on the floor here," she said, not looking away from the quill. "Maybe you should pick them up."

Terrano laughed.

Robin ended up picking up the papers Raven had noticed; he frowned as he started to shuffle them into a stack. "Were these on the floor when you arrived?"

"They were," the chancellor replied. "It is possible Professor Melden dropped them when he entered his office and found the body of one of his students on the floor. Are they of relevance?"

"Well…they seem to be the test. I mean, the test we're supposed to have in two days. With answers. Maybe Professor Melden was carrying it with him from somewhere else when he entered his own office. It would make sense if he dropped them when he saw the body, but…" Robin shrugged. He then got down on hands and knees and looked under the desk.

Papers were scattered under the desk, as well. More papers, all of a similar kind. Robin cursed under his breath. This test was *way* too long to be finished within normal exam hours. But that was Melden all over: fail most of them to give himself an excuse to look down on them. Not that he appeared to need much in the way of excuses.

"If you are concerned that they are magically augmented in some way, you may relax," the chancellor said.

That wasn't Robin's concern; it hadn't occurred to him that they would be. Melden would have had to ask one of the professors who *could* use magic to alter them, and there was no way he'd do that.

"These *are* the test. Can you check to see if he was carrying these papers to his office when he discovered the body?"

"Yes." The chancellor turned to Killian, whose Avatar was once again in the room. "Please convey my personal request for information to Professor Melden. His presence is, however, unnecessary."

Even Killian grimaced, but he nodded. Silence ensued until he spoke again.

"The professor was not carrying anything; all of his necessary work is contained *in* his office, in his opinion—an office which is currently inaccessible. The test was therefore in the office for the duration."

Meaning Alderson—or someone else—had been carrying it.

"There's no way Melden just handed the test to Alderson. He wants us to do better than the Barrani students, but not this way. This would be cheating."

The chancellor held out a hand, and Robin deposited the stack onto it. "It does indeed seem to be test material."

Robin flinched. "I didn't read more than I needed to to put them in the correct order." Melden would be *enraged* if he knew Robin had handled anything at all. Even a brief glimpse would have been inexcusable.

"Witnessed," the chancellor said, a momentary wry grin adorning his lips. It vanished pretty quickly.

"Alderson may have been carrying these papers when he died. Before he died."

"Go on."

"There's not much that would cause him to break into the office itself. I mean—most of us would assume it's impossible."

"As it should be, yes."

"He may have intended to enter the office, read the test, and then put it back wherever it was he found it. If Melden noticed the test missing, the entire student body would hear him raging. And the test would—obviously—have to be changed."

"The offices are warded," the chancellor replied. "And unless Mr. Alderson dragged Professor Melden here and forced him to open his own office, there is no way he could enter it."

"That's what I was thinking, as well." Robin frowned. "But he clearly did gain entry: his body is here."

Killian had been utterly silent since his brief interaction with Melden.

Robin continued to pick up fallen objects: two quills, one inkwell—capped—and one narrow strip of torn cloth. Being on hands and knees, he was closer to the corpse; he held up the strip of cloth, trying to color match it with Henri's clothing. Whatever it was, Henri hadn't been wearing it.

He then turned away. Henri's was not the first dead body he'd encountered, and it wasn't the first time a body had belonged to someone with whom he'd been familiar when they were alive.

No—that had happened long ago, when the concept of death had yet to fully dig its roots in and blossom in the terrible understanding of loss and fear. He pushed himself up, hit the underside of the desk, and cursed liberally before crawling out from beneath it.

"The wards are your construction, aren't they?" Terrano asked Killian.

"Yes, as you well know, the wards on the doors—which are considered standard outside the Academia—are my construction. All of the professors who choose to do so have similar door wards. One or two have chosen old-fashioned locks, as they call them; most choose wards as they are familiar with that paradigm.

"There is no way that Henri Alderson could have entered this office without bypassing the wards."

"Which should be impossible."

"Indeed."

"I could do it."

"Yes, but you wouldn't require the door to be open. I highly doubt Henri could simply partially disperse and walk through a closed door."

"Yeah, me, either. He was a bit of a drip."

Killian blinked. Which would have been funny, but Raven did the same. "Drip?" she asked.

"I picked it up from a friend. It means kind of whiny. Like a wet blanket."

She turned to Robin.

"That's what it means when he uses it," he told her, hoping she wouldn't ask for longer explanations. He turned back to the chancellor, whose eyes were red. "Henri couldn't have expected that he could open this door on his own."

"You believe someone else accompanied him."

"It's what would make sense. Either that or someone told him that at a specific time, the door's ward would not be active—if he came at that time, he could just open the door and walk in. I mean, I guess someone like Terrano could have walked through the door and opened it from the inside."

Terrano rolled his eyes. "For Alderson?"

The chancellor turned to Killian.

The Avatar shook his head. "I have no accurate internal record of Henri Alderson's movements. I have internal records of his activities on previous occasions, but...there is a...hole in my records, one which I would not have noticed were it not for this investigation.

"While it is technically possible Terrano could have done what Robin has suggested, I find it highly unlikely. Terrano can seldom be moved to act in his own best interests; I cannot imagine he would be easily moved to break rules in anyone else's—his friends being the exception."

"Thanks," Terrano replied, in a tone that implied the opposite of gratitude.

The chancellor clearly didn't believe Terrano had had any hand in the office incursion. Or the death. "When did you lose track of Mr. Alderson?"

Killian's eyes were once again black tinted with chaos. "Perhaps nine in the evening."

It was Robin who said, "Do you have any internal memory of what occurred on campus between nine in the evening and maybe four or five hours later?"

"Yes," Killian replied. The *yes* was almost sibilant. It was the first time hearing Killian's voice made Robin feel apprehensive. As if aware of Robin's sudden discomfort, he paused. His eyes slowly resumed their normal appearance, but it was another few minutes before he attempted to speak again.

"I know where you were," he said when he had control of his voice. "I know where Professor Melden was. I know where

Serralyn was. Where Valliant was. I can trace all of the presences of the Barrani; the first two deaths were among the Barrani students.

"But I cannot place Henri Alderson. And, Chancellor, Robin was in the baths. If I do not fully and carefully examine my memories, Robin went to the baths, bathed, and returned—as expected—to his room."

"Raven?"

"I cannot track Raven at all, except in the way any of you could. I know where she is at the moment because I am with her. I know when she is with Robin because he is aware of her. But my memories, such as they are, are...blurry. They are probabilities based on my knowledge of the patterns of the daily lives of the students."

"Did Mr. Alderson meet with anyone, or have a conversation about this test?"

"Several. He was highly concerned about his ability to pass the test, and even more concerned with his fate as a student of the Academia if he failed it. His position here was granted—as almost all are—but he was recommended by Professor Melden; perhaps he felt his tenure was reliant on the professor. His thoughts and the discussions that arose from them are clear.

"But he spoke with several people—those in his class. He did speak with Robin about the test."

Robin nodded.

"When you say that Robin bathed and returned to his room, you consider that memory suspect or inaccurate?"

"It is entirely inaccurate," was Killian's quiet reply. "Robin did not finish bathing. Raven came to fetch him, and she dragged him out of that room."

"Pardon?"

"Last night. Last night where there is a ripple effect in my records, Raven found Robin, interrupted his bath, and fled with him."

"This would be at the time you lost track of Henri Alderson?"

Killian nodded. "I would not have noticed the break had it not been for Raven's unusual reaction."

"She knew there was a danger."

"It would appear so."

All eyes turned to Raven, who was playing with the quill. She didn't look up when the chancellor cleared his throat. Robin immediately moved to her side and tapped her shoulder; she looked up then.

"I think he wants you to tell him why you knew there was danger," Robin said, voice low.

She blinked several times. Robin didn't cringe, but it took effort. It wasn't a question Raven could easily answer; she was more likely to come up with an explanation for why she drew breath or ate food. But he also knew it was important for very obvious reasons—the body on the floor, for one.

Raven looked at Robin beseechingly.

It was the look she gave him when they were forced, by either an errand turned job or the need to haggle for necessary supplies, to interact with other people.

He'd been honestly surprised when he saw Giselle with Raven, because that meant Raven had somehow gone to speak with the woman called the grey crow. By herself. Without Robin to run interference or to interpret. She'd nonetheless managed to communicate clearly enough that Giselle could bring her to the Academia.

"Raven isn't used to talking to other people," he said, his tone apologetic. "She finds it hard to explain things."

"Raven is sensitive to danger?"

Robin considered this, but not for long. "Yes."

"And you are certain of this because some of those dangers occurred in your life prior to the Academia."

He nodded. "Raven would sometimes come to find me; she'd

take me to a hiding place she'd found, and we'd stay there until she thought it was safe not to hide."

"Those dangers were not obvious to you?"

"Sometimes they were absolutely obvious. Sometimes they weren't. Raven has uncanny instincts. I wanted to survive. I never argued with her when she wanted me to hide."

"Did you ever ask her how she knew?"

Robin hesitated. "Once or twice."

"Her answer?"

"She didn't really understand the question. She doesn't like to talk much—she never has."

"We could use a few students who do not overvalue constant verbiage," the chancellor said. "Very well. I will continue investigations from here. I expect that classes—yours—will be highly disrupted for the day, but it is better, in my opinion, that the schedule is kept; I do not wish the students to be able to self-isolate at this time." He frowned.

"Perhaps we are not yet done here, but you and Raven are. You may now return to your rooms."

Robin turned toward the door that led to the waiting room, and from there to escape. Standing between the two doors, one open, one closed, was Arbiter Starrante.

Raven looked up instantly; her expression brightened. She immediately lifted both arms—although she was seated—and brought them trailing down in surprisingly graceful movements.

Starrante had already begun a similar greeting, but his was arrested as his eyes rose from his body, weaving in what Robin now identified as shock, *surprise* being too weak a word.

He spoke, but he didn't speak the Barrani that was customary for the librarians.

Raven replied in Elantran. "It's a feather," she said. "It's mine." Then, with a trace of self-consciousness, she added, "Robin found it."

He really, really wished she hadn't said that. "I didn't find it the way Raven finds things," he quickly added, turning to the chancellor. "Killian told you that Raven found me and dragged me off to a hiding place last night, right?"

"Continue."

"We found one, but it took longer than it normally takes."

"I told you, this place is no good!" Raven was defensive now.

Robin continued. "It was a storeroom in a basement level. Or it looked like a storeroom—there was nothing there but crates and boxes. One of them was a small chest—the type you might put on a desk. We were stuck in hiding for hours, so I opened the chest."

"It wasn't locked, then."

Raven said, "Yes, it was locked."

Terrano, curse him, snickered; Robin flushed.

"And you happened to find the key?"

Raven, distracted, shook her head. "No, he picked the lock."

Robin knew he'd wanted Raven to become a student of the Academia, but almost forgot why. "I did pick the lock." He tried not to sound defensive as he added, "We were there for hours, and we had nothing else to do. The box was covered in dust—all of the crates were."

"Killianas?"

"I am investigating, Chancellor. Raven let me know of both the location and the room's contents when they returned to their room."

"I see. Was this a room of which you were not aware?"

Killian said nothing.

The chancellor didn't have oversight of the librarians. The three Arbiters were a fief onto themselves. The chancellor controlled access to the library, but even that was controlled at the librarians' request. He nonetheless turned to Arbiter Starrante. "Why is the quill of interest to you?" His tone was low and a little on the loud side, and his eyes were a darker red.

Robin was grateful that Barrani was the tongue in which the Arbiters usually conversed, because Starrante's Draconic reply was almost deafening. Both Robin and Terrano immediately brought hands to ears. Raven didn't. Her glance bounced, with apparent lack of concern, between the Wevaran speaking Draconic, and the chancellor.

Who opened his mouth to reply in kind. This close, Robin could swear his teeth were rattling. He wanted to know the answer, but it was clear Arbiter Starrante thought the information should be—for at least now—restricted.

Robin therefore grabbed Raven by the hand and dragged her out of the office. She was clearly interested in whatever it was Starrante had to say, but she also wanted to return to the room; she followed Robin's more forceful lead.

"I saw a quill," Robin told Killian as they jogged across the quad. "Anything in that chest, I saw. Raven and I saw the same thing. The quill didn't change shape or texture when she touched it; she didn't just pull it out of nothing the way she did the piece of glass or the new piece of metal. If you don't believe me—"

"I believe you," Killian replied. They were both speaking in low tones. "But the storage room that Raven found clearly exists—and it has obviously existed in relation to this building for a long time. But it is not part of me—or not part of what I understand myself and my boundaries to be." They made their way through the front doors—which Killian opened— and from there through the gallery and the doors to the lecture halls. Classes were in session, which meant they had a pretty clear run to the dorms.

Robin exhaled in relief when his own door was at his back. He even leaned against it. Raven had run into the room and looked around in obvious disappointment. There was only one desk.

Robin wanted to know what she'd asked of Killian. Instead, he retrieved the chest he'd taken from the storage room. "I kept it," he confessed.

"If it was a room of which I was unaware, and the dust had not been disturbed, I would say the supplies contained therein are never going to be claimed. Were there other personal effects?"

"You said you were investigating." It was Raven who answered, arms folded; she looked distinctly unhappy.

"I am, Raven. And I hope to have your desk ready within the week. I told you it would take time." He gestured to a new table in the room's center, between the two beds. It was a small dining table; two chairs had been tucked beneath it, but they weren't important. The food was, and as promised it was plated and waiting to be eaten.

Robin was hungry. Raven, sadly, was not.

She stomped across the room, reached the corner nearest her bed, and sat on the floor. But she frowned before she could draw knees to chest as she so often did. "Robin, what is that?"

He glanced around the room, but there was nothing unusual in it.

Clearly she'd had a very frustrating day. She rose, stomped back to where he was standing, and caught his hand, dragging it up for her inspection. He'd forgotten that he'd picked up a piece of cloth under Melden's desk.

"A scrap of cloth," he told her. "I picked it up because I wanted to see if it was something that could have been torn from Alderson's clothing. It wasn't. It doesn't match what he was wearing."

She frowned, the ferocious look of focused concentration meaning he could say anything, at any volume, and she would fail to hear it. She thrust a hand out; Robin placed the strip of cloth into it. He then pulled out a chair. Since Raven was no longer interacting with him, he could eat; she probably wouldn't notice. If she had questions, she'd ask; she wouldn't

care about table manners. Table manners had been entirely absent in most of their friendship because there had been no tables. Not like this one.

Not even like the dining hall with its long benches and the
milling students attempting to stake out a space nearest the
more obvious luminaries in the classroom. Knives and forks
had been an unnecessary luxury; sometimes food had been
whatever wasn't so rotten it would poison you, and hands and
mouths were enough.

It was the food that Robin loved here—the lack of scarcity,
the abundance that meant if he ate quickly enough he could
have *more*. But the knives and forks and cups had felt oddly
natural, given his childhood in the warrens. They came hand
in hand with abundance.

So, too, the room in which this new table had been placed:
walls that hadn't half fallen over, a ceiling with no gaps. Warmth
when it was cold. Cold had been the second thing he'd quickly
learned to fear.

"Can I keep this?" Raven asked.

"Is it a treasure?"

"Maybe? It's not like the glass or the metal, but it's shiny."

The shininess of which she spoke seemed to Robin to be the
cloth's natural sheen; it wasn't like the metallic pins and pieces.
But it was a scrap of cloth.

Killian cleared his throat, reminding them both that he was
still in the room. "I do not believe the chancellor would agree
to your keeping it."

Raven turned to Killian; she was annoyed. "Why not? It's
Robin's."

"I believe Robin retrieved it from under Professor Melden's
desk," he replied. "While it is possible that the scrap was somehow lost there before Henri Alderson was killed, it is unlikely.
I keep the offices clean."

"The professors don't?"

"If I left cleaning to the professors, half of them would have rooms that could cause possible student injuries. I must also express reservations about the quill."

"It's mine."

"It was found, yes, but it was found by Robin."

"He said I could keep it."

"I am aware of that. But there is something unusual about it. There are obvious preservation enchantments on it; there are similar enchantments surrounding the box. I am willing to allow the quill; it is not, to my knowledge, part of the investigation. But the cloth, I request that you return to Robin."

"He doesn't want it!"

Robin had mostly finished eating. He silently explained to Killian—or to anyone like Killian who could somehow read his thoughts—that the one thing that you absolutely could not do with Raven, *ever*, was attempt to part her from the very few things she considered hers. You could touch her stuff if and only if she offered you the chance, but you couldn't *keep* or *take* any of it.

"Ah, but it was not yours to give away," Killian pointed out. "And I believe the chancellor might find it relevant. No, I do not know how." He turned to Raven and held out a hand. She wasn't happy. But she had yet to deposit the strip of cloth she'd been examining into her pouch.

"People have died," Killian told her. "We do not know why or how. It is possible that some of the how can be discovered should we take into account papers, the test, the cloth. If we know how, we will be closer to preventing other deaths." His hand did not move.

Raven turned to Robin, almost beseeching; he recognized the look, and felt a deep pang of guilt. "He's right," he said, which were not the words she wanted to hear. "I can't explain things in any way that will change his opinion; it's not like haggling or asking for directions.

"If we can find the killer, the students—including us—will be safe. If we can't, Killian will be damaged. I didn't think it would be important—it's just a scrap of cloth. But if Killian thinks it might be, we have to let him have it." He then turned to Killian. "If, on the other hand, we find the how and why of the deaths, and the cloth is still present and no longer important in the investigation, could you give your word that it will be returned to Raven?"

Killian considered the question—as he had always considered Robin's questions—with care. "Yes," he finally said. "Yes. I can give my word to Raven that in that circumstance, it will be returned to her." He then turned to Raven. "Will that do?"

Her expression made clear that she knew it was the best she could hope for, but her nod was hesitant, disappointed.

"Raven, lunch?"

"Not hungry," she said, folding her arms. She once again retreated to the corner. From the corner, however, she said, "Can we have the windows back?"

"If you promise you will not attempt to remove the glass again, yes. The glass is not found; it is not lost. It is part of the room, and the room is part of me."

Robin cringed and turned toward the corner. "Think of the parts of the building—all of them—as if they're Killian's fingers or toes. You can't keep those without injuring him."

"But there was glass here—broken glass, found glass—and that wasn't part of him?" Her forehead was pressed to her knees, her voice therefore muffled.

Robin considered the question in much the same fashion as Killian had considered his. "No," he finally said, frowning. "I don't think they were part of Killian. That's probably why he couldn't easily touch them. Raven, were the windows made of the same type of glass?"

She lifted her head, her brows furrowing in exactly the way they did when she thought he'd asked a particularly stupid question. "Yes."

13

Raven couldn't be coaxed to the lunch table, so she didn't eat. But she did push herself off the floor when Robin was done. Killian left the table in the room, but cleared it. He waited until Raven was on her feet, then said, "Your duty was interrupted by the discovery of the third body. It is, however, of import.

"Robin?"

"I don't quite understand what you want Raven to look for," Robin confessed. "Hiding places?"

"Indeed. There should be no hiding places within the Academia campus. There should be no areas of which I am unaware. Clearly there are. I would also like you to take the cloth scrap with you to the chancellor's office." He glanced at the chest on Robin's desk. "I will leave the contents of the chest with you, but I am concerned about the diary."

"I haven't read it," Robin began.

"I would not criticize any attempt to do so—curiosity is natural and in many cases it is to be encouraged. It is why the Academia exists." He hesitated. "But if that room—that hiding place—was the repository of things that have entirely evaded my notice, I am uncertain that it would be advisable. People hide things for many reasons; the diaries of which you have vague memories would have been hidden by children who desired privacy to express things that could embarrass them.

"That is not always the reason such things are hidden as people age." He paused, and then added more gently, "I am uncertain that you could even read the language."

"Have you looked at it?"

"Yes."

Robin felt hugely deflated then. But it was something abandoned in a dusty, ancient storeroom, and right now, he had more things to worry about. "Raven?"

She glared at Killian, but nodded.

There were so many things to discover in this place. Raven's initial reluctance to remain had given way to greed—but Killianas was a problem. He wanted to keep the scrap Robin had given her, and she resented it. She resented his vanishing of the windows. She didn't resent his food—she hadn't been hungry, but Robin was. Robin had always needed more food. More warmth.

More hiding.

She worried about Robin. She almost never worried about people. Robin had been wrong about this place. Wrong about Killian. It wasn't safe here. In the warrens, it was safe. It wasn't safe for everyone, but it was safer for Robin.

No, she thought. Maybe that wasn't true. Robin looked as if he felt safe here. The warrens were safer for *her*. Killianas didn't think there should be any hiding places here *at all*.

She'd missed Robin. She'd missed him enough she was willing to talk to the grey crow. She was willing to think about the grey crow's name, about the grey crow's knowledge, so different from her own. Why? Why had she missed him? She couldn't remember.

She stared at the hand he offered, so different from her own. Looked up from hand to Robin, to Robin's face. It was familiar and it was different than she remembered. Cleaner, maybe. Less gaunt. She had kept Robin safe in the warrens. She *had*. But Robin was happier here. Here, where it wasn't any safer.

Why was he like this?

Why had she missed him?

"I'm sorry about the cloth," he said, his voice the Robin-quiet voice she had learned to like. It was almost like music, but it was nothing like music. It's just that it made her feel the same as some music did. She took his hand.

"Did Killian ask you to look for hiding places?"

She nodded, but added, "I think he wants to know because he wants to break them."

Robin shook his head. "He doesn't want to break them. He wants to know because he can't see them. He can't see into them." Robin exhaled, different from the usual exhalations of normal breathing. "Something is killing students. I think he's afraid that that something is *in* the hiding places—the places he can't see. The places he doesn't know how to find himself."

Raven frowned and shook her head.

"Has no one ever found your hiding places before?"

"They're *hiding places*," she said. She tried not to be frustrated, but knew she was failing.

"But in the warrens, the hiding places changed, right?"

"Yes?"

"Doesn't that mean someone else found them?"

She almost forgot to walk because she turned to stare at him. "They *change*," she said. "If other people could find them, they wouldn't be hiding places."

Robin blinked; he forgot to walk, as well. "I don't understand."

She accepted then that he had never really understood. She'd hoped that he would learn. "You came with me," she finally said.

He nodded. He smiled then. She liked his smile. Always had.

"I trusted you." Past tense. She felt something heavy grip her insides—that happened sometimes. Too heavy. Too much like chains. Or pain. Or both.

"Raven—I still trust you. I will always trust you. Didn't I jump out of the bath and run where you led? If you tell me I need to hide, if you take me to a place we'll be safe, I'm always going to follow." His hand tightened briefly, but not enough to hurt.

She felt better. She didn't understand why. This was why she'd always avoided people. And why she hadn't avoided Robin.

"I don't understand," he continued.

She waited for him to start walking, but grimaced. It was Raven who could find hiding places, not Robin. But she couldn't just…walk into them. She couldn't just sense them. Hiding places didn't *stand out* if there was no need for them, no danger that drove her to reach them.

"But even if I don't understand, I promise I'll always try. Even if I don't understand, I still trust you." He shook his head. "Words are hard."

"Not for you."

"Words with other people aren't as hard, no. But I don't really trust that many other people. Most people use words better than you do. But most people can't be trusted. I'll take the trust, thanks." He looked down the hall. "Maybe we should go to the chancellor's office first."

"Why? There's no place to hide there."

"Killian asked me to take the piece of cloth to the chancellor. If there are no hiding places you can sense right now, we might as well do that. Killian gave his word that he'd return the cloth to you if at all possible after the investigation.

"And the faster we find the killer, the faster it'll all be over, right?"

Raven brightened. She knew Robin said this because he wanted her to *want* to help. She knew. But…she did want to help because she did want her cloth back. She'd almost forgotten. "You didn't look at it properly, you know," she said, pulling him along as she began to walk. "I wanted to show you why it was interesting."

"You can still do that. We're not at the office yet."

She shook her head. "I will. When I get it back." She paused, and then said, "Do you think there'll be more glass?"

He stiffened a bit. "If you only find glass or metal near corpses, then I hope not."

"There was real glass in the windows. Those weren't beside bodies."

"Did you really try to take the glass from my windows?"

"Only once."

The chancellor was not particularly happy to see them, but did let them into his office. "Killianas said you have something for me."

Robin nodded immediately, disentangling his hand from Raven's. He then walked to the desk behind which the chancellor sat, and gently placed the yellow silk on the desktop. "It was under the desk, along with the scattered test."

"Why did you not hand it to me when we were in Professor Melden's office?"

"It's a torn scrap of cloth," Robin replied. He didn't want to answer the question. He didn't want to say: *because I thought Raven might like it.* Even thinking the words made him cringe internally. Henri Alderson was *dead*. No one knew how. Or why. The test had seemed significant to the investigation.

But if he'd stopped to think, the cloth would have seemed important, as well. He knew he was reddening.

"I am, however, grateful that you brought it to me. Killianas says it is not native to any clothing he has created within the Academia. Before you get too excited, most of the students in the Academia wear their own clothing. In only a handful of cases is the student clothing supplied by Killianas."

Robin was one of that handful.

"Killianas does, however, create all of the robes worn in the dining hall at dinner."

"Was Alderson's clothing created by Killian?"

The chancellor smiled. It was a sharp smile, lacking in warmth, but it was genuine. "Funny you should ask that. Yes. Mr. Alderson's clothing was also crafted by Killianas."

Alderson was not from a background of wealth. He wasn't, to Robin's knowledge, from the warrens—but he might have been. Maybe Alderson had hoped that education could change things. Maybe, like Robin first was, he was drawn to food and the guarantee of warmth in the winter.

The chancellor cleared his throat. It was a rumble of sound, a reminder that while the chancellor looked human, he wasn't. "I have been asked to grant you an extended leave of absence from your classes."

Robin wilted. "Extended?"

"Killianas was not aware of the storeroom you discovered. We are now excavating the dust haven to ascertain whether or not the contents were deliberately hidden. It is troubling to Killianas, and it is therefore of grave concern to his chancellor. We would not have been aware of its existence were it not for Raven.

"Killianas believes that Raven has a gift for finding places over which he has had no current oversight. For obvious reasons at this time, I consider the finding of those places essential. I have some familiarity with sentient buildings; I have very little experience with those that have been almost destroyed, as Killianas was. I do not understand how they experience injury or near death; I therefore do not fully comprehend how to heal them or repair their architecture.

"Killianas has informed me time and student activity will do both. He is reviewing what he knows, and he is investigating in his own fashion. But protection of the Academia was oft left in the hands of its chancellors. I am that chancellor. I am, perhaps, a touch vain: I do not believe any chancellor prior to me has carried so much of that vital weight in such a circumstance.

"But I believe I am the right person for that duty. I understand that some of your teachers will be less than pleased that you have been pulled from their classes—it implies the lessons are of less value. And I am aware that the burden of catching up to lost lessons will be entirely and perhaps unfairly placed upon your shoulders."

Robin said nothing. The truth was, he loved most of his classes. He loved the lessons. He loved being able to ask questions of people who could give him answers—even if he was mocked for being ignorant because he asked them. The mockery wasn't fun—but if that was the price to pay for engaging with the material, he'd pay it. Here, no one pulled knives on you as an angry greeting. They just had words.

Or so he'd thought. But three people had died. The murderers could have hidden in the storage room. They could be hiding in the places that Killian couldn't see. But their crimes had occurred in places Killian *could* see. It was as if he'd been blindfolded for just long enough for the killers to strike.

"Professor Melden was ill pleased when he received the request, but I believe he will be somewhat distracted in the immediate future." The chancellor now turned his attention to Raven. Robin's shoulders began to tense.

"Killianas has explained what occurred in his own words, and he has explained what occurred in Robin's. I would—if at all possible—like to hear about what occurred from your point of view. We know that you came to drag Robin from the baths to safety. We do not know how you sensed danger. It would be of great aid to us and to the safety of the other students if you could explain it.

"If you cannot, however, it will not reflect poorly on you or your possible tenure as a future student. The value of words is frequently understated, but the ability to navigate their use is an essential component of most communication. Those who develop an affinity for clear communication have an advantage over those who do not if interaction is necessary.

"It has not, I perceive, been a necessity for you in the life you led before you met Robin. You may not consider it a necessity now. But if we understood how you become aware of danger, how you perceive it, we might prevent further death. We might end that danger in the Academia."

To describe Raven's expression as skeptical would be generous.

"Can you end weather?" she asked.

"Some mages can, yes. Killianas could, should the need arise, but his control extends only to the periphery of his campus. Do you believe that the danger you sense is like weather?"

She considered the question. "Maybe."

"I don't think she thinks they're the same," Robin said.

"Allow her to speak for herself," the chancellor replied. His gaze had not left Raven.

"They aren't the same," Raven said promptly. "But they are. I know when it's raining, because it's wet. Water falls. I know when it's windy because wind tugs at things, and if it's *really* windy, you can get stuff in your eyes. I know when it's hot. I know when it's cold."

The chancellor nodded. "And when there is danger you know when you are in danger?"

She smiled and nodded.

"What does danger feel like to you, Raven?"

She blinked several times; from long experience Robin knew she was considering the question she'd been asked from as many angles as she could, as if it were an actual physical object she could hold in her hands.

"It's not like rain or snow. But maybe it *is* like rain. It's just there, but while it's raining, it's everywhere. Hiding places are like buildings when it's raining, not like umbrellas. If you hide, the water doesn't reach you, can't hit you, can't make you wet." She frowned.

"Robin feels cold more than I do. Robin feels heat more, too. Doesn't make sense," she added. "But sometimes in the winter even I feel the cold. And sometimes if you can't get out of the cold for a bit, you die. There's never been a cold that could kill everyone. But there's the kind of cold that could kill anyone who can't find warmth."

"And the danger is like that kind of cold?"

"It's like that. Sometimes it's just mild. It can't harm most anything. Sometimes it's like killing cold, but—not cold." She frowned again. "Or maybe it's more like rain—like the kind of rain that breaks ships in harbor. Like it would drown anyone if they're stuck, if they can't get out of the way."

"Was last night's danger like that?"

"Maybe. It was strong."

"Did you sense such dangers when you lived in the warrens?"

She considered the question again. "Not for a long, long time." She hesitated. "Not until Robin. But—it wasn't as bad as this. It was just bad."

"Good bad?"

Her smile grew as she nodded several times, a certain sign of Raven's approval. "It was easier in the warrens, though. Easier to find hiding places."

"I see. Could you perhaps offer us warning when you feel that danger?"

"Us?"

"Someone who is not Robin. Killianas would be preferable, if it were at all possible."

It was Robin who said, "Killian didn't hear us. I mean, he didn't hear me. It's almost like he wasn't there at all."

The chancellor was less tentative when talking to Robin, as if such general kindness was a wasted effort. "Almost like? Did you attempt to make contact?"

"I called his name."

"When you were with Raven?"

Robin nodded. "It was an emergency; I had to move quickly. I called his name, and when he failed to answer, we ran."

"Killianas?" the chancellor said, in a tone of voice no one would ignore.

"Chancellor," Killianas replied, appearing by the chancellor's desk.

"You heard all of that."

"There is nothing in this office I cannot hear. I am confident of that if nothing else. Yes. I did."

"You did not hear Robin?"

"No. He remembers calling my name, but I have no memory of intercepting that call."

"And you cannot hear Raven at all?"

"No."

The chancellor's frown had a subtle hint of fang in it. His eyes were orange, not the red that usually indicated he was on the edge of burning everything down. When he exhaled, it was a stream of smoke and irritation.

"I hate to do this," he said, looking at Robin. "I am *almost* of the opinion that it is reckless and unnecessary."

Robin had no idea what the chancellor was referring to.

"Shall I fetch him?" Killian asked the chancellor.

"If you feel it wise, yes. I am very torn."

"I do not feel it increases the danger."

"Not to you, no. The last person I wish to ask any sort of favor of is Terrano."

"Shall I negotiate before I ask him to join you?"

"Negotiate?"

"Raven's situation is exactly the type of occurrence Terrano finds fascinating. You may be able to offer him unfettered, un-interrupted access to the Academia for the duration of the dif-ficulty, but emphasize Raven's unusual apprehension of danger. And my inexplicable inability to hear students during that time."

"You believe he will follow Raven?"

"I think it likely, yes. If he can't, however, that gives us more information with which to work."

"Very well. Please inform the Arbiters that I will be visiting the library this afternoon."

Killian visibly winced.

"Is this a difficulty?"

"The library queue for visiting students has been somewhat stressed of late, given the interruptions. I don't imagine you wish to engage the Arbiters while the students are actually in the library?"

"Of course not."

Killian nodded. "I will speak with Terrano and the Arbiters. At what time do you wish to visit?"

"Now."

Robin had never quite realized that Killian could be cun-ning, even manipulative. He wasn't certain he hadn't been bet-ter off in ignorance.

Killian, however, found this amusing. "Why is it called ma-nipulation in one instance and inspiration in another?"

"Different goals," Robin replied, as if Killian were one of his many teachers and this was a test question.

"I see you've been paying attention in ethics class. And if you are wondering where I learned this, let me pose you a coun-ter question. When could I not? Given the many professors and students who have studied here, I could not help but pick up some of the general behavior. Especially the whining about homework and grades. I will, however, spare you the whining;

even I find it somewhat irritating if it continues too long. And believe me, it does.

"The chancellor is wary of being obligated to Terrano because of Terrano's very close ties with Sedarias An'Mellarionne. You're aware that they're close friends. You are aware that they are namebound. They call themselves the cohort; it's simpler than listing twelve names. The chancellor has some prior experience with various members of that cohort.

"What you may not know is they were trapped for centuries within the Hallione Alsanis; they were exposed far, far too early to the wild power of the green, and they were changed. It is why Serralyn says they aren't considered Barrani. The chancellor approves of Serralyn; if all Barrani students were as she is, the Academia would flourish almost immediately.

"The unusual closeness of the cohort makes it difficult to interact with them as entirely separate individuals."

"They're very different people, though," Robin said. "They argue a lot."

"I agree. The chancellor believes they are, as well, but with reservations. The name bond of the Immortal can be abused; in the worst case, knowledge of the true name can be used to force obedience."

"That hasn't happened." Robin was certain.

"It hasn't happened *yet*," Killian replied. "What Serralyn told you in the dining hall is true: they have eternity."

"You said they were together for centuries."

Killian nodded. "Enforcing obedience would shatter trust— and the cohort trust each other completely. The chancellor understands that Serralyn and Valliant want to study in the Academia to learn, not to leverage knowledge for power. But he is wary of Sedarias and her current political struggle.

"If he asks Terrano for a favor, Sedarias will be aware of what he does here, and she may attempt to leverage the chancellor's obligation to Terrano, if the Academia can be used in her struggle for stability within Mellarionne. If, however, I point out the advantages to Terrano, he will not be acting as a favor to the chancellor, but for his own amusement."

"But...that's all he ever does."

Killian smiled. "Indeed. I do not share the chancellor's concern, but the chancellor is the head of the Academia. I believe Terrano's perception of the Academia—and of me—may lead us to answers. But there is the possibility that Terrano will end up remaining in your room."

"Why not Serralyn's or Valliant's?"

"Raven is in your room."

Terrano joined them before the dinner hour. Raven intended to start her exploration not in the main building—through which they'd run the night before—but across the quad in the administrative and office building. She'd been hesitant because the idea of describing the location of hiding places so that Killian could destroy the hidden quality struck her as very, very wrong.

Robin's explanation that other things could hide in those places where Killian couldn't see them hadn't made much of a dent in her discontent. But Killian also accompanied them, in full form not simple voice, and the two, Raven and the building's Avatar, conversed as much as Robin had ever heard Raven converse.

But perhaps he'd never heard her speak with someone who intuitively understood the questions she was asking. It had taken Robin a while to get used to it; Raven could ask a question out of nowhere, often while Robin was speaking.

She did this with Killian; Killian would answer, or counter with a question of his own.

Killian didn't intimidate her, not that he tried. But Raven was willing to express almost open hostility to Killian, which was extremely unusual; Raven usually didn't interact enough to take anything personally. Could a person be comfortable with some-one and at the same time angry, annoyed, or even dismissive?

Terrano joined them midargument, falling behind to keep pace with Robin. "Have they been doing that all morning?"

Robin nodded.

"She's looking for spaces that Killian can't see, right?"

"Yes. Killian believes she can find them—she found one last night. It doesn't make sense to me, but it seems to make sense to him. It's just—I thought all of the campus was part of Killian."

Terrano nodded, his gaze on Raven.

"So how can he just forget about it? I mean, wouldn't that be like forgetting you have a hand?"

Terrano's eyes looked normal. "I admit it's not Killian that's causing confusion. It's your friend."

"Because she knows when he's lost track of part of himself?"

"Exactly. Killian has enough control that he can find the parts she indicates, he can pull them back into his awareness. You talked to the chancellor, so you know that Killian was injured. If I were Killian, I'd've just recreated the entire Academia from scratch. I think if he'd done that, there wouldn't be missing bits."

"Was there a reason he didn't?"

"Probably. I know with the Barrani High Halls the entirety of the High Halls were transformed—but the building hadn't been injured, exactly; he was forced to withdraw in order to focus and concentrate all of his power in one tiny area.

"Helen—the name of our home—*was* injured. But it was a self-inflicted injury. I'm going to have to ask her whether something like this could happen to her." He glanced at Robin. "Care to come over and visit our house?"

Robin blinked. "Would that be okay?"

"Normally, no—you've got classes. I mean, you in theory have one and a half days a week free, but those get pretty loaded up with homework. But you've been given a bit of a leave of absence so your friend can investigate the Academia. I think it might be helpful if we could introduce Raven to Helen."

"When?"

"You could have dinner with us. The chancellor doesn't like it when students leave the campus in the evening—but it's pretty safe if we exit via the fief of Tiamaris. I'd bring you back if you had to return in the evening, but you could also just stay over. I think."

"You think?"

"Well, *technically* it's not actually our house."

"But you live there?"

"We're guests. Or roommates. It's tricky because Helen is sentient, but she's kind of the landlord, and Kaylin's the tenant."

"Kaylin?" The name was familiar. "Oh—you mean the Hawk? Private Neya?" She was one of the few Hawks Robin had ever talked with, because no one approached the Hawks that patrolled the warrens. It was her investigation that had eventually allowed Killian to fully wake up. Robin liked her, and wondered why all officers of the law couldn't be more like her.

"Corporal Neya, and yes. I'm sure she'd be fine with it, but sometimes Helen gets picky and worries about permission." Permission was clearly something Terrano considered an inconvenience. At best.

"Maybe you should get permission first?"

"Fine."

"I'll need to ask Raven. I think she finds dealing with Killian and the Academia exhausting; the only reason she wants to stay is the glass. She's not likely to find a lot of glass in Helen, is she?"

"I don't know. None of us understand what the glass and metal bits actually are." He exhaled. "It's a good thing Killian is with us."

Us. Robin noted the word, but didn't argue. He agreed. With Killian at her side, there was almost nowhere Raven wouldn't be allowed to go.

★ ★ ★

Raven spent time searching the administrative building. Her expression was possibly the sourest Robin had ever seen it, and she gave Killian the side-eye frequently. But he did open doors when she requested it, and he didn't ask why. She grudgingly explained that hiding places varied in size—not her words—and Robin quietly took over the explanation when she sent him a half angry, half pleading stare.

It was much easier for Robin to explain, because Killian could hear his thoughts, hear his struggle to find the right words. Raven didn't have that advantage, if it could be considered an advantage at all.

"These places can be of any size?"

Raven snorted.

Robin said, "Yes. There were times when both of us could barely fit, and times when we had a bigger space than this office." The office was unoccupied. Raven hadn't asked to enter any of the offices in use. But there were a large number of offices that weren't occupied, and she was intent on examining most of them. She was also worried. If Killian was present, maybe anything that seemed remotely like a hiding place would disappear.

What Robin couldn't understand was how there could be hiding places here of the type Raven could find outside of the Academia. He couldn't understand how they could be the same. Maybe they weren't—but Raven certainly thought they were, and he'd always trusted Raven when it came to those spaces, because his survival had depended on it.

In the end, the offices of the professors—or former professors—withstood three hours of searching. Terrano, frequently easily bored, was almost literally drifting away, but Killian remained focused—as did an increasingly annoyed Raven.

Robin knew the moment she found the trace of what she was seeking.

14

She'd once called it a smell, and once called it a sound. By inference over the years he'd come to understand that neither of those words was exact, neither a description of why she knew. No, it was like all of those things, in thin layers, stacked on top of each other until they had enough weight she could sense and find them.

"You are astonishingly perceptive," Killian said as he watched Raven. Her posture had changed. The irritation that had girded her expression since she'd arrived in the administrative building left her; her brow furrowed and her eyes narrowed as she focused.

She reached out to grab Robin's hand. He let her, their fingers entwining so naturally he felt, in the moment, that he had always run to safety holding that hand. It wasn't true; he could intellectually pick out several instances where his life had been under threat in the recent past, and there had been no Raven to follow.

What he knew and what he felt didn't mesh. He didn't argue with emotions. He'd learned not to let them rule him, but he accepted them otherwise. As long as he had control over how to react or act when in the grip of strong emotion, they didn't hurt anyone.

Raven's hand tightened as she sped up.

This, too, was familiar. She had almost always sped up when she neared a hiding place, as if, in the final leg, something was in close pursuit. Even when the streets were empty. He'd half wondered if she found hiding places only in emergencies—and he really didn't like the direction that thought was traveling.

Killian was here. Terrano was here. How much danger could there be?

But no. No. She used to tell him when she'd found new hiding places—and she'd found them when there was no emergency, no immediate threat of death. He tried to relax into the comfort he'd remembered so clearly, but couldn't.

In the streets of the warrens, he'd had nothing left to lose. He'd had no fixed home. No family. One friend—but that friend *was* his safety.

In the time he'd spent in the Academia, even as an initially unwilling prisoner, he'd become attached to the place; to Killian, to the students, to the professors, to the librarians—especially Starrante. All of that could be lost to him. He'd known it from the moment he'd been offered the choice: leave or become a genuine student.

Until then, as an unwilling prisoner, the fear of losing this place hadn't occurred to him. He'd had no choice. No one had asked him if he wanted a place where he couldn't freeze, couldn't starve, didn't have to run from random acts of violence. Had they, he would have been suspicious; he might never have arrived in this place at all.

But he had, and things had changed, slowly at first, and then so quickly he might have blinked and missed it. Now, there was no place in the world he'd rather be. It's why he'd sought Raven, in the warrens. She could live in safety here, without hiding. She could be warm, fed, clothed. But more, she was what the Academia needed. She was what Killian needed. He had felt it in his bones, had believed it completely. Still did.

Robin couldn't lie to himself. No matter what the chancellor suspected, he knew he wasn't as worthy as Raven. He didn't have as much to offer. Raven had—as a child in the warrens—saved another child when both had no power, no money. She had always offered help, when she appeared.

He had taken it because he was desperate. But he hadn't really *thought* about what it might cost her—he'd had no time, no mental space, for anything other than anxiety and despair.

And here she was, doing something she resented at Killian's request—because no one else could do it. Robin wanted to help Killian, but he couldn't. Whatever Raven had, Robin didn't.

It had never made him feel so useless before.

"You are not useless," Killian said. "Were it not for you, we would not be here, at this place, with Raven."

"It's *Raven* who's useful," Robin said. He'd forgotten Killian was with them—Killian who could hear everything if he paused to listen. He was clearly listening now.

Raven didn't comment; Robin knew it was because she wasn't listening. Whatever Killian and Robin were blabbing about had nothing to do with what she was doing, and she'd always been good at blocking out idle chatter. But even if she'd heard it, she wouldn't judge it, wouldn't be offended by it. She never had.

Robin seldom considered what made a good friend. He would have considered it now, but Raven's hand tightened, cutting off his circulation. "Robin! Robin!"

"I'm here."

"Look!"

He did. They'd entered an office. It should have been empty, because it wasn't in use. All of the unoccupied offices had been. This one, however, looked used. It wasn't the dust; there *was* dust, but not nearly as much as there had been in the storage room. Books adorned the shelves in the waiting room; chairs, older and more worn, were bracketed around a table that had seen better days—someone had carved initials into its surface, among other things.

Had Raven been inspecting any of those things, he would have understood. She wasn't. She had opened the door to the interior office—where the professor who had once occupied this room likely did most of their work—and was staring, almost transfixed, at the wall opposite the door.

The windows in the office were far larger, and far more ornate, than the windows in the offices in use; they spread across the far wall widely enough that from the door, the wall looked entirely composed of paned glass. Not just paned; the panes were colored and patterned—the metal holding the panes in place more intricate than the Academia's normal windows.

She was transfixed; Robin realized she'd forgotten about hiding spaces or investigation at all. He could see what she saw. He was certain they all could.

"Raven—is that real glass?"

Mouth half-open, she nodded as if words or speech had deserted her.

"Killian," Terrano said, "is this glass yours?"

Killian failed to answer. The Avatar might have been a statue.

"Do you know whose office this used to be?" Terrano asked.

Again, there was no answer.

"Robin, can you go get Starrante?"

Robin shook his head. "I'm not sure he'll be able to come this far. He can travel anywhere in the main building."

"It shouldn't make a difference—it's all the Academia." Terrano stared at Robin, still attached to Raven by the hand. "Never mind. I'll take care of it."

Robin was surprised when Serralyn practically burst into the office, but he shouldn't have been. When Terrano said *I'll take care of it,* he'd probably asked Serralyn, at a distance, to fetch Starrante. Starrante was fond of the Barrani student.

"You could have given me more warning," she snapped. "I was in class, and unlike some people, I haven't been given permission to skip."

"I will remedy that," Killian said. It was the first time, since Raven had seen the window, that he'd spoken out loud. "My apologies for the short notice."

"Why are you apologizing? It's Terrano's fault, and he's not."

Terrano rolled his eyes. Robin had time to look away before the eyes became the overly large and disturbing mass of chaos.

Terrano was cheeky and friendly; Serralyn, however, was better with words that conveyed actual information. Robin therefore turned to Serralyn, although Raven was still glued to his hand. "What does he see?"

"I'm...not sure. It looks like a window to me. It looks like a window to Raven—I mean, she sees the glass. I don't know what regular glass looks like to her, but—she sees the window. You?"

"Windows—stained glass, very fancy, but...windows."

Serralyn glanced at Killian. Killian said nothing.

"Is this a hidden place?" Serralyn asked. She glanced at Raven, and when Raven failed to answer—or acknowledge the question at all—she transferred her gaze to Robin.

"I don't think so. I think there *is* one in this office—but it's less important to her than the glass. And the metal bits. A hiding place would be more important if she had a pressing sense of danger—but she doesn't."

Raven moved toward the window. "It's not yours, right?" she whispered.

"Please refrain from touching it until Arbiter Starrante has had a chance to see it as it is," Killian replied.

Serralyn nodded, and turned to Robin. "It shouldn't take too long. Starrante is coming. He attached a thread to me so he could join us immediately, which is the only reason I'm here in person."

★ ★ ★

Arbiter Starrante appeared in the waiting room, a safe distance from the door as long as you weren't a chair. He was chittering quietly, the Wevaran equivalent of muttering to himself, but that changed as he managed to make space for himself to enter the door. Killian generally enlarged doors, or made them taller, to accommodate the needs of the various students; he didn't touch this one, which meant a reshuffling of everyone standing in the office.

Raven was fine with this—she wanted to move closer to the windows.

It was Starrante who stopped that. "Do not touch the windows. Do not approach them any more closely than this. Terrano, that means you, as well."

His body was almost the width of the doorframe; he had to squeeze himself through.

Serralyn grimaced and apologized.

"You did the correct thing," the Arbiter replied. "Caution in such circumstances is better than convenience."

"Arbiter?" Killian said.

"I wish to know how long this room has been like this."

"I do not know."

"Do your records extend to the time when it was occupied? Do you recall who claimed these offices as their own?"

Killian considered the question for a time. "Neither the furniture nor the window in this office were created by me."

"Professors were allowed to bring their own possessions into the Academia?"

Killian nodded. "As are students. It is seldom that a professor might desire to bring a window of this size."

"Do you believe it was created here?"

Killian nodded.

"Not by you."

"No."

"Nor with your knowledge."

"I have no memory of this window. I have very little memory of the office. The professor who last occupied it left when the Towers rose and the Academia vanished."

"His name?"

"Cordantas. He was unusual for a Barrani. A colorful person. Do you remember him?"

Starrante's arms rippled; yes. "He came frequently to the library, especially toward the end; the entrance to the library could not be removed from the Academia at that time."

Serralyn blinked. "Could it be moved now?"

"It is just barely possible now, yes—but it is not guaranteed. You've realized that the library is its own space?"

Serralyn nodded. "And the Arbiters have control of it, in concert."

"It is more fractious than that, but yes, in essence." It was Killian who answered. "The library was not built as part of the Academia; it existed before the Academia came fully into being. But the portal that allows entry to the library was stable; it is my suspicion—never fully confirmed—that the choice of location for the Academia was contingent upon that portal.

"It is the Academia that anchored the library. It is one of the Academia's highest priority expenditures of both attention and magic. I do not know what would become of the library should the Academia perish. Only the Arbiters could answer that question—but I do not believe they would choose to do so."

"Were it relevant," the only Arbiter present said, "we would."

Terrano frowned. So did Robin. They both turned to Starrante, but it was Robin who spoke. "I believe the man who attempted to install himself as chancellor wanted access to the library; I don't think he cared about the Academia at all. He wanted it to be functional, but only so he could reach the library."

Killian frowned. "He could not be accepted as chancellor without the agreement of the Arbiters—that is how tightly woven the integration is. Were he to somehow retain complete control of me, they could simply deny him access."

Starrante said, "This is all very interesting, but I believe we have more pressing concerns."

The three turned once again to the window; Starrante had enough flexibility in eye position that he could move several of them in different directions, and split attention evenly that way. Robin wondered how he could process what his different eyes were seeing; he knew he wouldn't be able to focus on more than one thing no matter how many eyes he had. Two was hard enough, some days.

He moved those two toward the window, because the eyes facing the window were the danger color.

"Terrano," Starrante said. "Please move closer to the window—but do *not* touch it."

Terrano nodded; gone was his usual oppositional pushback. He moved slowly toward the window.

Raven screeched. Literally screeched. She grabbed Terrano by the arm and pulled him back, pulled him away from the window just before the glass began to bulge in its frame. The frame bent slowly, but the glass seemed almost like blown bubbles, expanding faster than the metal that theoretically contained it.

Killian gestured; a barrier rose on the other side of the desk directly in front of that window.

"Perhaps these windows cannot be approached at all," Starrante said, sounding almost unperturbed.

"What *are* they?" Terrano demanded. Given the shape and size of his eyes, what he saw wasn't what Robin saw. Serralyn's eyes remained normal, but she glanced at Raven, who was breathing heavily, and with great effort.

Robin crossed the room and gently disengaged Raven's hand from Terrano's arm. She caught his hand and grasped it tightly enough it was almost instantly numb. She was no longer looking at the window; her back was toward it, the luster of new, whole glass completely forgotten.

He wanted to know why.

"Raven, what is it? What's wrong?"

"You mean besides the fact that the so-called glass is trying to *escape*?" Terrano snapped.

Robin turned to the window; Raven grabbed his face in one hand and turned it away. "Don't look," she whispered. "Don't look."

"What will happen?"

"You don't want glass shards in your eyes. You just don't."

Starrante's eyes swiveled to Raven, then he spoke. Raven understood him, but shook her head fiercely.

"I won't look," Robin said, "but Killian's protecting us."

She shook her head, and then shook it again. She spoke in the odd clicking chitter of the Wevaran.

Starrante's eyes almost popped out of their sockets, but Starrante wasn't Robin; he, apparently, was allowed to look toward the window with at least some of his eyes.

Starrante's eyes bobbed frantically in Killian's direction. "Killianas! Killianas, *withdraw*!" Killian failed to move. Robin didn't quite understand what Starrante wanted the Avatar to do. The Avatar was an extension of the living building—it wasn't the building itself. Even if the Avatar vanished, Killian was always going to be part of the room.

But Killian had taken a piece of glass from Raven's hand, and it had blackened the hand of the Avatar.

"Why is it dangerous for Killian?" Robin asked Raven.

"It can hurt him. This glass can hurt him."

"It can't hurt anyone else?" Robin asked.

"Terrano won't be hit. Serralyn's not looking. It's *glass*, Robin. It's only dangerous if it hits your *eyes*."

"Starrante has eyes."

Raven nodded, obviously far less concerned about that. Robin would have asked, but he heard the particularly uncomfortable sound of Starrante spitting web. In theory the Wevarans could weave strands, but not before they'd mostly spit them out. If Robin was not to look at the window—and Raven hadn't released her death grip on his jaw—he could look at Starrante, and did.

Starrante's webs could be used in at least two different ways that Robin had observed; no doubt there were more that he hadn't seen. The first was what he did now: he created a web. It wasn't Killian's barrier, which looked, to Robin's eye, more solid; it was a web that extended from ceiling to floor in front of all of the room's occupants—including Killian's Avatar.

"Terrano!" Robin shouted.

But it was to Serralyn Terrano looked. He grimaced and said, "I hate my life.

"I got it. Robin, stay with Raven—and make sure Serralyn does the same."

It was Raven who grabbed Serralyn, freeing Robin's face to do so. He was certain he'd have bruises along his jaw. But she no longer told him not to look; the strands of webbing seemed far more safe to her than Killian's barrier had been.

Terrano's entire body elongated, and Robin looked to the window because watching the Barrani youth stretch and thin—unevenly—was more disturbing than glass that seemed to be slowly turning from flat panes to globes.

He heard the metal crack first, and was surprised. Raven sucked in breath, but Serralyn closed her eyes. Starrante spit webbing, and ejected it in a thin stream through the gaps in the web they sheltered behind.

The webbing struck bits of metal as they fell away from what had looked, to Robin's eyes, like glass. He noted that the webbing only touched the metal, in one case before it was so bent out of shape it broke.

Raven, so enamored of glass, stared with almost dull eyes. It was the first time Robin could clearly remember being worried for her. He'd never seen her respond so listlessly to glass before. Until it had started to change shape, she'd been as excited as a friendly puppy.

"Raven?"

She stared ahead. "Terrano is strange," she said, without looking in his direction.

"Stranger than I thought," Robin agreed. "Will he be okay?"

"Probably," Serralyn said. Her hands were balled in fists, and her eyes remained closed.

"What does he see?" Starrante asked, continuing, between syllables, to spit targeted webs.

"It's not glass," she whispered. "I mean—maybe it was glass when we first entered, but that's not what it is now."

"What is it? Serralyn—what does Terrano see?"

She shook her head. "I don't know." She opened one eye, grimaced, and kept it open.

"He's going too far," Raven whispered.

"I know," she said through gritted teeth. "I know, but we're holding on to him. He won't get lost." Wincing, she added, "You said you wanted to meet our other friends, didn't you, Robin?"

Robin nodded, queasy. He could barely see Terrano now. No, that wasn't true. He could see something clearly—it wasn't transparent—but it looked *nothing* like a Barrani. Nothing like Terrano. It was amorphous, like an oddly colored piece of paper that had been twisted into a variety of different shapes and still retained those creases. He could see no other distinguishing features, and was grateful that there were no eyes, no mouth.

"Well, you're likely to meet at least one of them soon. I'm sorry."

"Why?"

Serralyn shook her head. "Arbiter?"

"It is too risky," Starrante said, leaving Robin confused.

"What Terrano sees is dangerous. It could kill us all."

"No, not where we are currently situated."

She shook her head. "Killian's barrier means nothing to whatever it is the glass has become."

Starrante concurred.

"Your webs *do* mean something. I think we need to preserve as much of that metal as we can."

"I am *trying*," Starrante snapped. "Its rigidity, its physicality, relied on the glass it contained in some fashion."

Serralyn lifted one hand. In the other she held a knife. It was a short dagger, common to the Barrani—and one of the few weapons the chancellor considered acceptable for reasons of utility. Robin was fairly certain utility didn't include cutting one's palm open, however. Raven flinched, although she hadn't seen Serralyn cut her own hand.

Robin watched as she then reached out for the web that stood between them and the window; she gripped that web with her injured hand. The glass, Robin noted, had begun to float free of the frame that had contained its parts, very like bubbles of different hues, different sizes. They seemed to have the same weight as bubbles would, given how they floated; were they actual glass, they would have fallen and shattered.

Serralyn tightened her grip, and then, to his surprise, she handed the blade to Robin.

"You want me to do the same?"

"Yes."

"Promise you'll explain why later?"

"Yes. We need your help. I'd ask it of Raven but I'm not sure Raven… I don't think it would have the same effect."

"Starrante?"

"He's busy; he's effectively already done what I just did."

"What do you mean?"

"Why do you think the color of the webbing is pink?"

Robin hated the sight of his own blood; he hated the sight of blood, period. He took the knife in shaking hands and drew it across his palm—but not hard enough to cut, to break skin. He tried three times, and then, hands shaking, he passed the blade back to Serralyn and held out his hand.

He expected her to be disgusted with his squeamishness, or at least visibly annoyed. She'd cut herself without hesitation, after all, and the best he could do was try—and fail. But she wasn't. She might have done this every day as a matter of course.

He held his hand steady as she cut his palm; it stung a bit. He didn't look at the cut.

"Use the bleeding hand to grab one of the strands."

He did as bid; Raven made no attempt to prevent it. He wasn't certain, given her oddly vacant expression, that she saw him at all.

But he felt something warm in his hands—something that didn't feel like webbing at all; webbing was usually far too slight to feel like anything.

Serralyn paled. "It's not enough," she whispered.

"It is enough," Starrante said, followed by a series of vehement clicks that Robin thought might be cursing. "Tell Terrano he must be prepared to move—quickly."

"He can't. He's shifted space a bit to buy us time, but we'll lose that if he steps back."

"We may lose Terrano. Killian understands some of the danger now; he has withdrawn."

He'd left his Avatar, silent and motionless, in his wake.

"I wish you'd said that earlier," Serralyn said through clenched teeth. Her eyes had shifted size and shape, not to the extent that Terrano's had, before he'd transformed into...something. Robin had no words to describe it. The only one that came to mind was *paper*. "Be ready. Robin—don't let go."

He nodded. Practical magical theory hadn't covered emergencies like this one. No wonder Serralyn hated that class.

The paper that Terrano had become began to fold slowly in on itself, from the outer edges to the center. Robin realized, as he watched, that Terrano was not entirely within the boundaries of Starrante's protective webbing.

"Starrante—" Serralyn began.

"I have him," the Weveran replied. "Hold tightly, both of you. I apologize for any discomfort this may cause."

Robin braced himself. Warmth of thread clutched tightly in hand became ice in that instant. What he was now holding was so cold it was painful. Serralyn winced; the free hand clutched the handle of the dagger tightly enough she was white-knuckled.

Robin clenched his jaw instead, watching as Starrante spit another web. This one didn't reach metal; it reached the folded mass the thinly spread sheet had become. Terrano. It was too large to drag through the gaps formed by strands of web, but that wasn't what Starrante intended.

The Wevaran could create barriers or shields with the webs they spun, but that was not what they had once been famed for. It was their ability to create portals of those webs, to use those portals to teleport between locations. Or, in this case, to allow others to teleport between locations.

The web Starrante spit attached itself to Terrano and spread. Terrano appeared beside Serralyn, his skin lined and wrinkled but recognizably himself. Serralyn's eyes didn't revert to their normal shape and color, but had they, they would have been blue. She wasn't happy with her friend.

Terrano shook the wrinkles out—which sounded way more normal than it looked—before he opened his mouth. When he did, words failed to follow; the bubbles of multicolored glass on the other side of Starrante's web exploded outward.

Shards flew, embedding themselves in the desktop, the walls, the floors—everywhere Starrante's web didn't cover. Robin watched.

It was over in an instant, in more ways than one. The window from which these bubbles of glass had emerged was gone. What faced them now was blank wall. The metal bits—the frame— were gone, as well, except for those elements to which Starrante had attached web. Those now shone, their surfaces more reflective than they had been when they'd served as framing for the glass itself.

Robin then looked at the room. He was certain shards of glass had struck every visible surface in the office. As he watched, what should have been shards began to melt or to sublimate. They left no marks, no scars of any kind, in anything they'd hit; Robin wasn't sure they would've caused actual wounds if one of the things they'd hit had been human or Barrani.

So much glass had stood on the far wall; it was gone now.

"You can let go," Starrante said.

Robin grimaced. "I'll try. I think my hand is frozen."

Starrante lifted the pieces of metal that had been part of the window. They were very similar in color and sheen to the small bits Raven had collected over time, but much larger.

"Raven," the Arbiter said, "I believe these are yours."

She blinked rapidly, the vacancy gone from eyes and expression. In its place was a growing and familiar excitement. "You found them," she whispered, although her hands had instinctively stretched out to take what Starrante lifted—suspended by web, not limb.

"Ah, no. I believe you led us to this office. Technically, you found them. And I do not believe it would do Killianas any good to retain these himself."

"But you could."

"Yes, Raven—I could. But not as easily as I believe you could or have. And nowhere near as safely. Killian is not present. The chancellor is absent, as well. In their stead, I believe I have the authority to ask you, and your friends, to examine the contents of this office for stray bits of glass.

"I would ask, however, that if they are found, it is only Raven who retrieves them."

The pieces of metal that Starrante had somehow preserved were far larger than Raven's pouch, but neither the Wevaran nor Raven seemed concerned with this bit of objective reality. Raven took the metal bits in her hands, examined them with barely suppressed glee—she was bouncing—and then withdrew her pouch of treasures.

She slid them carefully into the pouch. They fit, of course.

"Raven's going to have to look," Terrano said. He sounded exhausted. He certainly looked it. "None of the rest of us can see them anyway, and I've got a headache." He looked at Robin, and offered a sickly grin. "Most of the headache is people screaming in my internal ear. You would not *believe* how loud they're being."

Starrante brought the barrier down and Raven rushed past where it had been standing, as if speed was now of the essence.

Whatever fear or gloom had enshrouded her had been thoroughly thrown off; she was squealing in the glee and delight he had come to associate only with Raven.

"Robin! Robin! Robin! Look!"

She bobbed up and down, crouching at the foot of shelves, crawling under the desk, running to the corners of the room that had not been protected at all. When she finally came to a stop, she was practically glowing; she was certainly humming.

She turned to Robin, although everyone was watching her progress. Her hands were full of pieces of glass.

15

Starrante clicked quietly as he watched Raven's progress; he said nothing that anyone else could understand. When Raven was done—and her excited announcement indicated that she had, in fact, finished her frenzied inspection—he lifted two limbs and waved them in Raven's direction.

She bounced over to where he was waiting, then held out her full hands.

The predominant color of the glass bits she'd found was normal: they looked, to Robin, like clean, broken glass. But nestled among them were colored shards; she seemed exceptionally pleased with those.

Starrante didn't touch any of the pieces, but his eyes were no more than a finger's width away from the small pile.

"Is it safe for Killian to return?" Terrano asked.

"It is now. It was safe until the moment the window began to transform. I am surprised that a window of that size had been tucked away, untouched, for so long."

"Are you certain it's been here for a long time?" Robin asked, frowning.

"That is my assumption, yes." Starrante's limbs moved, but

most of his eyes had returned to their resting places on his body. "You have reason to believe the assumption is incorrect?"

"I don't know what the window is. I mean, to all of us, it looked like a window."

Terrano cleared his throat. Loudly.

Robin grimaced. "To *most* of us it looked like a window. Raven found it because Killian has us looking for hiding places on the Academia campus. Killian was with us when she headed to this office."

"And these hiding places are places of which Killian was unaware—and therefore has no oversight?"

Robin nodded. "Finding those places allows Killian to… have oversight, I guess?"

The discussion dimmed Raven's enthusiasm, but honestly, not by much. Robin understood. She had never found so much glass at one time. Everything that had happened before this treasure hunt was no longer a priority: only the treasure was.

Robin was used to doing the talking. "Raven thought this office contained a hiding place."

"Did she find it?"

"We all got distracted by the window. Even Killian."

Raven said, "The inner office. The inner office was the place to hide. It's gone now," she added, in a tone that implied it wasn't important. Robin could almost see her mind working as she considered hiding places and windows. Maybe other hiding places in the Academia had windows, and those windows became glass that she could pick up and keep. The first one hadn't, but that one had had the feather, which she lumped together with the rest of her inexplicable treasures.

For as long as he'd known her, she'd gathered her treasures—but she'd never found so many so quickly before. When she was excited, when she was lit up with joy and glee, she was almost incandescent, and the terrible desire to *share* would overwhelm her. It was the only time she ever lost all sense of her surroundings; she would make a beeline to Robin—wherever he was, whatever he was doing—her steps a dancing bounce. Sometimes she looked like she could bounce out of her skin.

That was her expression now. She'd been disgruntled searching for places that Killian meant to immediately destroy, but she'd lost that wariness, that look. He tried not to think of that vacant, empty stare. She'd passed through it to return to her excited, ebullient self.

If she found *more* hiding places, she'd find more treasures.

Robin wanted to tell her that it wasn't guaranteed; he didn't want her to get her hopes up only to see them dashed. He turned to Starrante.

"I think we need to know what the glass is. And the metal. What did you think they were when you first saw them?"

Starrante, however, deflected. "Raven, what do you do with your treasures?"

She looked confused by the question, as if she hadn't or couldn't understand it. "Do?"

"You keep them for a reason, yes?"

"They're treasures."

"Why are they treasures? Why are they something you've searched for?"

She blinked again. "Because they're treasures."

"Do you know what they used to be? The glass isn't whole; it must have existed in some shape—like the window—before it was broken."

She nodded.

"Why are the broken parts of something else important to you?"

Her exhalation was loud, and just shy of disgust. "Because," she said, speaking slowly, "they're *treasures*."

Starrante wasn't going to get anything else out of her for the moment. Robin had been curious the first time she'd shown him her treasure, but he accepted that it was important to her.

Maybe because he'd been young at the time, or maybe because his own family—

He stopped. He stopped, swallowed, and backed away from the abyss. Now was not the time, if there was ever such a time. The past was done. It was gone. The past wouldn't give him any answers in the present, and Killian needed those answers. The Academia needed them.

Robin did not want to lose his home again.

Raven insisted on returning to their room the moment Starrante returned to the library—vanishing as he did in a portal of his own making, his eyes the wrong color. Robin wondered briefly if the library would be open to students anytime today or tomorrow; Starrante clearly suspected something about Raven's treasures, but felt he either did not have enough information, or could not speak directly about it to those who didn't. Both were bad.

When Raven was ensconced in their room, Serralyn took a seat on Robin's bed. Terrano had decided to float, but his face was mostly normal. They were arguing, but silently; Serralyn's eyes were blue.

Terrano's were blue green; he was resigned but not angry or frightened. "Serralyn wants me to leave," he told Robin, "because she doesn't think you can handle a face full of Sedarias."

Serralyn's frown reached her brows. "Sedarias is the political friend I told you about. She's very attached to Terrano and she finds it difficult to easily forgive his recklessness."

"How can she be attached to him and not know he's reckless?" It was a sincere question. "I've known him for weeks, and I know."

"She expects him to be a little more cautious when it comes to his own safety." Serralyn was paler. "He could have died there. It was very, very close."

Terrano rolled his eyes. "Did I die?"

"You still might; Sedarias is really angry."

"Yeah, but she can't come here without permission, right? Here is definitely safer than home."

"Helen won't let her kill you at home."

"Won't stop her from trying—only succeeding," was the glum reply. "Look—I know it was dangerous, okay? But Killian was at risk. You heard Starrante. He could sense something, too."

Too.

"What did you sense?" Robin asked. "Why did you do what you did?"

"You saw the window, right?"

"We all did."

"It didn't look like a window to me. The lattice of metal around the glass? It looked more like bars, like a very pretty cage. To my eyes it didn't look like a bunch of glass or colored glass, it looked like something pressed against the bars of a very tiny cage, desperately seeking a way out. It looked alive."

"It almost looked that way after you started to approach it. I mean—the glass started to bulge. But to me the individual panes looked more like bubbles. Like blown bubbles."

Serralyn nodded.

"Yeah, and that was bad." Terrano shrugged, the motion too stiff. "I don't think the glass—such as it is—was ever meant to interact with our reality. I could see it because I was mostly not interacting with our reality, either. The glass is dangerous. And, Robin? I searched the room after it was safe. I watched Raven carefully. There *were no shards* until Raven picked them up. Just like near the body in the quad. I won't say she didn't see them, but it's like they didn't exist until she touched them.

"And now she has a bunch of pieces of glass. They look like glass to me. They look like glass no matter what I do with my eyes. They looked like glass to Killian when he attempted to touch a shard. You saw what a broken shard did to him, right?"

Robin nodded.

"Starrante was afraid of what very large, unbroken shards would do." Terrano exhaled. "Everyone thought the window was responding to me."

"You don't."

"I did—until Starrante shouted at Killian. But I think Starrante was right. The glass was responding to Killian, and I wouldn't bet on his chances of surviving if the whole thing had made contact with him."

"Which…doesn't explain what you were trying to do."

"I was trying to shield Killian, obviously."

"You looked like a weird, giant piece of paper."

"Yeah, I sort of felt like that, as well. It's definitely not comfortable."

Serralyn clearly disliked the almost casual way Terrano spoke. "Sedarias believes he literally spread himself too thin—she thought he could center himself more carefully. She wasn't certain what flying shards of glass would do to Terrano, but no one thinks it would have been *good*."

"I'm fine. I heard Raven's warning," he added, glancing at Raven. She was occupied with shards of glass; she'd carefully emptied her pouch onto a tabletop and was now playing with the pieces the way a child might play with tiny dolls.

"Eyes?"

Terrano nodded. "She wasn't worried about them hitting me or even cutting me. Just about them getting into my eyes. I mean, it seems obvious—who wants shards of glass to pierce their eyeballs? But it seemed like more than that. And frankly, if the glass is somehow alive, it makes it sound a lot more creepy."

"But why do you think it was attracted to Killian?"

Terrano shrugged. "I know it can't be just the Academia—Raven had glass bits before she came here. If I understand, she searched you out because she had new things she wanted to show you. She's always had them?"

Robin nodded. "I'd never seen the metal scraps before, but I knew about them. And it's the metal scraps that Starrante was trying so hard to preserve. I think you might be right."

"I'm always right."

Serralyn snorted.

"Right about what?"

"They were bars of a cage. If they could hold or contain whatever it was you saw, they might be important to us."

"Sure. If we had any idea how to use them. I highly doubt we could take the pieces he saved, melt them down, and fashion something that could serve as a cage."

"Probably not, or he wouldn't have given them to Raven. But I think he might think they're necessary. I'm more concerned with the idea that random glass bits can be found across the city. I mean—it *looked* alive to me, but it didn't exactly speak or attempt to communicate. It might not be sentient."

Raven said, "It is."

Everyone in the room turned to look at her back. There was no fear in her voice, no sign of emotion; she was absorbed in pieces of glass. It was the tone she used when she was busy but felt information needed to be conveyed.

"Raven?" Serralyn said.

Raven didn't respond. Robin approached her and gently touched her collarbone. She looked away from her glass.

"I think Serralyn wants to ask you a question?"

"Oh." Her expression said *now?* But she dutifully turned to the Barrani student.

"If the glass is sentient, are the pieces in front of you like body parts?"

Clearly Raven had had her fill of blatantly ignorant questions. "No."

"I don't understand."

"Why?"

"Maybe we're not using the word *sentient* the right way. Are dogs sentient, to you?"

Raven frowned. "Maybe? Some dogs are smart. And some dogs are good friends. Some are sneaky. And some are mean. Sort of like people."

"I won't ask the same question about cats. What about wasps? Mosquitos?"

Raven shook her head. No.

"Barrani?"

Terrano snickered.

"Barrani are sentient. Robin is sentient. *I'm* sentient. Killian is."

"Is the glass more like dog-sentient or Barrani-sentient?"

Raven shrugged, which meant she wasn't sure.

"Have you ever seen a window like the one in the office?"

Raven frowned, tilting her head to the side. Robin expected, from her expression, that the answer would be *no*. The answer was, "I don't know. I think so? I recognized it." She continued to think. "Ask Starrante."

"Ask Starrante if you know?"

Raven nodded.

Robin didn't exactly expect conversations with Raven to make sense, at least not at first, but this was the most confusing one he could remember. He couldn't tell if she meant Serralyn should ask Starrante if *he* knew, or ask Starrante if *she* did—which made no sense.

Serralyn accepted the answer. Then again, it was an excuse to go to the library, and she generally loved those. But she wasn't out of questions yet, even if Raven was out of answers.

"Could those pieces of glass be used again?"

"Used?"

"We can melt glass, blow glass, use shattered or broken pieces to re-create things. I mean, normal glass—what most of us call glass."

Raven nodded.

"Does this glass work the same way?"

This time, Raven smiled. "Maybe!" And then, as if Serralyn's question had been a prod, she immediately turned back to her scattered treasures. "Maybe."

Both Serralyn and Terrano watched Raven work; neither asked further questions. Terrano had recovered enough that he was willing to examine the glass from what he called different perspectives. Raven didn't appear to notice, as Terrano didn't touch a thing.

But Robin turned to his desk. "Serralyn, can I ask you a favor?"

She glanced instantly in his direction, nodded, and joined him at his desk. "Homework?"

"That's going to be ugly," he confessed, "but no. Hopefully we finish inspecting the campus in the next day or two—I'm starting to have nightmares about falling permanently behind."

"You haven't missed too much so far."

It had only been a day. Robin shook free of the anxiety; worrying wouldn't change anything. "Here." He opened the small chest he'd taken from the storage room.

"What is that?"

"I think it's a diary—it's handwritten. But... I couldn't read the language."

"It's not Barrani?"

Robin shook his head. "Or not Barrani I recognize; mostly we learn High Barrani, but Larrantin says there are a lot of dialects the Academia isn't teaching yet." He handed her the diary.

She frowned. "This isn't yours, then."

"We found it in the first hiding place Raven found. It, and a lot of larger, dustier boxes. Killian knows where the space is now, and I think the chancellor is having it excavated. Killian didn't see much harm in letting me hang on to this—it's not like anyone's using it now. There was a quill in the chest, probably part of a set with very dried-out ink. Raven has that."

"Oh?"

"It was a feather, it was new, and it was in pristine condition—I think it's the first time I've seen her add a feather to her collection."

Serralyn looked to Raven, and then looked down at the book she held, clearly torn. She settled on the book, but pointed out that the feather was not among the treasures spread out on the table.

Robin hadn't noticed, but Robin didn't pay a lot of attention to what Raven did with her treasures; he couldn't pick out specific pieces from the mess. Serralyn and Terrano could. All Barrani students could, if they put their mind to it. They could remember what they'd seen. Serralyn didn't have to read a book more than once to know its contents by heart. It wasn't immortality Robin envied the Barrani—it was the *memory*.

She opened the diary and frowned.

"Not a Barrani dialect, then."

"No. But the letterforms look familiar to me. Whoever wrote this had terrible handwriting, I think. Do you want me to try to translate it?"

He did, but she'd just implied—heavily—that she didn't recognize the language. "I mean, it's a diary, right? If it were written by a former student here, it's probably going to be pretty boring."

"Are you worried that you're prying into someone's privacy?"

Robin grimaced. "A little, yeah. I mean, if it was written by a human student, no—they've been dead for so long, they couldn't possibly care. But if it was written by someone Barrani or someone immortal, they could still be around, somewhere."

"Do you mind if I take it with me?"

"Go ahead. It's not doing me any good."

Raven said, "It's not doing you any harm, either."

They both turned to Raven. Robin said, "Will it harm Serralyn?"

"Don't know. Make her take the box, too, if she's taking the book. She can leave it there when she's not looking at it."

Serralyn immediately set the book back in the box, as Raven called it, and examined the exterior of the small chest. It had no obvious markings. "Was it locked?" she asked.

Robin nodded.

"And you picked the lock?"

He nodded again. "It wasn't magical. It wasn't warded. I mean—it looks like the kind of chest you give a kid, and those aren't really magically secure."

"It doesn't look like that to me, but maybe our customs are different." She closed the chest's lid. She then opened the lid again without difficulty. "No key?"

Robin shook his head. "If we'd found the key, we wouldn't have had to pick the lock."

Serralyn winced.

"Is there something wrong with the box?"

"No—with the administrative secretary. Our friend has arrived, and she wants to see us now. Right now. Terrano?"

"I'm not sure the chancellor wants her on campus in her current mood."

"He might allow it—she came with a Hawk." Turning to Robin, she added, "That's Teela. She's one of us."

"They're supposed to work in pairs, and I don't suppose any of the rest of you are Hawks."

"She's probably off duty. But still: Hawk. And Sedarias." It was clear which of the two was more intimidating at the moment. "Terrano, come on. Sedarias's temper isn't getting any cooler, and ignoring her always makes it worse." She paused and then added, "Robin, you can come meet her if you want. It might take some of the heat off Terrano."

Robin glanced at Raven, who shook her head: *No.* She'd

had enough people for the day, or at least this part of it, and she was busy studying her treasures. He just hoped she'd be in the room when he got back.

Serralyn led; to Robin's surprise the ever-quiet Valliant joined them before they'd exited the building. His eyes were very blue, and the look he gave Terrano should have shriveled the irreverent Barrani had Terrano any capacity for shame.

They walked across the quad, catching stray attention; given the color of Valliant's eyes, they weren't required to actually interact with any of the other students. If they drew a crowd of curious onlookers, it would be at a very safe distance.

Two Barrani women were exiting the administrative building. Robin could almost see a physical dark cloud emanating from one of them. Terrano cringed and fell behind Robin—as if Robin would be any kind of useful shield against an angry Barrani.

Suspicion became fact as the two Barrani stalked across the road to the quad. One of the two looked calmer. She wasn't wearing the Hawk's tabard, but Robin guessed she was Teela, a person he had seen before. The other, dressed in clothing far more suited to formal gatherings than school, must be Sedarias. She was *angry*.

Terrano muttered an apology.

Valliant reached out and grabbed Terrano by the shoulder. "No you don't," he said. "You're not leaving us alone with angry Sedarias."

Robin wouldn't have been surprised if Sedarias had drawn dagger and attempted to stab Terrano, but he was a bit surprised when she attempted to slug Terrano in the mouth with a very closed fist.

It passed through his face. Though it seemed Valliant was somehow capable of pinning Terrano in place, he clearly wasn't capable of forcing him to remain physically corporeal. Terrano was really, really strange.

Serralyn, silent until that moment, turned to Sedarias. She didn't speak.

Sedarias's eyes were practically black, they were so dark. Her hands remained in shaking fists. *"What,"* she demanded, *"do you think you were doing?"*

Terrano didn't answer, at least not with words Robin could hear; given Sedarias's facial expression, she could—and she didn't care for what she'd heard. But she replied silently as Robin watched. Serralyn didn't bother to introduce him, for which he was grateful.

Teela, however, stepped around Sedarias, Terrano, and Valliant; Serralyn was already hanging to one side, out of the immediate radius.

"Robin," she said, "I am here with the chancellor's permission."

"As a Hawk?"

"As someone who has some expertise in investigations, yes. The Hawks—and Imperial Law—do not hold sway over the Academia; it functions as a small fief of its own, absent Tower. The chancellor, however, retains his role as one of the lords of the Dragon Court, and the Emperor holds him in high enough regard he is willing to second some of the Hawks at need." Her professional expression softened. "I hear there is some need.

"Would you mind guiding me to the chancellor's office?"

Robin wasn't certain Teela needed a guide; most of the Barrani didn't. They remembered how to get from place to place if they'd managed it once. He glanced at angry Sedarias when she raised her voice, then he nodded quickly.

"I'm sorry about that," the Imperial Hawk said as they entered the building. "Sedarias is very close to Terrano, and she worries."

"Given Terrano, that's not really surprising. I thought Serralyn was going to strangle him, and Serralyn doesn't lose her temper. Are you really here to see the chancellor?"

"I am. Would you care to fill me in on what I'm to see him about?"

"I believe I can do that," Killian said, appearing from midair to the left of Teela, as Robin currently occupied her right.

"Killianas," she said, with a clipped nod.

Killian proceeded to fill her in on the bare facts: three murders—two Barrani, one human—within the span of the past week. No known cause of death. The Barrani bodies had not been sent to the Halls of Law to be examined, but Robin had a suspicion the human one would.

"None of that explains Terrano," Teela told the Avatar, turning once again to Robin.

"I think we might as well wait until we get to the chancellor," Robin told her. "No point in repeating myself."

Teela hadn't lied; when she knocked on the doors, they rolled open. If the chancellor was surprised to see Robin beside the Barrani Hawk, he made no sign, indicating that both should enter the office. Teela did; she had no reason to find the chancellor intimidating. Robin followed, feeling out of place.

"If you would care for a drink, help yourself," the chancellor told the Barrani Hawk as he came around his desk. "I can never remember what Barrani prefer, and beverages preferred by my kin tend to be corrosive to other races."

"I will indulge, as I'm not on duty," Teela replied, giving the chancellor a probing glance before she turned to the cupboard he'd indicated. "I was surprised by your invitation. I would have come earlier, but things have been hectic at the office, and I wished to be firmly off duty to assess the difficulty."

The chancellor nodded. He chose a chair and sat heavily in

it. To Robin's eyes, he looked tired, which was unusual. "What has Robin told you?"

"Nothing. Killianas informed me of the three deaths, but it is not the three deaths that occasioned my visit today."

"You'd heard."

"I'd heard of two of them, yes. I assumed the first was entirely political."

"As did I."

"The second, in my opinion, was not."

"Does An'Mellarionne concur?"

Teela rolled her eyes. "She can see the political in anything, as you must suspect. But the human death alters that supposition."

Of course it did. Humans weren't considered political in the Barrani sense—especially not poor students from the wrong part of Elantra. In the Barrani view, that would be almost all of it, but the Barrani were willing to offer grudging respect to those mortals who were rich and relatively powerful.

"However, that is not the reason Sedarias chose to visit the campus. I am not certain whether you've had a chance to speak with Arbiter Starrante or Killianas about the events of the afternoon."

"Killianas delivered a brief report, and I have an appointment to speak with the Arbiters after dinner. So no, I have not."

"Robin?" Teela asked, in a pleasant tone that did nothing to change the substance of command.

Robin exhaled. He was hesitant to mention Raven, but he had no story to tell without her. "There's a new prospective student."

"Your friend Raven?"

He blinked.

"I'm part of the cohort that includes Serralyn, Valliant, and Terrano. I know what they know."

"But you're a Hawk?"

She chuckled. "Indeed. Sedarias would find it humiliating to be associated with me were I not a lord of the High Court in a position of certain authority. Given the deaths on campus, and the initial possibility that they were politically motivated by Sedarias's enemies, she has been keeping me apprised of campus activities. If you wish a bit more privacy, you're going to have to avoid Serralyn and Valliant."

"Not Terrano?"

"No one can avoid Terrano without serious effort and more violence than you're capable of inflicting."

"So...you already knew about Raven."

Teela nodded.

"Did Serralyn talk about the hiding places?"

"Not very clearly—and that is something I, at least, would have an interest in. My understanding is that Raven can find places on the campus that elude Killianas entirely. Which should not be possible."

"She can. I didn't—" He hesitated. "I didn't expect there would be any. Killian *is* the Academia. He's the physical geography of it. The quad, the buildings, the dorms—it's all part of him."

"Are you aware of every part of your body?" Teela asked. "Are you aware of the knot in the back of your hair?"

He immediately reached up to the back of his hair, and was embarrassed to find it *was* knotted. "No."

"No, indeed. Are you aware of the length of your toenails?"

"Maybe?" His toenails were under a layer of shoe and sock. "Is it like that?"

"I believe it might be. And, as you suspect, it shouldn't be. You have no direct control over your hair or your nails; Killianas can transform any element of the Academia, saving only the portal that leads to the library. But if you attempt to think of these hiding places as if they were the back of your head, it might seem less concerning."

Robin doubted it, but nodded as if he didn't. That was just good manners. "Raven found a hiding place last night. She found one this afternoon—a different one. But this one…"

"This would be the room in which Terrano attempted to kill himself in a new and interesting way?"

"I think he was trying to make certain Killian was safe," Robin protested.

"From what, exactly?"

"From the window that looked like it was exploding in slow motion?"

Teela blinked. "You will have to describe it. What Terrano saw, we didn't see clearly." At Robin's expression, she exhaled. "Terrano is the most flexible of all of us. I would be considered the least flexible. He is capable of standing to one side of actual, physical reality. Sometimes he goes farther afield. We can see what he sees to a certain extent—but it's filtered. Unless the change is minimal—just his eyes, for example—it's hard to relate to what he perceives; he is often using senses that we do not naturally possess. And what Serralyn saw was…masked somehow, possibly by the Arbiter."

"But you all saw the window?"

"We saw the window, yes. It was stained glass, and Serralyn believes some of the motifs and colors have historical significance."

"To who?"

"That's the question, isn't it? She's already deepened her areas of research; I'm not certain Sedarias is best pleased by this." Teela's grin made clear she wasn't too worried. The grin vanished. "We saw the window, but when it began to bulge it seemed—to those of us who've seen the effect—like an arcane bomb had exploded on the other side of the glass, and the window was exploding in slow motion.

"But Terrano saw something different, and Serralyn did not clearly see the effects of that explosion."

"I don't think it was an explosion," he replied, choosing his words more hesitantly.

"I would be very curious to hear what you think."

Robin glanced at the chancellor, whose eyes were reddening. He felt it unfair that he was now the point person when he was a new student who understood very little. Shouldn't Starrante be here instead? Or Terrano? Or even Serralyn, who seemed to have a far greater understanding of at least theoretical magic than Robin?

He straightened his shoulders. *Stop whining. They're asking you, and you have a stake in the fate of the Academia. A greater stake than any of the other people you're thinking should be answering instead.*

"Sorry—I don't want to get in trouble with the law."

16

"The law—as you call it—has no jurisdiction over the Academia," the chancellor said. "An'Teela is here as a personal favor; she is consulting, not arresting."

"So you only have to be terrified of the angry Dragon sitting behind the chancellor's desk," the Hawk added, her grin returning. Her eyes, however, remained blue.

Robin then explained what he had seen, starting with Raven's sour attempt to find—and destroy—hiding places, Killian in tow, and ending with events that occurred after the window had either exploded, melted, or been deserted by glass that Raven had indicated was possibly sentient.

"Sentient?" the chancellor said before Robin could finish the sentence that contained that word.

"I didn't understand it, either, and Raven's recovering—she doesn't spend a lot of time with other people, and after the window fell apart, Starrante—" As the chancellor cleared his throat, Robin backtracked. "—*Arbiter* Starrante preserved what Raven calls metal bits. He seemed to think they were at least as important as preserving Terrano.

"Before you ask, I have no idea what Terrano was doing. I

only know he thinks he was trying to protect Killian. You're going to have to ask him, but I don't think he'll be able to come to the office anytime soon."

"Oh, he won't," Teela said. "Sedarias was terrified that we'd lose him, and he forgot the cardinal Sedarias rule: do *not* make her worry. I'd be surprised if he's back at the Academia before the week is out—but Terrano's hard to cage. And to be fair, given the two Barrani deaths, Terrano is worried about Serralyn and Valliant; he's not just loitering on the grounds because he's bored."

"For which I am grateful," the chancellor added. "My imagination is not up to the consequences of bored Terrano."

"It really isn't, and we're getting sidetracked. I'd like to return to sentience. And to one other comment you said Raven made—which Serralyn did hear."

"Which one?"

"Don't let the glass shards get in your eyes."

Robin nodded. "That would be common sense for any glass, though."

"Yes. Is that why she said it?"

"No. No, I don't think so." He exhaled. "This isn't the first time she's found glass."

Teela nodded. "No. Serralyn saw her pick up a piece of glass—a larger piece—from beneath the arms of a dead Barrani student. Until she did, no one could see it; after, it was simple glass."

"Not simple," Robin said. "Killian couldn't touch it. His Avatar tried—it didn't go well. But—" He frowned. "It's hard to think of it as a problem that only affects the Academia. It's the same with hiding places. Raven found them for us in the warrens, which have nothing to do with the Academia. She also found glass and some metal bits outside of the campus— she'd never been on the campus before Giselle led her here.

"So whatever the problem is, it's not just Academia related.

I mean—of course Killian wouldn't be aware of hiding places outside of the Academia, but they still existed."

"What did Raven feel you were hiding from?"

"Gangs? Thugs? People who'd sell us into slavery in the fiefs?" He paused, and then added, "Cold. Rain in the colder season. Fire, once. I never thought much of the hiding places beyond the fact that she'd found them and we'd be safe. They seemed mundane to me—but I was used to being overlooked. We both were." He tried to keep bitterness out of his voice.

The past was the past. He had nothing to be bitter about here. Well, maybe Melden, but Melden was probably not going to be condescending to his students in the immediate future. And Robin owed the chancellor everything. His best, not his worst.

"Raven found them?"

Robin nodded. "Raven found them. She found me, as well, if she thought we'd need someplace to hide. I know she's a bit odd. I know she doesn't really care for most people—it takes work for her to talk. But she's *solid*. She was there for me when no one else was; she cared for me when everyone who'd ever cared was dead."

"I see. I will now ask an intrusive and difficult question; you are not obligated to answer it."

Robin tensed.

"Do you remember the people who did once care about you?"

He swallowed. Nodded.

"They did not deliberately abandon you?"

"No!" His hands had become instant fists; he forced himself to unclench them. Swallowed. He shook his head, not trusting his voice.

"Raven found you only after your family was gone."

Robin nodded.

"And she continued to find you when your situation was more dangerous than the norm for the warrens."

He nodded again.

"You noticed nothing unusual about the places in which you both hid?"

"No—but I didn't notice anything unusual about the storeroom, either. It was dusty, there were cobwebs, and it was dark. To me it was warmer and safer than our usual warrens spots."

"How long did you remain in the first Academia hiding place?"

"You'd have to ask Killian for an exact time. We stayed until Raven said it was safe to leave."

"Do you know how she knew?"

Robin shook his head. "When we were hiding in the warrens, we didn't talk—we didn't want to attract attention. And later, it didn't seem as relevant. I did ask her when I was younger," he admitted, his chin dropping. "But I couldn't really understand her answer—she's way better with words now than she was then."

Given she wasn't terribly good now, the chancellor's surprise wasn't surprising.

"But I swear, sir—Raven isn't causing any of these problems. It's not like she brought whatever it is with her—things were happening before she arrived. And she's trying to help Killian in her own way—she's doing something only she can do."

"Robin," the chancellor said, calling his name to stem the flow of words, because Robin was marshaling more of them, "I have no intention of ejecting Raven from the Academia. Even if she is not suitable student material, she is, as you've pointed out, aiding Killian—if somewhat reluctantly."

"I think that'll change."

"Oh?"

"The first hiding place we found had a quill—she added that to her treasures. The second had more glass than she's seen in one place in her life—I think. Even if it didn't, she's now probably doubled her glass collection, and more than doubled her metal collection. She thinks there's a possibility that in the Academia, hiding places lead to treasure. Killian said she could keep them," he added in a rush. "And Starrante—Arbiter Starrante, sorry—seemed to feel that they were best left with Raven, as well."

"Did you not find it odd that Raven seemed so comfortable communicating with the Arbiter?"

"Of course I did—but, well, it's Raven."

Teela raised a brow. Robin couldn't raise his separately.

"Raven knows things. She can't explain how she knows them—usually if you ask her, she just looks at you funny. To her, it's just something she knows. She surprises people in both directions. There are things she doesn't know, things she doesn't understand the way most of us do. You just…kind of get used to it." He knew it was a weak finish.

Teela, however, nodded. She turned to the chancellor. "I would, with your permission, like to petition Arbiter Starrante for an interview."

"I have a few words to exchange with him myself."

Teela turned to Robin. "Will you be accompanying us?"

The chancellor clearly didn't care for the question. "I believe Robin has a task that Killian set him."

"I'm sure it can wait," Teela replied. Robin remembered then that she was one of Serralyn's close friends. Her cohort. Even if she was an Imperial Hawk. Teela probably knew what the task was, because Serralyn knew.

He was grateful that he'd never had much in the way of secrets, because it was impossible not to talk to Serralyn, and if he'd understood what Terrano said, everything Serralyn knew, the rest of her friends would know. He wondered idly if they cheated on tests that way. He doubted it.

"It can," Robin agreed. "Raven is tired, and she needs alone time. Even if I go back to our room now, we're not going exploring for a while."

★ ★ ★

Robin had questions for Starrante, but given the presence of the Hawk and the chancellor, he was pretty sure he wouldn't get to ask any of them. Even if it was possible, the chancellor wasn't best pleased that Teela had invited him to tag along. He understood why.

Raven had difficulty explaining concepts she knew well to anyone else. But Starrante didn't. Starrante had been excited to meet Raven; he had expected, on some level, that he could speak his tongue and she would understand it. And she had.

If Raven couldn't dislodge explanations, the Arbiter could. Robin still trusted Raven. He didn't think that would ever stop. And he still wanted her to be a student in the Academia. But questions he had never asked, or had asked only once, in distant childhood, had now returned with a vengeance. If he believed Raven had answers she didn't want to share, he would have put a permanent lid on that curiosity.

Robin had things he didn't want to share, either.

Hers weren't deliberate, though. If she were present, she would have been mildly annoyed—at best—that Robin was wasting time asking questions whose answers were so obvious. She wouldn't have considered the questions themselves a breach of her privacy. Raven had little concept of privacy.

She didn't seek privacy because she had things to hide. She just didn't like people.

The walk to the library portal was so silent, Robin almost started talking just to make noise. He didn't, but it was close. Most silences didn't bother him, but this one was uncomfortable.

"They are angry," Killian said, materializing beside Robin. "But they are not angry at you, and they are not specifically angry with each other."

Neither the Hawk nor the chancellor looked back.

"No; they cannot hear us. It is within my capabilities to have private conversations; I do it seldom because it is taxing."

"Can they hear me?"

"Not unless you wish them to. I do not consider this keeping secrets from the chancellor," he added, smiling gently. "Raven is not what you are."

Robin shrugged. "No two people are the same."

"No, but you know that is not what I meant. She is not human, Robin. She has never been human. She has never been a child, either."

"She has been—she was my age when we first met, and she's my age now."

"I will not argue with your memories. She is, in appearance, your age now. If you met her when she was your age as a child, that would make sense. If she were as she appears." He lifted a hand. "She is not pretending to be something she is not, in my observation. She simply is what she is. How she is perceived—when she chooses to be perceived at all—appears to be irrelevant to her.

"It is not irrelevant to the Arbiters, and it has become vitally important to the chancellor. It is of import to An'Teela because Serralyn, Valliant, and Terrano are here—although An'Teela does not believe anything could kill Terrano short of his own recklessness."

"Raven would never hurt them!"

"An'Teela understands that. She is not here to harm Raven in any way. But three people have died on my campus. I have no records of how or why; the chancellor is unaccustomed to investigations of this nature. But there was one clue that the Hawks might normally consider a start: the test. The test and the small bits of cloth in the professor's office. She is aware that Imperial Law is not in force in the Academia, but she is also aware that she can investigate and present information to the chancellor as if he were her commander, and he will act on it.

"In my opinion, it is better that the Hawk takes on the investigation."

"She has less to lose?"

"Much less."

"And you?"

Killian shook his head. "I should not require outside help; the questions being asked are all questions I should be able to answer. The chancellor believes I have not fully recovered from my long, suspended animation. I believe that, as well. But I am now less certain."

"Why?"

"Because Raven is finding places I could not see," was Killian's soft reply.

"You think that's deliberate."

"Do you not?"

"I don't know every inch of my own body," Robin replied. "So no. I can't tell you what my toenails look like right now; they probably need cutting, but that's a guess. So it doesn't feel as wrong to me as it does to you." He reached out and placed a hand on Killian's shoulder, stopping an inch from contact as he realized that buildings probably didn't need gestures of comfort.

"That is wrong," Killian said, voice soft. "We are buildings, yes—but we are alive."

Starrante was waiting for them when they walked through the "door" to the library. The chancellor and Teela went first; Killian stood back and Robin walked after them. "The library," he said, "is not under my jurisdiction; I cannot enter it. If you wish my presence, Starrante will have to come here."

They entered the library, and as usual, they walked into a world of books. The walls, the towering shelves that disappeared into the distance, there were so many of them. This was Serralyn's favorite place in the world, and she was desperate to finish this academic year because then she'd be a senior, with more opportunities to visit it.

Robin found it intimidating. He could read, but he couldn't read the variety of languages Serralyn could, and he was still much slower than she was. Books were language on the page, to her; to Robin they were *work*. But if he did the work, they yielded bit by bit, and offered him the knowledge that she attained so gracefully, time after time.

Starrante lifted arms in greeting, and Robin lifted his, as well; he knew the greeting by heart now, and could perform it—imperfectly—by instinct.

"I did not expect to see you today," Starrante said, his tone making clear that he was pleased, not annoyed, by Robin's presence.

"Killian's made sure that I don't have to attend classes for the next few days. Raven and I are supposed to be searching for hiding places. Places that Killian isn't aware of."

The chancellor cleared his throat. He did not lift his arms in greeting the way Robin had, but neither did Teela; they weren't here to be social.

"Apologies, Chancellor," Starrante said. He turned toward an empty space across from the chancellor, and Arbiter Kavallac joined them, walking from what looked to be a portal. Arbiter Androsse was not far behind. "We have been much absorbed in research."

"All of you?" the chancellor asked, his tone conveying surprise.

"Yes," Kavallac replied. Her eyes were red. Androsse's eyes were indigo. Starrante's—those that were exposed—were also red, but brighter. It was a congregation of emotional fire. Robin didn't bother to check the Hawk's eyes; he imagined they now matched Androsse's. The three elder Arbiters were of one mind, and that couldn't be good, given the circumstances.

"What is happening to my Academia?"

Kavallac chose to answer the question that had been asked of all of them. "You are aware, of course, of the deaths; we will refer to them only within the context of our research. Arbiter Starrante was summoned to an office within Killianas's domain—in theory—in time to view what would otherwise have been called a window. Whoever decided he must be summoned did Killianas a great favor." Kavallac turned to Robin. "We have seen and heard your friend, and we have reached an agreement."

Androsse said nothing, but the air around him chilled.

"It was Raven who found the office that contained the window; it is Raven who is now the binder of those elements of window that would have proved dangerously inimical to Killian. If she is willing to do so—later—we are willing to have her search the library in a similar fashion."

Robin was glad his jaw was attached to his face; it would have hit the floor otherwise. He glanced at Arbiter Androsse; the Arbiter nodded.

"What *is* the glass?" Robin asked. His voice barely wobbled.

Kavallac was the Arbiter who appeared to be taking point in the conversation. "We are, ourselves, uncertain. We initially believed it could be an element of Shadow; that would be best for all concerned."

Anything that made an incursion of Shadow the better option was not good news. "And now?"

"That is the question. Had this occurred only upon the premises of the Academia, it would be different; you have assured us—and we believe you—that it has occurred elsewhere. What is not clear to us is the existence of 'hiding places.' Hidden spaces within Killianas would, again, be grave cause for concern.

"You are aware that Killianas existed in a state of hibernation; you must be aware that this is not a state for which existences such as Killianas were designed. His existence was tenuous at best, anchored by the Towers that protect Elantra—and the rest of our world—from falling to the Shadow at the heart of *Ravellon*. It is why we considered Shadow to be the primary focus of our initial research. Not all Shadow is contained in *Ravellon*. Some escapes. Some has been caged within buildings similar in construction to Killianas.

"And some is not bound by the Towers. Killianas was in no position to defend himself while he slumbered—but the Towers were built entirely as safeguards and defenses against Shadow."

Robin didn't know a lot about Shadow. What he knew was that Killian was in danger, and if Killian was in danger, the Academia could disappear. It was Robin's home. It was only the second home he'd ever had, and he was old enough now that he couldn't just be swept away in the unwanted changes—not without trying to do something to stop them. He turned to Starrante.

"Do you think the deaths—and the glass—are related? Do you think something is trying to affect or injure Killian?"

"The deaths are clearly related to the glass in some fashion; were they not, Raven would not have found glass at the site of at least two deaths. We had assumed—and here, Terrano might be better at explanations—that there were some extradimensional difficulties; that something that exists in a space adjacent to Killianas is attempting to exit that space at Killianas's expense. This would not require communication; it is a type of invasive activity of which we might remain in ignorance.

"Such difficulties have occurred—very, very infrequently—in the past. Understand that reality is built in layers. Killianas occupies all of these layers, within the space constructed around him by the Ancients. But there are life-forms, living beings, that might exist in spaces to which we have little access. They are not like us; the difference between them and Wevaran and humans render racial difference on *this* plane moot.

"If Killianas can be made aware of these beings, he has the best chance of interacting with them in a fashion that might convince them to leave or avoid the area Killianas occupies. I believe young Terrano is doing research in a far cruder fashion on this very subject."

"But we found test questions and answers at one of the murder sites."

"Indeed. And that changes the complexion of the problem a great deal. Henri Alderson was a nervous child; he was afraid—constantly—of failure. Professor Melden accentuated that fear, and I believe it was the lever of *fear* that led, indirectly, to Henri's death."

"You believe someone offered Alderson a way to enter the professor's office to view the test," Teela said.

"Given the test and the location in which Henri was found, we do, and that changes things significantly. It strongly implies that someone—someone who has access to our campus—also has access to whatever it is that is shedding the occasional piece of Raven's glass.

"And now we must turn to Arbiter Starrante, because Arbiter Starrante believes he recognized some element of that glass."

Starrante clicked and coughed before settling into the Barrani most commonly spoken at the Academia. "When I was young, when the world was young and new, and when the Ancients still walked and touched the world—the many worlds—they had created, the *thoughts* of those beings could develop a sentience, a will, a chaotic life of their own. Some of those lives became Ancients in the fullness of time; the Ancients did not live—or die—as we lived and died." He glanced at Robin, and added, "Immortals perish. It was rare for my kind to perish after we left the nest, and imperative that we perish before we did or could. The Barrani kill each other with, in my opinion, wild abandon."

Teela raised a brow but didn't argue—it was pretty hard to argue with accepted, demonstrable fact.

"But the thoughts of an Ancient could become reality. Focused, intentional thoughts changed landscapes, transformed entire races. As I said, we were not Ancients in form or function. But we—who are immortal—were not the first of the lives those Ancients created in their own youth."

This surprised no one present except Robin—but for Robin it was almost like myths and legends had decided to climb off the page of one of Serralyn's many borrowed books. There was an aura of unreality to what was now being said. Starrante spoke of this time as if it were factual history, but it was a history so distant it would have been impossible to differentiate from legend or myth had it not been Starrante speaking.

He turned to Robin. "If I tell you not to think about Professor Larrantin, what is the first thing you do?"

"Imagine Larrantin, of course."

"I can tell you not to speak of him. You will not speak of him. I can tell you to avoid him, and where possible, you will do exactly that. But I cannot control the ebb and flow of your thoughts. No more can most people. What they control are deliberate actions." His eyes brightened, his limbs quivering.

"When I was very young, very new—and full of the brash confidence that youth often inspires—I was taken to view containers composed of the type of glass Raven collects. The containers varied in size, in shape, and in color, but they were housed in frames of metal—the metal that Raven also collects in lesser quantities. The glass was not inert; I was warned not to touch it. I therefore did not. I could *think* about touching it; I could consider the consequences. I would not have survived attempting to disobey my guide." Robin could almost hear the smile in the words, although he couldn't see it.

"I was told they contained the thoughts of the Ancients, those thoughts that had not been given voice, not been given deliberate will. Standing in that museum, I was as close as we could come to those thoughts, for the Ancients were beyond us in all ways."

"But…why did they exist? I mean, why were they bottled and put on display?"

"For safety, I think. For our safety. I was too foolish and young to ask that question, to my lasting regret. Perhaps it was a gesture of respect; perhaps it was because those thoughts *could* persist, and were they allowed to fully form, to take shape, they too would develop sentience from the chaos out of which the Ancients were born."

"And that would be bad?"

"If what has killed our students is related to those ancient repositories?"

Robin understood that if the one question had been smart, the following one had been painfully stupid.

Starrante's voice, as he continued, was gentle. "There are some thoughts, Robin, of which we are not proud. Some anger, some resentment, some envy. We do not wish them to define us, and we struggle to contain our reactions to those feelings. They are harmless unless we act on them.

"I believe—and I have never been certain—that the Ancients chose not to act on some of their thoughts, but those thoughts persisted." He lifted an arm before Robin could speak. "If Raven spoke of sentience, I believe this is what she meant. I cannot be certain, and I hope to be allowed to speak with her soon."

"This is interesting," the Barrani Hawk said, in a tone that bordered on icy. "But it is theoretical and historical nostalgia. My concern, if your guess is correct, is that Alderson entered the professor's office looking for test answers. He could not have entered that room without permission, but he did.

"I think it likely that someone on campus offered him a chance to better his mark, and he took that chance. If that is the case, it strongly implies that among the student body there is at least one student who is not only aware of these…thoughts… but is actively working with them in some fashion."

The chancellor's eyes were scarlet red; his lower eye membranes were lowered, and his eyes seemed to leech color from the rest of the room.

"What we cannot know yet is whether or not this force, whatever it is, requires death in order to grow stronger or further its own ends. There are magicks—forbidden and highly illegal—that used life-force as a source of power. I am not a scholar of this particular type of antiquity; I am simple Barrani Hawk."

The chancellor snorted, exhaling actual smoke.

"Lannagaros," Kavallac said. "She is not entirely incorrect."

"Can you answer her question?"

"It was not a question. As you must know, we do not have answers, but we have been researching what we know of magicks performed that required living sacrifices to attempt to come up with answers or theories that might lead to answers. It is Androsse's opinion—"

"Androsse is fully capable of speaking for himself," Androsse snapped.

"Arbiter?" the chancellor then said, turning to Androsse.

"It is my opinion that the deaths serve at least one purpose. They weaken Killianas. Three students have died in the past week. At this rate of death, the student body will be whittled away, and with it, Killianas's ability to assert and retain control over this space. While it will not affect the library directly, it affects access to the library."

"Do you think they seek the library?"

"I think it likely. It is what the previous attackers desired, and it would not be the first time aggression centered around control of this space. There is a reason there are three Arbiters, and at that, three who were considered exceptionally powerful exemplars of their race."

Teela exhaled slowly. "I will require permission to fully investigate as a Hawk."

"Imperial permission?"

"Yours, Chancellor. The Academia, like the fiefs, is not beholden to Imperial Law, of which I am an agent. With your permission, I will begin investigations of the purely standard kind: I will question the students."

"Which students?" Robin asked, half dreading the answer.

Teela glanced at him. "All of them."

"All of them?"

"Every single one." She turned to the chancellor. "If you have specific rules that do not follow the Imperial paradigm, please make those clear before the end of today." She paused, and then added, "Presuming, of course, that you wish me to investigate. You asked me to come in as a consultant, but did not ask me to take over this part of the investigation, and perhaps I am getting ahead of myself."

"Don't play games," the chancellor rumbled. "If you follow Imperial standards, I will accept—with gratitude—your aid in this endeavor. Will you bring in your partner?"

She shook her head. "I will, however, deputize a student—again with your permission."

"Very well."

The Barrani Hawk turned to Robin. "Congratulations, Deputy Private."

17

Robin stared at the Barrani Hawk, and then turned to the chancellor, opening his mouth. Before words could leave it, the chancellor lifted a hand.

"You are not in class, with Killianas's permission and at Killianas's request. I am certain An'Teela will not be here for more than a few days, and I would prefer that you be deputized over other candidates."

"I would not suggest Terrano, regardless," Teela told the chancellor.

"No, of course not. Robin's appointment, however, will not be seen as political; he is not Barrani, and he is not a human from one of the families of the human caste court. I consider Robin a critically important student," the chancellor continued, his eyes darkening. "And if he is deputized as your partner, he will investigate with the most feared of the Barrani Hawks by his side. I will be exceptionally displeased should harm come to him on your watch."

Teela frowned. "I see."

"But Killian already gave me a job," Robin pointed out.

"Yes. But as you've said, Raven requires some privacy and

recovery; if she didn't, you wouldn't be here at all. While she retreats from contact with other people, you will aid the Barrani Hawk in her inquiries."

Robin exhaled on a nod and turned, defeated, to Teela. "Can I skip the part where you interrogate the professors?"

Teela chuckled.

Raven was, to Robin's relief, still in his room when he finally managed to return to it. So were Terrano and Serralyn, which was less of a relief.

"We heard the news," Serralyn said, looking around Robin to see Teela on the other side of the doorframe.

"And came to offer condolences?"

"No—we came to see what Raven was doing. I think she's ready to keep looking for hiding places."

Raven was seated at Robin's desk, his desk being both her favorite thing in the room and the source of her discontent. While she did have a bed—and a chair—she did not have a desk. Killian's offer to create a desk similar to Robin's had been met with surprising resistance on Raven's part. Robin was curious; he wanted to see the finished desk, but the finished desk wouldn't appear until he and Raven had completed their investigation of hiding places within the Academia.

"She may be ready for searching, but I'm ready for dinner," Robin told the room's occupants. "I'm not sure I can face another dusty storeroom or an office with exploding, sentient windows on an empty stomach."

Raven made a face, muttered something about Robin and food, and went back to what she'd been doing. Which was, to Robin's surprise, looking at the diary that had been locked in the box taken from the storeroom. "Serralyn is reading it," Raven said. "Slowly."

Serralyn nodded. "The language is archaic, but Androsse

had suggestions of where I might start to look if I wanted to attempt to translate it."

"What language is it written in? I mean—it had to be a language that existed when the Academia did."

"That doesn't narrow it down much." Serralyn folded her arms. "The Academia was in this physical location, more or less—but in the before times, portals existed between the Academia and a number of other places. Not all of them were native to our world."

Robin hadn't known that.

"Killian said those portals would never be open again, because they relied on *Ravellon*—on what *Ravellon* was before the fall." At Robin's expression, she said, "You know Shadow, right?"

He nodded.

"Shadow comes from *Ravellon*. It exists in *Ravellon* in its purest form, and the Towers were built—the Towers that almost destroyed the Academia—to prevent that Shadow from leaking out in the rest of the world."

Robin nodded again. He'd inferred that from things Killian had said.

"We thought there might be a chance that something leaked out of those ancient portals to kill students here—or to, you know, leave the diary and emergency supplies."

"In a storeroom?"

Serralyn's voice grew softer. "Starrante said that before the Towers rose, Shadow had begun its transformative destruction. The portals in *Ravellon* were still active, and the worlds to which they led—according to his kin—began to…wink out. Like stars being extinguished. During that period, refugees fled the worlds that were being destroyed or devoured, taking only what they considered essential to their survival.

"I don't include diaries in that," she added. "But the diary was here, not somewhere else; they could be words written by one of the refugees who managed to escape *to* the portals in the Academia. Sorry I wasn't clear.

"The physical structures of the portals don't exist anymore. There's no ancient, empty spaces that used to be active; there's nothing."

"You've looked?"

"Well, it occurred to us that there might be some lingering transformed Shadow that had somehow managed to…leak through those ancient portals. I mean, something is killing us."

"How did this even come up? Weren't you just talking about the diary?" Robin didn't consider himself slow, but trying to follow Serralyn's thoughts gave him the equivalent of mental whiplash.

"When I was trying to figure out which variant of Barrani I should be studying," Serralyn replied. "Most of the written historical stuff is in one era's version of High Barrani or another, but there are some shifts in dialect, depending on the original home of the writer. None of this looked like Barrani to me. I've never studied Androsse's language—I'm not sure it's even spoken anymore. They're called Ancestors, but…it's a misnomer. They look like Barrani from the outside, but I'd be surprised if their blood was red."

"You took the book to the library?"

"Do I look stupid? I transcribed a couple of pages and took those."

Terrano broke out laughing, which earned him a sharp glare. "Sorry," he said, clearly not meaning it. "Didn't mean to interrupt."

"Androsse recognized the language but said it's not, at base, the same grammatical structure as Barrani in any form; it's not his people's tongue, either, but far closer." She hesitated, and then said, "He was clearly interested in what I'd transcribed; he wanted to know where I'd seen a language that is, in his opinion, dead."

"What did you tell him?"

She shrugged. "He doesn't expect honesty." Which wasn't an answer. "But he was helpful in directing me to books that might have more useful grammatical information. So I've been struggling a bit with those. Professor Skornov is a linguist, and I've also enlisted her help. She was practically glowing. No, I'm not taking the diary to her, either—but I'm happy to transcribe as I go, and she's happy to get what I've transcribed."

"She didn't ask you where it came from?"

"I think she's happy to assume it came from a book in the library. There are way, way too many for her to have seen even a tiny fraction of so far, and because the library is so vast, we have to be pretty specific when we ask the Arbiters to find us anything."

"Was there anything interesting in the pages you did take to Androsse?"

"Define *interesting*. To us, no. It was, as it appeared to be, a diary of sorts, and the beginning was what you'd expect. The writer was new to the Academia, and she wanted to capture her first impressions. I'm not sure this is going to be earth-shattering, either. It's a student diary. If it weren't for the location you found it in, I'm not sure anyone would care. Except Skornov, of course."

It wasn't Skornov Robin was worried about; it was Androsse.

Teela, silent until that moment, said, "You've already ascertained that whatever we're facing didn't come from the remnants of the portals?"

"We have," Killian's voice said; he had not materialized in the room. "But I would like Raven and Robin to investigate the room in which those portals once stood. The Ancients did not destroy that room—I, in theory, did. But it was on the eve of my own destruction; the Ancients did not consider those portals a threat while I was active, and as their intended raising of the Towers would destroy me utterly, it was irrelevant."

"You weren't destroyed," Robin said.

"No."

"So it's not entirely irrelevant."

"In theory, no. And when Serralyn says investigations were done, she refers to Terrano. Terrano visited that ancient room."

"It was part of you, right?"

Killian hesitated. After a pronounced beat, he said, "It was part of me in the same way the entrance to the library is. I did not create the portal to the library; I believe I was built around it. I became its anchor."

"And the other portals?"

"I was not meant to anchor them in the same fashion, but what lay beyond the structures I could create were not technically a part of me; they were a blend of my work and the work done on the other side. It was not a small undertaking; all portals were confined to one large room. Come. You will see it for yourself."

"Dinner first?" Robin said, trying not to sound too whiny.

Raven snorted, a clear indication that he'd failed.

To Robin's great relief, they arrived at the very beginning of the early dinner hour, which meant lines were short and professors were absent. That would change soon; the professors rotated dinner shifts at the high table. For the students, dinner wasn't a terribly structured affair; you picked up a plate, you went into the kitchen, you came back, and you ate at your own speed. You'd be in trouble if you started a food fight—which discouraged food fights but didn't entirely prevent them.

Robin had spent too long in the warrens to consider food a hilarious weapon.

The Barrani Hawk didn't join them for dinner; she left Robin with Serralyn, Valliant, and Raven and headed toward the high table as it began to populate. Robin groaned and started to get to his feet, but Serralyn caught his arm and gently pulled him back to his seat. "You didn't want to have to be in the presence of the professors, and she's decided that's smart. They can't do anything to her. Even the most respected of the Barrani scholars here will have some idea of who she is; the new ones will *definitely* know.

"They won't cross her, and if she's a bit harsh, they'll swallow it with pretty smiles. They won't do the same if you happen to be there as a witness, and the Barrani have long memories."

"What about the mortal scholars?" he asked.

"She's not worried about them."

No, of course not.

"But they won't be any happier if she manages to injure their pride, either. And they'll be even less happy to have a mere student witness it." Serralyn grinned; her eyes were mostly green. "She's going to make a full report of everything to the chancellor. Everything. So you won't miss anything important."

Terrano, who joined them on the bench, elbowing a space for himself between Serralyn and Valliant, rolled his eyes, which happened to be blessedly normal. "Even with a full report, he won't miss anything important. You know why I refuse to be a student? Those guys are ninety percent *boring*."

Serralyn frowned. Valliant rolled his eyes.

"Teela's pretty boring when she goes all official, too." He helped himself to a roll from Valliant's plate.

"You visited the portal room?" Robin asked.

"Yeah. It's not really a room," he added. "It's a hall. A big hall. There are railings on a second level, and a gallery—I think there were two floors' worth of portals to and from other places. But there's nothing there now. Empty gallery, empty floor, bare walls. I'd be interested to see what Raven thinks when she sees it."

"I'm glad to see you survived," Robin told him.

Terrano winced. "Sedarias was angry. She's still angry."

"Because Barrani have long memories."

"Something like that. She thinks I'm reckless."

"Because you are," Valliant murmured.

"Not more than I've ever been. I mean—I haven't changed."

"Yes—and she thinks it's a miracle you've survived. But it's Sedarias. She doesn't trust miracles."

"If it weren't for us, she wouldn't trust *anything*. Are you going to eat that? What, don't look at me like that—I'm technically not a student and the cook on duty realizes that and shoos me out. You can just go back for more."

Robin listened to them bicker. He had no siblings, now. He'd had a sibling once, he was certain of that—but she was gone. Raven smacked the back of his head. Hard. He turned to her. "What was that for?"

"Bad thoughts. Eat. Now."

He started to eat. She was right. There were places he shouldn't go. Things he shouldn't touch or poke. She'd never left him alone when he sank into the despair of loss and abandonment. He glanced at the Barrani cohort. Valliant was focused entirely on his food, which he ate deliberately and slowly, leaving Serralyn and Terrano to squabble.

But Terrano and Serralyn weren't squabbling. They had both frozen for one arrested moment. Valliant glanced at them, his lips compressing. He cast one glance at the food on his plate, then rose as they rose.

Robin started to rise, as well, but Raven caught his sleeve. Her eyes were wide now, and she raised a hand to his shoulder, pressing down on it in silence. He knew the gesture. He understood the expression. She wanted to flee.

She wanted to hide, and she wanted to take Robin with her.

He knew the Barrani Hawk had gone to talk with the high table, but noted that she was nowhere in sight; the professors had taken their seats. Two were missing. He frowned, trying to remember which of the two she might be talking to, but Professor Perella was frequently late when she was on early lunch duty; she was the first-year coordinator, a den mother of sorts to the kids like Robin who had no other families and no real familiarity with a place like the Academia.

Who did that leave?

Raven's grip tightened as the two and a half Barrani students headed away from the table. He couldn't see the Barrani Hawk, but he knew they knew where she was. Terrano winked out, and Robin rose instantly.

Raven didn't speak. Robin turned to her; her face was pale, her eyes wide; her lips were compressed as if to stop any sound from escaping. He had always followed her when she found him and caught him by the hand or arm; he had never asked her why. The why had always been obvious.

But they weren't in the warrens now. They weren't alone. They weren't young children, newly orphaned, without family. They were—or would be—students in the Academia. The chancellor was not a member of a terrifying gang. He was a *Dragon*. Robin had friends. They were Barrani, yes, but he trusted them. He reached for Raven's hand.

"Come with me," he said.

She looked at him. "We need to *hide*. We need to hide *you*."

He could see Serralyn speeding up, Valliant just behind; he'd lose them if he didn't follow. They were Barrani. Teela was Barrani.

But the first two murder victims had also been Barrani.

"Can we hide them?" he asked, watching them go.

Her hand tightened on his. He trusted her, had always trusted her, and always would.

"I have to go with them," he said, voice low.

"Why?"

"You don't have to come. They're not your friends. Go. Hide—I promise I'll find you when this is done."

Raven's hand tightened again; his fingers were almost numb now. But she didn't attempt to pull him away, and she didn't attempt to release him. He thought she would argue, and he felt a spasm of pure guilt.

"Robin. Let's go."

He nodded then. "Killian!"

Killian failed to answer. Just as he'd failed to answer on the night Raven had retrieved Robin from the baths and dragged him through the Academia halls to a safe place.

"Raven, can you go to the chancellor's office and tell the chancellor that there's trouble?"

"No."

He exhaled. "Okay. We're going to have to run—toward them. We don't want to lose them."

She nodded. Robin had made the decision, but Raven had always been faster on her feet. He was still surprised when she began to run, dragging him in her wake.

Raven didn't want to run *toward*. She wanted to run away. But she understood toward. She had run toward, before. She had had to find Robin, after all. Once she'd found him, though, she had always run away. She'd always run to safety. Robin had followed.

He'd been small. He'd been clumsy.

She knew he thought of *her* as clumsy. As awkward. But she knew that he trusted her. That he accepted her. That he had never asked anything of her. The first time, she'd expected he would. He was terrified. He was alone. The streets would kill him because he couldn't see them clearly; he saw them the way people saw them. She could taste his fear then.

She could taste it now.

It was a different fear. It was layered with many, many things. When she'd first met him, the fear had been pure; now it was messy, complicated. She should have let go of his hand. It wasn't safe now. It wasn't safe if they weren't hidden.

She could no longer see Terrano. He had run ahead of the

other two, and he'd run *quickly*. She didn't know where he'd
gone. She knew only that he was running away from safety.
He was running away from any place in which they could find
shelter until the danger had passed.

And she knew that Robin wanted to follow him. She didn't
speak; speaking was hard. If she had, she'd have told him that
she'd be safe. She was Raven. It was Robin who'd be in danger.
It was hard to find places that Robin could fit into with her. It
was much, much simpler—much faster—to hide on her own.

But Robin wanted this. Robin wanted to follow.

Robin wanted other people to be safe. Raven had never worried about other people. Only Robin. She could barely find
room for Robin in the warrens. She could barely find room
for him here. Smaller spaces wouldn't fit him. She didn't think
she could find places that would fit all of the people. Maybe
Terrano. Terrano could fit anywhere. But she didn't think that
was true of the others.

Or of Robin.

He wanted to go *to* danger. She exhaled. She exhaled all the
old wishes, the old fears, the old duties. Maybe it was time.
Maybe Robin could find his own spaces, his own safety.

Maybe Robin didn't need Raven anymore.

Wouldn't be the first time. It had happened before. Before
and before. She had found people who needed her. She had left
when they stopped, when she could no longer hear the cry of
their heart—someone had described it that way. She'd thought
it odd; she knew what hearts were. Had seen them pierced, had
seen them exposed—followed swiftly by death.

But the thought persisted long after the words had faded.

She had never needed anyone. She had never needed friends.
People did, or so she was told. Robin called her friend, and
Robin needed her—but it was different for Raven. Raven found
Robin when Robin needed to hide. Raven didn't need to hide,

not that way. She was used to being unseen—it was like being invisible.

Robin was no good at it. She'd taught him, and he'd learned—but she knew it was almost pointless because Robin *wanted* to be seen. Robin, whose hands were outstretched whenever he thought it was safe. She'd tried to tell him safety wasn't *real*. But he'd said it could be once, when the hiding place was too small and they were huddled together as if they were almost one person.

Maybe not forever. But the hiding place was real. Robin and Raven were in it. While they were in it, they were safe.

Robin had been a bit stupid when he was young. There were so many things he hadn't known. So many. She'd taught him what she could.

But Robin thought it was Raven who was stupid. And Robin taught her things, too. The reading. The name. The having of a name. As if Raven were a person, like Robin. Robin was the only one who liked her glass. Robin was the only one who was happy when she found pieces, when she showed them to him. He didn't understand it was her work—he didn't understand why she loved them.

But he understood that she did.

She liked to show him things. Sometimes, as he grew older, she would find him just to show him things—not because he needed to hide. Not because it wasn't safe.

Why had she come to this place? This place wasn't Raven's. It wasn't the warrens. It wasn't part of the city she knew; it wasn't part of the lost city. Robin didn't need her here. She hadn't heard him. If she couldn't, he was safe—he was safe from the things that Raven knew how to hide him from.

But she had wanted to see Robin. Not to hide him, but to… share. To show him what she'd found. To be seen.

Did Raven need Robin?

★ ★ ★

Raven could run without pause for longer than Robin had ever been able to run. She'd been impatient but not unkind; when he was younger, and his legs shorter, she would half drag him—as she was dragging him now—as if the pull of her hand could make up for the weakness of legs and lungs. He had longer legs now, but less reason to run; he caught up with Serralyn and Valliant before they'd made it out of the great hall that led to the dining room.

Raven, however, kept running; she practically dragged Robin through the small gap between the two Barrani. Robin tried to slow, but Raven was having none of it.

"Raven—where are you going?"

"Terrano."

She pulled past Serralyn and Valliant, while Robin murmured hurried apologies; she didn't lose them, though. The moment she spoke Terrano's name, they sped up to match her pace.

"Terrano what?" Serralyn demanded, far less winded than Robin was.

"She's following Terrano."

"She can see him?"

"You can't?"

"No, we can't."

"He's going to Teela, right? Raven is following him. But he's moving pretty quickly."

"No talking," Raven snapped. "Breathe."

When Raven slowed—when she was willing to slow—they were still within the main building. Teela was interviewing professors—or that was the theory—so she shouldn't have been far from the dining hall. This was pretty far. Teela had been in the dining hall. She left it. But the professors she was seeking should have been close by. Professor Perella. Robin grimaced; he couldn't remember who the other teacher was supposed to be. Professor Perella always took the early dinner; the chancellor always took the late one. The rest of the professors rotated positions, although some—like Larrantin—would often skip meals entirely. He was brilliant and disliked crowds. Or people in general.

But he also lost track of time; a student minder often had to stop by his office or the study hall to make certain he was on time for the classes he was meant to teach. On good days, the classes were interesting; on bad days people barely breathed, he was so irritable.

Was she interviewing Larrantin?

But no—every Barrani student, and every Barrani scholar who had sought a place in the Academia after the announcement of its reestablishment, revered Larrantin. He stood outside of the power structure, the political structure, that defined their external lives. Larrantin had gone down with the Academia on its final day; Larrantin had returned with its resurrection.

Then who? Who?

The Barrani Hawk wasn't in the hall. Terrano, however, was. Robin couldn't see him, but Raven could.

"Serralyn?"

She nodded, grimacing. "I can't see him with my own eyes unless I reconfigure them."

"Don't bother," Valliant said. "Terrano's here. Teela was here, as well."

"Where?"

"Where Terrano is standing."

Nothing was there, in Robin's view—not even Terrano. He took a step forward and Raven yanked him back, shaking her head.

"How do you know Teela was here?" Robin asked.

"We saw her." Serralyn exhaled. "She's part of us. She's part of the cohort. But we lost her for a long time, and we don't want that to happen again."

"So...you can see what she sees?"

Serralyn nodded. "It takes more effort, with Teela. We've done it for centuries; she's only had a few months to get used to it. And she can shut us out far more effectively than we can shut each other out. She wants privacy. We grew up without any."

"You know she's still alive?"

"For now. She's somewhere else. Terrano's trying to find where. In her eyes, she's standing in the hall we're standing in now. But the hall is almost empty."

The air grew colder. "What do you mean, empty?"

"It's the same hall but there are no other people in it. No students. No us." Serralyn exhaled. "She thinks she's speaking to a...student? Teacher? He's a bit fuzzy. I can't tell. But she can hear us. We can reach her. So she knows something's up."

Raven said, "Glass. Tell her."

Serralyn nodded, caught in Raven's orbit just as Robin had always been. "Terrano's trying to figure out how to get to where Teela is. But he says—" She stopped speaking as Raven's eyes widened. "Get back!"

Raven was already yanking Robin back up the hall, not to hide, but to reach an alcove in which a large painting had been hung. Serralyn and Valliant followed, moving far more swiftly—and gracefully—than Robin would have moved on his own.

The floor they'd been standing on seconds ago suddenly let out a brilliant green glow, a flare of warning light; the stone from which it emanated cracked and shattered, shards flying in all directions. To Robin's surprise, Valliant lifted his arms in a broad, circular sweep, stopping at the top of the motion, hands clasped. Robin could see a pale, shimmering wall of light envelop the alcove.

"I can't hold it long," Valliant said through gritted teeth.

Robin stared at the Barrani student. This—this was *magic*. Real magic, not theoretical magic, not historical magic, not the webbing that was a physical and natural part of a Wevaran, or the fiery breath that was natural to Dragons. This took study, will, effort.

Robin had never been tested for magical ability. In theory, that would happen in two or three months. He wasn't looking forward to it; he was certain he would fail. He would have no talent, no natural ability. He would disappoint the chancellor.

But Valliant clearly had no need to subject himself to that scrutiny.

"Edges," Serralyn said, in theory to Valliant. She meant for Robin—or Raven—to hear the words.

Raven nodded and pulled Robin firmly behind the center of Valliant's wall. "Should I get Terrano?" she asked.

Valliant almost lost the wall as he turned to stare at Raven.

Serralyn was more measured. "Can you?" she asked, curiosity in the question, not disbelief.

"Maybe. Should he be here?"

"Yes. He can't reach Teela."

"I can't reach Teela," she replied, as if Serralyn had asked. "Tell Teela—"

"Don't let shards get in her eyes. But, Raven—she doesn't see glass."

"Small glass. Bottle. *Something.*"

"We'll make sure—go get the idiot."

"Can't you just call him?" Robin asked, uneasy.

"He's stuck."

18

"He's stuck," Raven repeated, with far more disgust in her tone—as if Terrano should have known better. But she let go of Robin's hand. She looked back as she left him, and then transferred her gaze to Serralyn. She didn't speak, but her expression made clear—embarrassingly clear—that she was leaving Robin in Serralyn's hands, and that Robin was both precious and delicate.

He reddened. He wasn't a child, but any argument to the contrary would make him look even more immature in front of his new friends; he bit back words, swallowing them with effort.

Raven left whatever protections Valliant had erected. She'd always been fast when she left; sometimes he could catch a glimpse of her back, but often she was immediately lost in the crowd—and given Raven's appearance, that should have been harder than it was.

But as he watched her back now, no crowd in sight, he understood. She wasn't lost in the crowd. She just wasn't *there* anymore.

"Did you know what she was when you met her?" Serralyn asked, voice soft.

Robin shook his head, feeling disloyal. She was Raven. He'd

known she was Raven. "I was a kid. I was maybe seven." But he didn't want to talk about that now. Or, if he was honest, ever. "Can Terrano see her now?"

"No."

"Can he see *anything*?"

"He's trying very, very hard not to be seen."

Robin lowered his voice. "By what?"

"That would be the question, wouldn't it? Don't move beyond the border of the barrier."

"But if whatever it is can't be seen—"

"I didn't say it couldn't be seen. Terrano can see something; he's trying not to *be* seen. Valliant's shield is partly based on Terrano's observations. Valliant is good at defense. I'm not."

"You're better at attacking?"

"Surprising, isn't it?" Serralyn smiled her usual smile, but her eyes were a very dark blue. "But I'm not nearly as competent as Sedarias, and Sedarias isn't as good as Teela. Who is here. Somewhere. Don't worry about Teela for now."

"Can I worry about Terrano?"

"It won't do you any good, but it's pretty hard not to, he's so reckless." She startled. Valliant, head bent, did not. "I think Raven has found Terrano. He still can't see her, but—he knows she's looking."

"Is he at least in a form that *has* eyes?"

"He looks mostly like himself. His eyes are probably dreadful, but Raven's seen them before. He doesn't know what he's trapped in. He tends to insert himself into places he was never meant to stand. Wherever it is he managed to wedge himself into, it appears to be a collapsing space. This wouldn't usually be a problem—but apparently entry was one-way."

"But why did he even *go* there?"

"Because he was trying to reach Teela. The space around her looks—to Teela—like this hall. It's *not* this hall, unless we've run off track. But Killian's not answering."

Robin nodded. "Raven wanted to hide—the last time she wanted to hide, Killian couldn't hear me, either." He paused. "Who did Teela think she was talking to?"

"Professor Laksone. New professor, first-year magical studies. He's well-known in the High Court."

"You don't think it's Laksone."

"I really don't." She cursed.

"What happened?"

Terrano stumbled into view. His cheek was bleeding. Serralyn reached out, grabbed him, and yanked him off his feet.

Robin looked for Raven.

Raven hadn't followed.

Terrano was a pasty, terrible white—tinged green, except for the cut itself, which was too bright. His eyes were black, lacking whites or any other color, but they were at least the right shape.

"Something's wrong," Serralyn told him. Fair; it was hard to tell with Terrano, who had previously turned himself into— as far as Robin could tell—a large magical *sheet*. He had long since given up on worrying about Terrano's physical condition.

Robin helped Serralyn guide her friend to where Valliant stood, palms facing outward, arms spread and trembling as if he was pushing back against a great weight. Terrano's eyes continued to be black; his sockets seemed almost empty.

"Was there any glass where he was?" Robin asked, brusque, the words almost a demand. He had knelt to the right of Terrano; Serralyn occupied the left. Down the hall he could see movement.

Sedarias had come in search of her friends.

She didn't have to be told. She knew what Terrano knew. Probably knew what Teela knew; the Barrani Hawk remained absent. So did Raven.

It was Raven he was worried about. She'd gone to fetch

Terrano from wherever it was he'd been trapped, and Terrano had returned. Raven hadn't. He and Raven weren't like these Barrani friends; he couldn't hear her thoughts. He could guess at some of them, he'd known her for so long—but he required her actual presence to do it.

Her brief stay at the Academia had made clear to Robin just how little he knew about her, how little he understood. She had been his friend—his only friend—for over half his life. It had never occurred to him to wonder what she was. Who she was. Why she could do what she could do.

In Robin's childish mind, she had been like him. Lost and orphaned and desperately scraping whatever living she could from streets that didn't care about their survival. Because they were the same, he'd never asked her about her life before they'd met. She'd never asked about his. What had mattered, in the time they spent together, was the present, the now. The hiding. The sharing the small scraps of food they could scrounge; the finding of clothing—that was mostly Raven.

He wondered if she'd taken clothing from bodies. Assumed she had. It didn't bother him; someone would strip the bodies. Might as well be Raven. The dead didn't need clothing. The living did, if they didn't want to join the dead in the winter.

But he hadn't asked. He'd assumed she was *like him*. They were orphans together. Desperate together.

Waiting, breath half held, he accepted that this wasn't entirely true.

She'd said she found him because she heard him. Because he sounded like her. He closed his eyes, his hands balled in fists tightly enough his nails hurt his palms. Raven didn't lie. Had never lied. Maybe she'd never needed Robin. Maybe Robin had been the one to need.

And maybe what he needed had never been just about survival.

Serralyn caught him by the shoulder as he rose. "Don't. Raven's not a fool. Things are really, really sketchy here. Terrano survives almost anything, and he's been injured."

"And I'm not Terrano."

"Thank god," Sedarias snapped. "Whatever god you happen to worship." Her eyes were indigo, her skin flushed with what Robin assumed was fury. "Come to the Academia. The Academia is *safe*." She elbowed Serralyn aside, which was easy because Serralyn had grabbed Robin.

"What do you think you're doing?" she demanded. Her grip was Barrani in strength; Robin thought it might fracture his collarbone.

"Finding Raven," he snapped back.

Her grip loosened. "How?"

Robin shook his head. He wasn't about to explain it to Serralyn—although he liked and trusted her. It was his history, his private history. His and Raven's. It was a cowardly, desperate history—but Robin had done nothing in it that shamed him. He'd done his best—his very best—to obey the last words of his mother.

Live, Robin. Survive.

He had never known when Raven would come, when she would swoop in, grab his hand, and drag him away. He had always trusted that when she did, it was for a reason, and he'd never questioned it. Never questioned how she knew to find him. In the early years, life had been so desperate, anytime they met was an emergency; any hiding was necessary.

As he'd learned the warrens, as he'd run across Giselle, as he'd been given little guide missions and courier runs, she'd come less often. Robin had never felt *safe*, exactly, but safer.

If Raven didn't need him, if Raven could survive without him, it meant she was looking for him, looking out for him. When he was in danger, she would come.

"I have to leave the barrier," he told Serralyn. The hall was empty. Empty of Killian, the driving force that kept the Academia and its students safe. Raven had wanted to hide. Robin had wanted to help. To help Terrano and Serralyn and Teela. Objectively, this was stupid, and he accepted that. They were *Barrani*. He was mortal, and at that, not even fully adult.

Raven had come with him anyway.

Raven had let him choose.

Raven had gone to Terrano's rescue—and only Terrano had come back.

He couldn't shake the certainty that Raven was trapped where Terrano had been trapped, that she was stuck there. He knew he couldn't go to where she was. But he believed that she could come to where he was—if he was desperate enough.

If he was in a danger that Raven recognized.

"It's not safe to leave—not yet."

"That's why I have to leave it now." He smiled at Serralyn; her hand trembled before she withdrew it. He'd always liked her, and he believed she liked him. It wasn't that he hadn't been in danger in the Academia before. But Raven hadn't been here then.

Raven was close now.

Robin inhaled, squared his shoulders, and walked out from behind Valliant into the empty hall.

He noticed one difference immediately: the hall was cold. His breath, when he exhaled, came out in a winter cloud; when he inhaled, he could feel his nostrils freeze. He couldn't see a danger here. There was no glass, no odd windows. "Serralyn, is Teela still in this hall?"

"Yes. But she's pulled back a bit. Not a lot. She's using one of Terrano's tricks—she's standing with one foot in a slightly different plane."

"So is the person she's speaking with?"

"Yes. For what it's worth, he's talking about scholarship in the Academia, and the attitudes of most of the students here. Poor," she added, in case that was in doubt. "But his words echo in a strange way; they're a bit tinny, a bit discordant. Teela's asking questions as if she hasn't noticed."

"Raven said something about glass."

"Teela knows. There is no obvious glass. Where are you going?"

"To where Teela is," Robin replied. "Because I think that's where the danger is strongest."

"No wonder Terrano liked you on sight," Serralyn said, her voice at his back. She hadn't left Valliant's shield.

It was stupid, but Robin felt a brief, sharp happiness at her words. "Tell me," he said, voice soft, "when I'm standing in the same place as Teela in the other hall."

Serralyn didn't answer, but it wasn't necessary; Robin was uncomfortably certain he would know. The air dropped in temperature as he walked toward where he thought she must be standing; he followed the cold, and as he did, the stones beneath his feet whitened, as if they were ice. They weren't—not to his eyes—but he'd spent winters on the streets in the warrens, and the soles of his feet knew bitter cold when he walked across it. Through it.

He looked ahead; the far end of the long hall contained milling students, but few in number—the last of the classes had yet to be finished in time to eject students for late dinner.

None of the students looked at Robin, although some looked in his direction.

The cold grew; he started to shudder, his body responding to the emergency of being in the dead of winter without a coat, gloves—some insulation against the worst of chill. He made no attempt to speak—speaking would be interrupted by the same shudder. Once, while trying to speak to Raven, he'd bit his own lip.

She had looked predictably disgusted, her expression the *what are you even doing* one he disliked so much. No one liked being seen as stupid. But he had stopped trying to talk, and she had held his hand, sliding an arm around his shoulder and huddling against him to preserve the warmth of their small bodies.

He closed his eyes, remembering. She had come in the first winter—she'd come often. She brought food in small quantities, and he'd tried to refuse it, they were both so hungry. But she shook her head, pushing stale bread and cheese into his hands. She found hiding places for them—hiding places against the winter cold.

He would not have survived without her.

This was risky; he knew it. But he had faced death before in these halls, without Raven to shelter or hide him. He accepted now what he had not quite understood as a child: Raven came to him when his life was in danger. She stayed until it was not.

If she was lost where Terrano had been somehow lost, Robin intended to be the beacon that would guide her home. Because death walked these halls; he was now certain of it. Not a death as clear as power-mad Barrani or the high caste humans that comprised the mortal caste court. Something other. Something different. Something that Raven could, nonetheless, sense and hide from.

He had always assumed Raven and he shared a fate and a situation in common: orphans, alone, in the warrens. Not until she had arrived in the Academia had he questioned that, but the questions had led to one conclusion: she wasn't human. They weren't the same.

That didn't mean she wasn't an orphan. It didn't mean she wasn't dirt-poor. And it didn't mean that she wasn't his friend.

What were friends, anyway? Weren't they people you could trust? People who had your back? People who would offer a hand if you fell and help you get on your feet? Weren't they people you would also offer a hand to when they were in need?

It didn't matter that she wasn't human. What mattered was that she was his friend, his first friend. He lifted his left arm, opening his hand. "Raven!"

His entire arm shuddered with cold; he felt it in his nostrils, his throat; his lips chapped instantly, as they did in the winter. Had he known, he would have brought a coat. But he'd had no coat the first time, either. He'd had no time to grab it, just time to run, the chill air freezing his chest, his face, his exposed hands.

He looked at the empty hall and saw a flicker of color, of motion, just inches from where he stood. Raven?

No. No—not Raven. It was a Barrani form, blinking in and out. Hair as dark as Raven's—as most Barrani hair was—but longer, shinier, far less tangled with dirt and dust. Robin almost lowered his hand as Teela continued to flicker in and out of his vision. He'd come for Raven.

But as he stepped forward, he bumped into the Barrani Hawk, before passing through her as she once again vanished. She was, in the seconds he could see her before she vanished, physically present.

The next time he reached out, it wasn't for Raven's hand; he reached for the Hawk's arm, hoping she wouldn't break his hand instinctively. His hand passed through her as he missed the timing. He had never tried to touch Serralyn or Valliant— no one sane approached Barrani in the warrens, and old habits died hard.

But Teela was a Hawk. She was used to people of all different races. Used to threat assessment. He was *almost* certain it would be safe to grab her arm the next time she came into view. If he could control the shuddering enough. He didn't try to speak, didn't try to call the Barrani Hawk's name.

Didn't try to call Raven's name, either, forgetting for a moment why he'd entered the hall proper in the first place.

He managed to grab Teela's arm the third time he tried; her arm was solid and warm beneath his palm. He pulled back, holding her with both hands to gain enough purchase to give him a chance of pulling her out of wherever it was she'd been standing.

He threw the whole of his weight backward. Had the Barrani Hawk been braced against it, it would have amounted to nothing; she wasn't. She threw her weight in the same direction, and she weighed significantly more than Robin did; he staggered back as she appeared, fully, in the hall. It was Robin who tripped over his own feet and landed on his butt.

Teela was here. She turned instantly toward Valliant, cursed under her breath, and gestured. Her skin wasn't pale; it was red, as if with cold. Robin's would be the same. "Do not move from here," the Barrani Hawk snapped. "Stay as close to me as possible."

Robin nodded, but he turned once again; turned to look for Raven, who hadn't appeared. He'd been distracted, he could admit that—but Teela had also possibly been in trouble. She was still alive—unlike Barrios, Lykallos, and Alderson—but she was a lord of the High Court. She had been trained in actual battle. If something was going to take her down, it had to be far more powerful than she was.

Or more clever.

He couldn't see the source of the bitter cold.

He couldn't see Raven. But the cold was now like sharp pins against his exposed skin: his face, his hands. Even beneath the folds of his shirt, he could feel the pinprick pain, as if a brush of sharp, hard needles were being rubbed against his skin.

He bit back a cry; the needles were *hot*. Hot against his exposed skin, and worse against skin that was theoretically covered.

Teela cursed. She looked down at Robin's face. Robin lifted

his arms to pull out whatever was lodged there; his fingers touched nothing.

Warmth spread. Pain receded. He felt his arms begin to go limp. He could hear the Barrani Hawk—her voice low, even, the words no words he understood. There was an intensity to them he would have found terrifying in different circumstances. He did not feel terror now. Warmth passed, as cold had; he felt numb.

Numb, but without fear, without worry.

And then, of all things, he felt a hand grab his hand; he heard a familiar voice shouting in his ear. Not a happy voice. Raven was *furious*.

The lack of pain vanished as she slapped him, left cheek, then right. She then grabbed his shoulders and shook him with force before lowering her hand to hold his. She glanced back at Teela, at Valliant, and snorted.

"This was *stupid*!" she shouted, and dragged him down the hall, stomping rather than running.

To Robin's surprise, she dragged him back to their shared room. "No hiding?" he managed to croak.

"No point," she snapped. Her eyes were narrowed. She released his hand only once they'd crossed the threshold.

"What about the others?"

"Safe." She looked like she wanted to spit. For good reason, sadly. "*Safe*."

"I said it was safe here because it was!"

She gave him the look reserved for severe stupidity and folded her arms. "What were you thinking?"

Robin exhaled. "I was thinking that you went after Terrano and you didn't come back. Terrano was trapped. I thought you might have pushed him out of wherever he was stuck and then got stuck yourself."

"So you tried *to die*?" she shrieked, her voice rising so sharply she sounded like an angry bird. Like her namesake. It didn't get better when Robin burst out laughing. She shrieked in wordless rage, which made it harder to stop laughing.

Raven, however, couldn't hold on to a grudge. Or a fear. Or, in fact, most emotions—it was, in her words, too much work. Robin only had to wait her out.

It took much longer than usual, but the rage slowly banked until it exposed the worry at its heart. So familiar, that worry. Painfully familiar. He could remember—

She reached out and smacked the back of his head. "Bad thoughts. No. *No*." She hit him again. When she was very worried, she reverted to old speech patterns.

"I'm sorry," he said. "I couldn't think of anything else to do. I couldn't see you. I'm not like the Barrani—I couldn't see what you saw. I didn't know where you were."

"And her?"

He blinked.

"Her! The Hawk!"

"Oh."

"What were you thinking? You could have died!"

"Ummm, I was thinking that if I grabbed her arm and it was solid, I could maybe get her out of wherever she was trapped. You saved Terrano," he added.

"I'm *me*! You're *Robin*!" She whacked him again for good measure. It had never really hurt, and in the early days, it was the only touch she offered. "I'm mad!"

"I'm really sorry," Robin said, meaning it. "I didn't mean to make you worry."

"You did!"

He hesitated. "All right, I did. But you always come for me when I'm in danger, and I was afraid you were trapped somewhere else."

She snorted. Snorted, but made a face and sat down, heavily, on the floor. "I was."

"You were?"

"Trapped." She glared at him.

"I didn't know it would work," he explained. "I just…"

"Just what?" Definitely suspicious now.

"I thought it might. Because you come when I'm in danger. You always know."

"You were in danger before I got here."

"Wait, how did you know that?"

"Terrano. And I didn't know then. I *didn't*. So don't do anything stupid like this *ever again*." She bent her knees to her chin, folded her arms around them, and hid her face.

It took Robin another minute to realize Raven was crying.

If he'd had anything in his hands, he'd've dropped it. As it was, he flapped around like a flightless bird. He had no idea what he should be doing. Robin hated to be seen crying. He'd never wanted anyone to see it. Raven, though, had never particularly cared about being seen—unless they were hiding.

She had never cared what other people thought or said; she hadn't seen how it was supposed to be relevant to her.

Still, he knelt. When she failed to move her arms, he leaned into her. "I'm really, really sorry. I didn't think about how much you'd worry—I just thought that you might be able to find me. I thought, if you were stuck, you'd be able to escape."

"How does that make any sense?" she demanded, although the words were muffled because she hadn't raised her head. "You almost died. You were so close."

"Do you want to see how everyone else is doing?"

"Don't care."

"But you like Serralyn and Terrano."

"They're fine." She lifted her head. "They're each other's problem, not mine."

"And you're my problem, not theirs."

"I'm not your problem. You're *my* problem. It's *me* who comes when you're in danger, not the other way around!"

"Until today."

She dropped her head again.

"Raven—I'm grateful that you found me. Every single time. I wouldn't have survived without you."

"I know that."

"But I'm not a kid anymore."

"Are, too."

"I'm not. Not a little kid, anyway." He hesitated, and then reached out and wrapped one arm around Raven's shoulders. "I'm taller than you now. I'm only going to get taller from now on. I can't just stay a little kid forever. I can't always depend on you to get me through life. I can't take your help and offer nothing in return."

"Why not?" She raised her head again, but this time she was genuinely curious.

"Because that—that's not friendship. I can't just take without giving anything."

"I'm not a merchant," Raven replied. "It's not like you're stealing."

"I didn't say I was stealing from you! But…it's like that. It's like the one merchant who would sometimes give us old food from his stall without charging us. We needed it, and we took it—but we never gave him anything back. Even a little."

"We didn't have anything, and he didn't care. He gave. We accepted."

"But we can't just do that forever."

"Why not?"

"Because we're not little kids anymore. Because we're not helpless. I'm not helpless."

"You are," she snorted. "If you weren't, you wouldn't almost have died." Her expression instantly turned. "You could have died."

"I told you—"

"No one else ever cared. No one thought they were stealing

from me just because I helped them." She paused, and then said, "No one liked my glass, Robin. No one but you."

"Wait. What do you mean no one else cared?"

She ignored the question, but she stared at him, her brows slightly raised. "I promised to watch you until you were older. Until you could fight. Can you fight?"

"Raven—promised *who*?"

"But you can't fight yet. You can't. You *almost died*." She frowned. "That's how people like you die, you know. They think they're helping. They think it's okay to die so that other people can live. I'm not like you," she added. "I don't need it."

"Raven, please. Who did you promise? Who asked this of you?"

She shook her head. "I won't die," she whispered. "I *won't* die. Don't do that again."

He exhaled. "I'll try."

"No. Promise." She held up one hand, pinky crooked. "You have to promise."

He grimaced and held up his pinky. "It's not like I wanted to die," he murmured. "I trusted you to save me."

"While I was *trapped*? Why?"

"I don't know. I just—I thought you could come to me no matter where you were."

"But I *didn't*. Terrano said you almost died in the Academia before I came. I didn't know."

"I think you couldn't hear me because you weren't trapped where I was," Robin replied, thinking about it seriously. "Where did you think I'd gone?"

Raven shrugged. "Maybe where you belong? Home?"

"This is my home," Robin replied.

But Raven shook her head. "No. Not this. One day, Robin. One day you'll go home. Then you'll understand."

"This is the home I want."

Raven nodded, anger forgotten. "It's the home you want

now." She slowly unfolded her knees. "I like it here. And I don't like it here. It's hard to feel both things at the same time."

"Is it? I like it here. I like food. And warmth. Shelter. Lessons where I actually learn something. Clothing that fits. But I don't like some of the professors, and I really don't like some of the students. I don't like the fact that something is killing people. Would I have looked the way the three dead students looked by the end?"

"You'd look like Robin," she replied, shrugging. "Just dead."

He almost laughed. She was hard to understand, but if you let her be herself, it was fine. "I mean: Would my body look the same as the other three?"

"I only saw two."

"Okay, would it be like those two? There was no cause of death. Nothing that appeared to have killed them. There didn't seem to be any obvious cause of death—but they were definitely dead."

"Oh. You'd definitely be dead."

"Well, yes. What I mean is: Would it be the same death?" She nodded.

"So whatever almost killed me killed the others?"

"Yes."

"Well," Terrano said, his voice far clearer than the rest of him. "That's a good starting point."

19

Raven snorted in what Robin assumed was Terrano's direction. She had none of Robin's questions, but he realized, as she glared at Terrano—or at least glared to the left of Robin—that she considered the Barrani youth enough of a friend that she could be disgusted with his stupidity. "Idiot."

Terrano wasn't afraid of Raven, and he materialized pretty much where she'd been glaring.

Before Raven could elaborate on Terrano's intelligence—and her expression clearly said she wasn't finished yet—Robin turned to the Barrani youth. "Where is everyone else?"

"Teela's headed off to the chancellor's, with Sedarias on her heels. Serralyn and Valliant are with her."

"Did Killian come back?"

"I was not absent," the Avatar replied. He remained voice only.

"You were," Raven said, giving up on Terrano's intelligence.

"I cannot disagree with the assessment; I did not experience it as you did. Or as Robin did. Had I, I might have told Terrano that what he attempted was extremely unsafe and therefore unwise. You are Terrano," he continued, his voice becoming far more serious. "But who you are is not separate in its entirety from what you are. Do not lose yourself in your attempt to extend your abilities."

Terrano rolled his eyes; clearly he'd heard this many times before.

"Should we meet them in the chancellor's office?" Robin asked Killian.

"Not if you don't like fire," Terrano answered before Killian could. He winced. "Angry Dragon. Angry Barrani—Sedarias, in case you were wondering—and worried Hawk. I think, unless the chancellor sends for you, it's safer anywhere else."

"Not anywhere else."

"Anywhere—we're not dead, are we?" Terrano sauntered over to Raven's bed and sat heavily. Raven, as usual, was tucked against the wall on the floor. She didn't hate the idea of having a bed to call her own; she just didn't see the point in using it. He winced. "Maybe I should head there, though."

"Why?" Raven asked before Robin could.

"Sedarias was *worried*. She needs someone to scream at, and at the moment, that's the chancellor. There's too much racial tension going on there."

"Why?" Raven asked again.

"Sedarias is Barrani. The chancellor is a Dragon."

"So?"

Terrano winced again, but accepted Raven's apparent ignorance. "There were three wars, loosely called the Draco-Barrani wars in the Academia." Or anywhere else. "Dragons, like Barrani, are immortal. We remember everything."

This clearly made no more sense to Raven. Robin lifted a hand in Raven's direction; she understood what it meant. He'd often done similar when they were attempting to talk to people in the warrens. People like Giselle.

"What happened to Teela?"

"Teela initially thought she was interviewing a professor.

Laksone." Terrano grimaced. "I'm not sure the real Laksone is any better than the one she ended up speaking with."

"You're sure they're different?"

"No. But Laksone is in the dining hall. He apparently arrived late. At the same time as Teela was speaking with him."

Robin nodded.

"Whoever it was, he's clearly studied Laksone to a greater or lesser degree—that whole monologue about feckless students? That's him, day in and day out."

Terrano didn't like Laksone. Fair enough. Robin wasn't fond of him, but found him more bearable than Melden. Laksone, however, was the magic professor for new students. Robin was not yet in his class, and was torn. He didn't want to subject himself to Laksone's contempt, but if he wanted to learn magic, Laksone was a necessity.

"Whatever is attacking students in the Academia has the ability to mimic professors. It may have the ability to mimic students, as well—I'm sure Alderson didn't get offered exam answers from one of the professors." Robin exhaled. "But whatever attacked me wasn't Barrani or human or even Wevaran. I couldn't see anyone at all."

Terrano's expression lost color as he studied Robin's face. "Tell me what you experienced. Tell me why you did what you did."

"Which part?" Robin looked at his feet.

Raven snorted.

"Start with the why."

Robin lifted his head and looked at Raven. Raven shrugged. She didn't care what Terrano knew.

"This might take a bit of time," he finally said, retreating to his own bed, where he sat in Raven's usual posture—but on something softer and slightly warmer than floor.

Terrano absorbed Robin's scattered story. The only time he interrupted was to make certain he understood what Robin was saying. Killian appeared in the room sometime between the start of Robin's explanation and the end; his eyes were dark, but they looked like normal eyes. He stood, as if bearing witness to Robin's tale. Or perhaps listening to the things Robin wasn't willing to share with anyone.

Anyone except a sentient building who had offered to become his home. His only home.

"Let me get this straight. You didn't run out there to pull Teela away from wherever it was she was trapped."

Robin shook his head. "Did she know she was trapped?"

"Yes, but only because the rest of us were here. Having a head full of other people's voices—especially furious, raging other people—is more of a pain in the butt than you could possibly imagine, but it has its uses. To her eyes, she was in a quiet hall. In the same hall we were in. But she couldn't see us, and she knew we could see each other—and you.

"She was interviewing the professor. He wasn't under any suspicion—well, not normal suspicion. Barrani generally make better Hawks than expected because they never trust anyone, and they're good enough at lying that they can assess whether or not the lies they're being told are social or important.

"Laksone wasn't lying. He was whining. A lot. Which should have been a bit of a tip-off, honestly."

"Why?"

"Because Teela's... Teela. She's a big shot in the High Court. She was considered a disgrace because she chose to join the Hawks to alleviate her boredom—but the disgrace didn't, and couldn't, stick. *Because* she's An'Teela, she can get away with doing whatever she wants. Doesn't mean she's not terrifying. Doesn't mean she's not dangerous. Most of the Barrani consider her a bit on the chaotic side—and everyone's more careful around powerful, chaotic people because you never know what's going to set them off—you just know that you don't want to be the trigger.

"But Laksone didn't seem to care."

"Larrantin probably wouldn't care, either."

"Yeah, but he's ancient and if he'd cared about leveraging power, he'd never have stayed with the ship as it sank. Laksone treated her as if she were a garden-variety Barrani. That's the right idiom?"

Robin nodded.

"She doesn't expect scholars to be particularly careful, which is why she didn't notice."

"But she didn't die."

"She knows something is killing people—Barrani and human—leaving no trace of either fatal injury or struggle. There's a reason she's feared—she's powerful in her own right. As a Hawk, she doesn't *use* that power. She lets the tabard do the speaking. Well, most of the time."

"Was she even trying to escape?"

"She was trying to tease out some explanation—if Laksone had one—for the empty hall they were both standing in. She's investigating and she actually takes that seriously. I'm not sure that whatever it was that trapped her there would have been able to feed on her; not immediately, if ever. If she hadn't been prepared, maybe."

"But you interfered while she was attempting to extricate herself." Terrano frowned. "I was trying to reach her in a subtle way. Didn't work."

Raven snorted loudly.

"What? I thought if I could get in there and pull her out before it noticed, she'd escape! It's what Robin did."

"It's not."

"It's almost exactly what Robin did."

"It's *not*."

Robin grimaced. "Drop it," he said to Terrano under his breath. "If you can explain how or why you got stuck, that might be useful. But I wasn't intending to grab Teela—I just went to where danger was. Did you see Raven?"

Terrano fell silent.

"I mean, when she went to pull you out of wherever it was you got stuck, could you see her?"

"Yes. Yes and no."

"Give me the no part first."

"Why?"

"Because that's the part you're afraid to talk about?"

Terrano shrugged. "I didn't know it was Raven. Until she called me stupid."

"She spoke?"

"It wasn't quite speech."

"Where were you?"

"I don't know. No, don't give me that look—I honestly don't know. It was dark. It was so dark. I couldn't see anything. I couldn't feel anything. You know that part where I said having a head full of other voices can be useful? It was useful. I knew who I was. I knew they were there, that I was Terrano. But I was trapped somewhere. They could see what I saw, which was pretty much darkness and nothing.

"And I could see what they saw. I heard Raven. Her voice wasn't...it wasn't the voice we currently hear telling me I'm stupid right now."

Raven was annoyed. Robin winced because, on occasion, when something really irritated her, she could go on for an hour.

"Raven—I can't hear Terrano."

"Stupid. Don't listen."

"I think it'll help us in the long run."

She snorted again.

"And then something pushed me. I mean, *really* pushed me. I hit a wall—what felt like a wall—and then it broke or shattered, and I was through it."

"That was probably Raven."

"No kidding. But I didn't see her, either. I couldn't hear her properly. I was just…not trapped anymore. You're saying she was."

Raven rolled her eyes.

"She was stuck, but I think she just didn't see a pressing reason to leave immediately."

"Because she was somehow safe there?" He asked this of Robin, but he was watching Raven.

Raven shrugged. She was done with conversation for now.

Terrano wasn't. There was often this kind of friction with Raven, but Robin had always accepted it. Conversation required two people, and if one no longer wanted to speak, it was over. He understood Terrano's frustration, though—this wasn't a normal situation.

"Do you understand where you were? I mean—how you reached that space at all?"

"Yeah."

"Could you reach it again?"

Terrano nodded.

"And it was a space you'd entered before? I mean, my understanding is you kind of stand in the same spot and then move sideways, somehow, to be in a slightly different plane."

"Yeah. It's how I go invisible. I can see everything you see, but I'm not all there. It was hard to get that right to begin with, but it's pretty natural now—here. I mean in the space you're stuck in. But whatever is happening to kill people, it's not quite happening here. I mean, it *is*, but I think it might be similar?"

"Wrong," Raven said, although she was now looking at pieces of glass she'd withdrawn from her pouch.

"What do you mean, wrong?"

"It has to come *here* to kill."

"So it's reaching from there? Could it have killed Teela, where she was?"

"Yes." She looked up from her glass piece and said, "Done talking."

"You're the only one," Terrano replied, wincing. "I think the chancellor wants to see us."

"Us?"

"I'd duck it if I could. Serralyn's on the way."

"But she can just ask you without leaving, can't she?"

"Yeah—but that wouldn't guarantee I'll show up." He grinned. "You're a student. When the chancellor calls, you have to listen. I'm not—and I don't want to be." He glanced at Raven.

"No," she said, without looking up. "It's safe."

"I will accompany him," Killian said to Raven, materializing beside Terrano. "Terrano is, however, correct: the chancellor desires at least your presence. If it is any consolation, Arbiter Starrante may join you in the chancellor's office—I believe the chancellor has sent out an urgent request."

She nodded, but didn't stand.

Serralyn arrived, grabbed Terrano by the arm, and dragged him out of Robin's room. Her eyes were blue. Dark blue.

Robin followed, and Killian closed the door behind him.

Robin didn't run through the halls. If the chancellor had summoned him, he had an excuse—but having to deliver the excuse to multiple different people negated any time savings sprinting would gain.

"I could intervene," Killian said. Killian never, ever looked like he was running. He could *walk* at a speed Robin couldn't match.

"They'll just be mad at me when you're not around. Trust me."

"I do," Killian replied. "But the chancellor is…in an unfortunate state."

"How red are his eyes?"

"Very."

Robin now understood exactly why Terrano wanted to duck out of command performances. He walked more quickly.

The one good thing about the chancellor's office was it could be expanded to fit any number of people. Killian had once told Robin that sometimes the chancellor prevented this expansion in the hope that visitors would reach the welcome conclusion that they were unwanted.

Today, they weren't unwanted. Robin stepped into the office the moment the doors opened, followed quickly by Serralyn and Terrano. While they didn't slam shut at his back, they closed pretty quickly.

The chancellor's eyes were blood red but faintly luminous; he had lowered his inner eye membranes, but remained seated. "I will forgo criticism, which I am told is well deserved," the chancellor said, glaring at Robin. "I wish to hear what Raven told you—if she told you anything. Not you," he added to Terrano, who had stepped around Robin to stand to his right.

Terrano glared at Serralyn, but his glare wasn't up to Sedarias's standards; her eyes, at this distance, were almost black. So were the Barrani Hawk's. The color shifted slightly when Starrante stepped into the room. Serralyn's lightened; the Hawk's stayed the same; Terrano's darkened.

Robin lifted his arms in a feeble greeting—the equivalent of whispering in a crowded classroom—and Starrante returned the gesture; half of his eyes were hovering in stalks above his body, all brown at the moment. Robin was certain they wouldn't remain that way.

"Robin," the chancellor said. "Please inform the Arbiter of this afternoon's events from your viewpoint; add any information that Raven might have chosen to share."

★ ★ ★

Robin was right about the Wevaran's eyes; they shaded from their resting brown to a scarlet almost matching the chancellor's. And more of the eyes rose.

Mindful of the angry Dragon, Terrano didn't interrupt, but he came close several times. There were natural openings for Terrano's input, but Starrante kept closing them.

What he wanted to know—what he was focused on for this part of the discussion—was Robin's sense of Teela's placement. He assumed that whatever it was Valliant was doing was defensive magic, which was of middling interest compared to extra-dimensional killers who could nonetheless mimic actual people.

Only when he had interrogated Robin until Robin was forced into repetition did he then turn to Terrano. "I would like to hear what you intended."

"I knew Teela wasn't where we were; I knew it looked almost the same. I'm not sure if that was simply because it was only slightly out of phase."

"You have some experience with that."

"Yeah. It's useful. I couldn't tell exactly where Teela was standing, but we all knew she was the likely target. So I intervened in an attempt to protect her, to build a bit of a barrier on the other side. It's not as trivial as it sounds."

"It does not sound trivial at all," the Arbiter replied, clicking.

"I thought I was already most of the way there," Terrano replied, shrugging. "I just wanted to…shield her. We'd pretty much figured that if we didn't do anything, she'd be the next victim."

Teela grimaced, but failed to speak.

"Robin said you 'got stuck.'"

Terrano nodded. "But it was worse than that. I could see Teela, or rather, see where she was in the hall she occupied. I *didn't* see whatever it was I walked into—and then I could see nothing at all. With my own eyes," he added. Sedarias didn't like it, but Robin remembered that the Barrani were really touchy about True Names, something Robin didn't possess.

"I would like you to think back about the experience of being stuck or trapped."

Terrano nodded. "I could feel walls. Ah, no, that's wrong. I couldn't feel walls—not until Raven arrived and pushed me out of the space in which I'd been stuck."

"And then?"

"It felt like the wall she pushed me through shattered. I landed on the floor—our floor, not Teela's."

"Maybe that's why Raven didn't get stuck," Robin said, thinking—as he usually did in Starrante's presence—out loud. "But that wouldn't explain how she found him or saw him to begin with."

"It is a difficulty," Starrante agreed, voice gentling. "But Raven is a complex creature. She did not wish to accompany you?"

Robin shook his head. "She's in a bit of a mood, so she's calming down with her glass. She was pretty angry with me."

"I admit that I have more sympathy for her position than yours in this situation. I understand why you took that risk— but it almost killed you, in my opinion."

"Almost doesn't count, though."

"That is the theory, yes. I would like to examine you to ascertain that no changes have been made and no subclinical damage remains."

"Can it not wait? I detect no significant abnormalities," the chancellor said.

Had he said it to Robin, Robin would have put an examination on hold forever. But he'd said it to Starrante. "We do not understand the mechanism by which they choose victims—or kill them, if it comes to that. Robin's experience, if it can be generalized, is the first solid information we've had. All of the

Barrani present could see the attack on Robin; it is their best guess that it was meant for Teela, but Teela's caution is legendary.

"Robin's is not. I wish to make certain—absolutely certain—that they are not somehow tracking Robin, and that no small alterations have taken place."

"And if there are?" the chancellor asked. "Are they changes you can reverse?"

"Possibly. I will not know until I examine him."

"Very well."

Robin was accustomed to having very little say. Given that he would have accepted Starrante's offer if left to his own devices, he said nothing. But he felt distinctly uneasy now.

He wasn't surprised when Starrante began spitting webbing; it was pale silver, not pink, which meant the act was not physically taxing for the Wevaran. Yet. What he hadn't expected was to have webbing placed against his face; it was quickly followed by a cocoon of similar strands. They were light, pale; had he been able to lift his hands, he wouldn't have noticed them at all. Unless he looked in a mirror, and he didn't exactly have one of those on hand at the moment.

Killian very helpfully changed that, which caused Robin to flush. The chancellor said nothing; Robin couldn't see his expression because Starrante demanded that he look straight ahead. At, in fact, the full-length mirror Killian had placed on the floor between Robin and most of the room's occupants. He was entirely enwrapped in strands of Wevaran silk; they were faintly luminous, and they spread out from his body as if Starrante had woven together thousands of strands but left a little bit of air in between.

It was warm in the cocoon. It was almost soothing. The day had been one stress after another, culminating in what Raven assumed was near loss of his life. He closed his eyes slowly, his chin tilting toward his chest.

He could hear people speaking beyond the cocoon's reach, their voices only slightly muffled; he could hear the Barrani Hawk and the chancellor exchange verbal barbs. He couldn't hear what the cohort of friends were saying, but Serralyn's Barrani became stilted as she joined the conversation.

She loved this place.

She loved it at least as much as Robin did, if for different reasons. He was certain that no one loved it more than the chancellor.

He opened his eyes when he heard Starrante shout. He didn't recognize the words used, but given the tone, it was probably just as well.

He felt an immediate pain—a burning heat from which he couldn't escape. He opened his mouth and it was instantly filled with webbing, which should have muffled any sound he might make.

Through it all, he could still breathe—he wasn't sure if that made things better or worse.

"I apologize for any discomfort, Robin," Starrante now said, in his usual clicking syllables. The webbing should have muffled the words; it didn't. The cocoon seemed to vibrate with Starrante's voice; if anything, Robin heard it far more clearly than he usually did. "There is an anomaly."

"Raven thought I almost died. She was angry."

"She was correct. You are not—what is the saying?—out of the woods yet."

"That's the saying." He grimaced. He felt the burning pain across his shoulder blades, the back of his neck, the base of his skull. He waited until the intensity banked—almost expecting it would happen when his bones broke under the pressure. "What have you found?"

"You said you were attacked by needles. Serralyn has confirmed that is what she saw, as well. They were not needles in any traditional sense; think of them as metallic tentacles."

Because that was so much better.

"They are unlike mosquitos," Starrante continued. "Mosquitos inject something that can displace the blood they require. I am not entirely certain that the purpose was to devour. I believe it's possible that they intended to inject."

"Inject what?"

"That would be the question. There are two areas in which there is...difficulty. You are not aware of what has remained in the injection sites—or rather, were not. I think, if left alone, it would kill you. In the best case."

Robin coughed. Dying didn't seem best case to him in any scenario.

"But I am extricating what was injected. Killian?"

"Arbiter?"

"Please ask Raven to join us."

Killian fell silent. "I am not certain she will do so."

"Tell her," Starrante replied, "that Robin is not yet safe, and her input may change that for the better."

Robin couldn't see clearly, but he did hear the door fly open, hit the wall, and bounce back. The strange thing was he *could* see Raven clearly, even through Starrante's webbing.

He grimaced. Raven tended to let anger go when she saw something shiny or interesting—but whatever had happened in the hall had thoroughly discomfited her. He was half-surprised she hadn't just left the Academia, going to wherever it was Raven went when she wasn't worried about Robin. But she *was* worried about him.

She stomped over to where Robin stood. The chancellor cleared his throat, but didn't speak. Robin couldn't be certain why—he assumed either Killian or Starrante had silently intervened.

"Arbiter Starrante," Killian said. "He gestured in a definitive way, and the chancellor now understands that Raven is not to be questioned yet."

Good. Had Robin been looking in the chancellor's direction, he would have silently pleaded for exactly that. Since he couldn't take an instinctive step back, he waited. Raven marched over and grabbed his left hand.

He heard a spate of ranting about his intelligence—or total lack of—as she gripped his hand. But her eyes did widen, the equivalent of Starrante's cursing, before narrowing almost to slits. Her eyes had become odd. Not in the way Terrano's did—they didn't make him queasy—but there was a muted light, pale and luminous, covering them.

The pain that Starrante's probing caused dimmed as Raven cursed. And she cursed loudly, and far more colorfully, than she usually did. Robin wouldn't have dared, given who else was in the room, but Raven had never really worried about that. She wasn't stupid—she didn't seek danger, didn't taunt gangs—but she didn't particularly care about the innate authority of people she'd assessed as safe.

Robin's assessment didn't match hers, but that was almost comfortingly normal. As was the lessening of pain.

"What are you doing?" Starrante asked, voice slightly sharper than it had been.

She responded in a language Robin couldn't understand, although the tone made clear that she wasn't being any politer.

Starrante was not happy. He responded in the language Raven had spoken. She replied. There seemed to be an actual argument in progress when the pain stopped.

"There is," Killian said. "It is both interesting and alarming."

"Am I okay now?"

"That," Killian replied, "appears to be what the argument in progress is about. The chancellor can only follow half of it, and dislikes the exclusion; the Arbiter attempted to speak in a readily accessible tongue, but Raven will not. I believe if you choose to join the conversation, she will."

"How easy is it to join a conversation in progress when I can't understand most of it?"

"I admit that could be a difficulty."

Robin grimaced. "Raven—what was wrong with me? What did you find?"

She turned to Robin and said, "Wait here." She looked distinctly unhappy, but turned toward the door before he could reply.

Starrante didn't remove the webbing, either; he waited for Raven's return.

Raven flew back into the room; Robin could see that she was carrying the pouch in which she usually put pieces of glass. He wondered, then, if there were pieces of glass trapped inside him—if that's what was causing pain when Starrante attempted to remove whatever had been injected.

It might have been deeply disturbing to watch the extraction— Robin found even the sight of his own blood disturbing—but Starrante kindly worked from behind Robin's back. He closed his eyes regardless, in case the mirror gave him a glimpse of whatever it was they were somehow extracting.

Until Raven crowed with both triumph and delight.

"Are we finished?" Starrante asked the now delighted Raven.

"Yes. You can let him out now."

The webbing that had been so carefully wrapped around Robin was withdrawn. Robin stumbled; his legs felt like rubber and they failed to support his weight. Dropping to his knees, he took several breaths.

"Robin, look!"

Raven held two pieces of glass in her hands. They weren't as large as the piece she'd found beneath the elbow of a Barrani corpse, and they were—to Robin's eyes—a different color. But they were undeniably glass of the kind that Raven collected.

"I almost have enough!" she said, a smile wreathing her face and banishing all exhaustion and irritation.

"Enough for what?" he asked. His throat was uncomfortably dry, and he coughed the words out rather than speaking them.

She frowned. "Let's go back."

"To our room?"

She nodded.

The chancellor cleared his throat. "Raven, might I detain Robin for a few more minutes?"

"Why? He's fine now."

"Because other students are not guaranteed to be, as you put it, fine in the near future."

"Oh." She tilted her head to the side, as if listening. "It's safe now."

"It becomes unsafe with very little warning."

She shook her head. "There's warning."

"There isn't warning that the rest of the residents of the Academia can perceive."

She turned to Starrante and pointed at him. "*He* can."

"He is not a resident," the chancellor told her.

"I can extend my stay if necessary," the Wevaran told the chancellor. "But I do not believe I will hear the warning if I am within the library. Very, very little can penetrate the library space without specific permission."

"If not for Raven," Serralyn said, looking down at the carpet beneath her feet, "we would have almost certainly lost Teela."

The chancellor nodded. "Arbiter, do you understand what's occurring?"

"I am not completely certain," the Wevaran replied. "But I now have suspicions. They are not particularly comforting."

"Nothing that has happened in the past week has been comforting." The chancellor's voice was a low rumble.

"Understand that I am not certain. I do not wish you to act

on this possibility as if it is the sole possibility." The Wevaran's eyes were the color of alarm, and his limbs were raised and stiff.

"Arbiter. Your help is greatly *appreciated*."

Robin would have told the chancellor anything he wanted to hear at this point.

"I believe that the reason there are corpses is they cannot withstand the attempt to create a suitable container. A vessel." He glanced at the pieces of glass in Raven's hand. "Had Raven not interfered, Robin would likewise be dead."

20

Robin turned immediately to Raven, who was, as usual, enamored of new pieces of glass. The fact that they'd somehow come from him made it hugely uncomfortable.

"Is this where the glass from the corpse came from?" he asked.

She shook her head. Paused. Frowned. "Maybe? Starrante wasn't there. I don't think there would have been glass from your corpse if you died."

Starrante clicked and coughed. "I do not believe that I would have been able to remove those pieces without your aid," he told Raven.

Raven shrugged, uninterested. Which meant he was probably correct.

Not for the first time since Raven arrived at the Academia, Robin wondered what she was. What he'd known about her in his childhood was that she was trustworthy. Reliable. Safe.

He remembered the first time she mentioned glass. She had come, grabbed him by the hand, and started to run, which was normal. By this time, Robin knew that if Raven ran—while attached to him by hand—he had to run, as well. He had to keep up; he could not ask questions. Not while they were trying to reach a hiding place.

After, though—depending on where they were hidden—he could talk. Sometimes she would answer; sometimes she would shush him, finger to his moving lips, and he would fall silent until Raven told him the danger had passed.

But on that day, she'd showed him a piece of glass. It was the first time he had ever seen her smile—or perhaps the first time he'd seen a smile so brilliant. Glass had nothing to do with food or shelter or hiding places, and most of Robin's young life had been those things; there was little joy in it. What passed for the echo of former joy was relief. Relief at food. Relief at warmth in the winter. Relief at a hiding place that wouldn't be found, no matter how close angry voices and footsteps got.

But Raven's joy had been infectious. Yes, he'd had no interest in glass, but her interest had been profound; it had the whole of her attention and, given the enclosed hiding space, almost all of Robin's, as well.

He'd tried to find glass for her after that—glass pieces as pristine as the one she'd showed him. That shard had looked newly shattered; sand or gravel hadn't worn it down or scratched its clarity.

He'd never asked her why she collected those pieces. What else could she afford to collect? Raven had no toys that Robin had ever seen—and Robin had lost all that he'd once owned when he'd lost his home. If not glass or the pieces of things richer people threw away, what could people like them collect?

None of Robin's attempt to find glass for her—to *do something* for her—had worked. The pieces he could scrounge had never been as clear, as pristine, as Raven's. He'd stopped trying, and only wished his younger self had understood the source of her treasures; that would have prevented him from feeling like such a failure.

That child was clearly still buried inside of him, because he did feel a lessening of that child's guilt. But that guilt had led him to search for Raven. He'd believed he finally had something he could offer her. Something to share with her—something that brought him almost the same kind of joy glass brought her.

But it was something she didn't want; it was something she didn't need, given how she'd rescued Terrano. It had been about what Robin wanted, what Robin wanted to give, not what Raven wanted.

"No." Raven stood and smacked the back of Robin's head. "Bad."

Everyone stared at Raven, and then at Robin.

"So... I guess you're used to that?" Terrano asked.

"More or less," Robin replied. "Sorry," he added, to Raven. She frowned at him. "You should be."

"Can we return to the glass?" the chancellor asked.

Raven shrugged but made no move to leave, which was Raven-speak for *I can't stop you.* Robin, with effort, didn't cringe. Most people were content to let Robin speak in Raven's stead because Robin was just better at talking. That had always been true in the warrens; Robin understood the warrens and the people who lived there, and he could explain what Raven wanted—or didn't want—on the rare occasions they got work.

But here, it wasn't the same. He didn't understand what Raven had done, how she had done it, or what she wanted—beyond the pieces of glass. He no longer understood how she found hiding places; he'd always assumed, because she avoided people, she'd found them exploring. She was small and quiet, fast on her feet; she could sneak into places that Robin couldn't.

She'd taught him some of that, but he'd never learned well enough to find a hiding space and return to it while on the run. He hadn't needed to because Raven always found him first.

"Mr. Alderson's body did not have glass associated with it. You did, however, pull a piece of metal from his mouth. I assume the metal was inserted the normal way—through an open mouth, in case you are about to ask."

Raven nodded.

"You knew that something would be in his mouth—did you expect glass?"

"Maybe?" She frowned. "Mostly, it's glass—but if you don't get there fast enough, it's nothing."

"The piece of metal would not...leak out, as you put it."

She nodded.

"But the piece of glass that you found beneath Lykallos did not have to be extracted."

Raven shook her head. "He was trying to survive. Magic. I think he pushed it out, but not enough, not in time."

Robin turned to Raven, daring the chancellor's annoyance. "Are *all* the pieces of glass you've found like that?"

She tilted her head. He'd asked her *where* she'd found these pieces before. But he'd never really asked her what they were because he knew what glass was. Until he didn't.

"Not all? Most aren't. But, Robin, you have to make the jar to call. You have to make it carefully, or it shatters. You have to be careful if it shatters—the shards can get in your eyes. Most jars... I don't think they're made *inside* people. That's bad. That's very bad."

"Is the glass alive?" the chancellor asked.

Raven took some time with this question, as if the question itself were an object she could examine. "No," she finally said. It didn't sound definitive, but at least it didn't tail up at the end like her *maybe* usually did.

"So something is alive and it's attempting to create glass jars inside of living people?"

"I think so." She then turned to Starrante. "Can you explain it? I'm tired."

"Where did you *find* her?" Terrano murmured. Robin glanced at him; the Barrani was both amused and impressed. None of the rest of his friends were, and Sedarias was glaring at Terrano almost murderously.

"She wants me to have some dignity," he told Robin.

"She is not a fool," the Barrani Hawk also told Robin. "She doesn't *expect* it."

Starrante, however, was waving his arms in a way that reminded Robin of people running around and screaming in a panic. His movements were so jerky, the panic could almost be felt.

"Arbiter?" the chancellor said in a much softer voice.

The Arbiter skittered in a tight circle, chittering and clicking. Robin looked at his eyes. All of them seemed to be extended, and most of them were scarlet.

"Maybe that's not such a great idea," Robin said to his roommate. "I think he's upset."

Raven shrugged. "People always try to make things complicated. It's not complicated."

"But you can't explain it."

"I'm tired. Words are hard."

"When will you find words less difficult?"

She squealed in frustration; had she not been carrying glass, her hands would have been fists. He'd never pressed her so hard, never demanded answers she was unwilling, or incapable, of giving.

It was wrong. It felt wrong. The murders were wrong, too. People had died, and if they couldn't figure things out, more people would join them. Robin among them. But it wasn't fear of that hovering death that caused him to freeze in place, that caused him to walk to where Raven now crouched, that moved his hands to rest, gently, across her shoulders.

"I'm sorry," he whispered. "I'm sorry, Raven."

She said nothing, drawing Robin into her silence.

"I guess it's up to Starrante," Terrano said. He turned to Serralyn and cocked his head in the Wevaran's direction. Serralyn immediately looked to Robin.

Raven sniffed, and Robin unbent, releasing her as he rose; his hands felt cold at the sudden absence of the warmth of contact. He met Serralyn's gaze. It was silently agreed that the two would approach the distressed Arbiter.

It was also clear that the Arbiter did have some understanding of what Raven had said. Raven, however, had never been big on explanations. She didn't need to explain glass to anyone else. Even people who now needed the explanation.

Maybe he'd been wrong. It was the discovery of the world's *why* that made the Academia so compelling to Robin—and Serralyn, and probably at least a third of the other students.

"I think Raven does understand," Robin said. "What she can't do is explain it. I don't think she thinks in words, so explaining is hard. She once said she has problems squishing things into flat words. Too many words are needed, and they don't necessarily tell people what she knows.

"She wants to help. As long as I've known her, she's wanted to help."

"Only you," Raven said. "I only had to help you." She lowered her head. "Only until you left."

Robin turned to stare at Raven's bowed head; at the line of her shoulders that had sunk, as well. "Until I left? The warrens?"

She nodded as she sank to the floor.

"But I came looking for you."

She shook her head. "I looked for you. I didn't know you were looking for me until the grey crow." She drew her knees close to her chest, encircling them with her arms. "I looked for you."

"You always did."

Her hair moved as she shook her head into her knees. "I found you. I didn't have to look. I knew where you were when I needed to find you."

"And this time you didn't."

She nodded. "You didn't need me." She lifted her head. "You

didn't need me anymore. You said you were in danger here—
and I didn't know."

"That's when the Academia was still mostly buried."

She shook her head, looked up at him, and smiled. It was a
sad, almost bitter smile, more filled with pain than anything
that resembled joy.

Robin froze. Breath deserted him. Her face didn't look like
Raven's face in his eyes; it looked very much like a face that he
had forgotten, that he had forced himself to forget. The similarity was gone as the smile vanished, but its effects remained
within him.

"Yes," Raven whispered. "Bad thoughts." She rose then.
"Don't have bad thoughts." Robin knew the expression that
transformed her face; he knew the posture of her body: she was
preparing to storm off—at speed.

Which is what she did. What no one expected was that she
would run through the very closed, very thick doors. Robin
could hear her cursing as she went.

She flew through the doors, racing down the halls, her thoughts
scattering, the words dissolving. It had been so hard to hold on to
them, and she almost couldn't remember why she'd even tried.

Why was she trying so hard now? She had never done it
before. Why had she found those broken pieces of glass? She
couldn't remember. She loved them; she loved finding them.
They filled her with the joy of both discovery and possession.
But *why*?

Those weren't even the right questions. She knew. She was
only asking them because she didn't want to ask the only question that was relevant.

Why had she left the warrens in search of Robin? He was
gone. He was gone, and without Robin, she was free. Why
had she tried to find him?

She had stayed because she discovered he *did* need her. Still.

Because he was in danger here, in this so-called safe place. She had a reason to stay.

But…she wanted a desk. She wanted a desk of her own. *That* was safe. Their room wasn't safe, but she wanted to stay where Robin was. Even if she could leave at any time. That room was—what had Robin called it?—a home. She'd never needed one before. Never wanted one. But she wanted to go back there now.

She started to do exactly that, but she'd made a mistake. She was angry, and she'd wanted to escape—so she had escaped. She hadn't wanted to wait for the doors to be opened. But she knew there were traps here. She knew there was danger. It wasn't danger to Robin. Maybe that's why she'd forgotten.

She felt the cold, the dark, and behind them, a will that wasn't her own.

She would not reach her room. She turned then—but she was too slow; she couldn't even return to where she had been moments before.

"You were interrupted, Arbiter," the chancellor then said, in a tone of voice that implied interruption was the work of cockroaches very likely to be crushed beneath his feet.

"No, not at all—it gives me time to gather my thoughts. I would like to return to the library," he added. "This requires research, and the tomes required exist only there now. But," he added, quickly raising an arm before the chancellor could speak, "I understand that you wish me to speak of my suspicions, without the proper grounding in research.

"And as the research is entirely theoretical, given the loss of things ancient and the deaths of those who might once have been considered the most preeminent of scholars, I ask only that you allow one other to be present for these deliberations."

"The other Arbiters can't leave—" Serralyn began.

Starrante conveyed his horror by cutting her off instantly.

"I would never, ever invite the others to this discussion—their disagreements cause structural damage. Or worse. No, it was not of the Arbiters that I spoke; it was of one of the professors."

"Larrantin," the chancellor said.

"Yes. He was old even when the Academia was at its full power, and I believe he may have insights into the validity of my theories."

Serralyn raised a hand, although it wasn't strictly necessary. "Yes?"

"He's canceled classes for the week."

"Since when?"

"Since just after the first murder."

"Killianas, do you know where he can be found?"

"In his rooms. They are situated within the dorms," the Avatar replied. "I will, with the chancellor's permission, attempt to invite him to this discussion. If he refuses, we may have to relocate, which could be difficult. I believe the Arbiter may be unable to accompany us, but I am uncertain."

"Why?" Terrano demanded. "His rooms are in the dorms—they're part of Killian."

"Larrantin chose to remain with the Academia when the Towers rose—which should have meant his death. And mine," Killian added, as if he were speaking of the weather or a small change in class schedule. "He was an adept of great renown. I believe Teela recognized his name and his significance."

Teela nodded. Terrano grimaced. "We all knew about Larrantin."

"Larrantin's rooms are larger than the rooms of most of the scholars resident within the Academia—and they are unusual in other ways; they are protected from external interference."

"From yours?"

"If I wished to destroy them, I could." Killian offered Terrano a rare smile. "I cannot, however, preserve what those rooms contain; I cannot simply interfere with them. Should I consider his research a true danger, destruction would be my only option. Larrantin spends most of his time in his office in the administrative building, unless his students either bore or annoy him."

"Or unless he's researching something?"

"Indeed. Larrantin has chosen to be responsible for spells of security and warding within his residence. I am uncertain as to their nature. But something as simple as a Wevaran portal would require permission; Starrante could not simply enter his rooms the way he might enter any other area of the Academia under my control.

"You, however, present a different security problem. I think Larrantin would either respect you or consider you enough of a threat he would attempt to destroy you. You would find it very difficult to break into his rooms. That was not meant as a challenge," the Avatar added in a more severe tone.

"Harder than the library?" Terrano asked, ignoring the warning.

"Possibly," Starrante said. "The library space is old, and as Terrano proves, there is always change. Larrantin would keep abreast of those changes in a way that the library does not. Or he could. But he, as I, have slept for centuries while research and scholarship progressed around us, unlearned and unknown. He has been quite focused on regaining lost ground—as he put it. He does not consider his rooms to be reliably secure in the fashion they once were."

"If Larrantin himself invited Starrante, Starrante could safely enter, but only then. And he is aware that people can be enspelled to act against their will. It has happened to the Arbiters before." Killian frowned and turned to the chancellor. "Larrantin has expressed a reluctant desire to join your discussion."

"So he'll come here?" Terrano asked.

"Ah, no. We will go to him." Killian nodded to Starrante.

"He believes he has left an opening for you should you desire to accompany us, but says he cannot make promises."

The halls to the dorms were sparsely populated. Most of the students heading to—or from—class or study period stopped to look. They knew of the Wevaran, but Starrante seldom walked through the public halls. A giant multi-eyed spider was always going to draw attention.

The rest of the people present faded into the background for most of the students, but some of the Barrani took several steps back when Teela walked by. They took several steps away when the chancellor asked if they had time to waste loitering in the hallways. This was repeated several times, but toward the end the halls were empty.

"It is not always safe to put other apartments close to where Larrantin works," Killian said. "While he is cautious, he is Barrani at heart."

"What's that supposed to mean?"

"The things upon which he is focused are of far more pressing relevance than the problems of strangers."

"I think you could say that about anyone," Robin said.

"Perhaps. But the consequences of that lapse are seldom as severe as when Barrani are involved."

Terrano shrugged. "He's right," he told Robin before Robin could argue further. "I mean, seldom doesn't mean never, but you can ask the Hawk if you want confirmation."

"The Hawk," Teela said, "is not discussing statistical probabilities of severe crimes outside of the Halls of Law. Even were I so inclined, Barrani crimes are not subject to the supervision of the Halls of Law. Punishment, such as it is, resides in the hands of the Barrani caste court, unless those crimes affect other races."

"In which case," Terrano said cheerfully, "the Barrani behind the crimes—or some of them—turn up dead. Usually near the Halls of Law."

"Why, exactly, are we discussing crime?" the chancellor asked, in a tone that should have killed the discussion.

"Because you have asked me to investigate a series of murders," the Barrani Hawk replied. "Those murders are likely not yet at an end; I presume my investigation is in service to assuring there will be no further deaths."

Robin wouldn't have dared to answer the chancellor that way. Clearly Teela *was* intimidating. The chancellor snorted smoke in reply, but swallowed any words that might have followed.

"Oh dear," Killian said, which caused the entire small party to freeze in its tracks—including the angry chancellor.

"What's happened?" the chancellor demanded.

"We may have to put off our meeting with Larrantin," Killian replied, frowning. "There seems to be an unanticipated problem in his research area."

"What kind of problem?"

"I am not entirely certain. I told you—Larrantin's abode tends to be very, very secure. I am aware of rudimentary difficulties when Larrantin is not within his own quarters, but can access very little information when he is there. It is," Killian added, "a preference he has worked tirelessly to enforce."

"Let us proceed to the professor's chambers," the chancellor said. "He has not rescinded his invitation, and we may be of aid."

"I am uncertain he will be appreciative," Killian informed the chancellor.

"I am uncertain that I care. If, however, you feel his lack of appreciation will harm the students, feel free to command them to remain behind."

Terrano had no intention of obeying any such command, which was clear to everyone present.

Killian hesitated, looking at all of the assembled group, half of whom weren't actual students. He could throw them all out—that was well within his power. The chancellor seemed content to leave the decision in the Avatar's hands, but was not content to wait—he began to walk down the corridor.

Terrano immediately followed.

The building sighed. With a very resigned expression, he turned to Robin. "I feel that you should return to your room, but I also feel that you will be upset upon reentry. You may be of aid. Touch nothing in Larrantin's chambers, even if invited to do so. My protections are frequently hampered in his rooms."

"Not his office?"

"No. Our agreement was that he keep his research entirely contained. If there is an error in containment, I will simply destroy his chambers."

"I see." Robin frowned and began to follow the chancellor. "Do you think the murders are linked to his research?"

"If I believed that, we would be meeting in the chancellor's office, if a meeting was required at all." He turned to Starrante. "I believe you have some idea of what this is about—one you have not yet shared. Please practice restraint."

The hall had no doors except for a double set at the end; it was not a short hall, either. Robin guessed that the professor's room was not in any way like the student dormitory rooms. This made sense, given the differing positions the students and professors held in the Academia, and Larrantin, being a living legend, would be at the top of the heap, if one set the chancellor aside in the hierarchy.

It hadn't occurred to him to wonder where the chancellor lived and slept; the chancellor seemed entirely wed to his office from dawn to dusk. Possibly later. If Killian knew, he didn't share in the chancellor's presence. But the chancellor had command of the Academia.

He certainly seemed to feel the weight of that command as he lifted a hand and knocked—heavily—on the closed doors. Silence replied, and he tried again. The third time, Robin had some doubts about the future structural integrity of Larrantin's doors.

There was no fourth time. The doors flew open so quickly they should have cracked as they hit the wall.

Larrantin stood between them, his eyes dark blue, his hair—unlike the hair of any of the rest of the Barrani—a mess. Larrantin's hair was white and black; it had been that way the whole time Robin had known him. Robin had assumed that Larrantin was somehow a truly ancient Barrani—which he was—but understood that his assumption about hair color and age was entirely mortal.

Barrani were immortal. He knew they were eternal if they could avoid war, assassination, and the power games they played with their many rivals. They threw forever away on the end of swords, in cups of poison, in magical conflagrations.

Or in rage at Dragons, because Larrantin was *angry*.

Robin could only see the chancellor's back, but assumed that his expression was similar.

"You were informed that we were on the way to meet with you, I assume," the chancellor said, the words an accusation.

"I was not told when, and I am currently occupied in a delicate alchemical operation. Timing is of the essence, and if you interrupt me, I may lose valuable work."

"We will wait *inside*," the chancellor replied.

Robin took a step back, collided with Serralyn, and stopped. He froze in place, as if his hand was in Raven's, as if Raven was sprinting. She wasn't; she wasn't here. But he felt almost as if she were—or as if she would be, if she could.

It was Terrano who said, "Robin, we have trouble." His voice was a whisper; when Robin turned toward him, Terrano was invisible.

He didn't want to catch the attention of either an angry Dragon or an angry Barrani sage, but something in the way Terrano offered the warning made the hair on the back of his neck rise. He didn't know why.

He turned to Killian. "Killian."

The Avatar was silent, facing the simmering confrontation taking place on two sides of an open doorway. Words were thrown back and forth, the voices rising and echoing in the stone halls.

"Where is Raven?" Robin demanded.

Killian did not answer.

"Killian—*where is Raven?*"

"Why do you ask me that now?" the Avatar replied.

Robin had no answer. He had asked in dread and by instinct as he turned toward the occupied door.

"I'll cover you," Terrano whispered.

"Robin—it is not safe," Killian said.

But it wasn't Terrano who came to Robin's rescue. It was Starrante. Hard to forget a giant talking spider, but Starrante could become so still it was possible. The Wevaran lifted Robin off his feet with one limb and dropped him unceremoniously on his rounded back. "Be careful, young Robin, of my eyes."

He was probably sitting on some of them, but they weren't extended. It was still not a comfortable thought.

"I will keep you as stable as I can, but we will need to move in a fashion that is difficult for you." He paused and then added, "I know you will follow us, Terrano—but attempt to trace the *exact* path I take. There will be difficulties for you if you do not, and I cannot guarantee—nor can your chosen kin—that you will survive them."

"Fine," Terrano said, appearing across Starrante's back just behind where Robin was seated. "Let's do it the easier way."

"Indeed." Starrante then said, "With apologies to all other parties involved," and launched himself toward the ceiling, spinning in place so that Robin and Terrano were upside down. Robin was afraid he would fall—he hadn't expected to be flipped upside down—but webbing caught him and held him roughly in place.

The Wevaran then skittered across the ceiling, at speed, leaping over the arch of the doorframe as if it were an insignificant hurdle.

"Starrante!" Larrantin shouted, his intense disagreement with the chancellor interrupted.

Robin didn't look back—in part because the webbing made it impossible to turn around with any speed, and in part because he didn't want to meet the eyes of one of his favorite teachers. Although it hadn't exactly been Robin's idea or suggestion, Larrantin wouldn't have been wrong to blame Robin for the intrusion.

Starrante had responded to Robin's sudden, bone-deep certainty that Raven was somehow here. And that she wasn't hiding on purpose. She wasn't safe.

"Where?" Starrante demanded as Robin attempted to orient himself to the upside-down view. He was in a long hall; the floor was the ceiling. There were arches—Barrani often didn't have internal doors within their private chambers—but the largest appeared to be to the right of where Robin was sitting.

"My right as I'm looking ahead," Robin said.

Starrante didn't bother to flip over and land on the ground; he continued his run across the ceiling, once again jumping over the arch of the open frame. The ceiling was more problematic once they'd escaped the hall; it was a huge, curved dome.

This time, Starrante did flip and jump to the ground. Robin braced himself, but the landing, if jarring, was soft. They were in a huge room that seemed part library and part study tables— except not really study tables, because the things across the tables weren't uniformly books. This was like a lab, a type of room that Robin had seen all of two times before.

The shelves went up the left side of the wall; spokes of light streamed down from windows on the right, although the windows seemed hidden by the angle of the shelving. Books, Robin expected, but there were glass shelves with doors that were obviously locked, and the back wall was stone with alcoves formed of pillars. In the center of that wall, one alcove was occupied by something that seemed at first glance to be a dark blur of movement captured and set on a pedestal.

Starrante cursed in his native tongue; Robin could feel it as a tremor beneath his legs. Terrano cursed the regular way. Robin could only draw enough breath to speak one word.

"Raven!"

21

It was Raven. He was certain it was Raven. He recognized everything about her: her height, the length of her arms, her hands and the fingers that had always been long and slender, her mess of hair, her tattered robes. It was only her expression he didn't recognize: she was genuinely afraid. She'd been afraid for him before—that worried, half-angry look, he was very familiar with.

But this one was different.

"Starrante—why is she like that?" He slid off Starrante's back, but Starrante grabbed him by the collar and dangled him above the floor.

"I cannot fully answer that question in the time it would take for Raven to be irretrievable. There are dangers in this place. I will create a web for you—but you *must* walk that web; you must touch nothing else. Do you understand?"

Robin nodded. "Can't you portal me to her?"

"Not in Larrantin's chambers. There is a reason we had to walk. I might escape his protections but I doubt very much you would survive it."

Starrante released Robin's collar, and he landed on the web by the Wevaran. "Run," the Wevaran whispered. "I am sorry."

Robin didn't understand what the Wevaran felt he had to apologize for; he had brought Robin here literally over the head of Larrantin, after all.

"I'll go with him," Terrano said.

"I would not advise it. Anywhere else, yes. Even in the library, once you've invaded it. Larrantin, however, is cautious and deadly in a way we are not."

"You don't think a Dragon and an Ancestor are deadly?" Terrano demanded as Robin began to sprint. The lab was much larger than it appeared to be. Starrante, however, moved behind Robin as he ran, spitting webbing ahead of his feet.

"Of course they are. So am I. But the library's defenses will not kill you. Probably. Larrantin's are far less kind. Understand, boy, that he was a Barrani of considerable power; he was respected for his knowledge, yes—but the bulk of the respect offered was offered because he was feared."

"I'm not afraid of him."

"Yes. Were you an actual student, your lack of fear would have some grounding in demonstrable fact. You are not. I urge extreme caution here; do not simply shift form or shift plane in these chambers."

Robin lost the rest of the conversation. Raven was standing on a pillar of some kind; he couldn't see chains restraining her. But her movements—while visible—were slow, as if she were trying to swim in deep water.

"Robin, no!" Starrante shouted as Robin reached out to touch his trapped friend. "No. If I understand anything that has occurred, you do not have to touch her. Call her. Call her now."

A wave of something that looked like orange light suddenly spread across the floor, as if it were flame without the texture. Not without the heat. The webs upon which Robin balanced held; the orange light did not change their color.

Terrano whistled. "Okay," he said in cheerful Elantran. "You win. I'm staying right where I am."

"Yes, you are. Starrante! How *dare* you!"

Larrantin had clearly not remained in the doorway that led to his rooms. Robin didn't look back. He assumed that everyone had followed, but that could be wrong. What he needed to do before Larrantin could reach him was reach Raven.

He considered stepping on the orange floor; that might work to call her back from wherever she'd gotten stuck. But he knew, instinctively, that this was different. If Raven had been stuck when she'd rescued Terrano, it wasn't like this. She hadn't been afraid then. She knew she could leave if she really wanted, and at least no one could bother her wherever Terrano had been stuck.

She was afraid now.

She was afraid she could never leave.

He didn't understand how calling her—as Starrante said— would make a difference if touching her wouldn't—but maybe if he did touch her, he'd be stuck where she was. The first time he'd tried this, it hadn't worked, but he'd never had to call her before. He had waited, as a child waited, a parentless child, as a person who was certain he had no control over his environment, who could only hope to survive it until he reached that mythical age of Adult, when life would suddenly become easier.

Raven came when she wanted, and left the same way. She helped him. But he couldn't cage her. He'd been afraid, every time, that she would never return. No one else had. No one but Raven.

He'd always been afraid to call her. He realized that now as her name clung to the insides of his throat. He'd been afraid to call and get nothing but silence and absence in return. If he could touch her—if he could grab her hand—he'd've done that without hesitation.

But calling her felt wrong. It felt dangerous. It felt— He couldn't explain it. And he was immediately angry at himself. What was he afraid of now? What did he fear? Rejection?

Anger at himself freed his voice. "Raven!" he shouted, lifting a hand, palm up, toward where she stood, a living statue. "Raven, come here!"

On the pillar, Raven turned, her movements jerky. Her eyes were open, and they moved toward Robin, toward the sound of his voice.

"I'm not sure this is going to work," Terrano said, his voice so close to Robin's ear that Robin startled.

"It's already started," Starrante told them both. "Keep calling, Robin."

"Can you?" Robin shouted back.

"No. Nor can Terrano or anyone else who is present. But neither can Larrantin. Call her and make her hear your voice."

"Raven!" She could see him—he was certain she could see him. She couldn't move. Robin wasn't certain why calling her would make a difference; she clearly didn't want to be where she was; she was trapped there.

But he understood the urgency in Starrante's voice. The Wevaran felt that if Raven didn't move soon, she would never be able to move from that spot again. She was the only thing Robin had retained in the bitter helplessness of his early life. She was the only good thing.

She was what remained of his family. The only thing that hadn't been destroyed. He had lost his home. He had lost his father, his baby sister, and in the end, his mother after she had fled to the warrens in an attempt to preserve his life. What remained? Raven.

Raven, who hadn't even had a name. He'd given her a name. She'd thought it odd and confusing, but she'd accepted it, and in the end, Raven is what she'd been called by anyone who interacted with both of them.

Why Raven?

Because her hair was black and sometimes it caught light like the wings of ravens did. And because he was Robin, he was a child, and the other mostly safe person he knew by name in the warrens was the grey crow. It made sense to give her a bird name, like his. Like the woman he now knew was named Giselle.

Thus the intent of a child, the self-absorption of a child, the desire of an orphan to build some kind of connection, some kind of similarity, in the absence of blood ties and home. It was the name he'd given her. It was the name she had lived in, grown into. She loved shiny things.

"Raven!"

Something shattered in the distance; he could hear the echoes of falling shards of glass. Raven leaped off the pedestal, her hand outstretched; it connected with Robin's and she fell against his chest; he caught her back with his free arm, pulling her in close.

"Starrante?" he shouted.

"You are fine," the Wevaran said in a softer voice, clicking. "Well done. Well done, young Robin. Raven, may I carry you?"

"Robin, too."

"Of course. Robin, too." He reached for them—by sticky web, which was much less comfortable than limbs—and deposited them on his back. "Terrano, stop that and come here."

"Fine," Terrano snapped. He, too, returned to Starrante's back. "It's safe on his back," he whispered to Robin. "I'd probably survive the floor or the walls, but you should stay with Starrante. Don't get down until we're out of this place."

Robin had no desire to get down. He understood that if safety existed, it was right here. Starrante was a giant spider, and yes, that could have been terrifying. But Starrante had always been the most soft-spoken of the Arbiters, the most genuinely concerned with the welfare of the students. Robin had been safe with Starrante.

Raven would be safe with Starrante, as well.

Larrantin strode toward them, his eyes indigo. "What do you

think you are doing, Arbiter?" His voice was thunder, almost literally; the syllables seemed to be caught and magnified—magically—by floor and wall.

"You have made an error in calculations," the Arbiter replied. In the distant doorframe, the rest of Robin's company had gathered: four Barrani and one angry Dragon.

"And how would you know? Have you stolen glimpses of my work? Have you examined my research and the formulations derived from them?"

Raven reached up and covered both her ears with her hands, letting go of Robin's hand to do so. "So loud," she said. Loudly.

"That," Larrantin said, staring at Raven, "belongs to me."

"Impossible," Starrante replied. "I believe she has applied to become a student in the Academia, and the chancellors have always taken a very dim view of experimentation on the student body. Recall the fate of Tantrelle."

"It *cannot* be a student—it can barely be a *she*. I do not know what game you are playing, but that creature is far more dangerous than you understand." Larrantin's eyes remained almost black in color, but he lowered his voice, and the floor's light and heat dimmed until it once again looked to be composed of stone. He turned to Killian. "Why have you allowed this? We have an agreement."

"We do," the Avatar said.

"This breaks that agreement."

"No, it does not. Raven is considered a prospective student of the Academia, and the safety of the students is paramount to my directives. If the chancellor commands otherwise..."

"You will obey him?"

"I will find a different chancellor," was the quiet reply. It dropped into the silence that only Larrantin had disturbed, its effects spreading outward in ripples, as if it were a stone dropped into a still pond.

Larrantin then turned to the chancellor. "You cannot possibly allow this," he said, with far more confidence than Robin felt. "You do not understand the nature of what that is."

"Then inform me of that nature," the chancellor replied. His eyes were red to Larrantin's indigo. The rest of the Barrani eyes were uniformly dark blue. Except for Sedarias's, but Robin had a feeling that her eyes were always far darker in color than those of her friends. "You may inform me here; the Arbiter, however, will not remain. Nor will the students."

Larrantin glared at Terrano. "Do you consider Terrano to be a student?"

"For the purpose of my request, yes." The chancellor transferred his glare to Terrano. "Leave. *NOW.*" The last was said in a Draconic roar.

Terrano was reckless but he wasn't an idiot; he left.

"Robin, you are a student," the chancellor said.

Larrantin, however, lifted a hand. "I wish to speak with Robin."

"You may speak with Robin in my office. I was informed that you were occupied and you would be unlikely to join us there."

"I was," Larrantin replied, as if the chancellor's requests were usually irrelevant. "But I was not fully apprised of the situation at that time." He glared in Killian's direction. "If it will calm your ire, Chancellor, I have been attempting to create a defense that might protect our students from the predations of the murderer who seems to be attempting to feed on our campus.

"I assure you I did not utilize my research and my magic in order to victimize…prospective students." He exhaled. "Very well. Please leave my lab; I will need to reset some of its defenses before I join you in your office."

Robin wanted to send Raven back to their room, but he no longer trusted that she would be safe there. He had no idea how she'd ended up trapped by Larrantin, and he knew

Raven wouldn't be able to explain it. He had hope that Lar-rantin could—but he was genuinely angry with the man who was among his favorite professors.

Raven only lowered hands from her ears when they were once again within the proper halls of the Academia, but she was both sullen and exhausted; she leaned back against Robin's chest. Robin had never seen Raven sleep; he was almost afraid for her.

"Stupid," she muttered.

Or not. He desperately wanted to ask her what had happened to her, but he kept the questions to himself. She wouldn't answer them right now—if she even could. Raven had been in what she would call a Bad Place; she didn't want to dwell on it while she was so tired. Or possibly ever.

Starrante walked slowly, as if giving them time to compose themselves. He was clicking as he walked, a sure sign he was thinking out loud. He often did this when he was returning books to their shelves. Or finding them, because without the aid of the Arbiters almost no one could find the specific books they were looking for.

Serralyn actually liked that, though—she liked the discovery of the unlooked-for books that might be treasures.

But he wasn't reshelving books right now. He was heading to the chancellor's office. The others had departed or gone on ahead. Even Terrano had jumped off Starrante's back to join his Barrani friends. Robin, Raven, and Starrante were there-fore the last to arrive at the familiar doors of the most impor-tant office in the Academia.

The doors rolled open as Starrante approached. Beyond them, the office of the chancellor was almost entirely unfamiliar. The desk at which the chancellor usually sat was unchanged, but nothing else was: the floors, the size of the room, the large stone table that stood closest to the doors, adorned on both sides by long stone benches. Chairs sat at either end of that table, and the chancellor occupied one—clearly the head.

"Come in," he said. "Killianas has made some adjustments to the room, in consultation with Scholar Larrantin. They are not, and will not, harm you; Killianas believes that these alterations will make the room secure against possible invaders. Starrante, move that chair. Robin and Raven can sit on the bench closest to you. Unless you prefer the ceiling or the wall."

"I wish to remain close to the children for the moment."

"Larrantin has given his word that he will make no attempt to harm either of the children unless he is attacked."

"The Barrani notion of attack has always been unpleasantly legalistic," the Wevaran replied, folding two of his arms. "I will stay. But yes, I will avail myself of ceiling." So saying, he climbed up a wall and onto the ceiling—just above where Robin and Raven now took a seat, as far from Larrantin as it was possible to get.

Robin knew this was a waste of time; Larrantin had been nowhere near them the first time Raven had run through closed doors—something he'd never before seen her do, but which hadn't truly surprised him—and vanished. But Larrantin had always been one of his best professors. He wasn't friendly, but he treated all of his students the same.

Larrantin thought Raven wasn't even a person. If he thought that, he would treat her differently.

"While I do not generally counsel trust of the Barrani," Killian said, "I would ask that—in this room, at this time—you trust Larrantin. He will not hurt Raven; he will not attempt to contain her in a similar fashion while we are here. He understands that both the chancellor and I consider Raven to be a prospective student. He will not attempt to harm her unless she attacks him and I cannot confine her attempt."

"We can't sleep in the chancellor's office," Robin said.

"There is no reason you cannot, should it be necessary, but the chancellor is unlikely to support that idea. He may, however, allow Raven to stay here if she is concerned."

The chancellor didn't even grimace. He had raised his inner eye membranes, which muted the red of his eyes, but not by much.

Teela remained at the table, as did Serralyn. Terrano, to Robin's surprise, had also been given a place. Sedarias and Valliant had not. Or perhaps they had chosen not to remain; he hadn't been here for that part. Larrantin didn't care for the benches, and was pacing by the side of the table.

When the doors closed, they also vanished; there were now no doors in the walls. No windows, either. Had the room not been so large, the lack of natural light or normal exits would have been claustrophobic.

To Robin's surprise, Raven relaxed, her neck bending as if she could finally lower her head. Her arms were trembling; he knew because he reached out, placing his palm over the back of her hand. She hesitated, and then covered that hand with the palm of her free hand, binding them together. "It's okay," she said, as if he were still the child she had met the first time in the warrens. "It's okay now."

"We don't need to hide?"

"No. We don't need to hide right now." She smiled hesitantly. "This is a hiding place."

"But Killian's here."

"Yes?"

"Killian couldn't even see the last two."

"Oh." She tilted her head, and then glared in Larrantin's direction, which was easy because he had stopped almost in mid-stride and was now staring at her, mouth half-open. "Maybe *he* told Killian something important. I don't know. It's safe here."

"Robin," Larrantin said. "Please come here."

Raven shook her head. She was attached to Robin by both hands, rather than the customary one; he stood, but remained pressed into the edge of the table.

"I'm sorry," Robin said, meaning it. He *liked* Larrantin. Larrantin could be easily distracted by what he was teaching and his lessons often ran amok as a stray thought caught his attention—which is why Robin paid attention to his lectures. They were fascinating when they weren't a chaotic mass of confusion waiting to happen.

Larrantin exhaled. His eyes, however, had become the standard Barrani blue, not the indigo they'd adopted from the moment he'd set foot in his invaded lab.

"Very well. I've been informed that Raven is your friend; I trust the source." He didn't glance at Serralyn, but Robin was certain that she was that trusted source. "You have known her for how long?"

"I don't know. Since I was seven?"

"Five," Raven said.

"Five."

"Where did you first meet her?"

"In the warrens, where I lived."

"And you called her?"

"Uhh, no."

Larrantin's expression made clear that he was at the end of patience. "Well?"

"She found me."

He turned to Raven. "The boy did not summon you?"
Raven shook her head.

"Did you make your way to his side on your own?" An undercurrent of worry—or possibly fear—underlay the question.

"Yes?"

"How?"

"Because he was Robin?"

Larrantin's frustration grew, but this time he turned to Robin. Of course he did. "Serralyn says that you often speak in Raven's stead if you understand what she meant to say."

Robin nodded hesitantly. Raven, however, squeezed the top of his hand in encouragement. He didn't particularly enjoy it when people spoke for him—especially not when he was present—but Raven had never minded.

"Sometimes," he conceded. "But usually only when we're talking to other people. Like people in the market, or people who have odd jobs—had odd jobs—for us."

"Odd jobs?"

"Deliveries. Or pickups. Raven was best for those—she could get out of the warrens and do the delivery without getting mugged or robbed. Better than I could, when I was young."

Larrantin's eyes were a different color—a gold with blue edges that Robin could not recall seeing before. The gold faded slowly, leaving blue behind. "They were jobs you had been tasked with?"

"Raven was better," Robin said, shrugging. "She'd go get glass beakers or tubes, or deliver requests for them. Sometimes she'd deliver other things—but in that range. Things given to kids."

"You asked her—Raven—to deliver mundane things?"

"No, not usually. She'd volunteer for some of the tasks, or we'd go together. Why?"

Larrantin lifted his head to look at Starrante, who remained on the ceiling, his many eyes pointing in different directions as he watched every occupant in the room.

Robin exhaled. "I don't understand why you seem so shocked."

"Raven," Larrantin said, a frown of disapproval around the corner of his lips, "did you volunteer to do these...menial tasks?"

She nodded without apparent shame, which was good because Robin certainly didn't feel any. "Robin needed money."

"For what?"

The scorn Larrantin had managed to conceal lit Raven's expression from within. "For *food*. He didn't want me to steal it."

"For food."

"He needed to eat."

"Mortal food."

"Yes?" Her hands tightened around Robin's.

"He did not command you to do this."

"No?"

Robin exhaled. "You're confusing her. She doesn't understand why you're asking questions that seem obvious to her."

Larrantin grimaced and once again began pacing.

"Why did you trap her?"

"There has been a subtle disturbance in the Academia," Larrantin replied. "It is not of the variety that would be easily countered by guards—or Killianas. To be countered, it must be perceived, and Killianas has demonstrable blind spots at the moment. I do not expect those to persist; in time, Killianas will be what he once was.

"But should his students perish, it will take far longer to reassert his existence. I have been a scholar for longer than the Academia has existed. Some part of the disturbance felt familiar to me." He looked up at Starrante. "Did you not sense it in Raven?"

Starrante did not answer.

"I had not yet encountered Raven; I have been much occupied with defense of the Academia. But there is, about her, the dark energy of the forbidden."

Starrante chittered at speed.

Larrantin replied in Barrani. "The trap was not set for Raven; it was set for that energy. I cannot divine intent when setting such a trap; I can divine physical essence. That darkness, that otherness, permeates the one you call Raven."

"You thought she was the killer," Robin said, voice flat.

"I thought that the being who emitted this energy must be contained if we wish to prevent further deaths, yes."

"You cannot build a jail that even you cannot break," Starrante said. "Raven is not the killer. When the next death occurred, you would become aware of that—but you would never be able to release Raven from the trap you created."

Larrantin nodded. "Release was not my concern in the creation of the defense. But, Robin, it—she—is dangerous. You do not understand what she is." He then turned to Raven. "Who called you? Who summoned you? It was not Robin—but it is Robin you have been serving. By whose command, little darkling? By whose life's blood were you anchored in place?"

"I won't tell you," she snapped. "It wasn't you. You don't need to know."

"Chancellor?" Larrantin said, voice soft, gaze fixed to Raven's face.

"What does he mean by 'life's blood'?" Robin asked Raven.

She didn't answer. But she didn't give him the disgusted expression that meant his question was a waste of breath, either.

"Raven?"

"Bad," she whispered. "It'll make you think bad thoughts."

Robin hesitated as he always did when Raven drew her boundaries. She didn't want to tell him. It had never come up before, because it wasn't a question he would ever have thought to ask. He knew, if he pushed, she would answer the question.

He didn't want to ask it.

Larrantin assessed the silence that remained unbroken, and finally shook his head in annoyance. "Killianas—map, please."

"Of?"

"The City of Elantra as it is currently constituted." That map appeared on the surface of one half of the impressive table. "And?"

Larrantin's smile eased the almost engraved frown he'd displayed. "*Ravellon*, before the fall. Place them side by side; cover the same geographic location Elantra now occupies."

Killian nodded; he had finished almost before Larrantin's instructions ended. The grey-haired Barrani turned immediately to the table; Robin had never left it. The chancellor stood, as did Serralyn.

Robin knew the name *Ravellon*: it was the heart of the fiefs, and the heart of the Shadow that, uncaged, would destroy their world. But Larrantin's *Ravellon*—the historical *Ravellon*—was far larger than the last of the fiefs, the fief the six Towers were meant to contain. It spread past the borders of the fiefs, and past the boundaries of Elantra, except where the harbor sat.

"Are these the same scale?" Robin asked.

Killian nodded. All of the city Robin knew was smaller than Larrantin's *Ravellon*.

He could see the lines that denoted the streets of the warrens in the Elantra he knew; could see the lines that denoted a different neighborhood, one with which he'd been familiar before everything had gone wrong.

Turning, he looked at Killian's *Ravellon*, at *Ravellon* before the fall.

Larrantin rolled his eyes. "Killianas, if you will?"

The two maps converged, the streets they marked in different colors. The lines overlapped; Robin could still see the warrens, but he could now see *Ravellon*, as well; he could see what had stood there before the warrens.

Starrante chittered.

"Yes," Larrantin said, nodding. "There was not much left of that section of *Ravellon* when the first hostilities broke out." To Robin, he said, "*Ravellon* was larger than Elantra. The fief that bears its name is very small in comparison. When Shadow came to *Ravellon*, there was combat, some particularly ferocious. Much of the *Ravellon* that once existed was destroyed in the conflagration.

"*Ravellon* fell in stages. This area, and this—Killian?—were lost immediately. Some areas of the city were not; the clashes were resolved in our favor. Shadow was vanquished without the loss of all life in the area. We had thought it destroyed; it merely retreated to a place where its work was harder. If we had known…" He did not finish. "Raven found you in the warrens."

Robin nodded.

"She did not come to your aid before you entered the warrens."

"No." He hadn't needed her. Not then. Need came later.

"Why did you go to the warrens?"

Robin shook his head. "I went with my mother."

"And where did you live before you entered the warrens?"

He was uncomfortable now. He could feel that discomfort grow, could feel the weight of it sprouting claws and fangs.

Raven stood, withdrawing one hand, and gripping Robin's hand tightly with the remaining one. "No," she said, glaring at Larrantin. "No more."

"It may be important," Larrantin said, not budging an inch as he returned Raven's glare. "You should not be here. You should never have been here. But you should not have been there, either. The fact that you could exist there—and can exist here—implies many things, none of them good if one is concerned about the survival of a species or two."

"Robin," the chancellor said, his voice almost unnaturally gentle. "Where did you live before your mother took you to the warrens?"

Robin shook his head. He tightened his hold on Raven, half wondering if she could run through the walls as easily as she had run through the closed doors of the office. And in running, take him with her.

She didn't move. She had turned to Robin, hand in his, waiting. As if she expected an answer. Or as if she knew what the answer was, and didn't consider it bad. He couldn't explain why it was bad—not without everyone else hearing it, as well. He felt the weight of everyone's stares as he finally lifted a hand; it shook.

"I'm not great at reading maps," he said, his words weak even to his ears. "And I didn't really talk about neighborhoods much—not by name. Not when I was a kid. But—I think it's here."

Terrano whistled.

Larrantin did not. "Killianas—please enlarge that section of both maps."

The chancellor leaned across the table, his eyes an unfamiliar color. Both he and Larrantin looked up to the ceiling, and Starrante at last condescended to descend.

"This neighborhood was not so severely damaged," Larrantin said. "But I am not entirely conversant with the migrations that occurred when the Towers rose. If I am not mistaken?"

Starrante's eyes did a little dance. "You know as much as I; we had no interaction with the outside world during the slumber of the Academia. Chancellor, Lord Teela, the history that we did not experience must now be left in your hands. In our time, however, the neighborhood you've indicated was once a ward for those whose research was more esoteric. There were protections woven into the streets, and gates—gates I do not see in evidence now—that stood before the fall.

"Mortals lived here. Some few Barrani, as well—those that could easily disregard the disapproval of their kind."

"Wevaran?"

"Yes. But we were never so numerous a people as mortals. We wove—that was our vocation—in concert with the mortals who made, who blessed, their small containments, their tiny spaces. Mortals die on their own; they are like little echoes of life, and they fade, will it or no. Certainly none of my people remained within these areas after the fall; they were summoned back to the heart of the city—the ancient heart—there to do battle in the last desperate attempt to preserve it.

"But there were workings in this place that may have survived the fall."

"It is not known for such things today," the Barrani Hawk said. "Robin—your family lived here?"

Robin nodded.

"There was nothing strange about your home or the homes that surrounded it?"

"Not that I recognized."

"Corporal?" the chancellor said.

"I will need either a name or an address," Teela said. "I assume you wish me to investigate Robin's prior residence."

Robin was quiet. "I...don't remember the number. But I don't think our home survived. There was a fire." His eyes were wide, almost unblinking—as if that fire were within him.

"Robin," Teela said, voice as gentle as the chancellor's. "What was your family name?"

22

Robin felt silence descend on him as if it were a smothering hand. He could barely breathe, and breath itself was a struggle.

Teela glanced at the chancellor; the chancellor frowned. "Larrantin?"

"Am I a simple errand boy, to cast a trivial spell at your convenience?" Larrantin snapped. Had Robin not been struggling to breathe, he would have laughed when Larrantin turned to the Wevaran. "Starrante, you do it."

Starrante clicked loudly. Larrantin rolled his eyes.

Throughout, Raven clutched Robin's hand so tightly he could barely feel his fingers.

"Do you know what they're talking about?" Robin asked, his voice a whisper, a thread of sound.

"Spell," she replied. When his confusion was mirrored on his face, she snorted. "On you."

"On *me*?"

Raven nodded. "She put it there. So that you couldn't answer the question."

"Raven—*who*?"

"Rianna. Rianna did it."

Robin lost his breath in a different way as the syllables of that name echoed in his ears. The room wasn't silent, but it might as well have been; all other voices vanished beneath the pull of their weight.

"Who is Rianna?" the chancellor asked.

Raven ignored him. She ignored the question when it came from Larrantin, but did look to the Wevaran when Starrante asked. The only person who she might answer was Robin, and Robin wasn't asking. Had no need to ask. He knew.

"She wasn't a mage," he said.

Raven tilted her head, her eyes narrowing. "Bad. Bad thoughts."

"She wasn't, Raven. I'd've known. If she'd been a mage—" He swallowed.

Raven shrugged. "Mage. Not mage. Doesn't matter."

"Arbiter, can you see the spell?" The chancellor's voice was a rumble. "It is not one I detected. It is not one Killianas detected. All prospective students are examined for magic when they first step foot on the campus."

"Robin was here before you were," Starrante pointed out. "It is possible that Robin—and the few students who chose to remain when the Academia was brought back—weren't as thoroughly vetted."

"That is not true," Killian said. He was watching Raven, not Robin, his face a mask of stone. "I can see no spell, no sigils that imply spells were cast. The chancellor cannot; An'Teela cannot. Nor can Larrantin. If anyone can untangle the meaning of this spell, it is you."

Larrantin frowned. "I sense no magic."

"Raven," Robin said. "What does the spell do?"

"Hides you," was Raven's prompt reply. "Not like I do. It's different hiding." She considered her words—he knew the slightly scrunched expression—before she spoke again. "If people are looking, I can find a hiding place for you. If there's danger, I can find a hiding place. Even here," she added, her nose wrinkling. "But some things are dangerous in ways I can't see. Or hear.

"She said, when you were older, the spell would unravel by itself, because you wouldn't need it anymore." She looked at Starrante. "Are we finished now?"

"Ah. No, I do not believe we are finished."

She glared at Larrantin but once again sat on the bench. Robin allowed his knees to bend, and joined her once again; their hands were clutched together, as if Robin were still that long-ago child.

"My apologies, Chancellor—but without Robin's cooperation, I cannot clearly see the strands of enchantment; I cannot break them safely without some sense of where they are or how they're powered. But I do not believe they are inimical."

Larrantin rolled his eyes. "Do not *believe*? Are we now talking about feelings or facts?"

The chancellor roared. Silence descended. "Gentlemen, this discussion can be had in your own space at a different time. I concur with the Arbiter's opinion, and it is not to cause Robin distress that we are here. We are here to discuss the school's defenses, and those defenses are not to entangle or threaten Raven."

"We do not know what Raven is," Larrantin said. "It is difficult, without some knowledge, to create strong defenses that do not overlap with her in any way. If we cannot understand what she is and how she exists in this space, we cannot prevent others like her from encroaching on our ground."

Teela stood then. "I have some investigations of my own to do," she told the chancellor. "I will leave to begin them." She then turned to Terrano, of all people. "You, get up. We're going."

"They're not finished here!"

"They've come as far as they can without external research.

I'm going to the Halls of Law. You're going to the High Halls. Speak to the High Halls; ask them what they know about both the warrens and the gardens."

"Gardens?" Robin was surprised to hear his own voice.

"It's what we call the district you once lived in. The warrens may have been historically more important—and the destruction inherent during the Shadow war far more complete as a consequence. The gardens are more of an unknown. They are a largely mortal district; I think one or two Barrani families own dwellings there—but they are not occupied by Barrani.

"It's considered a more moneyed neighborhood. People want to live there; no one wants to live in the warrens. If you fled to the warrens for safety..." Teela didn't finish the sentence. "Raven should hold her nose and speak with Larrantin." All of this had been said in Elantran. She exhaled. "I think Robin should either return to the warrens, or ask the information broker to visit again."

"Information broker?"

"Giselle."

"Why?"

"Because she knows the warrens, and she knows both of you. There might be information there she would never think to volunteer."

Raven clearly thought this was a great idea, given her expression—Giselle could talk to the professor, the chancellor, and the Arbiter, and Raven could hide in the room. With Robin. Robin wondered if she'd let go of his hand anytime in the next several hours. She continued glaring at Larrantin; Teela's suggestion, while fair, wouldn't be possible in the near future.

"He didn't mean to trap you," Robin began.

"He did."

"He didn't mean to trap *you* personally. He was just...trying to trap things that don't quite belong in the same space as the rest of us."

"Like me," Terrano said, grinning broadly.

Raven's shoulders relaxed slightly; her hand didn't.

Larrantin was annoyed. "If the chancellor does not see fit to continue this meeting—"

"I do. But if we are to discuss the particular direction of your defensive research—and its early test case—would you not prefer that Raven be absent? She will not—from experience—be able to give you answers upon which you can act, and she is almost at the point where any answers at all will not be forthcoming.

"However, I do have one suggestion."

Larrantin's eyes narrowed in totally justifiable suspicion.

"Killianas has asked Raven's aid in a matter that directly touches upon Academia security: she is to find what she refers to as hiding places within the Academia campus."

"Hiding places?" Larrantin turned to Robin.

"Pretty much exactly that, sir. She can find places where we can hide that won't be found."

"Won't be found by who?"

"Whoever is dangerous? I don't know, exactly. Raven's always found hiding places when I needed to hide. She's found a couple on the campus. But the thing is, the places she finds, Killian can't see."

Larrantin froze. "I beg your pardon?"

"He can't see them. Until we take him there, they're in his blind spot."

"He *is* the Academia. How can they be in a blind spot?"

"I don't know. Killian?"

"Robin is correct. I was unaware of the locations Raven found until I was led there—by Robin, not Raven. She is not inclined to reveal hiding places; she says it destroys them."

"Why?"

Raven didn't answer. "I think," Robin said, "it's because Killian knows where they are, and we can't hide from Killian."

"Why would you want to hide from Killian?"

"We don't," Robin said quickly.

"We do," Raven said.

"We don't. Killian *is* the Academia. Killian *is* home."

Raven just stared at Robin. "He's not my home." When Robin opened his mouth, she continued before he could speak. "He's not dangerous. He's not like the other things we run from. But everyone needs to hide sometimes. Everyone."

"She showed Killian where those hiding places were," Robin said in a rush. "And Killian asked her to find other hiding places in the Academia. But...when we needed the first one, Killian couldn't really see anything. Not where we were. We ran through the main hall—he didn't notice us. He couldn't hear me. I don't think it's *just* about hiding places."

Larrantin's eyes—dark to begin with—had darkened significantly by the time Robin had finished. "Killianas."

"It is true," the Avatar replied. "The chancellor is aware of the deficit—but he would not have been had it not been for Raven and Robin. Both times Raven sensed danger, danger was present. An'Teela and Terrano would be far more acquainted with that danger."

"An'Teela—" Larrantin began.

She lifted a hand, and not in the *I have a question* way. "We can discuss this at length when I return. If you are willing to trust my instincts, my instincts tell me that some external investigation is required. You, however, might join Terrano when he visits the High Halls; your information, or the information you receive, might have more weight, given your grounding in the difficulties of that distant past." Her eyes were at least as dark as Larrantin's. "I do not understand why you chose to absent yourself from the High Halls in the past, but the High Lord has changed at least three times since then.

"Regardless, we are leaving. Robin?"

"I will send for Giselle," the chancellor said. "I do not think it safe at present to send Robin and Raven to the warrens." He rose from the head of the table. "We will reconvene in the morning."

Robin and Raven returned to their room, but there was no peace in it.

"Rianna was my mother," Robin said when they'd entered the room and closed the door firmly behind them. Not that it mattered; Killian could still listen in. There was nothing about the students that Killian couldn't know, but he was prohibited from *sharing* private information without permission.

Probably.

"Yes?" Raven took up her position by the corner of the room, on the other side of the bed she'd pushed out of the way.

"My mother wasn't a mage," Robin continued.

"I don't know what a mage is. But she was like you, just powerful."

"I'm not a mage."

Raven nodded, the nod equivalent to a question mark.

"If she'd been powerful, we would never have had to run to the warrens. People wouldn't have died."

"Other people would have died, just not yours." She shrugged, folded her knees to chin, and wrapped her arms around them. "That's normal, though. We don't want our people to die. We don't want our people to abandon us. We don't care about people we don't know. Caring about strangers is *hard*."

"I was a stranger," Robin said quietly.

"Not to me. Not to her."

"How do you know?"

"You're her child."

"No—I mean, how do you know she cast a spell on me?"

Raven blinked. It was the expression she got when the question he'd asked made no sense. She considered it for some time, a sure sign she was trying to find words. "I think I was there," she finally said.

"You think?"

"It's hard, at first. It's always hard at first. Like…you had to learn how to speak and walk, right? Maybe like that."

"You were a baby?"

"No?" She snorted. "Babies are helpless. And stupid. They don't *know* anything. I knew things. I knew how to hide. I knew how to run. I knew how to find things."

"Like glass."

She smiled—a real smile, a full-on burst of happiness. "Like glass. I almost have enough."

"For what? For a desk?"

"Maybe? Killian has to make me a desk," she added, speaking more loudly.

"I am attempting to do that," Killian's voice said. His physical body didn't follow. "But I do not think the glass you found would make a good desk."

"Not yet. It's broken. But you can make whole glass from broken bits."

"Perhaps. Perhaps not. It is not glass as mortals understand glass. But, Raven, why have you been collecting it? Why is it important?"

"Because."

Killian waited.

"She doesn't know how to put it into words," Robin said quietly, seeing her familiar expression. "She doesn't know how to explain it to us." It made sense—without Raven, they wouldn't even see the shards she'd been collecting. "I think Starrante— Arbiter Starrante—has some idea."

"He is conducting his own research as we speak. But, Raven— this is not the first time you've protected someone, is it?"

"Yes? Maybe? No?"

Robin was interested in the answer, as well. It was another question he'd never asked. Raven had always been his age— from the moment she first ran into his life, to now. He had assumed that she, like he, was an orphan in a city that didn't care; how could children be called upon to protect other people? He untangled her answer to the best of his ability. "You didn't protect someone like me."

"No."

"But you did protect something."

"Yes."

"A person? A person like Larrantin or Starrante? A person more like me, but not me?"

"No one is like you," she said, and smiled. "But Wevaran, maybe. I don't remember. I don't remember the way you remember. But I can speak to Starrante. He can hear me. I think— I think I was a different shape, then. A different size. Wevaran live forever. I could learn to speak, and it didn't matter how long it took.

"But those words—Wevaran words, Barrani words, your words—aren't really words. I could speak *real* words. I can speak them now."

"Don't," Killian said, a note of alarm in his otherwise placid voice.

"No. You might understand me. Robin never would. Language is for communication. Communication is for understanding. It's very important." She stared at the far wall, eyes wide. "I don't remember who said it. Or why. But I remember now. I'd forgotten. Words like yours are hard."

"Why do you need glass, Raven?"

"I *don't know*." She swallowed air and words, rising to walk in a tight circle. Thinking. Robin waited. Killian waited because Robin did; Raven's thoughts would become words soon, given her expression. "To build a space," she finally said, the words tentative, as if in speaking them she was also testing their truth. Her gaze was upon the wall, and within the murk of memory she couldn't disentangle. Or so it seemed to Robin. "To build a space for Raven." She turned in the direction of Killian's voice, as if she could see him. Given what Robin now knew, she probably could. "He's growing. He'll grow up. When he's adult, that's the end of it."

"That's the end, unless..." She shook her head, her eyes narrowing, the expression one of accusation.

"Why have you never discussed this with Robin?"

Raven's lips compressed.

Killian might not hear Raven's thoughts, but he had spent enough time observing her that he knew what her expression meant. "I will see you in the morning. The chancellor expects you both in his office after breakfast."

After breakfast became *after lunch*, as an unavoidable delay had occurred according to Killian. Raven and Robin were once again on hiding-place duty until then. Raven found nothing, but she was annoyed with Killian, so that could have been deliberate. She felt that he had somehow tricked her into answering questions he had no business asking.

Robin pointed out, as gently as possible, that murders were likely to continue if they didn't understand exactly what was happening. If Raven could, for example, explain to Starrante—Robin had given up on meaningful discussion between his friend and Larrantin—how she knew there was danger, they might be able to work with that. It would save lives.

It could, as Robin stressed to her, save the lives of people he knew. Some of those people had already died, and he didn't want any more deaths. A shadow of his early childhood held nothing but death and loss whenever he crossed its path—he didn't want it to become longer or darker.

Raven didn't believe discussion would change anything. "I can't breathe for you. If you're drowning, and I breathe, you don't get air."

"But this is—it's magic, right?"

She snorted and stomped ahead of him to the chancellor's office. The doors opened as they stood in the doorframe. Standing by the chancellor's desk was an older woman both recognized: the grey crow.

She smiled as she caught sight of them. "I hear you've been causing a bit of trouble?"

"Not us," Robin replied, returning her smile. "But it hasn't managed to kill us yet."

Her smile faded. "That serious, then? Raven?"

"It's *worse* than the warrens here."

"What, this fancy place? Worse than the warrens?" The grey crow laughed.

Raven didn't. She was watching Giselle, her head tilted to one side, as if something about the grey crow was familiar in a way she couldn't place. But she shook her head and nodded. "It's worse. I think more people die in the warrens, though."

"What kind of school are you running here?" Giselle drawled, turning to the chancellor; he had remained seated behind his desk, which was probably smart.

"A school in which Robin desires to learn," the chancellor replied, his voice rumbling.

"That doesn't impress me if the students are dying."

"It should. Imperial Law with regard to Dragons is not enforced here. There is one ruler of the Academia: me."

Giselle did not appear to be either intimidated or impressed by what was clearly a threat.

It wasn't an entirely credible threat, in Robin's opinion. The chancellor exhaled a steady, visible stream of smoke before he spoke again. "I believe I have paid your fee for information; your opinion about my Academy is neither required nor desired.

"Our students are neither slaves nor prisoners. Should Raven or Robin choose to withdraw from the Academia, they will be allowed to collect their things and return home."

"Raven?" The grey crow wasn't stupid. She didn't bother asking Robin.

But Raven shook her head. "I stay with Robin. If Robin is here, if there's danger here, this is where I must be."

"Why?"

"I—I want to be here. I want to be where Robin is!"

Giselle's eye narrowed, although her lips turned up at the corners. "That is almost an excellent lie. I believed it for a moment."

"It's not a lie," Robin said.

"Ah, yes. It's not a lie on the surface. It's a lie by omission. I have no doubt that Raven wants to be where you are. But that is not what she said. She said she *must* be here. Raven. Why?"

In a very small voice, Raven said, "Because the price was paid."

Robin was surprised she'd answered. She treated the grey crow's questions very differently than anyone else's. That made sense in the warrens—but the Academia wasn't the warrens. Here, Giselle was a visitor, a guest. The grey crow was at the center of the only semisafe web in the many overlapping webs that comprised the warrens. But she was Giselle, a mortal; the chancellor was a Dragon.

More surprising, more unsettling: Giselle seemed to understand the answer; something in her expression made clear that she'd had suspicions, and they'd been confirmed. Somehow.

"For how long?" Giselle asked.

"Until Robin is adult."

"Is the murderer hunting Robin?"

"I don't know."

Giselle turned to Robin then. "I thought you'd be safe here. With this Dragon, with Killianas. The things that could kill you are the usual things: Barrani, ambitious mortals. In civilized places, they have to be more subtle. Usually."

"And Raven?"

"I wasn't worried about Raven's safety." Giselle folded her

arms. "Chancellor," she finally said grudgingly, "ask your questions."

"I find your own questions oddly compelling," the chancellor replied, his eyes orange red. "But they lead to questions I had not thought to ask. Do you know what Raven is?"

"She's Robin's friend. And his guardian. The warrens don't have guardians in the traditional sense." Her smile was a thin, unkind edge. "I'm not cut out for it, myself. There are laws in the warrens, unspoken, that everyone obeys. Robin wouldn't have survived there were it not for Raven. I gave him odd jobs, and I observed him as he grew—until the day he disappeared."

"Did you search for him?"

"He wasn't in the warrens. Outside of the warrens, my contacts are less reliable."

"And inside?"

Giselle's smile deepened. "You wouldn't have called me here if you didn't already know the answer."

"I have assumed—as most will—that the warrens are dangerous slums. Imperial Laws are haphazardly enforced there; the only Hawks that patrol those streets are Barrani. Mortal Hawks don't generally survive unscathed."

"We don't take kindly to outsiders. If you can't lend a helping hand, you don't get to make the rules. You might try to change them—I'll give the Emperor that much—but mostly, we're ignored. We like it that way."

Robin didn't.

"Does the name Rianna mean anything to you?"

Giselle's gaze swiveled to Robin, which was good; Robin couldn't move.

"What does it mean to you?" the grey crow countered.

"It meant nothing until the moment we were told Rianna was responsible for an enchantment laid upon Robin—an enchantment we cannot detect. Raven can."

Giselle nodded. "I know the name."

"It is not a common name, even among mortals."

"What the boy can't tell you, I won't. If this Rianna cast a spell—and if it can't be detected, I'm inclined to doubt—"

"It can be detected. By Raven. We would not know of it otherwise."

"Then have her explain it."

Raven snorted. "Robin is my friend. It's meant to protect him."

"How?" the chancellor demanded.

"She didn't want him to talk about some things. She thought it would be bad. For him. She thought he wouldn't know who to trust—in the warrens, it's hard. Even here," she added. "She didn't have time to teach him so he'd understand. She was dying."

"So she made this instead."

"And he has no choice."

"It's bad," Raven replied. "It's all bad thoughts. Robin doesn't need them. Not yet." Her tone said *not ever*. She had always hated it when his thoughts strayed in the wrong direction: that of loss, of death, of resentment—even envy for the child he had once been, who had had everything.

He was certain he had been happier for it, for the reminder that there were still things he valued, his life among them. He had not felt constrained by external spell, hadn't even noticed it until yesterday, when he could barely breathe because he had tried to answer a simple question. Ah, no, a complicated question.

"Giselle, you knew Rianna."

"We met, yes. But she was from the gardens; the warrens were my home. What possible connection could two such disparate lives have?"

"That is the question, isn't it?" The chancellor rose. "These two sections of Elantra stand upon the remains of lost *Ravellon*. The warrens were gutted—or so history tells us; whatever stood there was destroyed. The gardens were not so heavily damaged. Once, in the history of *Ravellon*, the warrens were important. The gardens, less so—or more subtly so. Were I to flee with my child—should I ever have them—it is not to the warrens I would flee."

"The warrens are only safe if the things hunting you belong in the rest of the city," Giselle replied. "But we each had our duties. Mine are in the warrens. Hers were not."

"She died in the warrens."

"She was dying when she arrived. When she crossed the border, dragging her young son—the only member of her family who survived. Those who killed her were political creatures; they did not, and do not, understand what they set in motion. They simply wanted her branch of the family to die out. Her husband was a lord of the human caste court; he was respectable, wealthy, a man of power in Elantra.

"And he had brothers, sisters, uncles, cousins—people who desired that power for their own. Mortals aren't a patch on Barrani, but in proximity to Barrani, they learn the same games; they just play them more desperately."

"Chancellor," Killian said.

Giselle frowned and turned in the direction of the voice; Killian, mindful of the presence of a guest, materialized.

"My apologies for disturbing your meeting, but An'Teela has arrived. She is accompanied by Terrano. I would have them wait, but I believe their information is of relevance to the discussion in progress."

"Let them in. Is the Arbiter with them?"

"No. Should I inform you of his presence when he arrives?"

"Yes."

Giselle was far less comfortable in the presence of the Barrani Hawk than she had been in the presence of the chancellor. It struck Robin as odd; the chancellor was the power here. Teela could do nothing to Giselle unless Killian desired it—and if he did, he could manage on his own.

Perhaps it was because Teela was wearing the Hawk's tabard. She hadn't come as a Hawk yesterday, but she was here as one today: she had a partner with her, another Barrani Hawk.

"Has this become official business?"

"Quite possibly," Teela replied. "Terrano, quit playing around."

Terrano emerged from thin air. "The High Halls remembers what used to stand where the warrens now stand. There was a reason it was reduced to rubble—to less than rubble—and the citizens who lived there perished. The Shadow was subtle, but strong; it had infiltrated one of *Ravellon*'s key sources of power."

"Power?"

"*Ravellon* was once called the living city," Terrano said. "According to the High Halls. Before he became the sentient heart of those Barrani halls—before he was chosen to guard and protect the race from the traces of Shadow, or worse—he himself dwelled within the warrens. It was not called the warrens then, of course; it was a highly desired place to live, to work, to study.

"There was, at the heart of the warrens, a web. He said that our lamps in the city are placed aboveground. The heart of the warrens lay beneath it, a gossamer web, a thing that was alive and almost aware, although it wasn't sentient in the fashion the High Halls or the Academia were. There were buildings that were sentient in the warrens; it's part of the reason the warrens had to be so thoroughly destroyed. The sentience of those buildings were infiltrated by Shadow, and by Shadow transformed. The buildings themselves were rooted in the web of power. Uh, he called it life. Like…life essence, something distinct from a living being.

"It might have been some form of an Ancient. I couldn't quite get a better explanation."

"That power was corrupted?"

"Not in a way that was noticed at the time. I believe the Ancients believed all had been destroyed. Certainly the buildings had, and the people who had inhabited many of them; some weren't apparently mobile. And after that? They focused on the core of *Ravellon*; they couldn't destroy it—they would have, if they'd had the power. Instead, in the end, the Ancients created the Towers, and the Towers rose to stand guard."

"And the warrens?"

"Well, in theory there's nothing in the warrens anymore." Terrano glanced at Raven. He then turned to Giselle. "Apologies for my manners. I am Terrano. To my left is An'Teela, a corporal of the Hawks, and her partner, Tain."

"I'm Giselle," the grey crow said, speaking Elantran to Terrano's brief Barrani. "I live in the warrens."

The Hawks exchanged a glance; to Robin's surprise it was clear that they knew Giselle from before her entrance to the Academia. He frowned and lifted a hand, as if he were in a lecture hall.

"Robin?"

He faced Giselle, who was watching him with a slightly narrowed eye. "There's something left in the warrens, isn't there?" When Giselle failed to answer, he turned to Raven. "Most of your glass pieces—you found them in the warrens, right?"

She thought about it; he could almost see her making a list of all the pieces and assessing their locations before she nodded. "But not all."

"No," Robin said. "Not all. Were the other pieces found in the gardens?"

23

Raven frowned.

"The map," Robin said. "You saw it yesterday. The warrens, you knew. The gardens were the other part of the city the maps showed."

Raven's frown deepened. Of course it did. Seen as flat lines, the map of the warrens looked nothing like the warrens to anyone who wasn't at least a bit familiar with maps, the language of maps. He began to walk her through streets by name, instead; to describe where the gardens started, where they ended, how far they extended on either side. Some of their delivery jobs had led them there. It wasn't that Raven didn't know—it was that she couldn't put the lines over the streets she did know, couldn't reduce them that way.

Her expression cleared. "Yes. Some were from the gardens. Why's it called the gardens, though? It's mostly streets and houses."

"I don't know. I mean, why is Coppertop a street name? Makes no sense, either. But—glass was found in the warrens and in the gardens. Anywhere else?"

"Here."

"Anywhere else in the city that isn't the Academia?"

"I don't think so. I don't wander the rest of the city. It's too far away."

The Hawks waited, at least one with interest, until Raven had finished. Teela then turned to Robin. "Robin, you said you lived in the gardens?"

He froze, but nodded. It wasn't pleasant, but he could nod with discomfort. He could still breathe.

"Was your father Lord Onuri?"

Breath slowed. His chest constricted. He couldn't be certain that this was caused by enchantment and not by memory. "Yes."

"And your mother Rianna Gardianno?"

He nodded again, his throat thick.

"You had one older brother, and one younger sister."

He nodded, the scene before his eyes flickering. Brother? He could not remember. Must not remember. But he felt it as true.

Giselle looked down at her feet—or the surface of the chancellor's desk.

Killian said, "Yes, Giselle. Giselle of Gardianna."

"That is not my name," Giselle said, eye slender, almost flashing.

"It is the name uppermost in your thoughts. I apologize for the invasion of your privacy; I have bent the rules that govern my existence, but have not broken them."

"Please do not do so again," the chancellor said, eyes as narrow as Giselle's. "You have not spent much time in sentient buildings," he told the grey crow. "I did not think to issue that order because you are very much the type of person who is adept at masking your thoughts. Do you know why unknown creatures are hunting here?"

"I did not even know such unknown creatures existed until you informed me, Chancellor. I did not know about mysterious pieces of glass, either," Giselle replied. She exhaled slowly.

"But, Raven, you say you found them only here, in the warrens, and in the gardens?"

Raven nodded.

Giselle folded her arms, compressing her lips. She met—and held—the chancellor's gaze.

Teela, however, took it from her. "I am certain you are wondering why we are present as Imperial Hawks and not friends of students," she said.

"*Wonder* is perhaps the wrong word. *Dread* might be more appropriate. You are going to make me waste my time conferring with the Emperor. I do not have that time, and I will be ill pleased for at least a century."

The Imperial Hawk might have weathered angry Dragon every day. "A murder occurred nine years ago. It reached the ears of the Barrani High Court; it cannot have failed to reach the ears of the Imperial Court. Investigations of that murder—and the fire that followed it—were severely hampered; the residence did not employ nonhumans to our knowledge, and the crime was deemed a crime under the auspices of the rules of exemption. It is seldom that humans invoke those laws—but the murder involved the family of a member of that caste court."

Robin was now staring at the floor beneath Giselle's feet, his head heavy, his heart loud.

Raven took his hand. Took it, held it, her grip slowly tightening. When he looked up at her, he could see she was assessing the path to the office doors.

"Chancellor, Arbiter Starrante has arrived. He is perhaps in an excited or anxious state."

"If Giselle and the Hawks have no objections?"

"I have," Giselle said.

"Teela?"

"I was present for the beginning of this, and would see it to the end. It is not, however, within the remit of my visit."

Raven looked up at Giselle. "He's a giant spider," she said. "But—he's important, and he protects Robin."

"A...giant spider."

"Wevaran. That's what his people are called."

Giselle exhaled. "Very well, little Raven. I withdraw my objections."

Starrante's eyes were extended, and they were waving—quickly—from side to side; if they'd been pointed, he'd look like a balding porcupine. He was carrying papers in three of his limbs, so his gait was far less smooth than usual. He skittered over to the chancellor's desk and dropped the papers there.

The chancellor rose. "Killian, I believe we need a different table. And a different room."

Killian's silent reply was a reconfiguration of what had been the chancellor's familiar office. "My apologies, Giselle," the chancellor said. "The others in the room are accustomed to these kind of alterations."

"I'm beginning to understand why Robin likes it here," the grey crow replied, her lips half-crooked in an odd smile, her gaze entirely fixed upon Starrante. "I have heard tales of Wevaran; I have never seen one. Nor did I expect to, in my life." She shook her head, and to Robin's surprise, she lifted both of her arms. The movements should have been awkward at best, but they were far smoother, far more practiced, than Robin's.

Starrante turned his entire body to face her, his eyes the color of surprise. "My apologies," he said. "I was in a bit of a rush and did not fully see you."

Robin was certain he'd seen her; he just hadn't considered her presence significant. To be fair, he'd considered no one but the chancellor relevant. Limbs relieved of the burden of paper, Starrante lifted them in greeting.

Giselle spoke.

Raven stiffened, but her grip on Robin's hand didn't tighten.

Robin didn't recognize the language; to his ears, it wasn't Wevaran, but he'd had little experience with its use by people who didn't have Wevaran vocal cords. It didn't sound like Raven's Wevaran.

Starrante replied in kind, and then, to Robin's surprise, lifted one limb and touched the grey crow's forehead. Robin was certain that he'd never seen anyone foolish enough to physically touch Giselle before; no one *wanted* to lose a hand.

He also hadn't expected—although Raven had, given her expression—the soft nimbus of light that surrounded Giselle's head, like a gentle tiara.

"It is still there," Starrante said softly, speaking now in the Barrani everyone in the room could understand. "Perhaps my research was pointless."

"It wasn't necessary, was it?" Giselle asked.

"It was necessary to ascertain the changing shape of this new city, this modern collection of living beings, and the ancient boundaries of what once stood in its place. Some of your streets—some of the streets the warrens have claimed—are unaffected, unrelated; some of the streets the gardens, as you call them, once claimed have been lost. But the heart of each endured.

"Understand that it has been long since I have walked any streets; I may be able to exit this building and walk in the quaint little park—but I cannot wander farther. I am the library's Arbiter until I die, and my kind are immortal.

"Your kind are not. They change with the passage of centuries, as a race; they change within a small handful of years individually, becoming nigh unrecognizable to those who have seen them once or twice in passing. Did you have a hand in Raven?"

"No."

"I see. She should never have been released, should never have been called."

It was Robin's hand that tightened, Robin who stepped forward in instant outrage.

"Rianna was desperate," Giselle replied. "She knew the line must continue, and the rest of her children, newly dead."

"Humans do not lay clutches, as our kind do; nor are they guaranteed to have only one hatchling survive. Surely within the broad tree of mortal lineage, a child could otherwise have been found?"

"I didn't ask. I knew what had happened to her family; she did not have the time, and if the warrens hides its own, she was not one of ours. There has been almost no contact between our lines." Her smile was almost bitter. "There is always a grey crow; there is only ever one."

"That is not the nature of crows," Starrante replied. "I did not recognize Raven when I first encountered her here. I would not have recognized her, regardless. What she is is not what she was—and what she was…" His limbs moved, waving gracefully in the air, as if he had no Barrani words for what he described.

Giselle nodded. "She is not what the stories describe, no."

"Did you know?"

Giselle shook her head. "The magicks of old *are* stories to me. Only a few of the customs that might once have flourished in a time long lost to us were preserved in the ruins. I was born to be the grey crow. I was taught."

"Giselle—what is the grey crow supposed to do?" Robin surprised himself by speaking.

She smiled, that expression tinged with her natural bitter caution. "Watch. Guard."

"Guard what?"

She didn't answer, but turned once again to Starrante, who had waited patiently. "I studied the language of ritual, but it was taught, spoken. You know the words. It was not so with the gardens; what she knew was more complete. But it was also incomplete, clearly. It is far too easy for my kind to lose the heart of such a story." She exhaled. "Robin came to the warrens not due to any malfunction in ancient rites and oaths;

he came to evade the treachery of the mortal, the political. If magic was involved in his flight, it was the magery gold and ambition can purchase.

"It was not what was feared in ancient tales. It was not the things for which we were meant to serve as sentinels and guardians; it is a mortal contrivance—but all races desire the illusion of power, because with power there is safety." Her smile was very unpleasant. "We live in the worlds in which we were born. We make our way through that world. Sometimes, we fall."

"Were you present when she called for help?"

Giselle was silent for too long. She bowed her head; Robin thought it was to hide the expression she couldn't quite control. "She was dying when she entered the warrens. She knew it. She had lost too much blood. She had attempted to stem the flow of blood—but she had lost her right hand, as well. Literally.

"I was not present, but I heard it: the sound of shattering. The cry of exultation, of freedom."

"Whatever it was she called upon, I did not see. But I saw her. I saw her child. We…argued, but it was brief; she had no strength for it, and there was no point." Something about Giselle was odd; Robin realized, belatedly, that she was speaking Barrani. She'd been speaking Barrani. "No discussion could change any of the events that had already happened.

"But from that moment on, there was a tension in the warrens that had nothing to do with people's daily struggle to survive. I cannot speak for the gardens."

"Raven," Robin whispered. "How *long* have you been collecting glass?"

"And metal bits?"

Robin nodded.

She shrugged, her brow creasing. "Six years? Maybe a bit longer. Maybe a lot longer. But before, it was hard to find them. There are a *lot* here."

Giselle's expression hardened. "Here? In the Academia?"

Raven nodded. She didn't see this as a bad thing—it was probably the only good thing about the Academia in her mind.

"Understand," Giselle said, speaking once again to Starrante, "we did not see broken glass. What I describe as the sound of something shattering didn't result in shards of glass."

"And metal," Raven said.

"That, either."

Starrante was silent, his eyes dancing slowly and methodically.

Robin tightened his grip on Raven's hand. "When Larrantin trapped you—" he began.

She hissed.

"Was it like that? Like where you were before?"

"Before?"

"Before my mother called for you. Before my mother asked for your help."

"She didn't ask," Giselle said quietly. "Raven, tell him."

Raven, however, said nothing for a long beat. It wasn't her confused nothing; it wasn't her dismissive *people are strange* nothing. She looked, for just that moment, far older than Robin. Far older than anything in the room except perhaps—*perhaps*—Starrante.

But her hand was still familiar, and she tightened it briefly around his. She didn't let go before she began to speak. "She did ask," she told Giselle, staring at the grey crow as if she had never seen her before, but should have. There was familiarity in Raven's expression, and none of the usual confusion. It was as if a different Raven existed within her, and was being forced to wake.

"She asked."

"What did she ask?" Giselle said, speaking far more carefully than she had ever spoken to any denizen of the warrens. Her visible eye seemed faintly luminous in the transformed office, reflecting a light Robin's eyes couldn't see.

"To protect her child," Raven replied. Her speaking voice was different. Robin would have pulled his hand away, but her grip didn't allow that without struggle. And if he were honest, he didn't really want to let go, either—but he felt that this entire discussion was something he shouldn't hear, shouldn't be part of.

"To protect him without drawing attention to him. To keep him safe, to keep him *hidden*."

"For how long?"

"Until he was fully grown. Those were her words. But she spoke them, with effort, in the old tongue. I knew what she meant. I thought I knew. But…" Raven shook her head. "The warrens had changed so, so much. The gardens. It was hard to *think*. You understand that."

Giselle nodded. "You were never meant to think our thoughts, speak our tongue. You were never meant to be… Raven."

"What was I meant to be?" Raven demanded, her usual voice returning.

"I do not know. I am not lying. I was not there when you were called; I heard the shattering. I heard the breaking of a long-held covenant, a containment, a vow. I came to find her, but she was dying. I thought you had killed her to seal the bargain."

Robin paled to white.

Raven, however, shook her head. "I told you. She was dying. She was bleeding. She could not staunch the flow of her blood. I thought—I think I thought—that she had called me to heal her. I thought the child was the offering."

The chancellor rumbled. Robin couldn't look away from Raven—as if his gaze was the only thing that kept her in place, that *made her* Raven. But he knew the chancellor didn't approve. He couldn't even explain to his oldest friend why her words were so terrible; she wasn't looking at him. She'd shed the confusion he found almost comfortable.

Because when she was confused, when he could explain,

when he could help, he'd felt useful. He'd felt needed. He'd felt like they were equals. Yes, Raven could find hiding places, and that had saved his life many times. But Raven couldn't talk to people; she could barely understand what they said half the time. At least in the beginning.

But he understood, in this room, with the grey crow, Starrante, and Raven herself, that that wasn't true. She had never needed him. She had no reason to live the life she'd been living by his side beyond…whatever had brought her here. She probably didn't need sleep—she'd never seemed to need as much as Robin. She'd never really been hungry, even when hunger was the only thing he could think of. She'd never gotten as cold as Robin, either.

She wasn't like Robin.

Maybe she'd been forced into the shape, the size, the apparent age, by a desperate parent—but she personally had no other use for it.

She had found glass. It wasn't the glass that had shattered when she had been called—he was almost certain of that. But it was like that glass in some fashion. Had the calling somehow broken other containers, other vessels?

Starrante had talked about containments created to house the stray thoughts of the Ancients—those beings whose very thoughts could create chaos, as if the most stray of thoughts had a life, a will, an intent of its own. To the Ancients, those thoughts were insignificant; to the races they had labored to create, the worlds they had made and populated, they were inimical, deadly. Or they could be.

Starrante had seen them. He had seen them in his distant youth. Perhaps he'd been curious.

The Wevaran had thought them lost—lost with *Ravellon*. But something must have endured in the ruins of that vast and ancient city. Someone must have tried to keep those things contained, somehow, to keep them from the much less grand city—or cities—that grew up around and in the ruins.

Robin hesitated. "Giselle," he finally said, finding his voice. "You said my mother shouldn't have done what she did. I think maybe Starrante agrees. Is what she did somehow responsible for the strange things occurring in the Academia? The chancellor can ask the Halls of Law if similar deaths are occurring with the same frequency in Elantra. They might not know for certain about deaths in the warrens, but they'll know about deaths in the gardens.

"Or is it mostly only here?"

"That is an excellent question," the chancellor said quietly. "Arbiter?"

"Neither I nor this woman can fully explain what has occurred. Perhaps she can explain some of the details that I myself was never privy to."

"I can't," Giselle said, voice flat. "I barely countenanced them myself; they were old stories, old mysteries, things that I half believed. And I was taught only half of them—that was the division. Half for the core, half for the threads wrapped around it. The other half would be the gardens, and with Rianna's death, they are lost."

Raven shook her head.

Giselle frowned, but didn't engage with the denial. Robin wished she would. "The core was called the labyrinth. Neither are things I can discuss in any environment but the warrens, and even there, it is only discussed with those who are chosen to enter. I will not speak of it further, here; I have already skirted the dangerous edge proscribed in the lessons I was taught."

Starrante's eyes froze on their stalks before they swiveled to face her.

"Surely that's what your notes implied."

"My notes were contemporary historical notes. And those

contemporary sources made clear that that section of *Ravellon* had been gutted, that it was dead."

"Do you still believe that?"

"Chancellor," the Arbiter said, without looking away or moving his body, "please. Read."

The chancellor picked up the three reports. He read in a silence interrupted only by breath.

"It was important enough that what stood here be either preserved or destroyed, there were several teams sent to it?" The chancellor exhaled a stream of smoke.

"Shadow threatened the labyrinth. That," Giselle said softly, "is what I was taught. I *believe* the stories imply that it was a site of solitary pilgrimages. People of all races came to the mouth of the labyrinth, and they walked it. They could leave at any time, but should they choose to abandon, they would not reach the heart of that maze."

The chancellor continued to read Starrante's emergency research notes. "It was felt necessary to destroy what had long lain at the heart of what is now the warrens. I am unfamiliar with the word that describes it," he added, frowning. "But some volumes state that a life existed at the heart of the labyrinth; it was sometimes called the source." One brow rose. "The source could not be reached in a normal fashion, and even the supplicants who came to walk the maze could not tread the same path twice."

Starrante's eyes nodded as paper rustled.

"It appears there were sorcerers tasked with the necessary cleansing," the chancellor said, continuing to read at a speed that Robin found intimidating. "I do not recognize all of these names, but I recognize perhaps half; it was not a small group, and it was not a group without significant power. I note one name in particular.

"If I understand what I am reviewing, this group was sent

to destroy what they feared could not be preserved in the wake of *Ravellon*'s fall. They knew by this time that the Shadow had spread to other worlds through the gates; they knew worlds had been devoured, defenseless against the danger about which they had no warning.

"They therefore understood that this world could meet the same fate." His brows rose as he lifted his gaze from paper to Starrante. Starrante's eyes bobbed, the Wevaran nod. "What was encased in the warrens was an essential part of the power that supported much of the city: light, environment, weather; in some rare cases, life itself. *Ravellon* at its height was home to many, many races.

"There was a sentience to it that even the wise did not fully understand; it could not be easily studied because of the mysteries; the criterion to enter it, to touch it, to interact with it was subjective, individual. If Shadow breached that labyrinth, if Shadow could walk it or seep into it somehow, the catastrophe would outstrip any danger historically encountered.

"So it was destroyed. Killianas."

"Chancellor."

"I believe that Larrantin was summoned from the Academia at the time to aid in the deconstruction of that essence; his is the most prominent name I recognize. Of the others, there are three, two of whom are now deceased. Dragons," he added.

"I have informed him of your desire for both his counsel and his presence; I have taken the liberty of recounting most of the conversation to this point so he will know what is being discussed, and possibly why."

Larrantin, who hated to be disturbed, appeared at the door of the office as if by magic. Probably was. He entered the room, ignoring the doors that shut at his back. He even managed to offer the chancellor a passable bow before he turned to Starrante. Starrante and Giselle. He gestured.

"Larrantin," Killian said.

"It is a rudimentary precaution," the scholar said, ignoring Killian's expression. "If what was discussed is relevant, I must be certain of the mortal who now resides in the warrens."

"Certain of what?" Giselle asked in sharp Elantran.

"That you are mortal. That you are not somehow infected."

"I believe the Academia would know."

"And I do not, clearly."

Giselle turned to the chancellor. "I am not a criminal."

Robin's silence was loud.

Giselle's smile was almost feline. "I have not fallen foul of the Imperial Laws. I am not going to be detained and examined by a Barrani scholar when I came here as a favor." But she turned to the Barrani Hawks. "You came here on official business. I'm no Hawk, and I'm certainly no saint. But if you would take my advice, leave Robin alone. For now, he is safe."

Raven snorted.

"As safe as he can be under these trying circumstances," Giselle then said—in Barrani. "You think of him as a witness to an unsolved crime—or rather, a crime suppressed by the caste court. You hope that he will choose to have that investigation reopened, as it is well within his rights.

"But he will die. He will die, and any sacrifices—intentional and ill-advised—that were made to preserve his life will be wasted."

"Giselle," the chancellor said. "I ask that you forgive Larrantin his trespass. He is ancient and ill-tempered; he treats everyone this way. Larrantin was one of the men who knew what the warrens once were; he walked the labyrinth about which you have only stories. I do not know if he could walk it during the cataclysm—but he was well versed in both its mysteries and what could be learned of what it contained.

"His interest in you, and what you might signify, predates the Empire. It predates the fall. I will admit to my eye you look like a middle-aged mortal, windburned, sunburned, wizened by life in the warrens, where you must be considered ancient by most of the children in the streets."

Giselle nodded, but grinned. "Ancient at my age is terrifying—not old enough to be doddering but obviously canny enough—or treacherous enough—to survive. People don't cross me more than once."

Robin nodded vigorously. "Most don't dare to try it once," he added.

"The value of reputation," Giselle said. "It saves the lives of idiots. Your eye is good, Chancellor. So is your money."

Larrantin's eyes were blue, and darkening. He stepped between Giselle and the chancellor, and he lifted his left hand, palm up, elbow bent. To Giselle—for he faced Giselle—he spoke words. The syllables were not familiar enough to Robin that he could count words; there were only a handful. Raven's grasp tightened enough that his hand went numb.

Giselle's eye went almost white—as if she'd rolled it up far into her head. She lifted her right hand, in the same posture although Larrantin was a good deal taller, and placed her palm against his. She spoke three loud, sharp words—different in every possible way from Larrantin's.

Starrante's breath rattled.

"Raven—Raven, what is she doing?"

Raven didn't answer. Robin thought it was because she couldn't hear him. She was staring at Giselle—no, at her hand, and at Larrantin's. Robin was surprised when she let go of his hand, and very surprised when she tackled Giselle, knocking her to the floor.

The light and heat that existed in Giselle's hand—and her eye—dimmed as the contact was broken.

Raven turned to Larrantin, a man she already had reason to detest, and screamed, *"Are you stupid?"*

Larrantin blinked and slowly lowered his arm to extend a hand to Giselle. Giselle didn't take it, but did push herself off the floor, her eye narrowed as she turned to Raven. "You saw," she said.

"I think everyone did," Terrano said. Terrano who in theory was not in the office.

"What did you see?" the chancellor demanded.

"Ask Starrante. I think it's up his alley."

Starrante appeared to be having trouble speaking or breathing. Robin had never seen the Wevaran like this before. He spoke two words—in his native tongue—and Giselle replied in the same.

"I see. I see. Giselle—if I may call you thus—are you Warden?"

Giselle turned to the Wevaran, her lips a compressed, whitened line. She exhaled slowly, massaging her hands. "Yes," she finally said. "For all the good it does or has done my family through the centuries, I am the current Warden."

"I do not understand Raven's presence. I do not understand why Robin's mother fled to the warrens. From the gardens, if any trace of the ancient source remained, she should have been able to do what must be done."

Giselle shook her head. "This is...the first time. The first time I have seen the beginning of the mysteries evoked. No one has spoken the words Larrantin spoke for generations. There are no notes, no journal entries, that would indicate that *anyone* has."

Larrantin's eyes were indigo. "The source survived the fall," he said, voice flat.

"If it were contaminated, as was once feared, the city would know. The High Halls would know," the chancellor said. He did not look particularly surprised at what he had heard.

"Much is hidden in the warrens," Giselle replied. "But no. Of Shadow, there is no trace."

"I will visit to ascertain that claim," Larrantin said.

"You will not," Giselle replied. "Let sleeping things lie,

scholar. We have other difficulties." So saying, she turned to Raven, glancing at Robin as she did.

"Robin's mother, Rianna, was not Warden; her duties weren't attached to the warrens. No, she was in the wealthy district— the gardens weren't attacked in the same way the warrens were in ancient history. She'd inherited the duties of her line."

"What duties?" Robin asked as Raven merely nodded.

"I said she wasn't Warden," Giselle replied. "She had some fancy title, but it was hidden, secret, the way some people's wealth is." Her grin was brief and sharply edged. He thought Giselle knew the title but wouldn't speak it here, where Larrantin was still glaring at her. She turned her attention to Raven again, although her words seemed meant for both of them.

"Title or no, she was the keeper of the hidden thoughts, the hidden presences. Or rather, guardian of the containments that let them sleep gently. Do you remember her?"

The hidden thoughts. The captured thoughts. The Ancients. Robin remembered what Starrante had said: he had once seen them in his youth in a vastly different age.

Raven nodded.

"I don't know how she chose you; I didn't understand the rites of the somnambulists. But it was forbidden. The waking was forbidden, and the rites for it, thought lost."

Raven shook her head. "Rianna had the right to call me. I came because she had that right." In a much smaller voice, she added, "I will sleep again."

"You were not the only thing released."

Raven tilted her head to the side. "Maybe."

"What do you remember, Raven?" Giselle's voice was surprisingly gentle.

"It was white. Blinding. I felt voices. Heard voices?" she said, looking to Robin.

"I don't know what the voices are—they might be felt. They're voices we can't hear." Of the last part, he was certain.

Larrantin was studying Raven carefully. "It is possible," he said at last. "It is possible that the imperfect mortal control, imperfect knowledge, released things collaterally. It was part of my research, in my distant youth: this inexplicable whispering of the Ancients. They are old," he added. "Older than some of the Ancients in those distant times. Raw, perhaps; inimical to the lives the Ancients wished to create and shepherd.

"The defenses I have attempted to erect are, in some part, based on those early studies; it is how Raven—your prospective student—came to be in my chambers. But there are, I believe, others. Students have died, and Killianas cannot afford their loss."

"If they are not as we are," Teela said, "they understand some part of the form and function. I met—I believe I met—one such creature; he had taken the guise of a member of the staff here."

"So do animals choose to camouflage themselves when they seek prey," Larrantin replied. "To ascribe intent of the type you suggest is dangerous."

Robin lifted a hand.

"We are not in the lecture hall, young Robin," Larrantin said, frowning. "But yes, by all means, speak."

"Alderson died in Melden's office. I think it's likely that someone—pretending to be a student—told Alderson he could find test questions and answers in the professor's office. If the creature didn't leave a trail of bodies in the warrens or the gardens, it might have spent time there learning about...us."

24

"An'Teela," the chancellor said. "By order of a lord of the Dragon Court, I grant you permission to access Imperial Records. If there were difficulties in the gardens of all places, some of that information will not make its way to the Halls of Law, given the interference of the human caste court. Look for deaths, murders, or disappearances in the gardens approximately six to seven years ago."

"Imperial Records are accessed at the palace," the Barrani Hawk pointed out.

"Yes, I am aware of that. I am aware of your distaste—or your people's distaste—for the palace. I will send you with a message bearing my seal; while delivering it, approach the Arkon and explain the urgency of the situation. He will understand."

She looked as if she would refuse. Tain stepped past her toward the desk, and waited as the chancellor scribbled a message. The Dragon gestured, and the letter curled in on itself until it was cylindrical. He gestured again, and a seal appeared in place. "It is keyed to the Arkon." A slight smile touched his lips. "The Emperor, of course, can also view it should he so desire."

"A visit to the Imperial Palace will have to wait. I came to speak with Robin on official Halls of Law business." Teela's eyes were blue and slightly narrow.

"Ah, yes. Taking Giselle's recommendation into account, I will assert my authority. He is an orphaned ward of the Academia. The decision is not in his hands, but mine."

"He is an involved party in an as yet unsolved murder. Investigations were halted because the human caste court claimed the murder as caste court business. They did not consult with Robin, clearly, and he is an affected party."

Murder, Robin thought, remembering the fires and the screams of a distant childhood—a childhood whose shadows were lengthening as if reaching out toward him.

The chancellor shrugged. "Bring me more information about the caste court business, and I will review it. Ah, you will also find that information in the Imperial Records; caste court exemptions are nonetheless investigated and retained; they are not retained in the Halls of Law Records because they have been rendered irrelevant to the Halls.

"Murders of notable men and women of power are never entirely irrelevant to the Eternal Emperor."

Giselle did not leave immediately; Larrantin hemmed her in. He treated her with more respect than he treated students, and a smidgen more than he currently offered the chancellor. Giselle, however, had very little she could tell him.

Robin wasn't certain that this wasn't because she honestly didn't know. He would have bet it was, but he'd seen her eyes—and hand—go white when it met Larrantin's, had heard her speak words in no language he recognized. What he knew about the grey crow was what the warrens knew. More knowledge had never been safe.

His name hadn't been safe.

Raven had been safe, and it was to Raven he turned now. "Should we head back to our room?"

"Not yet," Giselle said. "I wish to speak with you both—without interference." This last was said to Larrantin.

"Our discussion is important for the defense of the Academia," Larrantin said.

"The Academia is not my problem," the grey crow replied, folding her arms.

"Robin—and Raven—are part of the Academia for the foreseeable future. This affects their safety." When Giselle failed to reply, he continued. "It is possible that whatever escaped—undetected—is searching for Robin for the same reason Raven protects the boy. The murders at the Academia happened when Robin was resident as a student; they occurred before Raven entered the Academia. It is reasonable to believe they were not hunting Raven.

"It is also, given the information we've gained today, reasonable to suspect they are hunting Robin."

"The deaths seem random." Robin's voice was quiet.

Larrantin frowned, but nodded. It wasn't an agreement.

"There's no indication that I'm being targeted."

"Perhaps not. But it was once believed that in the area you now call the gardens lived somnambulists who could, in emergencies, bind the things that should remain forever sleeping. If what I have seen here today is any indication, it is possible that Robin, of that line, has that ability, if not the knowledge."

Giselle's smile was slender; it was the bad smile. "That is a possibility to consider, but I will leave it in the hands of scholars; an information broker from the warrens is unlikely to be helpful." Her eyes narrowed. "Robin's flight to the warrens occurred in a time of desperation. An'Teela and the Hawks assumed that the family was murdered for political reasons. What if that was not the case?

"It might explain why Rianna—of all her long line—was the first to attempt such a calling."

"She could not have done that in the gardens?"

Giselle smiled. "That would be my assumption. I cannot confirm. The somnambulists had duties in the warrens from time to time; they are oddly linked neighborhoods in modern Elantra."

The chancellor's eyes were crimson.

"I realize our mysteries and rites are imperfectly handed down, master to apprentice. It is possible that Raven's waking was loud enough to affect those that must sleep. It is also possible that someone or something sought access to the forbidden in the gardens, and they could not gain that access without destruction of its guardians.

"Robin escaped. If the loss of the entire family was necessary, Robin would be a threat. And if the survival of the line protected that which must be protected, the risk of the calling of Raven was the lesser risk." She turned to Raven. "If you know, Raven, tell us."

Raven shook her head. Robin couldn't tell if she was refusing or if she didn't know; the shake could mean either.

"Raven." It was Starrante who spoke. "It has been a very trying week, but we require some of your attention now."

"We need glass," Raven told him, voice grave.

Starrante's limbs wavered.

"If you can find this glass, does this mean that something has escaped its confinement?"

"I...think so?" She glanced at Robin.

"Is Robin's survival essential?"

"Yes."

"For personal reasons?"

Her deliberation was longer now. "Yes."

"You said Robin's mother called you. Summoned you. Raven—what were you before you were called?"

"Sleeping. Dreaming."

"Dreaming?"

"Old dreams," she said. She lifted her arms in an odd dance; it was Wevaran. She made no other sound. "She paid the price of my waking. She asked me to protect Robin."

"Asked?"

Raven nodded.

"Could you have said no?"

"She paid the price."

It was his mother's death they were talking about. She'd taken him to the warrens. They'd run. Her clothing was singed and blackened on the left. Robin couldn't remember why. He couldn't remember if his own clothing was likewise burned. He couldn't remember anything that might have called Raven.

"Robin does not command you."

"No one commands me. I agreed to stay until Robin is adult, and safe. Not until he dies." Her hand tightened around his. "But... I want to stay. I want to stay until then."

"And is that what the glass is for?"

She tilted her head to the side, as if questions were physical objects that had to be carefully studied. "Yes. No."

Starrante didn't find this confusing. "Is the glass a containment? Can you find what escaped?"

"Not yet. Not ready yet."

"When will you be ready?"

"Soon." She hesitated again. Then she turned to Killian. "Your windows are glass."

"My windows are constructs; they are not glass."

"They're real glass."

"That isn't possible," Starrante told Raven. "The windows here are the province of the building's sentience and the miasma from which it draws substance. The glass you have shown me is no part of Killianas. The glass that you found in the quadrangle was not part of Killianas; the glass in the hidden office was likewise not part of Killianas."

She said, "It was. It was part of Killian, but he wasn't aware of it. He won't lose it now."

"Killianas did not make that stained glass window."

Killian, however, lifted a hand. "Raven, was that window—before it shattered—part of me?"

"I think so?"

"I have no memory of creating it."

Here, she rolled her eyes. "Yes."

"But you have glass now, in your pouch, that came from that window."

"Yes."

"Can you leave the Academia campus carrying that glass?"

"Yes."

"Will it remain in your pouch?"

"Yes."

"Will it sustain its shape and form if you carry it? Or if Robin does?"

"Yes. It doesn't have to be in the pouch."

A window formed in front of Robin and Raven. It wasn't attached to the wall; it didn't seem to be attached to anything. Looking through it, Robin should have seen the far wall of the office. "I wish you to break that window."

If Robin had expected argument, he got none. Raven, still holding on to his hand, walked over to the tall, wide window. Its clear glass looked out on nothing but clouds in motion.

Starrante moved, as well; Robin could hear the sound that preceded web-spitting. "I am ready," he told Raven, although Raven had asked nothing of him.

Raven nodded, lifted her free hand, and drove her fist through the largest pane.

The pane shattered.

Everyone in the room could see it: the chancellor, the Hawks, Giselle, Larrantin. Terrano became visible.

"We can all see these shards," the chancellor said. "I presume."

"I can," Larrantin concurred.

Raven ignored them both; she was catching shards of glass—with Starrante's aid—as they fell. The glass shards didn't fade or vanish as they scattered. Raven grabbed the largest pieces first. She then turned and handed one to Killian. Killian frowned, but accepted it; this time, there was no explosion.

"It is not the same," the Avatar said.

Raven nodded. "It isn't because it's yours. But it's real. We can use this."

"I could not touch the piece that you found in the quadrangle."

"You could. It just hurt. Some glass will hurt you. Some might hurt me. Most won't." She had opened her pouch, and she continued to gather the glass. "Does it hurt?"

"No. It is of me, but it is not analogous to a body."

"Do you notice that it's missing?"

This time, it was the Avatar who was silent—he was considering the question Raven had asked. She didn't look back; she continued her work, absent her usual unfettered glee. "Things I create can be consumed. The chancellor wishes the students to eat real food. I could, however, feed the student body. I would not notice the absence."

"And the window is like that?"

"It should not be."

Raven strode over to Giselle; she offered Giselle a piece of glass.

Giselle looked at it. "You want me to take it when I leave?"

Raven nodded. "Just to see."

"I can take it," Terrano offered. "The chancellor doesn't want me here anyway."

Raven shook her head. "Not you."

"Why not?"

Her expression in response was sour. "Because you don't

stay *here*. You move around. If you carry it, something that isn't *here*, where we are, might notice it first." She exhaled. "I think they already have."

"You think the glass that you found on the campus was once part of Killianas?" Larrantin's question was sharp, harsh; it was not doubtful.

"Maybe. I think that the attacker was trying to build a body within the students' bodies. Then they could be here."

"Why is here important if this is not where they live?"

Raven grimaced. "The gardens are here. The gardens are the binding."

"They want freedom?"

"They want freedom," she agreed. "To create and destroy, to change, to transform. They want to eat thought, to digest it, to expand what they can be until it is solid and inevitable."

"Shadow?"

"I don't know what Shadow is," Raven replied, which was a shock to Robin. Even in the warrens, people knew about the Towers—the fiefs in which they stood were very much like the warrens.

"Raven, do you know all the sleepers meant to be contained in the gardens? Can you hear them?"

She shook her head. "They're dangerous. They're dangerous for Robin. They're dangerous for anyone here. The warrens had other dangers. I hide Robin when there's danger."

"You cannot kill his enemies."

Her brows furrowed; she considered the statement stupid.

"Of what use is the glass? You said you almost have enough. What do you intend to do with it?"

She glanced at Robin, and then away.

"Raven," Giselle said in her steeliest voice, "answer the question."

"Make a jar. Make a sleeping jar. For them."

"And for yourself?"

Raven looked down at the floor. "I want to stay with Robin."

"You need to make a container for yourself?"

"I want to stay. I can't without it. I have to return. I have to dream." She then shook herself. "But not now." Turning to Larrantin, she said, "You trapped me. It was a bad trap."

Larrantin nodded, unperturbed.

"Can you trap other things the same way?"

"Probably. But you were the only one to whom my defenses reacted."

She nodded. "I wasn't hiding."

"And whatever you believe is responsible for the deaths on campus is."

"Until it attacks. Until it needs to attack."

"My defenses are not—yet—that sensitive. I would, in other circumstances, consider Killianas to be the better choice. Possibly Starrante or his few remaining kin. The nature of their webbing means they have some familiarity with traversing different planes of being."

"Perhaps we might work together," Starrante suggested. "Your magics are the magicks of your people; mine are, as you suggest, different. If we combine them, we might be able to create a more responsive net."

"Can you create one that young Raven won't trigger?"

"Yes, I believe so." He then turned to Raven. "Can you explain to me, Larrantin, or even Killian how you intend to use the glass you've collected?"

"So that you understand it?" She shook her head. "I might be able to explain it to Robin. If Robin knows, Killian will know, and Killian can explain it to others." She lowered her chin. "I'm not sure I can, though."

"We'll try," Robin said quickly. "Let's go back to our room, and we can talk there. Raven finds groups stressful when she's trying to think." He then turned to Giselle. "Want to see our room?"

Giselle nodded, glass shard carefully held in her left hand. The grey crow made it look like a weapon.

The discussion that was to start between the chancellor, the Arbiter, Larrantin, and Killian began before they could leave the office. Larrantin led with a much more technical explanation of the spell that had trapped Raven. Terrano clammed up, given the possibility that he'd trip the defenses simply by walking invisibly through them. He whispered to Robin, "I can't understand a tenth of what they're saying. Teela can understand more. Go back to your room—we'll meet you there after they've finished."

Robin was surprised Terrano was allowed to participate.

Killian smiled. "Terrano has practical experience most here do not. His input may prove valuable. It is to be hoped it does not prove enraging."

Raven fell in beside Giselle. Both were utterly silent. Giselle was not the usual visitor to the dorms, but she'd always carried herself with an air of subtle menace. Or unsubtle, if called for. The students, at least, kept their distance.

They made their way without incident to their room.

Killian—present as Avatar—opened the door from the inside.

Robin stopped as Killian stepped back. The room he could see beyond the physical Avatar looked almost unchanged, which was a bit of a relief: it was normal, or what he'd come to think of as normal.

No one spoke until the door closed. "I would like to take basic precautions against intrusion." Killian sounded almost apologetic.

"No," Raven snapped.

"We cannot be certain the killer is hunting Robin, but we cannot be certain they are not."

"If it's dangerous and you make a room like the windowless, doorless conference room, Robin can't run. We can't hide." She folded her arms and glared up at the Avatar.

"I would accept her assessment," the grey crow said as she slid past Raven into the room itself. She looked around, almost as if inspecting it for dust or mess. "You don't have windows?"

"We did," Robin replied. "But... Raven thought they were real glass, and Killian didn't want her messing with them."

Giselle walked over to Robin's desk, pulled out the chair tucked beneath it, and sat, left elbow on the chair's lower back. In her right hand, she carried the shard of glass.

"You wanted to speak with us."

"Yes. Can we have some privacy?" Giselle asked Killian.

Robin shook his head. "Killian can hear most of our thoughts anyway."

"Giselle is careful," Killian said before Robin could continue. "Her thoughts are almost opaque. You are not so adept, and as you are aware, I cannot hear Raven's thoughts at all."

"You can," Giselle told the Avatar, an odd half smile crossing her lips. "You can hear her when she speaks."

"That is not generally considered the same thing."

"Not generally, no. Raven, come and take this."

Raven did as ordered, opening her pouch to add the piece to her collection.

"Killian?"

"I will remain," Killian replied.

Giselle exhaled. "If I understand what you are, you were not always the heart of a building. Or a campus."

Killian nodded.

"You must have lived before the fall of *Ravellon*." At his nod, she continued. "You must have had some interaction with *Ravel-*

lon, given the location of the Academia itself. Did you never attempt to visit the maze?"

"No. I was not a scholar. I was not an adept. I was not a mage. I was a teacher, an administrator, and a swordsman. I was known for my ability to handle logistics intelligently, and at a low cost to the lives of those who must do the work. The mysteries of the labyrinths, the hidden dells, the wild green in the West, were of little interest to me; I might have studied them had they disgorged monsters, obvious threats.

"But I became the heart of the Academia long before the Towers rose. Larrantin seems to understand at least the base functions of what remains of those mysteries; if you wish information, he would be a far better man to ask."

"No. The maze is not, now, for Larrantin. I do not believe he could walk it. I do not believe he could reach its heart."

"Have you?"

She smiled, but did not answer.

"You believe all of these things are connected."

Giselle nodded. "I am certain of it. I retract any unkind words I may have leveled at the woman who served the gardens; I understand the desperation, now. I understand what she feared. It is far, far more dangerous than the pimps and thugs the warrens oft produce but not on an individual level. Any thug with intent could have ended Robin's life. Dead is dead.

"At least if it stays that way." She exhaled. "The strands that bind the warrens to the gardens are ancient, invisible to the naked eye; there is no door, no window, no path that leads between them—not one that can be perceived by most people. There were once, or so we were told; I'm not of a mind to believe it.

"But the caged thoughts of gods—the wild anger, the desire for destruction, the need to vivisect, the search for…something, even the desire for peace, warmth, comfort. Who could comfort gods?" Giselle shook her head. "This is more than I have ever said to one who will not become the grey crow after I fall. We are cautioned—even forbidden—to speak of our hidden duties.

"Men seek power; it is in their nature. There is power in the caged thoughts, for even the thoughts of gods are alive; they are not like our thoughts. When they fight for dominance, they are not like us. We might be of two minds about any specific issue, but neither of those two minds will destroy a city or a small country if let loose. These thoughts could.

"But they were the Ancients' thoughts, barely given voice; they could not be killed or destroyed."

"They were considered too precious?" Killian asked.

Giselle chuckled. "Hardly. It was simply impossible. Even the attempt was dangerous: our thoughts lacked tenacity in the lee of theirs. We could easily become agents for the driving thought we attempted to suppress. We *could not* kill them, or we would have, and the long stewardship of my people down the centuries would be over. I like being an information broker. I like being the grey crow.

"And for the vast majority of my life, that's what I've been. But this—this has weight of a different kind. I wasn't certain I believed it when I first began my lessons. But I learned. We did not house them in the warrens, so close to the heart of the maze; it was too great a danger, and our skills were not the skills of the Gardianna or Gardianno. Too close to the source of power, the thoughts became waking dreams, waking nightmares; they gained strength and solidity; they transformed what they touched.

"They were not like Shadow; we understood them, and they were singular in their goals, if *goal* is the correct word.

"But these thoughts could not be too distant from the warrens, for it was the power at the heart of the maze that allowed them to be lulled into sleep or stasis in their cocoons. They were housed in the gardens, and their sleep guarded there."

Robin, seated on his bed, had leaned forward as Giselle

spoke; he couldn't look away from the lined visage of the grey crow. He could almost see the wings of the bird for which she was named, and blinked twice to clear the momentary illusion.

"I am almost certain you will find mortals and their allies at the heart of the trouble the Academia now faces. It is possible that one—or more—have been infected, have become the carrier and servant for the caged thoughts. These thoughts cannot exist without specific forms, but they corrode and distort their vessels if those vessels are not properly prepared.

"I believe that is why there have been deaths in the Academia. I don't believe the deaths are related entirely to Robin or his line, but I cannot be certain. It is possible they require more vessels to carry the essence; to accomplish what the wakeners desire. It is a foolish, foolish game. We don't touch the tools of the gods because we're not gods; they *will* change and shape us.

"Most will die of the attempt. It is clear that this is not considered relevant."

"Wouldn't it make more sense for our enemies to seek people in the warrens or the fiefs?" Robin asked. "I'm from the warrens," he added quickly. "I'm not the only person who went there to disappear. The Hawks don't learn of most of the disappearances there. Here, the deaths are going to be noticed."

"Yes. Yes, it would make more sense, especially given the location of the Academia as it now stands. But there are far fewer Barrani in the warrens or the fiefs."

"And Barrani would be better vessels?"

Giselle shrugged. "I'd use them over mortals if offered the choice; they live forever. But there might be no choice. If the work of the somnambulists, as we called them, was completely undone, everyone would know. Towers couldn't contain them in the same way Shadow is contained by the Towers.

"The thoughts themselves...some are like questions, like problems, like things that were considered without rigor. They desire completion."

"And we can't."

"We can't even *understand* them. It's not safe." She exhaled. "Raven?"

"There's glass here," she said, her voice almost a whisper.

"Pardon?"

"There's glass here. Killian's glass. More glass here than in the warrens or the gardens."

Killian nodded; his eyes were now black with colored flecks. "Glass of which I am not always aware. Perhaps they are aware of my blind spots, my weakened state."

Raven joined Robin on the edge of his bed, very carefully handing him her pouch of treasures. "You have to build them."

"Me?" If Robin's jaw weren't attached to his face, it would have fallen off. "I know *nothing* about building containers for the stray thoughts of gods!"

Raven nodded, as if this were obvious. "Doesn't matter. Learn."

He stared at her.

It was Giselle who spoke. "Can he, Raven? Can he learn?"

"Only Robin," she replied.

"And if he fails?"

"He can't capture what's free. Not yet. Maybe not ever. But he can fortify the sleepers, so that nothing else gets loose. It's not one thought that will destroy. It's all the thoughts, at war. It's the arguments between them."

"Where do you come in, then?"

Raven smiled. "If the glass is broken, if the thoughts escape, I can be called."

"But you were called to protect Robin."

Raven nodded. "Bound to him. Bound by her life." She turned to Robin, a hint of fear in her eyes. "She said you could do it. If you lived. You could do what had to be done."

"I don't even understand what has to be done!"

Raven nodded. "You have to learn. I can't teach." She exhaled. "I can gather. Killian can help now."

"Larrantin suggests," Killian said, "that Robin requires more than rudimentary classes. And he also suggests a more 'comprehensive' testing suite to determine whether or not Robin has the necessary talent to pursue those."

"If it gets me out of Melden's class, I'll take it," Robin said.

"The chancellor did not seem to find that condition amusing."

Robin winced.

Raven looked up. "Giselle," she whispered. She reached out for Robin's hand, clasped it tightly, and rose, pulling him off his feet.

Giselle nodded. She rose, as well, turning to Robin. She lifted her left hand, palm toward him, her expression neutral.

Robin stared at her hand, remembering Larrantin's brief contact. Then, Giselle had spoken words, even if Robin couldn't understand them. Now, she said nothing. Her hand wasn't glowing. Her eye was the normal brown.

Raven elbowed him. "Try," she said urgently, her hand tightening on his. "Killian!"

Killian blinked.

"Tell the others—it's now. Something is trying to enter the Academia." To Robin, she said, "We have to hide."

"Robin," Giselle said, voice far more commanding.

"I don't know the words of the spell," he whispered. Raven dragged him toward Giselle, glancing over her shoulder in the twitchy way she always did when she needed to hide. No, he thought almost bitterly, when she needed *Robin* to hide.

"If Raven is correct, you don't need them."

"Larrantin spoke to you in a language I don't know. You responded to those words."

"Larrantin is not of us, not like us; in order to approach the maze at all, he had to study, to learn. In theory, many made that attempt. I can't tell you what it was like in practice, it was so long before I was born.

"But if your mother believed you have the gift, those words aren't necessary. You only have to *be*."

"Robin," Raven almost hissed.

Years of obeying Raven when she spoke with that edge caused Robin to reflexively raise his right hand, to turn the palm toward Giselle, whose eye was narrowing, and to place it flat against hers.

The white light that had haloed Giselle returned as their palms met; her eye was once again almost silver. This time, her hair seemed to lengthen, to trail back down her shoulders, to darken in color. Her face altered, the changes subtle: the shape of her chin, her jaw, the loss of the lines age, sun, and wind had worn there. He wouldn't have recognized her had he not been touching her hand.

She was Giselle. She was the grey crow. She was shelter—rough and almost inhospitable, hidden, as so many things were hidden, in plain sight. In the warrens.

He cried out in pain, pulled back; she let him go. "Look at your hand," she said as the light died.

He turned his right palm toward his eyes. There, as if burned into his skin by killing cold, lay a small sigil on the mound of his palm; it stung.

"If I were my ancient Ancestors, I could send you to the maze from this place. I'm not." Giselle turned to Raven. "Take him and go. I will do what I can to confuse the invaders."

25

Raven was attached to Robin by hand—the unburnt hand. Her grip was familiar, tight; her stride lengthened the moment Killian opened the door to their room. She practically leaped into the hall, and Robin kept pace. He didn't speak; he could tell, by her desperate sprint, that they needed to hide.

That she thought they needed to hide.

On the previous occasion, she'd found a place to hide in the Academia. Given Giselle's words and the mark on his palm, he knew she wouldn't even look here. She meant to run all the way back to the warrens, Robin in tow. He would have been a lot more comfortable if Giselle was running alongside. He could infer that she meant Raven to lead him back to the warrens he'd been so grateful to escape, but the warrens were much larger than the Academia campus, and she hadn't mentioned *where* in the warrens they were supposed to go.

He didn't have breath to ask Raven; she didn't slow until she'd left the building, and barely slowed as she hit the quad. She paused for breath—moving from sprint to jog—without lessening her desperate forward momentum.

He'd run this far by her side before, dragged by her urgency; this time felt different.

Above their heads, a storm loomed; clouds tinged grey and green gathered, adding texture to the heavens. He tried to look up, but Raven didn't slow; he stumbled. She yanked him forward, shaking her head; he couldn't see her expression. Didn't need to.

He could feel an odd electricity in the air, something that caused the hair on the back of his neck to rise. He hoped that whatever Larrantin had set in place was once again active. Raven wasn't on the campus—but something else was. He could sense its presence.

And he could see that he wasn't the only one. Ahead of where Raven now ran, the quad wasn't empty; students were looking up, and then away—to shelter. They expected rain.

Robin expected worse now. His hand hurt; it was throbbing as the clouds moved.

"Don't look!" Raven shouted over her shoulder. "Don't look."

Robin didn't ask why.

"They're here," he whispered.

"Don't look," she said again. "Run."

But he could see a familiar student—a human student, older than Robin by at least four years. Admission didn't take age into account—although in time, it probably would. Robin's clothing, Robin's style of dress, marked him as poor; this student—whose name evaded Robin—dressed in a way that practically screamed wealth.

With wealth came power—anyone who lived in the warrens understood that.

The student caught his eye—and he and Raven caught the student's attention.

Robin found the strength to sprint then. Something about the student was off, wrong: his eyes were pitch-black, no visible whites, and Robin could see them clearly at this distance. He shouldn't have.

The student shouted. Robin assumed it was either a command or a name; it was followed by a loud *"Wait!"*

He was clearly used to being heard and obeyed; what followed when Robin failed to slow was something akin to a scream of rage. This, too, reverberated, reaching Robin's ears as easily as if the student stood directly beside him.

He sped up.

Raven's hand tightened. She wasn't given to cursing, and she hated it when Robin did; it was a waste of breath. Breath he needed for running.

He couldn't hear his feet hit stone; he couldn't hear footsteps behind him. Just the shouting, but that banked as sprinting increased the gap between them and the lone student.

He was surprised, then, when something grabbed his shoulder; he felt its grip as if it were a cold mail glove.

Raven pulled at him; she hadn't looked back. Robin lifted his free hand to dislodge the hand that had grabbed him; he could see that it wasn't armored, even if it felt that way.

Raven had said *don't look*. Funny, how obeying all of her curt, quick commands had become so natural; he glanced at the hand, grabbed it with his free hand, and jerked it off his shoulder. As he did, his palm flashed light and heat; he could hear the scream behind him as the hand fell away.

He almost looked then. Maybe, decades from now, obedience wouldn't be so natural. But Raven never wasted words on pointless warnings.

Instead, he glanced at his palm; the mark that had seemed like an ice burn was blue. It seemed more like a tattoo now; the pain was gone. He was shakily certain he'd managed to wrest himself free of the hand because of this mark.

Raven could run forever, in Robin's experience. Robin couldn't. But she didn't allow him to slow until they had left the neighborhood surrounding the campus and entered the fief of Tiamaris. There, they moved at a jog as she ran toward the bridge. Only when they reached it without incident did she look back, over Robin's shoulder. Her frown was instant.

He looked down at his shoulder; it was black with soot.

"They won't follow this way," she said. "Not to Tiamaris."

"Why not?"

"Tower."

"The Academia is a sentient building. They don't have trouble hunting us there."

"Damaged. Tower is whole." She frowned. "Run, now. We need to hide. We need to hide before they find us."

And by *us*, she meant Robin. She always had; he just hadn't realized it. He had so many questions he wanted to ask her. So many things he wanted to know. But to ask them, they both had to survive.

The urgency of her grip lessened; she didn't let go. Letting go was the silent sign that things were as safe as they were going to get.

"Do you know where we're supposed to go?" Robin managed to ask.

Raven's nod was clipped and unaccompanied by words.

He had memories of running to the warrens. Memories of the way the buildings changed, the way the street itself narrowed, weeds springing up between stones that had seen better decades. He had memories of the streets, crowded with stalls and wagons, everyone practically standing on top of each other, there were so many people.

Those memories overlapped with his view of the streets as Raven ducked around people. He'd had practice following the flow of her movements; she left enough room in the gaps between pedestrians for Robin to slide through if he kept up.

"Stop! Thief!"

If he'd had the strength, he'd have yanked Raven to a halt. They were running. They weren't well-dressed. There weren't a lot of people who would easily draw attention and fit the shouted description—and Robin and Raven were young enough it wouldn't seem dangerous to catch them.

Raven hadn't heard—or if she had, she didn't consider it her problem. She wasn't a thief; she hadn't stood still for long enough to steal anything. If he hadn't been so out of breath, if he hadn't been *almost* certain that the voice lifted in command wasn't a normal, human voice, he might have laughed. She had never been good at people, had never learned to care about how she was judged by strangers.

It was the only way he'd been useful to her.

But she'd never needed it at all. Anything he'd taught her— to read, to hold a conversation of more than two words—was irrelevant. He'd been proud that he'd had something to offer her. Proud that he could do things she couldn't. He had never been helpful to his family, now lost.

He couldn't save his family. Couldn't even save his mother, who had picked him up and run, run, run—just as Raven was running now, hand in his, stride wide and desperate as she sprinted, burdened by Robin, to the warrens. Whatever happened to the wealthy in the warrens was still safer than what had happened just outside of their home.

Death was death.

Robin, even then, had wanted to live. He had wanted to live until the moment his mother had died—and then, he had wanted to follow her. He'd been so young.

These were the thoughts that Raven had always interrupted, as if she could hear them. Maybe she could. He didn't know what she was now. Didn't understand what she could—or could not—do. He was torn between betrayal and a terrible, gnawing guilt. She had stayed by his side because she'd been summoned. She'd protected him because of that summoning. Did she have no will of her own? Was she somehow enslaved?

Had she ever really been his friend?

Her hand tightened, as if she could hear the doubt. She didn't bother to tell him to stop thinking bad thoughts.

Raven came to a stop, which Robin appreciated only after he'd been able to draw several deep breaths. He was sweating; his legs were trembling. They were standing to the side of the well. There was more than one well in the warrens, but this, unofficially, was where Giselle could be found during daylight hours. She kept an eye on the well; it was the safest well to visit unless you intended to cross her, in which case, there was no safe well anywhere.

People weren't afraid of Giselle, for the most part; she was like a force of nature. If you didn't cross her, she wouldn't kill you. She didn't buy children—or kidnap them—and she didn't have a taste for excessive cruelty. Unless she intended to make an example of you.

There was no grey crow here today. No one occupied her leaning spot against the wall. She could come back at any minute, and no one wanted to be the person who had to move.

Raven, unlike other people, had always seen an empty patch of wall that stood in shade when the sun was hottest; it served as a windbreak when the wind rolled in from the harbor. People gave her the side-eye as she marched—Robin's hand in hers— toward the wall, toward Giselle's spot.

She leaned against the wall to one side of where Giselle would have stood, which was mostly safe. But she pulled Robin back to the exact spot the grey crow usually occupied.

He could hear the sharp intake of breath from people gathered in ones and twos around the well; some were jeering, some philosophical. It didn't matter to them if a young kid with more bravado than brains angered the grey crow—it wasn't their problem.

Robin hated to be the center of attention. That hadn't always been true, but the warrens had taught him it was better to be overlooked. Better to be unseen. Being seen, being powerless, had other consequences; the warrens had taught him that, too. But it hadn't ended him. It hadn't killed him.

Because Raven was here. He leaned into the wall, closing his eyes.

He hadn't expected to fall through it.

Raven had been holding his hand from the moment they fled the Academia to the moment they arrived at the grey crow's well. He could still feel her grip, but he couldn't see her. To be fair, he couldn't see much of anything. It was dark where he'd landed, and the landing wasn't soft; he lay against stone. His eyes acclimated to the much dimmer interior light. There were no windows, but in the distance, he could see the yellow glow of lamps.

He turned to Raven.

She wasn't there. The sensation of her hand in his faded as circulation returned to his fingers. He wondered if her absence meant he was safe. He looked at the hand Giselle's touch had burned; in the dim light, he could see the outlines of a rune that glowed a faint, pale blue.

He gained his feet and began to walk, quietly, toward the distant light. As he did, he saw that he was in a hall, stone to either side, but against the walls, ivy or something similar grew; its leaves were shiny, and reflected the light the rune cast when he lifted his hand to touch them.

Age seemed to have descended upon this hall, this floor, but the vines themselves weren't ancient; they couldn't be. They were alive, just as Robin was. Things ancient and things new blended as he continued down the hall.

He whispered Raven's name. Silence returned; he didn't try again.

Giselle had talked of a maze, a labyrinth. This was a simple hall. A long hall. He walked it, keeping his steps deliberately light as he listened. He could hear his own breath; could hear, with effort, the beating of his heart. He could hear no other sounds that implied anyone else was present. But the light ahead grew brighter as he walked toward it.

When he was almost at the end of the hall, he saw that it opened into a large, round room; the ceiling was shadowed, but he thought it domed. The light resolved itself into lamps that ringed the round walls. One burned in the center, but as he approached it, it moved, lifting itself from a small pillar, as if it were being carried by invisible hands.

The lamp drew closer as he stood surveying the room. If there was an entrance to a maze, he couldn't see it; the hall he'd landed in led here, but there were no exits or entrances.

Given the events of the past week—or less, which was almost impossible to believe—he wasn't surprised when he heard a voice.

"Gardianno, is it already time?"

He looked over his shoulder, saw no one, and accepted that the invisible person was speaking to him.

"I don't know," he said quietly. "I don't know why I'm here. I only know that Giselle said this is where I had to be."

"Come here, child."

He flinched at the word *child*, but accepted it. He approached the lamp. As he did, what had been invisible became clear: the lamp was held by a person. Long hair, the color of lamplight, fell down their back; he couldn't tell whether they were male or female. Or neither.

The person lifted a hand, palm out, just as Giselle had done; he lifted his in response, and pressed it against the light. He felt nothing: no flesh, no friction; he might have been moving his hand against the cool, pleasant air.

"You seek power," the voice said.

Robin hesitated. He felt like a fraud. "Something has been broken. I've been told that I can mend it, that I can stop other things from breaking." As he spoke, he realized that he was carrying, in the hand that Raven had gripped so tightly, Raven's pouch. Raven's treasures. "I don't know how."

"What do you carry?"

"A pouch. A bag of Raven's treasures."

"Raven?"

"A friend. My first friend. She gave these to me."

"You will find little need for the coin of your realm in this place." There was amusement in the voice then. "And little use for it."

"Oh, it's not gold." He very carefully untied the strings that kept the pouch shut. "It's glass. It's Raven's special glass. And metal."

Silence. The light faltered, and the person at whom he looked seemed to freeze in place, as if they were a thought that had been entirely abandoned as they confronted unexpected information.

"Please wait here."

Robin had no way to leave, but nodded anyway. The light remained floating in place, and the translucent person carrying it remained there, as well. He used that light to examine the pieces of glass, but didn't empty the pouch as Raven often did. To Robin's eyes, Raven's glass had always looked like glass; he'd handled it with care because the shards often had sharp edges.

Here, the light hit it differently; it was as if the glass itself was absorbing the illumination, echoing it. He frowned, and fished around in the bag for a colored piece of glass; the effect was the same: the base color didn't change, but it brightened as it absorbed light. The light itself didn't diminish. He set the shard—a bright green one—back in the bag, and this time pulled out one of the metal pieces. There were far fewer of these, but they came from the same source.

He held one up to the lamp.

The effect of the light on the metal was very different. The metal didn't absorb light the way the glass shards had; it didn't become brighter. Professor Caldon would be delighted to be given even a piece of this, because it was new, unknown. And why had he thought that?

The piece he'd chosen was one that might fit a stained glass mosaic; it was slender, like pencil lead but shorter. As he held it in his hand, it elongated, and a small lattice formed; the small piece was part of the whole, too large to easily fit the bag unless he was willing to bend or break it.

Raven would have loved this.

Raven wasn't here.

He was wrong about one thing: the small lattice fit in the pouch. The opening of the pouch elongated to accommodate it. Robin had thought it strange that everything Raven had gathered always fit a pouch that seemed too small for it. Now, better taught, he simply assumed it was magic. Practical magic, like streetlamps or hot water.

He chose to pull out a flatter piece of metal next. Holding it up to the light, the metal grew, once again, into a distinct shape, a whole shape. It was flat, circular—it seemed almost like a lid.

Windows. Jars. Two different types of glass: separation or containment. The glass itself didn't change shape or color, but the metal did, as if it were the necessary structural element.

"I understand," the voice said.

Robin looked up, once again returning things to the pouch. He wondered when Raven had left it in his keeping; he had no memory of taking it from her.

"Maybe you could explain what you understand to me?"

The neutral expression of the transparent person didn't change. "Gardianno, you must ask."

"Ask *what*?"

"For the power you seek. We can hear them now: the restless thoughts. We hear other voices in harmony with theirs. Something has frayed and broken. We do not have the power to repair it; that was left in your hands. But you must move quickly now. You should not have left it so long."

"Who do I ask for power?" *And knowledge*, but Robin left that part silent.

The image smiled. "You will know. Go now."

Once again a hand was lifted. Robin tucked the pouch inside his shirt and lifted the hand that bore the rune. Nothing touched it, but when the image lowered their hand, Robin's rune was glowing a brilliant, steady gold, tinged with blue and green. "Walk forward now. Walk into the unknown."

Robin turned toward the walls; they were the same. Lamps were posted just above the height of his head, but there were no doors, no halls. Ah. Not even the hall he'd traversed to get here.

"Seek," the image of a person said, then lifted the lamp, extending an arm toward him. Robin grimaced, but lifted his own hand to take the lantern. When he touched it, it became solid, although it was a delicate thing. He wondered if the glass sides were true glass as Raven perceived it, but he had no intention of breaking it to find out.

Lamp in hand, he turned once again; the walls remained solid.

He closed his eyes and stepped forward, the light of the lamp adding a subtle red to the darkness beneath his eyelids.

Eyes closed, he could now hear something: movement, a hint of a whisper, possible footfalls. He wasn't certain whether he wanted to walk toward noise, or away. In the end, he chose toward. His own steps were taken carefully; he couldn't see and didn't want to walk into a wall by accident.

But when he touched bark, he opened his eyes. The round room was gone. What replaced it appeared to be a forest. Robin had spent the life he could remember clearly in the warrens, where there wasn't a lot of forest. He'd seen trees, but not a congregation like this; he lifted the lamp and looked ahead; the trees went on forever.

There was dirt beneath his feet, not stone; he'd been sent somewhere else. It didn't look like a maze to his eyes.

But he could see flickers of movement ahead of where he stood; he turned to look back. Nothing seemed to be behind him—literal nothing. Forward, then.

He tried to remember anything his mother might have told him that would be useful. Or his father. Nothing came to mind; his mother's last words did, and he flinched. *Survive, Robin. You must survive.* He remembered the blood, the swelling of her lip, the way her eyes were reddened with weeping; remembered her labored breath, because words required breath. Her last words. Her last command.

He had no memory of Raven. No memory of the summoning.

No memory of shattered glass in the distant gardens.

But Raven believed he could do this. Whatever this was.

The flickers of motion grew brighter; he thought he would see the person who had offered him the lamp, and walked confidently toward them. But he froze before he reached the light, because the light was wrong; it was the wrong shade, the wrong shape, more grey than white, more diffuse.

He was grateful for trees then; he could duck behind a wide trunk, breath held.

His fear was loud. It made his heartbeat loud. *Raven.*

No answer. He hadn't expected one, but he'd hoped. He chose a different direction. He wasn't certain if the light could sense the light he carried, because he couldn't understand what the light was.

But light was reflected—and absorbed—by something on the ground perhaps four yards from where he stood, and he moved toward it.

Glass. Glass shards. Pale green in color. Kneeling, he retrieved them and put them carefully in Raven's pouch. There was no metal here, but it was a small miracle he could see the shards, and the light they absorbed made clear they were Raven's type of glass.

He wondered if it had been window or jar, or if it had been a lamp. Wondered what it might be in the future, if it could be anything at all.

He rose. He felt the hush in this forest shift, as if silence was now a pressure, a weight. He began to walk more quickly, searching for sign of a path.

He met three things as he walked. The first was Giselle.

She didn't speak, didn't seem to see him at all; she was grey and white, an apparition, a phantasm. His hand, when he reached out to test her solidity, passed through her. He noticed. She didn't. But she turned toward the lamp he held, her expression drawn, tired. He spoke her name; she didn't react. She wasn't here.

If she was somehow guardian, guard, or Warden of this place, maybe it made sense. Maybe this was a lingering echo of her will, her intent. He walked past her, certain that her presence here, even as an illusion, meant he was heading in the right direction.

The second such apparition was Rianna, his mother.

Shorn of physicality, she wasn't bleeding, wasn't dying. Nor was she gasping for breath with failing lungs and a world of pain in her expression. She stood, her shoulders back, her gaze beyond him, her lips slightly compressed. He didn't call her, didn't try to catch her attention; like Giselle, she was apparition, not ghost. But it would be much, much harder to remain unnoticed, unseen, if he made the attempt. He couldn't bring himself to experiment.

He knew she was dead. She would never return. He would never hear her voice again; never be carried, put to bed, read to, or lectured. One day had destroyed the years that still lingered emotionally, even when memory was hazy. He stared at her face, her familiar face; it wavered in his vision. He was grateful Raven wasn't here. She'd've smacked him. She'd've said it was *bad*.

It was. It was very bad. He stood frozen before Rianna, his arms stiff by his sides by force of will. He wasn't the child he had been. He wasn't a child. He demonstrably didn't need his mother. But it took him time to find the rhythm of breath again; time to find thought, to try to piece together what he'd seen so far.

Giselle. Rianna.

If this phantasm of his mother was here, just past Giselle's, he was certain he was on the right path—although *path* was the wrong word. He was stumbling forward, uncertain that forward was the right direction. But it was better than standing still.

It was better than standing, as he was, at the precipice of grief.

He stumbled forward, found his footing, and continued walking. It was that or remain stuck in this yearning, this loss.

Perhaps he hadn't escaped it; perhaps he never would. He had lost track of what forward meant, where it was, what he was searching for. He didn't expect the third apparition, or perhaps he was still trying to process the vision of his mother. He had no portraits of the family he had lost, nothing but his life itself to remember them by. Seeing her, even if she wasn't here, was a gift and a knife, both.

"Yes. It is the price love exacts."

He stumbled again.

"And it is costly enough for some that love dies; what is left behind is emptiness and the hungering desire to fill it somehow."

He blinked and turned toward the voice.

"No, child. Not yet. You are not yet done. But I have been watching you, and I have been listening."

He hadn't spoken anything but Giselle's name.

"That is not her name," the voice said.

Robin almost felt like he was walking with invisible Killian in the halls of the Academia.

"I am like, and unlike, Killianas of old. His functions are not mine, and his flexibility—the envy of those who were chosen to serve—not mine.

"You are Rianna's son."

Robin nodded.

"Tell me, child, of your companion."

He knew, without asking, that she meant Raven.

"Indeed. Why do you call her Raven?"

Robin shrugged. The voice moved as he moved, neither leading nor following. He looked ahead. Once again he saw lights flicker, but this time they seemed to spread, becoming mist or fog in the distance. He frowned.

"Yes, it is dangerous, as you perceive. Your instincts are good. But why Raven?"

He felt mildly stupid, and then deeply defiant. "Because she had no name, and she needed one. I couldn't keep saying *hey, you* every time I saw her."

"Did she not think to tell you that names are dangerous?"

Robin shook his head. "She seemed confused, but in the early days most things confused her." In spite of himself, he smiled.

"And Raven?"

"I was Robin. I always hated that name," he added, his smile rueful. "But it's mine. And the whole warrens knew the grey crow. I also had a bird name, and her hair reminded me of ravens' wings. So, Raven."

"I see. You were very young. Had you been taught, it is not a mistake you would have made."

"It wasn't a mistake," Robin replied. "It was deliberate. She's saved my life so many times I've lost count. She brought me food. She led me to shelter in the winter. The first winter, especially." He exhaled slowly. "I gave her a name she could use as her own because she didn't have one. I thought she'd forgotten hers. She was so odd; she seemed feral to me.

"Feral, like a creature in the wilderness who knew the wilderness far, far better than I did."

"So you gave her a name to tame her? To domesticate her?"

"No! She was a *person* to me—not an object. She can't be owned! She couldn't be owned then!"

"No. Not by you."

Robin wanted to shriek in frustration. He held it in, aware that Killian would have found the action mildly curious, but not disrespectful or threatening. He had no idea about this disembodied voice, and had to struggle to care. "Not by *anyone*. Not by you, whoever you are. Not by my mother, not by Giselle. Raven's a *person*."

26

"Is she, now?" The light from the lantern bled into the space to Robin's left; in it, he could now see robes in the rough shape of a person: two arms, two legs—very unlike the Wevaran he might have expected.

"If that is more comfortable for you, I can adopt that form; this is…a faceless, neutral form. Wevaran were seldom greeted with comfort by your kind, even those who worked in close proximity to them."

Robin shrugged.

"Your Raven is not a person in the same way you are."

He bit back a sarcastic reply. Clearly he'd spent too much time around Terrano and sarcasm had rubbed off.

But if it came to that… "Starrante isn't a person the same way I am. Killian isn't. Terrano isn't. Serralyn and Valliant aren't. Larrantin isn't, either. I know a lot of people who are nothing like me. Raven's one of them."

"Is that why you sought the labyrinth of the ages, child?"

"No."

"No? Did you not have a desire to change Raven's essential nature?"

"No."

"I see. Then why did you come? What do you seek?"

"You already know. I need to somehow rebuild the webs and containers that keep the thoughts of Ancients asleep. They need to dream."

"And how do you intend to do that?"

"If I knew, I wouldn't be wandering around in a forest listening to you," he snapped.

To his surprise, the form did shift, the apparition becoming, limb by limb and eye stalk by eye stalk, Wevaran. "Starrante, you said?"

"Arbiter Starrante."

"That would explain much. I sense his traces in you; he has taken an interest in your education. Tell him he *must* proceed with caution. You are young and too ignorant." The voice gentled; if the form was Wevaran, the voice wasn't. "Ignorance can be alleviated, and you have much to learn."

"And you'll teach me?"

"No. That is neither my privilege nor my duty; I cannot leave this place, and you cannot remain here long. What remains here is transformed." At Robin's expression, she said, "Mortals *are* change, but that change is based in your nature. You will return here, and you will not be the boy you are now; your knowledge will be greater, for good or ill. Even the shape of your thoughts will alter; what you will become is not what you are now.

"But you have the instincts of your distant kin. Learn to trust that." Eye stalks bent in a way that implied frown in Wevaran. "What are you carrying?"

"A lamp?" When the figure failed to speak, he said, "Oh, do you mean the glass?"

"I referred to the pouch in your hand."

Robin removed the pouch from where it rested against his skin. "The pouch contains glass. Raven's glass." He opened it and withdrew one shard. Its edges were sharp enough to cut the careless, and he was annoyed enough to be careless. At least the cut was clean and shallow.

"Glass? Is that what you call it?"

"It's what Raven called it. And it looks like broken glass to me."

"I see. And why are you carrying it?"

"I don't know. I was holding Raven's hand when I fell through a wall. She didn't come with me, but the pouch did."

The apparition sighed. "Child, she is a guardian. She was created to be a guardian in times of trouble. There are protections woven into this place that have stood the test of time, but we could not know how the world would change beyond our reach. We could anticipate danger that was obvious to us in the very distant past, and we built defenses against it.

"But we knew that life would evolve, and as it did, it would present different dangers, dangers that we had not, and could not, anticipate; the Ancients continued to create, to will life into being. Change is life, but it is also, in the wrong circumstances, the end of life. There was power in the Ancients—in their blood, which is eternal, in their thoughts, which shaped worlds and formed language.

"Change is necessary," the apparition continued. "Learning involves change; by learning, by gaining experience, understanding is deepened, and thoughts evolve.

"It was not always so with the Ancients; it was not in their nature. It is, however, in yours. In the mortals, the youngest of the many creations. But you are descended from the line of one who wove sleep. It is not so prized a skill these days; it is not elevated or valued.

"When the Ancients walked, your Ancestors were essential. The Ancients have not walked for so long mortals have forgotten their existence. And the somnambulists have not been trained or taught; what purpose would their lessons serve? Only here, in these places, are the old ways followed; only in these places do the restless, unfinished thoughts of the Ancients sleep."

"There was power in them?"

"To you, yes."

"No, I mean…power that could be used for other purposes?"

"An odd question. They were of the Ancients, and as such, they had a power the simpler creations did not. But they could not simply be *used*. They could not easily be accessed, could not be moved to change or retreat. They are like questions that have no answers—and it is only answers that might complete them, might set them permanently to rest."

"What if someone—like me, say—wanted to reach the power inherent in them?"

"That is not a good question to ask; I perceive you have reasons for it."

"We think it's possible that someone stumbled across the sleepers; that they reached them or touched them or disturbed them enough that the containments—the sleep—were shattered."

The Wevaran eyes didn't rise or swivel. So. They knew. "We did not touch their power. It was too risky. There was power here, in this hidden place, that was far safer. If someone could breach the defenses that surround the captive thoughts, they might have attempted to enter the labyrinth instead."

"What if they didn't know it existed?"

"If they knew nothing, your family would not be dead. The magic of mortals is slight; it touches the world in which they live. But some adepts can reach beyond that world in their experiments. It is possible that there was enough similarity in thought and desire that they echoed a dreamer, and touched that dreamer."

"But—did they shatter the containment?"

"It is a metaphor that is not entirely apt, but not entirely wrong. Glass is found in windows; windows separate interior from exterior. Someone has broken or shattered the windows. They cannot yet enter the interior; the interior is protected. The door is locked."

"So we have time?"

"You have already seen the power of a dream on the edge of waking. People have died. That will continue. In dreams closest to the surface of waking, the captives have will; they do not have the strength to fully become. But it would not surprise me if the people who entered that almost waking dream have been given inexact instructions. The thoughts are imprisoned; they desire to be free. There is a locked door that stands in the way.

"The key to the lock cannot be found. The door can."

"Door?"

"Rianna. And now, child, you. If you live, they cannot breach that barrier. They believed that you—and all of your kin—were dead. That is my supposition. But the door did not yield."

"So you think they came to the Academia to find me?"

The apparition chuckled. "The interest in the Academia is, in my opinion, entirely separate. There is no way that they can track a simple mortal child with any ease. It is possible they knew where your mother fled, but I do not believe they knew that you survived."

He began to walk, lifting the lamp as he did so. "Someone came to the Academia; they could disguise themselves as people who lived or worked there. One of my friends thought they meant to…pour glass *into* living people."

The apparition froze in place. Robin thought it would remain there, but a sense of urgency now drove him forward.

The voice caught up with him, or kept pace with him; the visible form did not. "If such glass could somehow be inserted into living people, they could become a container for things that otherwise couldn't survive or thrive in your world. Our protections are rooted, grounded, in your world. And the Academia—

as any sentient building—has raw material of which they might make use.

"They did not know who you were, I believe. They have been hunting in the Academia because they can make use of the same numinous ether Killianas can. I wish to discuss the Academia at length, but we do not have time. Suffice it to say that we all thought it lost when the Towers rose. That it was not lost is a miracle—a miracle of hope, intention, and the diversion of power granted the Towers.

"But found, it was weakened. If a mortal stays in their sickbed for months, they cannot simply rise from bed and return to the life they lived prior to their illness. It is not so different for Killianas; he is alive, if not in the fashion you are. He has lost the equivalent of your muscle memory, and he must build it anew. It was not something considered by the Ancients when they built him."

"Are you like Killian?"

"No. Killian and his constructed kin—the Towers, the High Halls, the distant Hallionne, and a handful of others—were created to house a living person."

"And you aren't a living person?"

"What do you think?" Robin could hear the smile in their voice. "I am not as you are, not as he is, or was. Robin, I, too, am sleeping. You are a dream that has caught my attention while you walk in this space."

"Could you wake?"

"Not while you live, little Gardianno. And not while the grey crow flies." This was said without bitterness.

"You don't want to wake."

"When you are having a beautiful dream, do you wish to wake? No; I am—and have been—content. Here, in the darkness, in the web of possibilities."

"But you...are you a thought? Like the ones held captive?"

"Nothing like, no. I was a thought given free rein. A small

thought; an unambitious thought. A thought about the nature of power, responsibility, and the sanctity of life—of living things, created by the Ancients, who walk toward the unknown future. That is, of course, inexact; it is a limitation of language. But even were you to understand the language of the Ancients fully, it would still be inexact; I exist as a thought not fully given the shape of words, the future words imply."

"I thought this was supposed to be a labyrinth."

"What does that word imply to you?"

"A maze? A place with passages that have to be navigated if you want to reach the center?"

"Or the exit?"

Robin nodded.

"Do you fear to be trapped here?"

Robin shook his head. "I probably should. I don't. But this… it's a forest. There are trees. There's no path."

"There is a path, child. You are creating it as you walk. It is your path. It is not Rianna's path; it is certainly not the grey crow's—she flies. If you have the shards of what you call glass, you must know what you intend for them. It is the question you will be asked, and you must answer it honestly or you will be ejected."

Robin nodded. He tried to clear his mind, tried to focus on his task. The problem being he didn't *understand* it. He knew he didn't want the thoughts—if they could be called that—to fully enter his world. The attempt had already cost lives—at least three, but Robin was uneasily certain that more had died outside of the Academia.

The attacks on the Academia hadn't started with the thoughts. Men seeking power—human and Barrani, in uneasy alliance— had somehow found the slumbering Academia, and had pulled it into a half-awake state. They were the reason Robin was at the Academia at all: he'd been kidnapped off the warrens' streets and dropped into a grey stone room. From there he had entered the campus with others who had been grabbed off the streets; it was a surprise that so many of them were Barrani.

The chancellor, however, had wrested the Academia from the hands of those who sought it for power; they had wanted to reach and control the library, of all places. As if the librarians—Wevaran, Dragon, and Barrani Ancestor—could not defend the space that now defined them.

But they'd almost succeeded in controlling the Academia, in leaving Killian catatonic, his halls easily and openly traversed by those who knew how to reach the building.

The chancellor's Academia was now Robin's home. It was a home he had grown to love, a home he wanted to preserve. It was a home he had offered to his only childhood friend, and her presence had led him here, to the labyrinth, to the private heart of the grey crow's power.

Focus, Robin.

He wanted the thoughts to sleep. He wanted the Academia to be safe. He wanted Raven to be safe there, as well.

"Choose wisely, child." Voice absent form. "For you have reached the end of trees."

He had, as the voice said, reached the end of the forest. The trees spread out in an uneven line to his left and right. Beyond them was a field: a flower field. There was no forward path, no building in the distance, no visible destination. He glanced to the left and right, and then continued forward, stepping carefully so as not to crush any flowers.

The flowers themselves were odd; he'd never seen any like them before. They were white, three-petaled; they grew close to the ground. He had never been interested in botany, even when offered at the Academia—he'd never lived in a place where the growing of flowers could be safely done. But even so, he tread carefully, finding places to put his feet that didn't crush what grew here.

What he found odd about the flowers was their scent: it wasn't uniform. Although the flowers looked similar, they smelled different; some were so strongly perfumed, they made him sneeze; some were subtle and softer. And some reminded him of favorite foods, not flowers at all.

They were childhood smells.

He remembered, as he knelt, sneaking into the kitchens in his old home. There were always people in the kitchens. He wasn't supposed to bother them while they worked, but they never seemed bothered; they had a high stool on which he could sit and watch and chatter. So much chatter, he was almost embarrassed now. It was a memory that returned to him because of the scent; it was a memory he had not recalled until this moment.

He rose carefully, and moved slowly, a step or two at a time; he knelt in front of flowers and carefully sniffed the scent that rose from their heart. Those scents that weren't familiar, he discarded; he ended up threading his way through this field almost by smell alone, pausing when they evoked memories.

The scent of alcohol: his father's birthday? He'd wanted to drink what his father drank. His mother said no, but his father said yes—as a present to himself.

The scent of wet dog. Which led to the scent of the pond behind the house. Had he forgotten the dog? Trouble. The dog's nickname. Robin couldn't remember his actual name, because Trouble is what he was called. He was a large dog, but clumsy, awkward, and far too impulsive.

The scent of powder. He hesitated there, but remembered: sister. Young, as he was young—although she had seemed much younger to his child self. Lost, as every other scent was lost, except in a memory that had not returned to him until now.

The need to survive had made the memories too painful. He could be paralyzed by loss, by abandonment, by the certain sense that the world was, or would be, his death. He rose and looked around; the field remained, the flowers with their varied, impossible scents the same as any of the other flowers.

He considered the fact that Giselle had called this the labyrinth, the maze. And that she had said that every attempt to navigate it was unique. He now understood why. It was a maze constructed of the suppressed memories and history of Robin. If Raven had come, if Raven were here, she wouldn't find the path that Robin had found; his memories, his experiences, overlapped hers, but they weren't hers.

But she'd find her own path, separate from his.

"No," the invisible apparition said. "She would not. Not her. Child, you don't understand how difficult it is to walk this path—you who are on your knees in this field, searching for lost things."

He would have asked her why it was difficult had he not found a flower that was almost scentless. Almost. But the subtle scent invaded his nostrils, crept down his throat, filled his mouth with the taste of blood. His blood.

His.

In the distance, he could hear his mother scream. She screamed his name: *Robin!* He heard, turned toward her, mouth full of blood. He'd been walking ahead of her, as he often did; she walked so slowly. He felt pain, a brief flash in his chest. Looked down to see blood spreading across his shirt. Were it not for his mother's scream, he would have felt confusion. He hadn't fallen, hadn't tripped, hadn't hit anything that would make him bleed.

But his mother's fear became his as he absorbed it.

He turned toward her, saw her expression as time almost froze. Behind her, fire blossomed across the horizon. Their house. Their house was on fire and Robin was bleeding, as if home and Robin were the same.

His mother was a mage. He knew it, although she almost never used the magic she was known to possess. Once, she'd spent an afternoon making bubbles and fireworks—but only once. Today, there was fire. Fire, lightning, and fear. He could see the crackle in the air as she ran to his side; could see fire melt stones in two lines to either side of where they ran.

She caught him in her arms, lifted him, turned to look back at the burning house. One or two people had staggered out, having survived the fire and the collapse of the left side of the building. Robin thought she would run to the house; was surprised when she began to run away, carrying him, her head bent over his.

He never knew the moment she, too, started to bleed; couldn't see what had caused it. Couldn't see the enemy that had attacked their home. But no, that wasn't true, was it?

He was carried; he'd thrown arms around his mother's neck. He looked over her shoulder.

Standing, arms raised, hands in fists, expression clear even at this distance was a man familiar to Robin: his uncle. His mother's youngest brother. Nothing else about him was familiar: not his clothing, not his stance, not his utter lack of warmth or affection. His face was twisted in fury as he brought his hands down. Robin felt the motion as if it were thunder. It destroyed the road beneath his uncle's feet. It destroyed the road at his mother's back.

But the road in front remained stable for just long enough that it didn't break beneath her.

He was bleeding; his chest hurt. He was too young not to whimper.

His mother said nothing he could understand. She spoke quick words, desperate words, magical words—words that weren't language. They weren't meant to comfort; they weren't meant to soothe. They were meant to protect.

Robin knelt in a field of white ash, ash in the shape of flowers. The memories that returned told him clearly that life as he had known it had ended permanently. There was no home to return to. There was no family.

He wasn't a child anymore.

But even if he told himself—and anyone who would listen—that he *wasn't* a child, that part of him remained: the desire to return home. The desire to once again be held in the safety of his parents' arms. The desire to spend time with his baby sister. To tag along with his older brother. All things that he'd rejected as a young child, because they were impossible.

Was it better not to have the memories? Was it better not to have that joy if the end was nothing but pain?

Everything has a beginning. Everything has an end. Who had said that?

Robin knew endings. He hadn't considered his life in the warrens to be a beginning; it was a beginning he'd never wanted, based on the loss of everything in his life except life itself. But it was the only life he had. He'd wanted to live. He'd wanted to survive. He'd wanted to believe that somehow, if he grew strong enough to survive, he could return to the home that had once been his.

There he could build again. He could make a family. He could have a family.

He'd never spoken the words aloud; he'd barely thought them after the first year, because Raven hated bad thoughts. The family he wanted was the one he had lost on that day. The house meant nothing without the family in it. Yes, in his first home he'd never lived in fear of starvation or freezing to death. But he didn't fear those things in the Academia, either.

And if the warrens weren't his choice, if the beginning had been one of terror and desperation, it had led to Raven, and to the Academia. To a different life, divorced—until this moment—from the life he had lost. In it, there were possibilities he had not dreamed of.

If he could go back in time to that day, if he could save his family somehow, if he could warn them of what was coming, he wouldn't be the Robin he was now. He wouldn't be a student in the Academia. He would never have met Raven, and she had been his only friend. Even in a life of plenty, he had seldom strayed far from home or family; his parents had been very protective. He'd had guards on the few occasions he had left his house, and his parents had been a constant presence.

He wouldn't have met Starrante. Serralyn, Valliant, Terrano. He wouldn't have stood in front of an annoyed Dragon, or entered a library that contained more books than Robin could read if he did nothing but read for the rest of his life.

He stood in a field of flowers, and he felt, as breeze moved their petals and leaves, that he could hear a distant voice; it offered him a choice. He could go back in time. He could warn his parents. He could change the past.

But he knew, listening to this attenuated voice, that this was a lie. It must be a lie, because his mother had enspelled him to prevent that terrible yearning, to deny him the ability to look back on that past, to dwell on it, to even *mention her name.* Maybe she knew that he'd end up here. Maybe she knew what he might be offered—or what he might ask. Maybe she knew that the asking itself was a failure, at a time when failure was disastrous.

More disastrous than the death of his family?

To his mother, yes. The only greater disaster would have been Robin's death—Robin, the one child she could still save.

Had she come here? Had she come here after she'd called Raven? Had she met this field or something similar, and been offered the same choice that Robin could faintly hear? *Choose, and you will get your daughter back. Your husband back. A home for your sons. You have served us well, and we will give you what you desire; use the power you know is here.*

Whether his mother had, or had not, faced this at the very end of her life, he couldn't say. But he knew what she would have counseled if she were standing beside him now, on this path that everyone walked alone.

He shook his head: no. "No. Even if I believed it could be done, I couldn't do it. It would destroy all the new possibilities in every other life, not just mine."

"You are certain?" As it spoke, as its question echoed, the apparition began to emerge from thin air. This time, however, it wasn't Wevaran. It wasn't—quite—human, but closer in form and shape.

Robin nodded.

"You are angry."

He nodded again, and attempted to exhale that anger, to separate it from himself. "It's a mean test."

"Mean?" The spirit laughed. "Perhaps. I will tell you this, you who have not asked. All of your kin who venture into this place face tests of their own. Some pass, some fail."

"But I'm the last?"

"No. And yes. They who were born to the power might find this place in dream; they might search for it if they know of its existence. But their ability to walk to the heart of this maze is decided in a similar way. It is by your desires and choices that you are judged. Some cannot enter the maze a second time— their desires have grown edges and weight.

"But, boy, desire is not, in and of itself, a great evil. Who does not desire the love of kin? Who does not desire a home and a family? It is not *desire* that is the weakness; desire simply means you're alive.

"Your reasoning to reject is of interest to me. What did you mean when you said your choice would destroy the new possibilities in every other life?"

Robin blinked. "If I had been offered this when I first arrived in the warrens, I would have taken it with both hands. I would have spent whatever remained of my life holding on to it. If that meant I was never to navigate the maze... I wouldn't have cared."

"It is why children are not taught the mysteries."

Robin hadn't been taught anything, either, and almost said as much. But he finished answering the question instead. "But if I hadn't lived in the warrens, I would never have met Raven. I would never have found the Academia. I would never be considered a student worth teaching. If I could go back in time, if I could save my family and my home, I would lose all of the things I value now. They couldn't happen. I don't know how lack of me might have changed the fate of the Academia—and I'll never know.

"But if I made the choice to give up the things I value now, nobody else would get a say. Right now, some people are in far better places than they were when I was a child—and they'd lose whatever they've worked for and gained without any choice at all. Their world would unwind, same as mine. Maybe they'd be reliving the worst years of their life all over again. I don't know. And I can't ask everyone living for permission, can I? I can't make a decision like this for everyone else."

"Why not?"

"Because I'm not a god," Robin replied, anger simmering just below the surface of the words. "I can't randomly make decisions for every other living being."

"No. No, you cannot." The apparition began to glow; what had been pale, translucent grey took on color: white, blue, gold, a flare of every color imaginable in the location a human heart might have occupied. "Very well, Robin Gardianno. You have come in supplication, and you have been heard." The apparition held out a hand, palm up, toward him.

"What if I had made the wrong choice?"

"Does it matter?"

"It does. It was—" He wanted to say *mean* again, but felt suddenly self-conscious, as if it were a word meant only for children to use. "Unkind."

"And you will face similar unkindness in the future that we cannot see. But you are allowed to pass into the heart of this hallowed place, there to make the request you have carried with you. Come."

Robin exhaled slowly. He lifted his hand—right to their left—and placed it against the transparent palm. He was surprised to find it solid.

The field beneath his feet vanished as the apparition absorbed all light present—saving only the lantern that he held aloft in his left hand.

27

The light did not return landscape to Robin's vision as he squinted, waiting for his eyes to acclimate to the brighter, stronger illumination.

"I see you found your way in," a familiar voice said. Robin turned—could easily turn—toward the voice, his eyes widening before falling into a squint again as he raised his hand to shield them.

"I fell through a wall," Robin told the grey crow. She was standing—not leaning—on what appeared to be stairs—stairs that led up behind her back. Her arms, however, were folded. Her entire body was translucent, like cloudy glass.

"The wall by the well?"

"Your spot, yes."

Giselle's smile was sharp. "Not a place for others to lean."

"We were trying to find a way into the labyrinth, and that seemed like the most obvious choice."

"We?"

"Raven and I."

Giselle's expression was sharp, odd. She wasn't smiling, but something about her gaze implied approval. "It was. I can't stay; I wanted to make sure you hadn't gotten yourself lost."

"Could you have helped me?"

"To leave, if you were lost, yes. You wouldn't be the first person I've led out of this place." She exhaled. "Your uncle was in line to be Gardianno. He was promising, sensitive, aware of his responsibilities. Or so they thought. But he could not find his way to the heart. The first time he tried, he came closest; the next two times, he struggled. There was no fourth time. In my opinion, there shouldn't have been a second or third."

"And if I had failed?"

"I would have argued that you should be allowed to make another attempt." He wondered with whom she would have made that argument, but didn't ask; he was certain she wouldn't answer. Or worse, lie. "But I've seen more of you than I did of your uncle. Your uncle, I was only aware of here, in this place."

"Can you tell?"

"Tell what?"

"When someone enters."

Giselle nodded. "I can't stay," she said again. "Things are a bit tense at the Academia. Whatever you need to do—and don't ask me, I don't know—you should do it fast." She paused, and then said, "Raven is here."

"Wait—she's at the Academia?"

"Yes."

A thousand urgent questions tried to leave his mouth at the same time; he clamped his jaw shut until they died, choosing only one. "Can you see them?"

Giselle didn't pretend to misunderstand. "Yes. The guardian is with you; it is only through the guardian that you can enter this place at all."

"You can enter at any time."

"I can—but I cannot make use of the power. I am a first line of defense. Robin: this is important. You need to focus on what you want. What led you here? What do you intend to achieve?"

"Can the heart of the maze reject my request?"

"Of course." Giselle closed her eye. "See you soon." She faded from view.

Robin inhaled. He was surprised at the taste of the air here—it was so different. In his hands, he held Raven's pouch. In his thoughts, his own fear. Raven had gone back to the Academia. Raven had left him here alone. Why? She was in danger there. Here, she was safe.

It was a bitter truth. For Raven, the warrens were safer than the Academia. Safer than Killian, who couldn't fully trust her. There was no Larrantin here to trap her. No rules that made no sense to her, which made them hard to follow. She wouldn't starve here, wouldn't freeze here. All of the fear and the struggle had been Robin's. He should have left her alone. Should have set her free.

But she wasn't free, was she? Whatever she was, she had been bound to Robin, to Robin's survival. He'd survived without her in the Academia. He *could* survive without her. Raven needed nothing the Academia had to offer.

Needed nothing from Robin. All of the need—he could see this clearly—had been his. He had been her burden.

"Yes," his companion said quietly, shimmering into existence by his side. "As children often are. But, child, there is joy to be found in the care. Do not forget that."

"There's death in it, as well," Robin replied, voice low.

"Mortals are tangled, always, in the imperative to survive. In the imperative to have their children survive. Children are your legacy, who cannot endure for eternity. Your mother made her choice; she understood that choices have consequences, and she paid the price for your survival.

"And you are, as she hoped, here. What would you have of us?"

He held out the pouch toward the translucent figure. "Teach me."

"What would you have me teach?"

"How to gentle the wild thoughts. How to put them to sleep again." He opened the pouch. From it, he withdrew the metals that had been transformed by lantern light. They retained their larger, unbroken shapes; the glass remained shards, although those shards were luminous now, lit from within by the light they had also absorbed, or were absorbing.

"Ah. I cannot teach you that. But come: we are sleeping in this place. Sleep, to us, is not what it is to you; we do not perish without it, and we gain little strength from it. It is a state that separates us from your waking world; without a conduit of some kind, we cannot interact with you at all."

People had died.

"Yes. And that is the conduit. I feel, child, that your prior losses and your current crisis are linked. But you have the ability that your kin lacks. If you call, the dreamers who have almost woken will hear you; they will come to you."

"To be bound?"

"No; they will come to you as moths to flame. It is that involuntary. That is the measure of your line's ancient power. Come. See the world that dreams create. See the power that resides in those dreams." They held out a hand, and Robin placed his palm across theirs.

Nothing changed. He withdrew his hand, or tried, but transparent fingers closed around it.

"Come," the apparition said again. This time, he could feel the rumble of the words ripple up his arm into his center. The maze's Avatar, the apparition that spoke on behalf of its ancient power, began to walk. Robin followed, certain that if he stood his ground, he'd just be dragged in their wake.

He was not surprised to see the walk that had once surrounded the back of the manor he'd once called home. He probably should have been. "You know this place?"

"I know it well. Generations of your people have called it home. You are the first who cannot. You could build it again."

Robin shook his head. He knew nothing about architecture, and even if he had, he understood that money was necessary. He had no money to speak of. He hoped that his tenure at the Academia would give him the skills with which he could earn money—but he'd never earn enough to re-create what was lost.

"I do not know what stands here in its place. Do you?"

Robin shook his head. "I didn't think about what I'd lost. My mother—" He shook his head again. "Spells were cast to prevent it. I think she was afraid that I'd mention my name, my family name, my old home, someplace where the wrong people would hear it. I had no way of defending myself." He had no way of doing so now. "I could run. I could hide. That was it."

"Will you find out?"

"Not now."

"Do you feel you owe your family justice?"

Did he? Was he walking this familiar path because he desired justice for the dead? He hadn't thought about it before. Couldn't. "I...don't know."

"Consider it. Come."

The walk changed, although the change was subtle; the stones were paler, newer, than they had been; what had once been loose flower beds—very loose—had been replaced by pristine, short grass. He looked up to see that this path led to stairs—shallow, few in number—that in turn climbed to a wide stone patio; the rails that enclosed it were low. Glass doors had been installed, and above those doors, a stained glass arch.

The building itself was not yet completed, but elements of it strongly implied that the parts that had been finished were inhabited.

"This stands in the place your home once stood. Will you enter?"

Robin nodded. He felt a sense of dread, and an unfamiliar sense of another emotion he didn't want to name.

They didn't open doors; they passed through them, as if the entire incomplete building that stood where his home had once been was a mirage, a phantasm. The interior halls were unfamiliar; even the shape of the interior had changed—at least here. Where he had been led, he now took the lead, following new halls to see where they joined with the damaged former building.

He found offices—three—on the ground floor, but he'd never been interested in the offices as a child. They were pristine, almost empty, as if decorative in nature. There was a large sitting room, entirely newly furnished, and a large living room that seemed to span at least half the building's length. In a room similar to this, his parents had entertained their valued guests; the children had not been allowed to join in, but had lingered, watching people arrive.

It was the kitchens he wanted to see the most, and he followed the halls searching for it, until he came upon the dining room. It was, like the living room, very large and expensively appointed; there were large bay windows on the far wall, and light illuminated a table that was not in use.

The kitchens were closest to this room. He found them and entered.

There were people working in them; they'd always been occupied. The woodstove was burning, and it was tended. He recognized none of the faces. There was no familiar stool, but the kitchen wasn't silent. Maybe that's why he'd loved it as a child: it never felt empty. He never felt alone.

The kitchen had survived the fire in more or less the same dimensions; the floors looked newer now, and one wall had been replaced. But the people who'd worked in those kitchens were gone—either let go or dead through no fault of their own.

He wondered, then, who lived here.

He was certain that he knew. He left the kitchen and began to walk deliberately through the areas of the house he had avoided, to see if there were people he recognized. In the end, there were two, and he found them—of all places—in the basement, near the cellars that the cooks used so much.

He hadn't loved the basement, half fearing that the rumored dungeons were real; he didn't like the lack of natural light, the lack of windows. But he understood, as he approached the downward stairs, that the stairs themselves were the ones he'd avoided in his childhood. They were old, and they had no rails, only a wall to one side.

Falling wouldn't hurt him here; he took the stairs urgently— fear of falling, fear of darkness, forgotten. Those fears would give him no answers.

"Fear seldom does. But if handled adroitly, it leads to caution, and caution is often necessary."

The ceilings in the basement were higher than expected, and the floors, once the stairs were cleared, smoother. The stairs had been worn by constant use, but the floors had not.

He went farther in and saw that the basement hall opened into a large room, a room with uneven walls, uneven ceiling; it looked like a rectangular cavern in which stonemasons had not been up to the task of finishing touches.

One man stood in the room, unmoving; to Robin's eye, even breath had stopped.

He had last seen this man in a memory the maze had dislodged and offered him: his uncle. He wondered if his uncle had taken his father's place. Or if he had attempted to take his mother's. But his uncle didn't hear Robin, didn't see him. Robin's gaze traveled beyond his uncle to the floor: it was carved stonework that radiated out like petals of wild growth; Robin's uncle stood at its center.

Robin couldn't tell if the pattern itself was new. He didn't remember the basement clearly. He certainly didn't remember this room.

But some echo of distant past returned as he looked at the floor. *This is your mother's workspace. The basement is not for the rest of us.* His father's voice. His father's, when it was his mother's that had so scarred him.

"Is this how he hopes to enter the space where the dreamers lie?"

The voice didn't answer. Robin was certain the maze heart was still here; he couldn't be here if it wasn't. But the silence felt ominous in this cavern.

The silence, the lack of light.

Robin stepped carefully past his immobile uncle. The kitchen servants had moved and talked and worked; his uncle did not. His arms were raised, his palms toward the ceiling that could barely be seen in the dim light, as if the pattern on the floor was not as worthy of his attention.

Robin knelt behind his uncle's back; he reached out to touch the floor, to touch the edges of the engravings here, as if by touch he could ascertain its age. It was stone, which he expected; it was warm, which he hadn't. He wanted light, and the lamp he had carried since he'd entered the labyrinth was in his hand, as if he had never set it aside.

He'd never consciously let go of it.

In this light, he could see two patterns. One, carved in stone, as if it were a symbol his uncle could rule over. The other was far more delicate; it left no mark on the stone, and could be seen only as trails of light. But the light formed vines and the edges of leaves, and in among those leaves were small, white flowers, three-petaled, clinging to the vines.

Here and there the carving matched the pattern Robin's lamp revealed, but it seemed random, as if his uncle had seen this pattern before but could not completely recall it. He had built this floor; Robin was certain of it. But the floor was just carved lines in stone; there was no sense of life in it beyond the warmth he could feel by touch.

This was his mother's room. He wondered if she once stood as still as his uncle now stood; wondered if she centered herself in the heart of the pattern as if she ruled it. He shook his head. She couldn't have. Not his mother. Not the mother who tended gardens—real gardens. He thought of her as a gardener, wondered if *gardens* came from that initial concept.

But he looked, now, at the vines of light, the leaves, the flowers; his sense that they were alive grew stronger. He knew nothing about gardening. Nothing. He would probably overwater plants until they drowned in fear that they were lacking. But even thinking that, he could see the way the vines grew wild, grew lumped together; could see the way the leaves were too numerous and the flowers—delicate and small—were overwhelmed.

It's not like they needed sunlight; they wouldn't have survived in this place otherwise. But he felt as if they did, somehow, and he began to nudge the vines, to move them, in place. They were solid in his hand, just as the guardian of the maze had been, although she had been ghostly and translucent to the eye.

He noted that the vines themselves were overgrown where they coincided with the carved stone, and he frowned. Stone, yes, but warm, as if it were sun-drenched earth. It became softer as he pressed his hand against it; he found he could shape the stone, but it was slow work, this shaping. The vines didn't avoid the stone that wasn't engraved; he could arrange them carefully, but it was still not quite enough.

He exhaled; it was soundless. He didn't exist in the same space that his uncle did, for which he was grateful. He had seen what his uncle could do, and even if the dread was magnified because the impression had been made when he was a child, there was still fact wrapped in that dread. He was not his uncle's equal in magery. He might never become his equal.

But he could do this. Because he understood, as the vines moved, what the glass must achieve: the vines across the floor were like bevels, like frames. The glass, however, was absent. He withdrew Raven's pouch, opened it, and looked at the glass that lay within, glowing faintly with light.

He removed a shard, examining the way the vines grew; he found a place which would fit the shard and set it down, nestled within vines of light. As if the glass had weight, the vines closed around it. He drew another broken piece of glass; he laid it in an opening of vine and leaf, and the vines tightened around the glass, fastening it in place.

He chose pieces that were clear at first—those were the largest—but as he worked, arranging vines and erasing engravings that lay beneath them, the glass he had placed was suffused with a white-green light, as if it were taking root. He had thought of jars, or glass boxes, or windows, things that had glass in the life he knew.

But this was different. All of the glass felt *alive* as he placed it in the space it belonged. He couldn't understand how Raven had found this glass; he knew she had found it both in the warrens and here, in the gardens—but if this was where the glass had been laid, he couldn't understand how she'd stumbled across it.

Didn't understand why, unless she somehow saw ahead to this moment: Robin, without her, carefully taking the pieces she had so joyfully husbanded and placing them where he knew they belonged. His uncle was still frozen; Robin wondered if time had stopped as he labored; if, in the real world, things moved glacially slowly.

No answer came as he worked, and he worked quickly. Giselle had said speed was necessary. Raven was in the Academia. He wondered if she would come—if she even could—if something went wrong here. If his uncle became aware that

Robin was here, working in silence, and destroying what he had attempted to build.

But no. His uncle had destroyed. Robin was attempting to rebuild what should have been here. Had he the power, he thought he would kill his uncle where he stood; had he a weapon, he might have tried. The chancellor frowned on weapons in the Academia, although swords apparently didn't count as weapons, given the Barrani youth who bore them. But he was aware that what he had asked the labyrinth for, and what it had granted him, was not revenge.

Later, maybe.

Later. But he could rebuild this to the best of his ability now, and hope that what he was doing would inhibit whatever it was that now roamed the Academia campus, shedding pieces of glass and leaving corpses in its wake.

The colored bits of glass that had come from the hidden office's cathedral-like window he found no home for here, no like harmony of placement or purpose; most of the glass shards were clear and he used those until he had almost emptied the pouch.

There were still spaces for glass, but he hesitated, almost afraid to empty the bag. He drew out the small metallic lattice, but there was no place for it in this pattern. Just space for glass, although there was too much space and too little glass. He wondered if, at one point, the entirety of this odd pattern had held glass like this. He wondered what the whole would look like, if it could be made whole. Wondered what practical purpose the glass served.

Raven's precious pouch was almost empty; it now contained the brilliant colored shards and metal pieces she had gathered, nothing else. But there was glass in the Academia—glass that, with Killian's permission, Robin might make use of here.

He rose, having finished as much as he could.

"I'm ready," he whispered, turning to stare at his uncle. "Take me back."

Silence was the only response he received; it continued for too long. Robin was clearly meant to take himself back—or at least take himself out of this basement, this unfamiliar building that had replaced his childhood home. Could his uncle undo the repairs? Could his uncle once again attempt to engrave his own pattern, half-understood, in what wasn't truly stone?

Yes, no doubt he could. Robin had no idea how long it had taken his uncle to make the changes he'd made. He suspected it had been the work of years, possibly beginning before his family had been murdered. But seeing his uncle standing at the heart of what he had attempted to create, he understood why his uncle had not become guardian. His uncle must have believed that power was a sword: it could be picked up and wielded by a person who'd been trained to its use.

The idea that it couldn't be uprooted and wielded had probably never occurred to his uncle, to men like his uncle.

But it wasn't a weapon; it was a garden. The power it contained was the power of life, of living things; it couldn't be uprooted without destroying much of it. Robin was certain of that. More certain than he'd been about most of his life. As certain as he'd been that the Academia was his home, the place he truly desired to stay. A place he belonged.

His uncle didn't see him. Couldn't see him. The place in which Robin was standing was not a place his uncle could stand. He could reach out to it, could strain to break in. Had probably done just that. But all of his attempts failed to understand the nature of this space and the labyrinth that lent it power.

And some of his attempts had cost lives, would continue to cost lives if he could not be stopped. Perhaps he knew that; perhaps this had traveled too far beyond him. It was a struggle to think it. The bitter sting of loss and betrayal simmered beneath the surface of Robin's thoughts.

But he understood: the labyrinth had accepted him because

it wasn't vengeance he'd asked for. He'd asked for the ability to do what he'd done here. There was only one thing left to do.

Robin left the manor far more quickly than he'd arrived; he left the changed grounds at a sprint. He could sprint without tiring, proof that his body wasn't actually here, even if he could see himself clearly. He paused only once on the road that led to the warrens, to look toward the fiefs, their Towers, and the Academia that could be reached from any one of them.

"Yes," the maze's guardian said, joining him for the first time since he'd been left in the bones of his old home. "The grey crow flies. You, too, must learn to fly." Once again, the guardian held out a hand; Robin placed his own in hers, and they began to run.

His feet were on the ground; he could feel the earth beneath the soles of the shoes he wore. He wasn't running *on* dirt; he was running down the street, dodging to avoid people and wagons. Or that was his intent, but the guardian dragged him *through* the wagon—and the horse that pulled it—and continued on her way.

He almost felt like she was Raven, in this place.

"I am not. I will never be like your Raven."

He bit down on words that served no purpose, on anger that was pointless.

"But she did gather things necessary to attempt to repair what was broken. I had not foreseen that."

More nothing. More forced silence. Why was he even angry? He knew: the guardian didn't consider Raven a person.

If Raven didn't consider herself a person, that was fine. But she *did*. She had her own goals, and even if some had been truly strange to Robin—broken glass collection chief among them—they were hers. She had things she wanted, things she dreamed of having. A desk. A desk of all things. But the harmless compulsion to pick up broken pieces of glass wherever she could find them hadn't been useless. It had been necessary.

"Are you sure I shouldn't go back and get my...body?"

The guardian snorted. "You are ignorant."

"That's why I'm a *student*. I want to be *less* ignorant." He ran, trying to catch up. He wasn't a child, to be dragged to his destination.

"You are often dragged to a destination."

That was different.

"How?"

"It just is. Raven's my friend."

"And I am not." There was no question in the words; for a moment the voice seemed immeasurably *old*. "Do not forget it, child. Come, hurry—we are almost there. Can you see it now?"

Robin had crossed the Ablayne by bridge; his steps made no sound and the bridge itself felt squishy beneath his feet. But he looked up at the question and stumbled, which was awkward given the speed at which they were running.

He could see what she saw, but it didn't look like the Academia to his eyes. It looked almost like the pattern in the floor of his former home: a thing of golden light, edged in green, in blue, in violet, and even in red; the air shimmered in place around it as it rose before his eyes. Which was ridiculous—the Academia had no towers, no buildings designed to look majestic and impressive. What was impressive within its many walls were the scholars, the students, the chancellor, the library— things meant to be experienced.

Yet he could see, as if all other buildings had become irrelevant or transparent, the shape of the building that housed dining halls, dorms, and lecture halls; could see, before it, the viridescence of the quad; could see the trees, liminal as they grew and extended shade and protection from sun and rain; he could see the streets—the streets that started in the fief of Tiamaris—that led to the circular road upon which the Academia sat.

Even the residential buildings seemed too new, too bright, to be real. He hadn't spent time in those buildings, but he'd lived in the dorms and attended the classes and been on the inside of the chancellor's office too many times: the Academia was real. As real as Robin.

They sped up, passing streets Robin didn't even register to reach the streets he could; they ran, following the curve of the road, until they reached the quad. There, the guardian let go of his hand. Robin stumbled to a stop and turned to look back.

The guardian's hands were gently folded together. "I wish you peace and success. I offer you no warnings. But you must return, both to me and to the place that was once your home, in the fullness of time. Whether you return alone or not is not in my hands."

"What do you mean?"

"The power granted you has been granted, but, child: you were not terribly *focused* in your expression of desire. It is not necessary, but it can complicate things. The heart of what you wanted, the maze wanted—but it is now intrigued, and its dreams shift and change even as we speak. It is subtle, but it is there.

"Go. Go and save the home you have chosen for now."

28

Robin ran across the quad; he moved around the students who were sitting there. They were very still. Not statues, not like his uncle, but all of their movements were slow. He recognized one or two, but they didn't see him, didn't demand attention or interaction. Had any of them been Serralyn or her friends, he would have stopped.

He ran across grass, beneath trees, and toward the wide, shallow steps that led to the main building. He ran through the doors—both closed—and into the hall.

He wasn't surprised to see Killian. Until Killian turned to look at him. Killian could see him.

"Robin?"

"There's trouble," Robin said, not out of breath although he'd never stopped sprinting.

"I had assumed you might be trouble—I didn't recognize you when I first sensed you on campus. Why *are* you entering like this?"

"I'll explain later if you can't pick it out of my thoughts."

"Your thoughts are highly obfuscated at the moment, no doubt due to your current plane of existence."

That didn't even give Robin pause. "Where's Raven?"
Silence.

"Where's Terrano?"

"I cannot see him." Killian's eyes were obsidian and unblink-ing. Robin understood then: Killian felt that something was wrong—but he couldn't see what. He had lost sight of parts of himself. Robin knew this; Killian knew it, as well. "I...do not know. The chancellor is distressed."

"Is he in his office?"

"I...do not know." If a building could pale, if a building could evince genuine distress and fear, Killian did.

Robin inhaled. He exhaled a single word. *"Raven!"*

Down the hall she came, arms flapping at her sides the way they always did if her hand wasn't attached to Robin. Her eyes were wide, unblinking, oddly luminous given the darkness of their color; they spread light across her pale face, but her hair was its usual tangled mess, and her feet—her feet were bare. Again.

She launched herself at Robin when she was ten yards away— he'd swear it was that far—and crashed into him. "Don't shout," she hissed. "What were you *thinking*?"

"I needed to find you. I needed to know where the dan-ger was."

Her brow furrowed. "Make sense." The command was curt.

"Giselle said there's danger on campus—and that I had better hurry. She told me you had come back here. Why didn't you wait for me?"

Raven was confused. "I did. I waited. And waited. And now you're here. Where should I have waited? The warrens? The grey crow's well?"

"No, here is good. Raven—do we need to hide?"

Raven nodded. "But we can't now. They heard you. I'm sure they heard you."

He could have asked questions, but could tell from her expression that she wouldn't understand them, or he wouldn't understand her answers. "Giselle says there's danger."

"You said that."

Robin exhaled. Now that he was in the Academia, the urgency he felt gave way to a much more visceral fear. He hadn't expected that; if asked, he'd've said he already *was* afraid. Why else would he have run here at top speed? Now that he was here, he was forced to come face-to-face with his own ignorance. What had he hoped to accomplish? Had he hoped that whatever problem he'd face would be immediately obvious, and the solution completely clear?

That had happened in his former home. He'd already lost that home. It wasn't, and didn't feel, like his anymore. He hadn't expected his mother to die. His father and his siblings were dead, although he hadn't seen them perish. The servants—those he'd known well, those who'd indulged him—were likewise dead. Of family, his uncle remained, and his uncle's children, and they *would never be* Robin's family. Ever. He had no home in the gardens.

But this place? The Academia? It was his to lose.

Or maybe, just maybe, his to save. "We don't want to run *away*. We need to run *toward*."

Her gaze flickered. "Toward?"

"I think I might be able to do something, if the danger is what the grey crow thinks it is." This sounded lame to Robin; he imagined it sounded worse to Raven.

"It's not safe," she said.

He didn't argue, because she was right. He didn't tell her he knew what he was doing, because that would be a lie, and he'd never lied to Raven. She hesitated, staring at him, eyes unblinking. She studied his face, his expression; a shadow crossed hers when she nodded. She held on to his hand, but she didn't insist they hide, didn't drag him to a place that couldn't be found. She moved at a brisk walk, as Robin had asked, toward.

Robin couldn't sense what Raven could sense, not even in his oddly heightened state. He didn't doubt that she could. He ran beside her, their hands a link between them.

"Why are you here?" she asked.

He didn't misunderstand. "I was allowed to go to the heart of the labyrinth. I was allowed to ask for help. This was the answer. I left the labyrinth like this. Most people can't even see me."

Raven frowned. "At all?"

"Most people aren't you." He recognized the hall down which they were running. "Giselle said that there was danger here. I would have come here first, but I was led to—to Rianna's home. I—I used almost all of your glass. I'm sorry."

"Almost?"

"Almost. Some pieces were the wrong color, the wrong shape—they didn't fit the pattern I was trying to repair."

She nodded as if this confirmed a suspicion. It didn't fill her with joy.

"Is that why you gathered glass? Is that why you looked for it?"

She hesitated for long enough he thought she wouldn't answer. "Yes. No."

Both, then. "Some of the larger pieces were the pieces we picked up from Killian's window. If he could give us shards like that, I think I could fix everything."

"Dangerous."

"Everything is." Robin spoke it as truth. "But not doing anything is more dangerous now. I can't run and hide forever."

"You can."

"I can't."

"Why?"

"When I was young—"

She snorted.

"When I was younger, then. Better?" At her nod, he continued. "When I was younger, I couldn't *do* anything. I couldn't survive on my own. I couldn't defend myself. All I could do was hide. If I hadn't, we wouldn't be here."

She nodded.

"But now I *can* do something. That's what I learned in the labyrinth. It's not valuable to most people. It *was* valuable a long, long time ago—but it's useless now. Mostly. Today, it's useful, because today, we're facing what people like me were meant to face."

Raven nodded. "That's not the danger," she said. Stopped. Started again. "No, it's dangerous, but not what I meant."

"You meant people."

"I meant people. People killed your mother. People are the reason I came when called. People can kill you. They can kill you if they know." She grimaced. "They'll know now."

"They won't necessarily know."

"You changed the window, Robin. You fixed it. They'll know."

He didn't have time to absorb and consider the words; he accepted them as truth. He could try to figure out how to live in his own skin, with his own name, in his own world, later.

"Are we going to Larrantin's rooms?"

Raven nodded, lips twisted briefly in distaste. She was never going to like Larrantin.

"Is Giselle here?"

"At the Academia?"

Robin nodded.

"Yes."

"Raven, is she *with* Larrantin?"

"Yes."

"Terrano? Serralyn? The chancellor?"

"Yes, yes, and no. Starrante is also with Larrantin."

"Will they see me?"

"Don't know." She tightened her grip on his hand. "Terrano."

Robin nodded; that was his suspicion, as well. Terrano and Giselle. But if Terrano could see him, the rest of his friends would, as well.

Larrantin's doors weren't open, which wasn't a surprise. Raven stopped at the closed doors; Robin didn't. Her hand was solid as she pulled him back. "The doors are dangerous."

"Let me try. I was able to enter the Academia."

"You were," Killian agreed. Robin jumped at the sound of the Avatar's voice; he had forgotten Killian was there. "Larrantin's chambers are, by agreement, unusual."

Robin could see doors. He could see nothing unusual about them. But Raven had been trapped by one of Larrantin's defenses. Robin tried to free his hand. "I have to try."

"Or you could allow me to open the doors."

"But you said you couldn't."

"I did not. I said Larrantin and I have an agreement. Emergency protocols, however, are excepted from the conditions of that agreement." He glanced at Robin and turned to Raven. "This is an emergency, in your opinion?"

Her nod was reluctant. If she disliked Larrantin, she was wary of Killian; she had chosen to trust him because Robin did.

"Raven, perhaps you wish to stand back. I can prevent Larrantin's defenses from entrapping you if I am here."

"But you're everywhere," Robin pointed out.

"That is the theory. But clearly I am not entirely whole." Killian smiled; he lifted a hand, palm out, the gesture an act of courtesy to Robin. The doors rolled open into the hall.

At least, the doors should have rolled open into the hall.

This wasn't a hall. He could see the rough outline of what might once have been hall, but it was blurred, smudged, the stone almost melting as his gaze touched it. What had once been walls were high piles of greyish mud slowly merging with floor.

"Killian?"

Killian stopped moving or speaking.

"I don't think you should follow us," Robin said.

"We shouldn't be here," Raven added. "None of us should be here."

"Do you know where this is?"

Raven didn't answer. If they had two hours, Robin could slowly pull an answer from her, because she did have one—but it wasn't one she could easily express in words. She was trying; he could see that clearly.

She'd always tried.

Robin stepped across the threshold, planting his foot in what he saw as mud. To his surprise, his feet didn't sink. He took another step, turned to the doors, and stopped. He'd meant to shut them. They were no longer there.

"I'm getting sick of disappearing doors."

Raven tilted her head to the side as if trying to make sense of Robin's words.

"You saw the doors we entered, right?"

She nodded.

"Did you notice they're gone?"

"Yes?"

Later. He could talk about it later, when he had both the time and the patience. "Can you see where the others are?"

She shook her head.

"Let's go find them." He could see what had once been the shape of halls in the mess it had become. He headed down the muddy mess toward what he hoped was the laboratory, or what was left of it. If his friends had grouped up anywhere, it was likely to be there.

Mud was the wrong word—it was just the most convenient one. "Raven, what do you see?"

"Dissolution. Confusion."

"I see colored mud." In places the mud was white; in some

it was a pale blue, a dark green. The semblance of walls—well, piles of tall mud—disappeared as he walked farther into what had once been Larrantin's chambers.

Raven's snort made her opinion clear, but she'd often found Robin's lack of vision frustrating: he didn't see what she saw, or didn't see it the way she saw it. She didn't believe Robin was lying to confuse her or tease her, but she didn't understand why they were looking at the same thing but seeing it differently.

If Raven had been summoned, she had to come from some-where. If she wasn't the girl she'd always appeared to be, she'd come from some hidden place, a break-glass-in-emergency con-tainer. Glass had been broken. Raven was here. But the place she'd been was, he thought, where he'd been walking since he'd been led from the labyrinth to his former home. It wasn't the real world. Probably why she'd had such a difficult time adjust-ing to it, seeing it, interacting with its people. Robin could see the real world, but most of it couldn't see him; to Raven that would render people irrelevant. If this was the state she'd lived in before, she could walk through people the way she could walk through walls.

She was his mother's summons. She was part of the gardens and its defense.

"Raven, do you know which dream is almost awake?"

"Yes?"

"Can you tell me?"

She shook her head. "There are no words, even your words. If there were words, they would already be awake, and the world would be different."

"But it's here?"

She nodded, but added, "You already know that."

"It was a guess."

She shook her head firmly. "You are the unbroken thread. You are the line." She spoke in familiar cadences. Ah. His mother's.

He was torn between anger and guilt, and picked no words to express either.

"She said you would know. When you grew up, when you grew into yourself, you would know. Maybe you're not grown up enough yet?" Her eyes and voice brightened as she said the last bit.

Robin tried not to feel offended and mostly succeeded. She was Raven, after all. Interpreting her words, he realized she was trying to tell him to be more confident in his guesses. To trust his instincts.

His instincts said that he was in the right place. But the entire space felt wrong, out of kilter, and this wrongness was expressed in piles of mud. He looked for something more solid—wooden beams, bits of doorframe. He couldn't find them. There was nothing that implied anyone could live here; even the dilapidated buildings in which they'd found shelter in his childhood had been places someone had once lived.

This wasn't part of the world he'd been born into. It was part of the world he'd inherited. He closed his eyes and listened. Raven's hand was still in his; it was warm, solid, a reminder that he wasn't alone. He'd never truly been alone.

He didn't intend to start now. He was aware of Raven, aware of himself, and as he listened he became aware of a third presence. He could hear murmuring that didn't resolve into words—even words of a foreign language. He would have followed the sound, but it was everywhere; it was in the mud, in the air, by his side, and in the distance.

"Raven—have I stepped into a dream?"

"Yes?" It was her *water is wet* tone.

The sound didn't give him direction. Raven had told him not to shout, not to speak loudly, or he would have raised his voice.

"Can you see Terrano?"

"Yes."

He exhaled in shaky relief. "Can you take me to him?"

She began to walk, and he followed; they were still attached at the hand.

The mud itself was hard beneath his feet; what it looked like and what it felt like were very different. The pile of white mud *felt* like stone. He wondered if the grey-green piles would feel like leaves; there had been alcoved plants in Larrantin's halls. The detail seemed important; he thought about it as Raven provided forward momentum. She didn't run, but she walked quickly, and Robin was content—as he had so often been—to let her lead.

Terrano stood in what Robin assumed was the lab in which Raven had been trapped. He wasn't alone. With him, no surprise, were Serralyn and Valliant. The Barrani Hawk was absent; the terrifying Sedarias was absent, as well. Starrante was on the floor, or what passed for floor in this melted mess, as was Larrantin. The chancellor wasn't here. Giselle was.

It was Giselle who turned as Robin and Raven approached. Her brow was furrowed, but her expression was otherwise clear. The lift of brows changed the lines in her forehead; for the first time, Giselle didn't seem ancient to Robin. He wondered how old she was.

"Robin."

He glanced at the rest of the people in the room, realizing that Giselle stood slightly apart from them. "They can't see me, can they?"

"Larrantin is aware, and the Wevaran will be able to converse soon. You are walking a path for which you are not prepared."

Robin nodded. "What does this place look like, to you?"

"A lab that looks like it's never seen use, it's so clean."

"Can the others see you?"

Giselle nodded. "And they are now wondering about my sanity." She smiled. "You will learn to do this, in time; you are too close to the labyrinth. What do you see?"

"I see the people—but they're barely moving. Or I'm moving too quickly. I don't see the lab. I know what it looks like normally; that's not what it looks like to me."

This time, Giselle's expression shifted into something focused and almost murderous. Robin had never labored under the illusion that the grey crow was kind or gentle. No one in the warrens made that mistake more than once; some didn't survive the first time. This time when she looked at Robin—her eye narrowed, her gaze focused—he almost forgot to breathe.

"We have a problem," Giselle said.

Robin, mindful of the respect her anger was due, simply nodded. "I think I can help with one problem. I don't know what the other one is."

"No?" She armed herself.

Terrano joined her; he'd had little experience in the warrens, and almost none with the grey crow; he glanced at her daggers, but shrugged. "How did you get here?" he asked Robin.

"Long story. Why are we in Larrantin's lab?"

"Short story," Terrano said, grinning. "Apparently we have a mage problem. And a magic problem. And a sentient building problem. The chancellor is attempting to deal with the last one. No one else can see you," he added.

"Giselle can."

"She's apparently transparent now, and I don't think that's going to last. No one can see me, either."

"Can they see Raven?"

"Strangely enough, yes. They can see her, and they can see that she's trying to hold on to something. What are you here to do?" Terrano looked around, frowned, and shook his head.

"Tell him to go away," Raven whispered.

"Raven says—"

"I heard her. Why?"

"They can reach you," Raven said.

"And they can't reach the rest of us?"

"They can't. Not the same way. You'll be in danger. Or you'll become the danger. Go back."

Terrano's frown deepened. He glanced at Giselle, and then at Robin; Robin must have looked grim. "Fine. I don't like it, though."

"Tell Starrante not to come," Raven added.

"Larrantin?"

"He probably can't." She tensed. Across from her, so did Giselle.

Robin understood why; the murmuring that had been background noise grew louder. He no longer had to make any effort to hear it. It filled the space he stood in.

But there was another sound, another murmur; it was different. Through what he assumed was the doorway to the lab, he could see someone approaching. They weren't like Giselle, Raven, or Terrano; they were a dark blur across the landscape—a smudge in the shape of a person.

Giselle's knives began to glow, a faint luminescent turquoise. Her smile was all edge. "I read about this," she said, her gaze going toward what remained of the door. "I read about it, I studied it. I never thought I'd see it in life. Are you ready?"

He wasn't. He'd never felt ready for anything in his life, except maybe classes on the day he was told he could stay. "Can they see us?"

"Yes—but not as clearly." Her grin was brief but genuine. "I always hated book learning. They'll be aware of us in this dream, but their transition to it is flawed and deadly."

"For them or us?"

"Both. I'll take care of the new intruder; that's my job. You take care of…everything else."

Robin nodded. He wanted to ask her what had driven them to Larrantin's chambers, but there would be time for that later. If there was a later. He armed himself, as well; he pulled Raven's pouch from its resting place against his side. He felt the cold of its absence keenly, although it wasn't his. He opened the pouch.

From it, he withdrew the first thing his hand touched: the small lattice. It was imbued with the same light as Giselle's daggers. He wondered if they came from the same source. Giselle glanced at it, and at him, but she said nothing. Her belief in him was terrifying.

He held the lattice in one hand. The pouch, he handed to Raven. Or tried. She shook her head mutely, and he slid it back into its place at his side, between skin and shirt. He had *no idea* what to do with the lattice. With the glass, the vines he could see had been his guide; he'd placed glass between their delicate stems, but that had been a lucky guess. There was no such pattern here, no markers to indicate where the lattice should go, where it should be placed, or even what it would do.

But somehow glass was part of this, and the metal that had become the object he now carried had come from the same source: Raven, her gathering, her pouch. It *had* a purpose.

It had a purpose in his hands.

He watched the intruder approach; Giselle simply stood her ground, waiting. The darkness-wreathed blur resolved itself, slowly, into a figure he recognized.

Grannick Gardianno. His uncle.

29

He had left his uncle in the manor. His uncle had been standing, hands in fists, expression strained; Robin was certain his uncle hadn't moved from that place.

"I don't think he's really here," Robin told Giselle. "I saw him in the manor. He hadn't moved by the time I'd finished. Whatever that is isn't my uncle."

"I think it is. It's an essential part of your uncle." She spoke with distaste, her gaze even.

"What happens if you kill this one?"

"I don't know. I don't know if he can be killed. I don't know if the destruction of whatever this is will also destroy him. I'm happy to find out."

"His real body is in the gardens."

The shadow showed more animation than the man in the manor had; the face, absent the color of human skin of *any* race, was twisted in a visage of…glee and anger. The shadow's eyes were the only thing about it that looked human to Robin; brown, with the normal whites. Everything else about its physical form was dark, condensed smoke. As he thought that, he realized he could smell something burning. It was a familiar scent.

Black smoke rose in wispy tendrils; it was pulled back and

absorbed by the form of a man. The solidity of the shape grew, but some of that smoke managed to escape, wafting upward into the darkening air. As if the form itself had been created by the burning of bodies, the sacrifice of the living.

Robin had spent much of his life being afraid. What he felt now was not fear; it was fury.

Raven's grip tightened. "Bad," she whispered. "Bad thoughts."

Bad thoughts? Was it bad to be angry—to be worse than angry—at the man who had murdered his family? It wasn't bad—it was natural. His uncle had destroyed everything. Everything but Robin, and Robin had only escaped because of his mother's sacrifice.

"Bad," Raven whispered.

Around him in this smudged, collapsed room, the voice of the dream, wordless, inchoate, rose. It grew. He could almost hear words. But words weren't necessary, just as they'd often been unnecessary with Raven: something in the room could hear Robin's equally wordless rage. His uncle couldn't, but the thing with which he traveled, perhaps the thing in which he traveled, could. Robin's unvoiced pain and fury was louder than anything his uncle could offer.

Offer.

He could feel the well of endless anger, could feel it as an absolute so large it overwhelmed every other human emotion, every other possible response. Robin trembled with that fury.

Raven's hand tightened around his.

There was no room for something as insignificant as worry in this mass of rage that resonated almost perfectly with his own. There was no desire to protect, to love, to be loved. There was no curiosity, no desire to learn, to understand. No need to communicate. This last, however, he understood. Something voiceless, something without language, couldn't communicate, and without communication, however imperfect, understanding was almost impossible.

His anger didn't abate; it didn't dissolve. But as Raven tightened her hold on his hand—an analogy for her presence in his life from childhood to the present—he understood. No person felt only one thing forever. No person wanted—or needed—only one thing. Robin might need justice—or vengeance—in this moment, but he needed Raven. He needed the Academia to be safe. He wanted to protect his new friends.

The dreams, the thoughts, were all of one thing, and only that thing. But rage was part of Robin. He couldn't shed it, couldn't ignore it; he could swallow it, sit on it, stop it from driving him forward, stop himself from doing things in fury he would regret later. It was part of him, but it couldn't be all of him. He could not allow rage to overwhelm every other part of his life. Not and remain human.

His uncle lifted one hand and pointed at his nephew, which answered one question: he could see Robin.

"You!" The eyes widened in surprise, but the voice was infused with the miasma of rage. In his uncle the dream of fury had found a champion. "How are you here? Why do you live?" He gave Robin no chance to answer. Around his uncle, smoke shifted and moved, streaming from that finger pointed toward a nephew that should have died years ago. A ripple of comprehension shifted the line of his uncle's face before it fell into a deeper rictus of fury.

From his uncle's hand came the channeled power of the restless dream. It wasn't the dream itself.

Raven shifted position, placing herself between Robin and that slow, inexorable smoke. It was awkward because she wouldn't let go of his hand. He tried to disentangle his fingers, but she tightened her grip.

Giselle stepped in front of both of them. "Children," she said, "should wait for adults."

Raven snorted. Robin didn't. He watched as Giselle wielded the knives she carried; they sliced through the smoke. The tendril she'd cut through lost form and density, dissipating before it came anywhere close to Robin. What was interesting was the confusion that briefly permeated his uncle's rage, becoming part of it.

His uncle couldn't see Giselle. Robin wondered if he could see Raven.

"Be careful!" someone shouted, the words echoing in Robin's ears. Terrano's voice, stretched and extended. For a moment, Robin thought Terrano was speaking to him.

Larrantin's voice made clear he wasn't. "We are *trying*." As Robin's uncle once again began to move toward Robin, he could hear other voices creeping into the space.

Robin frowned. "Giselle, can they see him?"

"They can see his appearance; it's solid. Apparently this isn't the first time he's taken the appearance of someone who otherwise belongs in the Academia."

"What does my uncle look like to the others? Do you know?"

"If you call that your uncle, you've got other problems. If you mean does he look like Grannick, then no."

"Then who?"

"To the great annoyance of the scholar, he looks like a cheaper version of Larrantin. Those weren't his words, but his words were mostly Barrani, and seemed to shock the Barrani students into momentary silence. He was detected before he could damage or kill another student; Larrantin engaged an untested defense mechanism. To do it, Larrantin had to be there in person.

"But this thing you're calling your uncle has had to work in person in a fashion, as well."

"I think he was the one who approached Teela as Laksone."

"Teela?"

"She's the Barrani Hawk. He's trying to fire again."

"You don't say. Now stop talking and do your job."

He nodded. The lattice felt warm in his hand. "Raven, you need to let go of my hand. I need both."

She shook her head in mute denial.

"Will I be in worse danger if you let go?"

"No."

"Will you?"

She didn't answer. Her silences had always had texture and weight.

He stopped trying to convince her. His uncle was the source of the worst loss Robin had experienced in his life, but Giselle's words made clear that that uncle shouldn't be Robin's target. He had to struggle to remember that.

He had power. The labyrinth had given him permission to use the strength of its voluntary dream. If he killed his uncle, the dream gathering in the Academia would have no conduit. Robin was certain of that.

He could kill his uncle. He could have revenge. Revenge for his mother, who'd bled to death in the warrens. Revenge for his siblings and his father. He could do that *and* detach the restless dream from its anchor to their reality. He could justify it. He could justify the use of that power. He felt the certainty take root and grow.

How exactly do you think you'd use that power to kill him?

He studied his uncle's face, his obsidian, slightly diffuse expression, his bloodshot eyes, his hands in fists. Robin realized as he did that his uncle was an older, darker mirror: he stood almost as his uncle had stood at the heart of the engravings in the basement of the manor, down to the fist in which he now gripped the almost forgotten lattice.

But his uncle's hands had been empty. Robin held Raven in one and the lattice, with its steady light, in the other. He was certain the lattice couldn't be used to kill his uncle; he thought it might be able to injure him if his uncle was kind enough to stand still. And he thought, as he took one steadying breath, that that wasn't what it was meant to do.

Here, facing this man, he wondered what his uncle's past had been like. Wondered if multiple failed attempts to reach the

heart of the maze in the warrens had etched failure into him
deeply; wondered if failure had been the place in which rage
had gathered and swelled.

Wondered how easy it would be to give in to fury and become his uncle.

Oh, he was certain he wouldn't murder whole families, including children, the way his uncle had. But his uncle had had
to start somewhere; had had to start at a place where his actions
seemed reasonable. It seemed reasonable to Robin that his uncle
die for his crimes. It would be reasonable to a court of law.

But Robin couldn't be that court of law; to do that, Robin
would have to surrender everything else. He would have to surrender the heart of the power that had kept stray thoughts such
as this in a safe and peaceful state of slumber. He felt it as truth,
as certainty. If he let fury rule him here, he would take a step
down a road he did not want to follow—and he wasn't certain he could turn around and walk it back. It was like taking
a wrong step and falling off a cliff—he couldn't simply reverse
that fall by moving his feet.

He *could* injure or kill his uncle, but the power to contain
the dream would be spent.

Raven said nothing, but her hand relaxed. She still didn't
let go. She wouldn't.

"Do I need the glass?" he asked her, looking not to his uncle,
but to the miasma that surrounded him.

No answer, but he'd only had faint hope. Glass was containment. The lattice wasn't. Even were he to fill the spaces in the
lattice with Raven's glass, it was a flat plane; it couldn't entrap
or contain anything. That wasn't the purpose of the lattice.
There were other metal pieces in the bag, but he'd only pulled
out two, and if one resembled part of a jar lid, it was useless if
he didn't have the jar. He really wished he'd taken *all* the pieces
out and exposed them to the light of the labyrinth.

But the lattice itself was warming in his hands. He couldn't go back in time; he couldn't leave this place—not now, with his uncle here, and his friends in the Academia under attack. How could he use it? How had the dreaming thought, the dreaming heart of the labyrinth, imbued it? And why?

Why could he walk in the labyrinth? Why did its Avatar say it was like the thoughts prisoned in sleep?

And why, damn it, *why*, had he *not asked* when he could have had the answers? He was always the first to ask questions in class when he didn't understand the lectures. He was always the person who was desperate to learn—he never feared looking stupid, even if his classmates sometimes mocked his questions.

But he hadn't done it there, where it counted. If he survived this, he'd go back and he *would*. Now, all he was left with was a tremulous belief that *somehow*, the very fact of his birth and his bloodline, his connection with a family he could barely remember, was all that he had. That, and a lattice whose warmth edged into heat. It was not yet uncomfortable, but it would be.

What was he meant to do? Why this lattice? If he set it down, could he find something else to throw at a thing he couldn't clearly see?

Raven tightened her hand briefly; it was a gesture of encouragement, as if she could hear what he didn't say. He inhaled. Once again, he felt the encroachment of a frustration that would lead to anger. He already had simmering anger; he forced the frustration back because it wouldn't help.

He stopped then.

How had he forced it back? How had he loosened its grip enough that he could function outside of its imperatives? He looked at his uncle and understood that his uncle had made no attempt to quell his rage; he had fed it, had allowed it to be fed, had been taken by the thoughts themselves and the power inherent in anything of the Ancients.

And people had died. People still died. His uncle was more than rage—would have to be more than rage and fury to be in this place, in disguise, at all. But he carried that miasma with him, within him. If Robin understood what he was attempting here, it was to find a different vessel. A vessel outside of himself, a vessel who could carry the miasma, contained, in a fashion far more easy to control.

Giselle's knives flashed, drawing his attention. She would kill his uncle.

She would kill his uncle and the thoughts would be uncontained. He said nothing for one long breath. If she killed his uncle, it was not on his hands; it was not his use of the power he'd requested by presence alone, the power he'd been granted.

He exhaled words. "Giselle—tell Larrantin to be ready. If you kill Grannick, whatever he's barely containing will be instantly freed in this room."

The grey crow cursed in familiar, comfortable, and particularly vulgar Elantran. "If you have a better idea, I'm all ears."

"And knives," Raven said.

"Don't you have somewhere else to be?" Giselle snapped; she didn't look back at Raven.

Robin did. Robin did, and he froze again. Raven's hand was solid. It had to be; it was twined tightly around his. But her arm wasn't; her body wasn't. Even her face was now transparent—except for her eyes; her eyes were solid. They just weren't the eyes that he was accustomed to seeing. He'd asked her if she was holding his hand for his sake or for her own safety; she hadn't answered, but that *was* an answer for Raven.

Somehow, in this miasma, her physical connection to Robin was now sustaining her. He didn't understand it completely, but had an uneasy sense that her existence depended on his childhood—a childhood that he was, even in this moment, leaving behind.

But she wasn't his servant, his slave, his convenience, his parent. She was his *friend*. Friends could last a whole lifetime. He wouldn't simply outgrow the need for friends, and the history of their time together almost defined him. Almost. But it did define Raven. He looked at the lattice. He looked at Raven. He thought he understood now what the lattice was for.

He wished he'd pulled anything else from the pouch of detritus; it wasn't *meant* for fighting. It wasn't meant for containment. It didn't help him do whatever it was the maze thought he could do by the simple expedient of being born to the right bloodline. It wasn't what he'd *asked for.*

But the maze had said it read what was in his heart.

Whatever it had read there, it had accepted. He turned to Raven. He held out the lattice to her. It was small—too small for the vines that wrapped around them and flowered in the grounds of his childhood home. But Raven wasn't as large as a manor, either. Raven wasn't a vine; he understood that the lattice was a metaphor, created and imbued by an ancient power he did not know and did not understand.

"This is for you," he said quietly. "Not the glass I thought—we thought—you needed in order to stay here and be Raven. It's something you can hold on to, something you can grow around. It's yours, if you want it." He held it out to her, to her translucent hand.

She looked at it mutely. She said nothing. Her hand didn't move.

"You're not *mine*. You don't belong to me. But you didn't belong to my mother, either. I don't know—maybe I've broken something that you used to be. Maybe I've changed it somehow. But you're alive. To me, you're a person. An important person. I don't want to own you. I don't want to create a jar that contains you. I want you to be Raven.

"I'm going to change. You'll change, as well. That's what life *is.* I can't own you. I can't be your master. I can't spend my entire life with you being nothing but a burden. Choose. Become."

She remained frozen, but her eyes went to Robin, not the lattice. "What if I change?"

"You will. But, Raven, so will I. Change is scary. But the Academia is change, to me—and I love it. Trust that some change will be change you love. I do." He exhaled. "You're like the thoughts of the Ancients. I don't know if you're awake now, or if you're like the maze. I only know that you weren't supposed to be called. You weren't supposed to be broken free unless there was an emergency.

"I don't want you to live like that. I don't want you to go back to…wherever it was you were trapped. I would if that's what you wanted—but you don't, either. That's why you gathered the glass. Not for me. Not for the containment. For the possibility of a different future.

"This is the start of it. This is yours. Not glass. Not a jar. Not a trap into which you get poured. A place where you can take root. A place where you can grow. Take it," he said when her gaze trembled. "I can't hold it for much longer."

She squeezed her eyes shut and moved her free hand—her transparent hand—toward the lattice. When the two—Raven's hand and glowing metallic lattice—came into contact, the light in the room changed.

No, Robin thought, it *shattered*. As if the miasma that had defined everything he could see had been a grimy film of thin glass around everything, it broke. He could hear the sound, but even if he hadn't, he could see the instant difference. He didn't understand why, but he could think about that later. There would be a later. He promised it, silently.

He could see the lab, the edges of the floor and walls blurred. He could see his companions, his teachers, and his new friends. It wasn't the lab as he'd seen it the first time; it wasn't quite solid. But it wasn't the terrible melted sludge, and it was no longer empty of everyone except Giselle.

The grey crow was here. She was armed. She was standing between Robin and something that looked like Larrantin.

Starrante chittered Robin's name: they could now see Robin.

He wondered if they could see Raven in the same way; he almost had to squint to look at her. She was glowing so brightly it was almost painful. Almost. But Raven had never been painful. Raven had never hurt him deliberately; it had taken her a bit of time to get used to how slow he was, how exhausted full-on sprinting made him, but she had.

The light was Raven-shaped. The voice with which it spoke was Raven's voice. "Glass," she said, her tone distinct, the words no more expansive than they'd ever been.

Robin immediately withdrew her pouch, the pouch she hadn't taken when he'd offered it to her the first time. He offered it to her now. She snorted.

He shrugged, his hand tingling as circulation returned to it. He then opened the pouch. Glass. Glass glittered here in several different colors. It wasn't the clear glass that he'd laid against the floor. He hadn't been certain why these had retained color and why he'd felt none of them were meant for the floor in the manor; he thought maybe they were somehow meant for Raven.

That had been wrong; he saw that clearly now.

This glass was meant for this almost waking thought. It was different because the thought had been somehow pulled out, extenuated, contained in a man who had had the potential to become what his mother had become. Robin wondered if he could also contain it, to keep it from destroying everything around it as his uncle had. It was an idle thought. He had more than enough difficulty containing his entirely human, entirely mortal rage. He wasn't certain he could contain anyone else's. Anything else's.

He couldn't touch the power that came with it; it came *from* the element he couldn't control.

Maybe his uncle couldn't see past the similarity, the familiarity, of the rage to understand that. Or maybe there was a reason he had never been able to approach the maze in a way that would allow him to take up the power the heart of it offered.

Robin pulled out a piece of glass—a deep purple. To his surprise, it rose from his fingers to hover in the air in front of his eyes.

"Robin!" Starrante chittered. "Move away!"

He pretended not to hear the Wevaran, and hoped Starrante wouldn't use webbing to pull him away when he didn't immediately obey. He took out another piece of glass: it was a deep emerald green, an echo of the hidden window that had once contained it. It, too, lost weight and the ties of gravity as it floated up, out of his hand.

Larrantin Two, his uncle's form in this reality, walked forward, glaring at Robin, all of his attention focused there, his expression suffused with rage and resentment. His eyes, however, weren't Barrani eyes; they weren't the dark blue of Barrani rage, the indigo of fury. They were brown. They were eyes very similar to Robin's.

He was far closer than he had been when Robin first entered this room. He did not seem to see the grey crow at all.

"Robin?"

"Not yet," he replied. Instead of pulling out one shard at a time, he emptied the bag of glass, gathering the metal bits that hadn't been transformed and returning them to the pouch.

Yellow glass rose; red glass followed; all of the pieces Raven had gathered from the hidden office floated at Robin's eye level in a semicircle. He could see the edge of that half circle from the corner of his eye. In any other circumstance, he would have been oddly amused that they formed the colors of a rainbow.

Not now. But he watched as those colors blurred together, as they condensed while retaining altitude, as they slowly emerged in a shape. The semicircle became circle as he watched; he ducked under that circle—stepping back, not forward into Giselle. The circle continued to condense, to become smaller; the colors began to bleed into the air. And he'd been right— the other piece of metal, the circular one, was a lid.

He understood that this was what must contain what his uncle had somehow called forth and now carried within himself, imperfectly. Almost without thought, he took the lid from the pouch and held it in one hand; the jar continued to float, as if nothing could change its position. He hoped that was true.

He found his own anger, which was far easier than he would have liked, and he held it out. He held it out and felt the air shift, felt an echo of sound grow into the only sound the room contained, stronger than the voices of those he wanted to protect. Raven no longer provided an anchor, not physically.

But she was the anchor he needed, regardless.

He understood the shape of his anger, the structure beneath it; he accepted it. It was his to own. He didn't despise it, didn't hate it, didn't hate what it said about him, perhaps because he believed anyone would feel anger—the anger that was rooted in such deep pain, the one led to the other. He was almost certain that his uncle had—deliberately or accidentally—resonated with this single thought, had drawn it out, and had seen, in a way Robin did not, how to *use it*.

But Robin understood how to use his own anger. It was instinctive. Like called to like, even if his human rage was a single raindrop in a vast, howling storm.

The Larrantin who faced Giselle staggered, stumbled; he almost buckled to the floor. His face when he looked to Robin was suffused in rage—but Larrantin's semblance slowly faded, leaving the face of Grannick Gardianno in its wake. "I will *kill you! You should have been dead!*"

The rage of disappointment was not equal to the rage of loss. Even had it been, the man who now found his footing and stood his ground wasn't Rianna. He wasn't Robin. He wasn't a man who had managed to walk the labyrinth to reach the heart of a maze that would judge him. Or maybe he'd managed to get that far once—but he'd been judged unworthy.

The power that Grannick had taken from this almost awake

thought was stolen. The power that Robin carried was given. And the power that Robin carried didn't depend on a single element of who Robin had become. It didn't depend on who he'd become as he experienced life. It depended entirely on Robin being Robin.

It depended on Robin's ability to acknowledge parts of himself he'd almost been afraid to touch, and to use them as wordless communication. He couldn't compel. He could not command. But in his anger, rooted in events that had been outside of any control when they'd happened, was his resonance. It was his only communication.

He focused on the feeling as he stood behind Giselle. He heard nothing, and as he closed his eyes, he saw nothing. He was alone here. Alone with emotion. Alone with the detritus of the past. It was Raven's *bad thoughts*; he almost didn't think at all.

But he knew the moment the thoughts touched him, because fury surged within him, and thoughts tumbled into memories and images and scents, into colors that had defined that day: red of blood and fire, white of death. He opened his eyes, then, to see the colors of things that didn't: grey of floor and black of Giselle's clothing; rainbow of a scintillating round cylinder. Yes, that rainbow had red and white, but never only those colors; it was rooted in here. It was rooted in what Robin could see in his life outside of this emotion, this moment.

He exhaled. He exhaled rage. His hands were shaking, in fists, his knuckles white; he cut his hand on the metal disc. Blood was fine. Blood was red. Pain was transmuted, almost always, to anger. He could feel the beat of a heart—that was his only word to describe it—as the thing his uncle had contained came to him, moving just as slowly as his uncle had, as if speed was impossible, as if it were literal storm clouds traveling across a very low sky.

Rainbows when they existed were part of the sky. He watched as the jar descended; watched as it lay across the metaphorical sky; watched as the clouds moved toward it. They did not move past it; they tried. But this was where they must be. This was where they must go. Robin knew it; the anger did not displace the sudden clarity.

He had no desire to destroy this; it was part of him. It was a fact of life. It was something that he himself had to push down, push away, lest it overtake everything and destroy his life—but he fully accepted its right to exist, because his own anger was just…part of him. A truth of his life. Sometimes it was good. Sometimes it was better to struggle with it; to calm it enough that it would slumber someplace deep inside.

Some part of himself entered that jar, that thing of not-glass. And with it, as if it were the greater part of his own anger, went the restless thought.

He lifted the lid that had cut his hand because he'd been clenching it so tightly, and very gently placed it on the jar that had been created out of broken glass, broken things.

The light vanished as the lid came down.

The *jar* vanished.

Robin's legs lost strength as his knees folded. He heard Serralyn's cry of dismay, Terrano's shock; felt something familiar touch his forehead—oh, Starrante.

He understood that the power of the labyrinth, the power of that singular dream, had deserted him. He'd done what he had to do, which was the only reason he'd been given permission to use that power at all.

Both of the things.

EPILOGUE

Giselle was not in the best of moods—something anyone who had any cause to interact with her assumed was her natural state. In the warrens, this served her well; had she looked friendly or kind, people would have been standing in line to attempt to take advantage of that perceived weakness.

Only those with emergencies dared to approach her on most days.

Which meant Raven had considered Robin's absence—a significant, lengthy absence—an emergency. Giselle had watched the child with curiosity over the years.

"She is not a child."

She had first seen Raven by Robin's side. Although it had been Raven who had dragged Robin to the well at which Giselle—when not working—could be found, it was Robin who had found the courage to speak to her; had he owned a hat, he would have held it in two hands, head bowed, as he approached. He was far too poor for a hat, and far too young—and weak— to strip bodies of the hats they might once have found use for.

She had not been surprised by that; she'd expected it. What

had surprised her then was Raven herself. She knew what Raven was. She could see it clearly; the liminality and the darkness compressed into a single form. She had spent her life learning and studying—something she had never much enjoyed. She'd enjoyed it more than starving in the streets of the warrens, which was clearly the fate that awaited her if she refused to learn.

She knew about the gardens.

She knew about the Gardianna—or Gardianno, as Robin would be called to those very, very few who understood the mysteries of the labyrinth. She knew about the restless sleepers that should not wake, ever. She knew that the power that slumbered at the heart of the maze redefined the word *sleep*. It wasn't mortal sleep. It wasn't mortal dreaming.

She remembered the first time she had entered the labyrinth; she had been trapped there for what felt like months. She'd always been an angry child; she'd grown into an angry adult. A competent, angry adult.

Why do you think you must live in the warrens?

It's the only way to reach you?

Foolish child. No. This is where you begin to understand the true flow of power.

Giselle, angry as always, made clear that this was not about power—it was about the powerless. Anyone with power left as soon as they could.

All people play games of power. All. It's the most desperate who play the most desperately; they have everything to lose. The meager gains are larger in their eyes, and the nature of the desperate is exposed constantly. Understand how the small games of power, with small stakes, are played here, and you will understand power.

And not how to have any of it.

Laughter then. *Do you think you are without power, child?*

She'd always hated being called a child.

But the power at the heart of the maze had been disturbed

by what it could sense in the distance: waking. Something was waking. Something was, quietly and certainly, wrong. Had the Gardianna finally failed in her duties? Had she passed on?

"No."

Not then. But not long after. Rianna had come to the warrens—Rianna, whose life had been lived in privilege and wealth, whose position in mortal society was almost at the top, when Giselle's was near invisible to anyone who didn't live in the warrens. She had come with a child. Giselle thought him maybe six or seven years of age—at the most—and he was wide-eyed, pale, and wet with blood.

Most of it was Rianna's blood. The wound was deep; Giselle had seen the like before more often than she cared to remember; had even caused worse in her time.

"I can't keep him," Giselle said, voice flat. It was true. A child of his age couldn't survive the maze; he would never be allowed to enter, and even had the maze accepted him, its guardian—Giselle herself—would not. Things magical and ancient could easily transform adults to their detriment—she was certain it would be disastrous for a child.

Such a disaster would likewise be disastrous for Elantra. For the warrens. It would be a gross dereliction of duty. Rianna knew this as well—or should have known it. The guardian of the maze had no children. Giselle was not a product of a respected and revered bloodline.

Truth be told, she'd had no desire to take the child in. She'd had her share of resentment, and children died all the time in the warrens. Rianna was the bloodline—but that bloodline was dispersed over generations; Robin wasn't the *only* one who could adopt the necessary duties.

Rianna accepted this; they had never been friends. They were bound together in only one way, and Rianna's duties had almost never taken her to the warrens. But Rianna withdrew the small crystal pendant the Gardianna wore, drenched it in the blood that would not stop flowing, and broke it. Hard to imagine that those delicate, slender hands could break anything, especially something as solid and small as a crystal.

It shattered. Giselle could hear it; the sound of breaking glass. It echoed—and echoed, and echoed—in the interior of Giselle's house. She heard Rianna's words, Rianna's plea, Rianna's commandment. She watched history unfold, as if the lessons she'd been forced to endure were finally, *finally*, becoming truth. Rianna summoned a guardian for her young child.

The guardian obeyed—it had been offered life's blood, and at that, the blood of the summoner, offered freely. All of the lessons she'd learned coalesced in this moment. There *was* power in the Gardianna, and there was—in cases of emergency—a last measure that could be taken. But it had never been taken, until now. Giselle considered the weakness of becoming a mother, of becoming so attached to a child, that one could do this. She had not interfered—it was too late, and if she was honest, she wanted to *see*. She wanted to see what emerged.

She had watched, silent, unseen in the heart of her territory. She had not spoken of what she had seen, nor would she: she was Warden. Those words were for journals, for diaries, should she ever feel the need to capture them.

She would never have guessed that the form this emergency guardian, this last-ditch attempt, would have taken would be a child's body. From her own lived experience, Giselle knew there wasn't much protection a child could offer anyone.

The first thing the guardian, in this diminished and highly unimpressive form had done was to grab Robin's small hand and drag him out of Giselle's house at a run.

It was years before she saw that guardian again, wandering the streets like a starving urchin, another orphan in her shadow.

She buried Rianna. She buried Rianna at the heart of her true home: the labyrinth. She understood the flow of power, just as her master had desired: Rianna's death was not necessarily about ancient, long-forgotten customs. It was about the seat of power. It was about the caste court. Rianna's husband had been called the Lord of Gardianno—a name that was a family designation to Elantra's lords of power. He had married Rianna, and he had taken the reins of political power in her stead, perhaps at her desire. He had occupied the seat on the caste court that governed racial human affairs within the Empire. Rianna had been as far above the paltry streets of the warrens—and Giselle—as it was possible to be.

He had died. Had been among the first to die. Rianna had died. They would look for the child, because the child was the heir to that empty seat. Giselle was unsurprised when the seat was filled—but it was provisional. They could find neither mother nor child, and if they did not have bodies, they did not have incontrovertible proof that Garrick Gardianno was now the line of succession into the future.

They'd looked.

They'd even come to Giselle, the fools.

Giselle gave them nothing. That wasn't always the case. She understood the games they played, saw the strands enter the warrens. Some, she cut off. Some she cultivated. Information flowed both ways—but of course they considered her knowledge irrelevant, so assured were they in the differences of their social status. They were powerful. She was not.

She was a woman they held their noses to deal with when necessary.

In the fullness of time, in the absence of Robin, Grannick would become the family head. He had already moved into the manor—to repair it, he said. Had Grannick not been powerful—and he was—some might have been moved to object. But he could stand toe-to-toe with Barrani Arcanists and emerge triumphant.

Had more time passed, he would have become the Gardianno by acclaim. It had not been a decade yet.

★ ★ ★

She did not expect that Robin would die; how could he, when Rianna had paid such a heavy price? She had half expected that Robin would return to the gardens, guardian by his side, and avenge himself and his family—but not at his age. Not yet. She had expected the guardian to become something more useful to Robin.

Perhaps that guardian had absorbed the context in which Robin now lived. Perhaps she had adopted warrens' rules without intent. Regardless, she remained a child in physical form; she aged as Robin aged. She often saw them running down the streets, Raven leading. She was surprised the first time the guardian brought Robin to her.

Raven gave him a little shove, and he stumbled forward— and introduced himself, his manners clearly the manners he'd been taught. They had no place in the warrens, but perhaps because of his youth, she found it almost charming.

What had shocked her was Robin's introduction of the guardian: *This is my friend, Raven. She doesn't talk a lot.*

And Raven's almost sullen response: *That's his job.*

Raven. Robin had *named* the guardian. The guardian who looked like a ragged urchin his own age. Robin had been looking for errand work, although he sheepishly confessed that it was Raven who really knew the warrens inside and out. He was learning, he added, but...maybe Raven would be the better choice.

Raven's eyes were downcast. Giselle's curiosity got the better of her—it was a failing she'd managed to survive, but she knew that couldn't always be the case. She gave Raven the errand. Raven delivered a message and returned with proof of delivery, and Giselle handed her coins.

Raven took the coins to Robin. Giselle knew how he spent them. On food—and not great food, at that. Robin survived. Raven saw to that. But she saw to it in a way so mundane it would be easy to believe she was a very odd orphan. On some days, Giselle believed it. Any hint of the power, the essence, of the guardian she had first seen vanished as the months—and years—passed. The guardian was Raven. Raven was odd.

And Raven was, as Robin said, his friend. Probably his only friend, given his lack of family, his lack of home.

Giselle's curiosity grew, and this was the danger with curiosity of this particular kind. Though she had refused to take responsibility for Robin, she watched him. She watched out for him. She was subtle—but given his age, she could have been obvious and he wouldn't have noticed. He knew he had no friends here. He knew that staying hidden was necessary—Raven saw to that. But he was, in his own fashion, a friendly child. He wanted to reach out. He wanted to build whatever community a young child with no power or wealth could build.

She wondered what would have happened to him if he had not at least had Raven—but not often; she knew the most likely outcome. The boy couldn't go to the foundling hall; he couldn't go anywhere it was possible he'd be seen. He'd have been dead within the week, if it took that long. Only here, alone and struggling not to freeze or starve, was he safe, and it was a rough, terrible safety.

When he was eight, she'd started to send him on errands she'd once reserved for Raven, and the people to whom he made deliveries began to hire him to do the same. Giselle only intervened if those deliveries took him outside of the warrens; she allowed Raven to take those jobs.

Raven and Robin maintained an age. They maintained a kind of ragged helplessness as time passed.

And then Robin disappeared. Robin disappeared, and Giselle wondered what would happen to the little orphan girl he'd named—and by naming, bound.

She is not a child. This is not where she should be, and you know this. She is meant to be a guardian in times of emergency—not one of the children you toss a few coins at.

"I know. But it's odd. I can't see in her what I saw on the day she arrived. Sometimes, in brief flashes, I can—usually when she's on the run with Robin. But almost never anytime else. She doesn't stay with him; they aren't always together. But…she's started to visit him when he's not cold or starving. She's started to spend time with him. She's started to show him things she's discovered.

"You say she's not a child—but to my eyes, that's exactly what she's becoming."

You must stop her.

"Why? She's harmless and she's devoted. She's in the warrens and she belongs here; she knows them at least as well as I do. Probably better, by this point."

Why do you want to allow this?

"Why do you want me to stop it? She's…" Giselle grimaced. "I think she's becoming herself—whatever that is in this context. I think she's learning how to be happy."

It is dangerous, grey crow. Do you not understand that? You are falling into the trenches of foolish sentimentality. She is not human. She is one complex, sleeping thought, the detritus of the Ancients.

"Is she awake?" The heart did not respond. "Is she more dangerous than the heart of all mysteries in this place?"

I am not awake.

It wasn't an answer, and Giselle knew it. But so did the heart of this place.

Giselle *did* have doubts; she accepted them. She had spent very few moments in her life that weren't riddled with doubt; if doubt had stopped her in her tracks, she would never have survived. What she did was make choices when confronting doubt; she had made her choice here. Her curiosity over the years had shifted to something stronger, something she couldn't be bothered to name.

She did look for Robin when inquiries came in; it wasn't

that he always checked in with her, or she with him. But he was gone. He'd disappeared. It happened sometimes. She was certain that if he had died, it was far from the warrens; she'd've known had he died here.

But it nagged at her, bothered her, pushed her; she continued to search—not for Robin, but for the information for which she was now famed.

And she found threads of power, slender threads that were the farthest reaches of a web; Robin had been trapped in it—but she was certain he hadn't been recognized.

She heard what Robin said to Raven in the moment that Grannick arrived in the labs of the intimidating Barrani scholar. Robin had once been fond of the man; Giselle wondered if he could retain that when he could truly learn to see. But she was focused on the abomination that was Grannick, Grannick's spirit form. She wanted to kill him; she was uncertain that Robin was ready for the fallout.

Regardless, if she wanted to effect his death, she would have to enter the gardens, bypassing the protections that existed to stop assassins such as she would become from killing the ruling lord; it was where his body was. She wasn't certain what would return to it now.

She was certain that his power—his impressive, terrifying power—would be heavily diminished. She was also certain that he knew Robin was alive. Robin was in the Academia. Something would have to be done.

Robin was not her responsibility. She had made that choice, following rules and laws that were far, far older than she would ever be. But still. Something would have to be done. She'd spent most of her life never touching or drawing on the power to which she was, in times of duress, entitled; she knew how to survive without it. She'd never depended on it; she never intended to start.

Yes, she thought, leaning against the wall and surveying her territory as she folded her arms. Something had to be done.

Raven, Robin, show me what you will become.

"Are you finally awake?" a familiar voice demanded.

"I am now." Robin opened his eyes to Terrano's face. He blinked several times, but Terrano remained, eyes slightly narrowed, forehead furrowed in concentration. Or annoyance. With Terrano it was sometimes hard to tell. "Raven?"

"She's in the corner by her desk."

Robin pushed himself out of bed. He was wearing clothing, which was a good start to what was probably not morning.

Raven was, indeed, sitting at a desk—but it wasn't a desk made of glass. It was the standard desk that most rooms started with, although Killian was more than willing to modify furniture at student request. One student's entire room looked like a battlefield might—after the battle was done. Killian hadn't even questioned the request, although he'd put his foot down at crows and vultures.

Raven hadn't had a desk of her own; she'd wanted a glass desk, and Killian had been uncertain about either giving it to her or creating it. Now, it didn't matter. Raven was opening and examining the small drawers—and the large ones. Robin assumed they were empty. He wondered if she would still collect glass pieces.

He got out of bed. "Killian?"

"I am here." Spiritually, at least.

"What time is it?"

"You have missed the late dinner hour."

Robin winced; he was hungry. But this hunger was nothing compared to the hunger that had dogged him as a child. He hoped his stomach wouldn't embarrass him by growling. As he looked past Terrano, he could see Serralyn; she was seated on the ground, cross-legged, doing what appeared to be homework.

"How long was I out?"

"Two days," Killian replied. "Your friends were concerned."

Terrano rolled his eyes. "We were worried, yes. Especially the bookworm in the corner. I'd've let you sleep—she kept nagging."

Valliant was not in the room.

"Killian can get you dinner," Serralyn said, carefully placing a bookmark between the pages of the book in her lap before she closed it and rose. Her eyes were a green blue, but the blue was moving toward green. "How are you feeling?"

"Hungry," Robin admitted. "But fine, otherwise. What happened?"

Terrano glanced at Serralyn, punting the question.

"Larrantin approached us—in class—and asked to speak with us."

"Us?"

"Valliant and me. Terrano warned us that the Larrantin that wanted to speak with us wasn't the Larrantin who otherwise taught our classes. Teela had already had that experience, but... Larrantin's cranky when he's offended, so we got permission to leave the class. No absentee slips or demerits. The other professors don't want to anger him, either. We went out into the hall. Terrano was having a *fit*."

"And you didn't listen to me," Terrano snapped, annoyed.

"But Giselle was there. She did something to Larrantin—he rippled, he almost dispersed before becoming solid again; we could see a hint of a different face, and we didn't stick around. Terrano led us back to Larrantin's lab—at a run. Larrantin let us in immediately—his defenses had picked up *something*. He didn't know what it was. Sedarias thought he'd refuse to let us in—and I'm pretty sure it was close.

"But the false Larrantin cast some sort of spell, sundering the hall containing Larrantin's labs from the rest of the Academia, somehow. And Killian was absent when the fake Larrantin was walking around the campus. I'm not sure why or how he knew to ask for us."

Robin wasn't, either. "The false Larrantin was an extension of my uncle," he said quietly. "He wouldn't know you. I think he killed the others randomly. You're saying he specifically asked for you and Valliant?"

Serralyn nodded. She then winced.

"What did you expect?" Terrano asked his friend. "Sedarias sees political machinations—Barrani machinations—in *everything*. She sees them in bread stands and candle stalls."

"This one seems like it might be genuine."

"Yeah, leave that for later."

Serralyn frowned, but otherwise ignored Terrano. "You know Teela wants you to give the Hawks permission to investigate a murder of a lord of the human caste court, don't you?"

Robin exhaled. "The murdered man was my father. I know what Teela wants now. But Terrano's right. Later."

"Fine." Her eyes were shadowed blue with worry again. "Larrantin let us in. I think he only did it because Giselle was with us. She said something to him in a language I didn't understand. If his eyes could have darkened further, they would have. But we all ran in, retreating to the room in which Raven was previously trapped.

"And whatever was following entered, as well—through closed doors. It was a bit tricky. Larrantin said it was essential that we not be touched by, not be in the vicinity of, the fake Larrantin."

"There's some *serious* magic in those rooms," Terrano added. "More than there was when we went there the first time." He grinned. "I guess he wanted to make sure that that never happened again."

Raven snorted, but didn't otherwise join the conversation.

Terrano picked up the story before Serralyn could return to it. "Starrante was actually in the lab already—I'm guessing the adjustments to Larrantin's enchantments are partly due to Star-rante's advice. He was…not happy. I mean, he was happy to see us, or as happy as a Wevaran in an emergency can be. But he was extremely unhappy at what was following us.

"Which made me decide to investigate."

"Which is when you saw me?"

"Not exactly. Giselle had kind of taken up position of her own—so it was clear to me that she was seeing something I couldn't. There's something strange about her," he added; from Terrano that wasn't criticism, it was appreciation. "I kind of wanted to see—or try to see—whatever it was she was seeing."

"You came a bit later. I'd like to know how."

"Long story," Robin replied, shaking his head.

Raven, on the other hand, said, "No."

"Good thing I wasn't asking you," Terrano shot back, annoyed.

Raven, as usual, didn't care. Would she learn to care? Would her reactions change? Robin shook himself.

"The others couldn't see you; Starrante was aware of you. Larrantin was annoyed, because his defenses should have made you stand out like a burning pyre. Probably literally."

Robin laughed in spite of himself.

"But…something was warping the lab itself. I'm not sure Larrantin's domicile would have remained entirely solid—or entirely under his control. It's interesting," Terrano added.

"And then you appeared—for everyone else—and Raven appeared, and Giselle became much more solid. Whatever it was that was attacking us kind of collapsed. But it lost Larrantin's appearance as it did. Did you see it?"

Robin nodded. "It probably won't surprise any of the Barrani students here. It was my uncle. My uncle is one of the lords of the human caste court. That was the role my father took before he was murdered."

Terrano winced. "No surprise from at least some of us. Teela—"

"I'm not ready for that yet," Robin replied. "I'm not ready to be the Gardianno in the human caste court—I don't think legally I'd be capable of that. In the best case—and the worst— I'd have to have a regent of some kind. And I do not want to have my uncle as regent because I'd like to survive." He hesitated. "I'm not sure my uncle will be capable of holding that seat; I'm not sure how much damage we did to him, but his body was in his home. If he's too damaged, the seat might go to my cousin; he was older than me."

"Later," Serralyn said softly. "I don't know what happened to you. I don't know if you can talk about it. Your friend seemed to think you couldn't."

"He can't," Raven threw in. She held a small drawer in her hand, and appeared to be examining it.

Serralyn walked over to Robin's desk and placed a small stack of papers—and two books—on the desk's available surface. "You've missed a couple of classes, which your teachers are willing to forgive if you don't fall behind. Melden's class is still on pause; he hasn't recovered from the murder in his office. Silver lining," she added. "That is the phrase?"

Robin nodded, exhaling. There was so much to think about. He'd have to make decisions going forward, some of which were likely to lessen his chances of survival. The warrens had been impersonal death, impersonal danger. This wasn't. Had he known his family's name, had he known the political power his family held, would he have attempted to claim it?

No.

No, he would have died. If he could have remembered, if he could have spoken his name, he would have been discovered and disposed of.

His uncle had seen him. His uncle wouldn't tell anyone that

Robin had survived, so Robin's life was already in danger going forward, through no choice or decision of his own.

But no, that wasn't entirely true. He'd chosen to interfere in the manor; he'd chosen to interfere here. If the manor and the lord's seat were of no interest to Robin, the duties, the hidden duties, of the family were; they were the responsibility his family had carried, and they kept the world safe.

These things were in Robin's thoughts, but they weren't the only thing; they weren't, twinges of conscience aside, the most important, the most pressing.

"The chancellor wants to see you, understandably," Serralyn said, her voice quiet. "But I think you need a few minutes before you face the Dragon in his den." When Terrano failed to move, she grabbed his arm. "So we'll give you a bit of time." She winced—someone in her large group of friends must have disagreed with her. But although they shared thoughts, they were very much their own people.

Serralyn dragged Terrano to the door, opened it, and pushed him out. She followed.

Robin turned to Raven when the door closed. "Killian?"

Killian didn't answer; perhaps he'd left the room in his own fashion. If that was the case, Robin appreciated him more than he could say. He didn't try.

Instead, he approached Raven, busy at her inspection. "He didn't make a desk of glass for you."

Raven didn't look up. "I don't need it now."

"You wanted a desk made of glass to...contain you?"

"Maybe?" For the first time, she looked up. To Robin's surprise, her gaze was apprehensive. He'd assumed she was just being herself: she'd never really understood that looking at people when you were listening let them know you were listening. Mostly, she didn't bother.

This time was different.

Maybe in the future, everything would be different. He'd truly wanted Raven to be able to make her own choices, to be her own person—as much her own person as Robin himself. But she'd been part of his life for almost all of his memories of it. She'd been part of his life because that had been her purpose; that had been the command laid upon her.

But without the command, what was Robin to her? Without the essence of the summoning to bind Raven to him, what would she do? What would she choose? It had been his only fear, his only anxiety, when he had given her the lattice, the metal trellis. He wasn't proud of it; he wasn't proud of it now.

The anxiety hadn't stopped him from doing what he knew to be right. Anything else was just a form of enslavement, wasn't it?

Raven's face scrunched up in near disgust. She rose, leaving her new desk behind. "Bad thoughts," she said, and whacked his shoulder. "Bad."

"Sorry." He exhaled. Raven had never liked lies. Lies of omission probably didn't count, but Robin pushed on. Just this once. He could say this just this once. "You had no choice." His voice was low. "You had no choice but to be my friend. If you had, you could have befriended anyone. My mother—my mother called you and bound you to me. It's not because you wanted to be anywhere near me.

"And now you don't have to. You don't have to be that guardian."

Raven nodded, waiting.

"I'm just afraid that now that you have a choice, you'll go somewhere else. You can go anywhere you want now. You can choose what you want to do, and I wanted that for you. I really, really did. But I don't want to lose you. I don't want you to leave."

"Stupid," she said, but her lips turned up in a half smile.

Robin shook his head. "We never know what life's going

to throw at us. We catch it, we adjust, and we change. We've changed so much since we first met."

"You changed," Raven agreed. "I changed. I found glass," she added. "It made me happy. I *wanted to stay*. You gave me a name. You taught me about people. People like you, not like me. But…they thought I was like you, just odd. You taught me how to run errands, how to get coins. How to *talk*. I can talk to other people.

"It's still hard. But maybe it won't be so hard later. I wanted to stay. You were growing up. You were becoming adult. I would have to go away if I couldn't find some way to *be*. I looked. I looked." Her smile was slight—but it had always been slight, except when she found pieces of glass.

"The glass," she said, as if she could hear that thought, "was containment. I thought if I could find it, you could make me a place that I could live in by your side. I want to see this world. I want to see what you see, and learn what you learn, and teach you what I know. That's what I want. That's my choice."

"And what if it changes?"

Raven shook her head. "Borrowing trouble. Bad."

Robin shook his head. He thought his legs would buckle and he sat heavily on the floor to avoid that embarrassment. Raven came to sit beside him, as she'd sat beside him in countless hiding places after he was safely ensconced. Tilting her head, she placed it against his shoulder, and this, too, was familiar.

"I want to stay," she said.

Robin put an arm around her shoulder and tilted his head so it rested on top of hers. "Then please stay."

★ ★ ★ ★ ★

ACKNOWLEDGMENTS

As usual, a book is not written on a deserted island.

This one was a bit harder because I had to start it so many times—which is not usually the case for a Sagara novel.

I want to thank Leah Mol, my new editor, for her patience as we figured out how each other works. (I've worked with a number of editors, and they all work slightly differently and notice slightly different things; she's worked with a number of authors, and *we* all work differently. Some authors, for instance, don't care if you move their commas, and some go nuclear—and until you start to work with an author, you don't actually know which variety they'll be.)

Sophie James, thank you for publicity outreach—it's not easy to work with Oscar the Grouch (that's me, in case anyone was wondering).

The marketing team, thank you for the Indigo promotion inclusion!

Kathleen Oudit, art director extraordinaire.

And all of the Harlequin proofreading department. Seriously.

On the home front, the usual suspects kept me as sane as I'm ever going to get: Thomas, Daniel and Ross, Kristen, John Chew, and, of course, my parents, Ken and Tami. Becca Lovatt and Ben Freiman, who let me take time off from the bookstore job to finish the book and its copyedits on time.

And my away team: Terry Pearson, who still reads these books in raw first draft and understands that what I need to know at that point is that he wants to keep reading.

(Special mention: West Patreon patrons who allowed me to whine about having to start this book multiple times, even though this is not actually a West novel.)